URANIUM — F.O.B. MARS

A guy's gotta earn a living someplace—and if it isn't on Earth, it might as well be on Mars. That is if the Syndicate would *let* you live on the red planet. Bert Schaun found himself washed-up as a round-the-world rocket racer, blacklisted by Thornton McAllister. He tried to make a new life for himself prospecting for uranium in the lonesome vastness of the asteroids.

But McAllister's fury hunted him even to Mars; the issue became a struggle to stay alive against the dangers imposed by McAllister's interplanetary power. And then Bert found that he was not only fighting for his own survival, but for the survival, too, of a whole race of Martian outcasts.

Singlehandedly, he had to combat genocide on the planet Mars!

**Turn this book over for
second complete novel**

CAST OF CHARACTERS

BERT SCHAUN
The fortune in uranium he had discovered made his life worth living—and him worth killing!

EMMA KLEIN
She was determined to buy whoever had sent her husband on a slow rocket to infinity the same one-way passage.

THORNTON McALLISTER
This interplanetary mogul would do anything to bury his son's bad name.

STEVE BABCOCK
Was he the agent of a syndicate of terror or of a kind of evil all his own?

GRECKLE
This Martian was despised as something less than human, but he proved to be more of a man than any one of his oppressors.

OSBORNE
What he really wanted to run his refinery was not a crew of workers, but a band of slaves.

THE

MARS

MONOPOLY

JERRY SOHL

ACE BOOKS
A Division of A. A. Wyn, Inc.
23 West 47th Street, New York 36, N. Y.

ONE

October 10, 2026

1

THE intercom winked to life and Bert Schaun caught the red glow out of the corner of his eye.

"Bert," it said as he took the cigar out of his mouth and turned in his swivel chair to depress the switch.

"Yes."

"There's a Stinker around here some'eres."

"There ought to be. This is Mars, remember?"

"I'm not kiddin', Bert. I mean right here on the lot."

"You sure, Sam?"

"Sure?" There was a laugh. "If you was standin' where I was a minute ago, you wouldn't be askin' that question."

"Okay. I'll be right down."

Bert sat a moment, his finger still on the lever, feeling a vague uneasiness. An alien wasn't using very good sense coming to Seven like that. He remembered what happened to the last one and knew he couldn't let a thing like that happen again.

Well, there was one thing about them: they were easy to spot if the wind was blowing in the right direction.

Bert sighed, put his ledger to one side, and got to his feet. As he did so, he glanced out of the open door and saw a young couple coming up the walk.

A young couple!

He started, finding the sight hard to believe. There weren't any people like these on Mars!

They were at the door now, standing at the jamb like visions from Earth: fresh, sparkling-eyed, smiling, and, it seemed, a little embarrassed. The girl was dressed in a frothy thing that clung to her like a glove and emphasized

5

her curves. Bert had become so inured to the practical clothing of Mars he found it difficult to take his eyes off it. The latest Earth style? It was white, neat, and without a smudge. When he did manage to look at her face, he was held by its youthfulness, the bright green eyes, and the strange tint of lipstick. An affectation?

The man was something from an advertisement for men's wear, clad in the latest thing for tennis. Odd, how styles for men never changed, Bert thought. The youngster was well-formed, muscular, and looked the picture of health.

"Can I help you?" Bert asked, reluctantly putting in force what he knew would annihilate the tableau.

"Are you Mr. Schaun—Bert Schaun?" the youth asked uncertainly, advancing through the door. The girl held his hand and came forward with him.

"One and the same," Bert said, smiling and coming around the desk. As he did so, he caught the full force of scent. The young people did, too, and winced.

"There's an alien around here somewhere," Bert explained. "Don't let it bother you. I was just going out to look for it."

"I—I've heard about them," the girl said, looking around as if she expected one to creep out from behind the desk.

"It's not in here," Bert said. "It's out on the lot somewhere."

"They tell me," the youth went on in a strained voice, "that you buy and sell spacers."

"That's right. Bert Schaun: Never Undersold. Guaranteed OK Used Spacers. Biggest dealer on Mars, as a matter of fact. Didn't you see the signs out there?"

"You mean there are other dealers on Mars?" the girl asked in surprise.

"Well . . ." Bert grinned. "Maybe there will be some day. Let us put it that way. Were you folks thinking of acquiring a spacer? If you are, you've come to the right place."

"Well," the young man said, "not exactly. I—"

"We're stranded," the girl blurted out.

"I think I'd better explain," the young man said, giving the girl a let-me-handle-this look. "My name's Dean. Spencer Dean. And this is my wife, Pamela. We were on our honeymoon—"

"We thought it would be fun to come to Mars—"

"Let me tell it, Pam," Spencer admonished. "You see, we took her father's yacht for the honeymoon. We didn't think he'd care, since we were getting married anyway. And we thought we'd land here and do a little sight-seeing and then go back."

"We didn't count on father," Pamela said. "He's disowned me."

"We don't know why, except maybe he didn't like the idea of our just taking the yacht without telling him."

"Oh, father's always had it in for you, Spence. Maybe if he hadn't tried to stop it I'd never have married you."

"So you came to Mars in a yacht on your honeymoon," Bert prompted.

"That's right, Mr. Schaun," Spencer said. "And now we can't get back."

"Why?"

"Father's issued orders."

"I see." Her father must be a big man to do that, he thought. And that explained why she was dressed as she was. And a space yacht—of all things! How out of place it must look beside all the stubby ore haulers on Mars!

"We have no fuel, and no money, no nothing," Spencer said.

"And you've come to sell the yacht, is that it?"

"Yes, sir," Spencer said militantly.

"You've got title, of course?"

"Title?" Spencer looked bewildered.

"Surely you know what a title is!"

"Oh, yes, of course. I—I just hadn't thought of that."

"The ship's in the family," Pamela said. "I guess I have a right to sell it, title or not."

Bert smiled. "I'm afraid not, Miss—Mrs. Dean. I'd have no protection, don't you see?"

"Yes, I see." The girl was crestfallen.

"And besides, I don't know what I'd do with a yacht. That's probably the last ship I could sell on Mars."

"It's a wonderful ship," Spencer said. "Room for more than a score of passengers, kitchen, bar, recreation room—"

"I'm not denying it's a wonderful ship," Bert said gently. "I simply couldn't buy it."

Spencer gave his bride a woebegone look and she answered it with an equally mournful face. Bert was amused. They had a problem all right, but it wasn't that tragic.

"You don't have enought fuel to get home, is that it?"

"We left Earth without even checking," Spence said. "We were lucky to get here. The gauge read empty when we landed."

It would take plenty of fuel to move a thing like a yacht back to Earth. And fuel was not exactly cheap, considering the length of the run and the size of the ship.

"Don't you kids have enough dough to take a frieghter home? There's always one leaving over at Four."

"We don't have a thing," Spencer said, shamefaced.

"You mean we should leave the *Pamela* here?" the girl asked, incredulous. "We couldn't do a thing like that!"

"The *Pamela*? Did your father name it for you?"

"Yes, he did, the stinker! Oh!" She put her hand to her open mouth. "I didn't mean that the way it sounded."

"I know what you mean," Bert sighed, walked back to the desk and sat on it, lighting his cigar. "I don't know what to tell you."

"I just couldn't leave the ship with *anybody*," Pamela said,

And I know what you're thinking, Bert thought. Well, he'd always wanted a space yacht. Or had he? He chuckled.

"What's so funny?" Spencer asked.

"Well, I'll tell you what I'll do," Bert said. "I'll advance you the money so you can go home on a freighter, and I'll take care of your yacht for you, Pamela, until your father sends somebody up after it. You'd better not leave on Seven's landing pattern, though. They charge ten dollars a day for that. There's room on the lot." He gestured toward the open window. "It runs back as far as you can see. I'll keep my eye on it and be responsible for it, if you like."

"But—but how will we ever pay you back if father really had disowned us?" Pamela quavered.

"I'll see that Mr. Shaun gets paid," Spencer said firmly. "I'll see to it somehow. And that's a promise, Mr. Schaun."

"Good boy," Bert said, moving behind the desk. "I'll bet you will." He opened a drawer, withdrew a cash box, unlocked it and counted out their fare, adding several bills for incidentals. "There," he said, passing it along the desk top, "that will get you to Earth all right. But there won't be any frills on the way."

"We've had enough frills," Pamela said.

"From now on it's going to be up to me," Spencer said seriously. "And there won't be any frills for a long time."

"I don't know how to thank you," Pamela said, suddenly brightening. "You've been swell, Mr. Schaun."

"Yes, we sure appreciate this, sir," Spencer said, offering his hand.

"Forget it," Bert said, taking the hand. "I was young once myself." Thirty-two must seem an awfully advanced age for them, he thought. "Will you do me the favor of bringing the ship over, Mr. Dean?"

"That I will, sir. Right away."

They turned toward the door and as they did so the faint aroma of an alien came through the window. Got to get out on that right away, Bert thought.

"Thanks again," Pamela said, turning and smiling.

"It's all right," Bert said. Then he had a sudden thought. "Say, who is your father? I'll need to know when he sends somebody after the ship."

"His name is McAllister," Pamela said. "Thornton Mc-Allister."

Bert jerked in his chair at the name, stared at her.

"Whom? *Whom* did you say?"

"McAllister. Thornton McAllister, Mr. Schaun."

"Oh. . . ."

"Good-bye, Mr. Schaun."

"Good-bye. . . ."

He watched them go: Thornton McAllister's daughter and the man she had just married, a likable young man named Dean, Spencer Dean; and he was filled with the wonder of life, of chance meeting, of events of other years. . . .

Thornton McAllister's daughter!

Once there had been two McAllisters: Thornton and Roger.

An old fury started to envelop him and he was moved to call the young couple back, but he did not.

Didn't she know? How could she *not* know?

Or maybe she did. It *was* possible.

And he grimaced at the thought.

Still, what difference did it make? It was so long ago and she had probably forgotten the name. A year isn't long, really, except to young people, and what happens to you to make it seem long.

It seemed an eternity ago.

Actually, it was a little more than a year.

That other time was September 4, 2025.

TWO

September 4, 2025

DAY OF THE 'Round the World Classic!

Two rows of giant flags, one on either side of the takeoff apron, fluttered in the light September breeze.

Fifty-six ships, contenders from a starting field of more than two hundred, were spaced equidistant from each other on the concrete, their noses pointed proudly heavenward, the early afternoon sun glinting from polished places.

Pennants and banners flew from buildings around the starting area and were carried by enthusiasts and rooters, a hundred thousand of them cramming the area, most of them on the apron out among the ships.

Hawkers sold balloons in the shape of jetcraft; concessions selling pennants, hot dogs, root beer, a half dozen flavors of lotofiz, ice cream, and candy bars, had more business than could be handled.

It was a perfect day for the running of the Twenty-Seventh Annual 'Round the World competition.

A TV crew was at work below the *Skysweep*, ship number 129. Rope held by workmen kept the crowd around the ship from overflowing into the actual scene of the interview.

"Tell me," the announcer with the red bow tie said to the man in coveralls leaning against the ladder to the ship, "how many races have you been in before?"

Bert Schaun, pilot of the *Skysweep*, frowned thoughtfully, then said, "Unless one of them got away from me somewhere, I think this will be the tenth."

"You've never won?"

"I've been second twice, third three times."

"Always a bridesmaid, never a bride. Is that it?"

11

The crowd laughed good-naturedly.

"Something like that," Bert said.

The announcer looked toward the dolly and nodded his head slightly. It began to roll forward for a close-up of the two men.

"With all that experience, you ought to be able to win this year, don't you think, Mr. Shaun?"

"I'll try, but there's a lot of stiff competition."

"What kind of a ship do you have?"

"It's a Powers-Yaus. Not the fanciest. But it's plenty fast. Worked it over myself."

"I've heard the best ship in the race is McAllister's."

Bert nodded grudgingly. "That Jaffenen job is a good one, all right. But it set him back plenty."

The announcer chuckled. "But you're going to give him a run for his money, eh?"

"I'll do my best. Have you talked to McAllister yet?"

"We were over there a little while ago. Tell me, Mr. Schaun, what will you do with the hundred thousand dollars if you win it?"

Bert Schaun pushed his pilot's cap back on his head and grinned. "You fellows ask me that each year. And I always tell you I don't want to think about it. Once I get it in my pocket, I may have an answer for you."

"Maybe we'll be seeing you after the race."

"I hope so."

"Well, we've got to move on now, Mr. Schaun. Good luck to you, sir."

"Thanks."

The announcer moved away, the dolly was rolled back, and Bert put his cold cigar back in his mouth and went into the ship.

Well, at least *that* was over.

He clanged the metal door closed behind him.

Operations was the scene of frantic activity. The building, with its open glass wall facing the takeoff apron, buzzed with static, bells, the click of machines giving the weather reports and checking co-ordinates in other parts of the world. Pilots raced in and out with last-minute requests or errands or orders. Uniformed men at the doors kept the curious out. Other uniformed men circulated around the inside, alert for any trouble.

Lights blinked on a giant board above the open wall, indicating the changing odds on the racers. The information came from the wagering center across the apron where people stood in block-long lines to place their bets.

Schaun was favored to win two to one. McAllister was second with three to one. The last man on the list was Agnew with one hundred and eleven to one.

Thornton McAllister glared at the policeman at the door, showed his identification, then pushed past him into the building, taking long strides because he was a big man. His hair was jet black beneath his black hat, and there was a flamboyant touch to his mustache that comes only from years of cultivation.

There was no mistaking where he was going. His destination was straight across the floor to the desk of the Chief of the Takeoff Pattern. If people had not moved out of his way, they might have been bowled over like tenpins.

At the edge of the open floor, his hands gripping the rail of the waist-high partition, his face a mottled red, McAllister thundered, "Mr. Duggan!"

Patrick Duggan looked up from a sheaf of papers he was thumbing through. When he saw who it was, he jumped to his feet. "Why, Mr. McAllister!"

"It's rotten, sir. Perfectly rotten."

"Sir?" Duggan's eyebrows raised as did the eyebrows of several people in the vicinity.

"You put Roger where he is on purpose!"

"Your son," Duggan said quickly, "picked his place himself. He asked to be put smack dab in the center of the pattern."

The elder McAllister snorted. "He must have taken leave of his senses then." He threw his hands in the air. "How'll he level off at thirty miles? There'll be ships all around him. He should have taken a fringe berth. Preferably one on the east side. Why didn't you tell him that, Mr. Duggan?"

"It shouldn't make any difference—"

"Difference! Why, it will make all the difference in the world!" McAllister's jowls quivered with rage.

"Not if he's first, Mr. McAllister," Duggan said calmly. "You don't think he'll be anything else, do you?"

"Eh?" What's that?" McAllister's eyes narrowed. "What do you mean by that, young man?"

"I mean it doesn't make any difference where the other ships are if he's first. He'll have the field to himself. He won't have to worry. After all, he does have the best ship, you know."

"That may be," McAllister said, unwilling to be soothed. "But you said *if* he's first."

"We're all pulling for him, sir," Duggan said, smiling. "After all, it isn't as if this were his first trip around."

McAllister nodded grudgingly. "Well, Roger *is* a fair pilot. That plus the ship ought to mean something."

Lanzer Murcheson, Chief of Operations, wearing a welcome smile, approached the rail and offered his hand to McAllister.

"Thornton McAllister!" he said warmly. "I was hoping you'd come to Operations. You'll be our guest, won't you? We'll have it all on the big screen here and there won't be too many inside."

One moment it was quiet, the sun flooding the area about the ships, now devoid of people. A bird flew in a long curve over the Operations building and landed atop ship number twenty-three. The second hand of the big clock at the end of the field completed its circle to sixty. Somewhere deep within the Operations building a relay clicked.

The next moment there was thunder, the roar of fifty-six reactorjets splitting the air at the same time. It would have ruptured the brain of anyone within a few hundred feet. But no one was that near. The hundred thousand people were in buildings and shelters about Simmons Field, watching the takeoff on television or seeing it through reinforced windows.

The bird on ship number twenty-three was still there, its claws still gripping the scored nose of the ship.

But it was dead.

As the ship shuddered, the bird's claws lost their death-grip and it fell to the blackened concrete below. Atop the ship it had suffered the indignity of death, and now it suffered the additional indignity of cremation.

The ships rose as one, slowly, then a little faster, then swiftly. Then they screamed high into the air.

People ran out of the buildings to watch them, careful to keep away from the takeoff and landing apron.

In no time at all the fifty-six ships had vanished from sight.

The 'Round the World Classic had begun!

The race had begun at noon. At 12:07 the screen in the Operations office went blank.

Immediately the face of Frank Nielsen, one of the nation's top sports announcers, replaced the picture of the speeding sports crafts.

"Well, it looks as if this will be the race of races," he said. "The fifty-six contenders were off to a fast start in this twenty-seventh annual running of the Classic. They were favored by a prevailing wind which rode them briskly into an eastward movement even before they reached the thirty-mile track. Fair skies made for fine ground observation and millions were out with binoculars and other visual aids."

"Damn!" Thornton McAllister said, squirming in the soft, cushioned chair next to Murcheson. "Where the devil is the picture of the racers? How's my son doing?"

"They're too far out over the Atlantic right now," Murcheson said. "We don't have a control point until Madrid."

McAllister looked at him aghast. "You mean there's no viewplane to follow them all the way?"

"Viewplanes are something else," Murcheson said. "We have them stationed along the route to follow the racers only a designated distance. If we had too many of them they'd be getting in each other's way. Besides, viewplanes can't go as fast as the racers ten miles above them."

"You had a picture all the way last year!"

"I'm sure we didn't, Mr. McAllister. I remember the race very well. I handled it."

"So do I remember it," McAllister said stiffly. "My son was in that one, too."

The view of Nielsen faded. The screen came to life with a long string of jetcraft high in the sky, looking like stars in the late afternoon sky over Spain.

"Number one twenty-nine, *Skysweep*, Bert Schaun's ship, is leading by two hundred miles," the speaker intoned. "Second is number seventy-two, *Lightning*, Baylor Evans' ship."

"Where's the *Mac IV*?" McAllister cried, getting to his feet.

As if it had heard, the speaker went on, "Evans leads number thirty, the *Mac IV*, Roger McAllister's ship, by three miles. Behind McAllister are three ships separated only by a few miles. . . ."

Bert Schaun checked the peripheral scanners. It was night, but the scanners showed the earth was below, where it ought to be, the stars were in their accustomed places, and there wasn't a single contestant behind as far as he could see.

He had long ago passed the control point at Madrid, had seen the long blue triangle pointing in the direction he should next assume, had noted with satisfaction the single red dot in the middle of it. That meant he was leading the field. Number one man!

Then he had passed other control points in rapid order: out of New York at 12 noon, Madrid at 12:16, Suez at 12:28, Cocos at 12:40. They had all indicated he was still number one man. He wondered how far behind the rest of them were.

The next point was Melbourne. About 12:50. He could afford to relax a little But before he did, he let his eyes roam over the dials and gauges. Fuel O.K. He could go a-round the earth a half dozen times on the pellets in the re-actorjet. Speed nudging 5.3 miles per second. He sighted down the infrascope, saw terrain moving slowly by thirty miles below. Australia!

He chuckled. No matter how long he raced he'd never get over how you had to point your nose at the earth to maintain a speed like that. Otherwise you'd go shooting off into space like a rock from a sling. He remembered other races and other pilots. Some of them suddenly went crazy and pointed the noses of their ships up and started building up to 7.1, and the next thing they knew they were on their way to infinity. Perhaps some of them are still on their way, he thought grimly. Unless something stopped them. A meteor, for example. Or the moon. Chances are they'd never get by the asteroid belt. At least not in sports craft like these. But of course they'd die of starvation before they ever got that far. Or their oxygen would give out. One was as bad as the other.

He glanced at the speed indicator. The needle wavered

a little under 5.3. He moved the speed lever over another
notch, saw with satisfaction the arm move up and pass
5.3. A red blinker on the control panel started winking
slowly, then faster. Bert moved the nose of the ship down
to twenty-nine degrees. The blinking slowed, then stopped.

Some day they'd go around the earth in a day. But they'd
have to build better ships than the *Skysweep*. And when
they did go around that fast they'd have to point the nose
straight down—or almost straight down—most of the time.
And then how could they get up any greater speed? There
was such a thing as diminishing returns, even in racing.

He looked at his watch. It was 12:48. The race was more
than half over! Only the last half, the breaking into sunlight
again, and he'd come roaring down to collect his $100,000
prize!

He felt sorry for McAllister. The kid had sunk a lot of his
father's money in a racer and expected to win because of
that. Didn't he know it took a little skill to run a ship?
You couldn't buy a thing like the 'Round the World Classic.
You had to train for it, work for it, dream for it. Just because
your father wanted you to win wouldn't insure your getting
it even if you were a good-looking guy like McAllister, could
spend as much as you wanted for a ship, and had a father
who could be counted on for a nice yearly appropriation to
the International Jetcraft Racers Association. How they
treated him to his face and how they laughed at him behind his back! Bert didn't like it.

Thornton McAllister gripped the arms of his chair with
sweating hands, eyes fixed on the screen.

Tiny flares moved slowly across it. First a single point
of light, then another isolated point, then several pin-
points together, followed by a mass of lights that looked like
fireflies over a garden.

"The racers are over Western Australia now," the speaker

said dispassionately. "In the lead position is number one twenty-nine, *Skysweep*, Bert Schaun's ship, which has maintained first place since the first. . . ."

"Damn, damn, damn!" McAllister said, running a dry tongue over dry lips.

". . . but number seventy-two, *Lightning*, Baylor Evans's ship, has been passed by number thirty, the *Mac IV*, Roger McAllister's ship, and now lags the *Mac IV* by a hundred miles. . . ."

"But how far behind—" McAllister started to say.

"Sh!" someone hissed.

". . . and the *Mac IV* seems to be catching up with the leader. . . ."

Bert sighted the Melbourne control point thirty miles below him, a green triangle, its lights shimmering like stars in the night. He wondered how many miles lay between the cluster of lights that formed each of the lights in the triangle.

A single red light winked in the center of the figure. He was still first! With a singing heart he corrected his flight, while over the control area, to continue his course in the direction of the thinnest angle. Good going, Schaun! He grinned. Unless something happened, he'd be the winner. But that long stretch over the Pacific was coming up. The control triangles on Fiji, Samoa and Hawaii would be small. You could miss them if you were off a fraction of a degree. The next big control point would be San Francisco. It was 3:50 in the morning in Melbourne. When would he see daylight? In time to see Fiji below? He guessed not. But surely by Hawaii.

He punched the button that set off the tracer rockets. Give the millions watching the race on TV something to see!

Now he turned on and enlarged the rear scanner view. He'd be able to tell how far behind the competition was by the glow of their tracers, if they came soon enough.

Almost immediately he saw the white glare of two tracers blossom on the screen.

Damn! Who could that be? He darted a look at the speed indicator. A little over 5.4. Whoever was piloting that ship must be exceeding that. And there was danger in getting too near 6. At 6 or over you had to keep your nose tilted at a dangerous angle and any misfire swept you higher than the forty-smile limit. It was cold out there. The thirty-to-forty mile limit had been chosen because, at the racers' speeds, the few molecules of air in that stratus helped warm the ship. But beyond the forty-mile limit the air fell off sharply and the temperature inside the ship went down quickly. If you went too high you had to jet to slow your speed, pushing down to the lower level again with backward thrusts.

You also lost the race.

Bert shrugged. If the racer behind him wanted to take that chance there was nothing he, Bert Schaun, could do about it. He advanced the speed lever another calibration. That would put his ship near the 5.5 mark. It was straining things, but it was necessary under the circumstances. But he positively would not go beyond that. No matter what happened—even if the other pilot came sailing by—he knew he'd never push his ship any further.

Now he could see the ship on the screen. A black notch in the edge of a small glow that would be the jet flare. Even as he watched it, it grew like a blob of ink on a blotter. And then he saw something else, something he didn't like. A change of color in the exhaust trail. It was no longer a healthy, yellow streak. There was a tinge of white to it.

You can't do that to a reactorjet!

But the pilot was doing it.

When the racer filled the screen, he turned off the scanner and tilted his chair to look through the rear transparent window. The ship was there and the white flare was no mistake. Slowly and steadily it was overtaking him.

Go ahead, you fool! Come on! Rev it up above 6, see if I care! But you'll never make it to the finish line!

He moved his chair again when the ship went out of sight in the rear window, turning to one a little higher in the aft section. There it was now, a sleek, black vessel barely distinguishable against the blue-black sky, spitting a silver plume that curved toward the direction from which it had come, a needle nosed earthward and coming toward him sidewise and above.

It was the *Mac IV*, no question about that now. Trimmest craft in the race. It put Bert's teeth on edge to see what the boy was doing to it, pushing the pellets that way, turning the tail so white. How did he manage to keep it on level flight?

It was so close Bert could look into the lighted control room now, seeing the components, the dark head that was McAllister's. He'd be laughing now, the way his ship was pointing at Bert's like a bullet, sliding slowly by.

Suddenly the figure inside the other ship moved. Then Bert saw the ship dart forward.

What was the matter with McAllister? Wasn't winning enough?

With a frantic hand Bert automatically thrust the accelerator to reverse jets and cursed McAllister. That's what the boy wanted. The sudden deceleration pulled him forward and the straps to his chair strained and creaked. Only by straining his neck could Bert see the *Mac IV* still gliding toward him, a huge object filling all the rear windows. He gritted his teeth and hoped the ships would miss.

There was a grinding crash that made the *Skysweep* shudder. The *Mac IV* bounced away.

Okay, okay. Bert swore. He threw the switch that canceled everything and the silence, after the steady roar of the reactorjets, was oppressive.

He looked upward, his hands ready to work the controls for any contingency. What was McAllister up to now?

And then he saw that McAllister would never be up to anything in the short time he had yet to live. A faint red glow filled the other ship. He could see McAllister working over the control panel frantically.

But Bert knew it was too late.

Let's get out of here!

Bert jammed the accelerator to full forward, hoping the jets weren't impaired by the crash. They weren't. They roared to life and he was thrown violently against the cushioned chair.

He might have looked back at the *Mac IV* if he had been able.

The brilliant flash from the exploding ship filled the control room of the Skysweep.

He was glad he hadn't seen it.

They revived Thornton McAllister by throwing cold water in his face.

He spluttered, breathed raspily, then looked around as if he didn't know where he was.

Then he sat bolt upright, his eyes wild.

"He killed him! He killed him!"

Hands helped him to his feet.

"Did you see him? Did you see that Schaun fellow? He backed up into Roger's ship. . . . He rammed him! *He killed him!*"

The face of Frank Nielsen looked out at McAllister, unperturbed. "Well, folks, we've just witnessed one of the tragedies of the twenty-seventh annual running, leaving fifty-five contenders in the race, though there seems to be little doubt of the outcome now. . . ."

THREE

"HERE," Lovell Gardner said, "let me buy this one."

Bert Schaun drained the last few drops in his glass, set it on the bar in precisely the spot from which he had removed it. He then stared at it.

"Harry," Gardner said, waving a bill in the air, "let's have another here."

Harry was in a hurry. The race was over, the pilots were flocking in. There was money to be made here and now. But he made time to stop after he picked up the empty glasses in order to say, "Tough luck, Bert. But everything will turn out all right."

Bert glared at Harry, then turned to Gardner. "Why is everyone talking to me as if this were a funeral? Hell, I keep telling everybody the kid tried to ram me, but all they do is nod their heads and look away."

"It's that Mr. McAllister, Bert."

"I came down ahead of everybody else, expecting to pick up the hundred thousand, and what happens? I get mobbed by newspaper and TV guys. Do they ask me how it feels to win the World Classic? Hell, no. They ask me did I or didn't I ram Roger McAllister."

"Why don't you forget about it for a while?" Gardner said gently, pushing Bert's refill toward him.

"I'm not going to foget about it. I won the damn thing and now I can't get the dough. It'll be a long time before anybody comes in at 1:28 again."

"You did make good time."

"Damn right I did."

"Even considering the incident."

"Even considering the fact that the kid went berserk and tried to put his ship through mine."

Gardner drank a little. Bert watched him as he did, not drinking himself. When Gardner put his glass down, Bert said, "You haven't said what you think, Lovell. Did he ram me or not?"

Gardner shrugged. "Hell, how should I know? I didn't see it. I was in ship number eighty-nine, remember?"

"But you could tell me what you think."

"What good's my opinion?"

"*I'd* like to hear it."

"Well. . . ."

Bert grabbed Lovell's forearm. "Damn you, Lovell! Do you think I rammed McAllister, too? Do you?"

Gardner pulled away, angry. "Of course not. But that doesn't pull you out of the hole you're in."

Bert frowned, returned to gazing at his glass. "Maybe you're right. But it would be nice to know how many people believe me and not that nutty McAllister."

"That's what I've been telling you. It's that McAllister guy. He's got them all believing you went after the *Mac IV*."

"Hell of a note." Bert downed the last of the drink. "I got a good mind to go punch his face in."

"That would help, wouldn't it?"

"What luck I've had, Lovell. I worked like hell to make enough to buy a ship, then I'm in the races for nine years, each year changing this and changing that to make the ship better and each year getting closer and closer, and then, the one year I get it in shape and everything goes off just right and I'm way ahead of everybody else, this kid comes along and tries to put me out of the running."

"McAllister says you're the one who went batty. He says you couldn't stand to see the *Mac IV* pass you by, so you decided to put it out of commission."

"Ha! I didn't have to do that. I was sailing along at a good 5.4. Then this McAllister opens up everything the

Mac IV has and he comes roaring up with a white tail—you know what that means."

"Too bad a thing like that doesn't show on the view-screens."

"Yeah, isn't it," Bert said dryly. "Well, he did, anyhow. He was finished before he got within a hundred miles of me. He was really pushing it, Lovell. All it took was that last whack when he shoved it against the *Skysweep*. That triggered it. Hell, when I looked over at his ship it was already red inside. That's when I got out of there."

"Where's your ship now?"

"They're looking it over. . . . Harry, let's have another."

A hand against his shoulder brought Bert around. It was Agnew.

"Sorry to hear about what happened, Bert," Agnew said. "We're all pulling for you though."

"Thanks," Bert said sourly. He turned to Gardner. "When these wreaths get shoulder high, I'll trade them in for a case of Scotch."

"You got these fellows wrong, Bert. They really are pulling for you."

"Just like you, eh? I'll bet if I asked, they'd have no opinion either."

"Hell, how could we—"

Bert waved him quiet. "I know, I know." He sighed and pulled his refill over to him. "Well, here's to the prize I won and won't get."

A speaker in the ceiling came to life. "Attention, everyone! Attention! Official results of the race have just been posted. The winner is Baylor Evans, ship number seventy-two, *Lightning*. *Skysweep*, ship number one twenty-nine, piloted by Bert Schaun, has been disqualified. Second place winner is. . . ."

Bert was on his feet.

"Hey, where are you going?" Gardner grabbed his arm.

Bert jerked free. "Where do you suppose?"

"It's just as I told you, Bert," Murcheson said patiently. "They looked your ship over, they took in the film of the collision, and they figured you could have done it. So they gave it to Evans."

"But I didn't do it!" Bert said. "McAllister's got you all so rattled you don't know what you're doing!"

Murcheson sighed. "I know how you feel, Bert, but I had nothing to do with the decision. That's what the Evaluation Committee's for, to look into matters like this."

"But nobody asked *me*. *I* was there. *I* was the one involved."

"But they couldn't ask *you!*"

"Why not?"

"Why, you'd tell them you had nothing to do with it."

"I had everything to do with it. I braked to avoid a collision. They misinterpreted it, the damn fools!"

Murcheson looked at him coldly. "Have you been drinking?"

"Sure, I've been drinking. What would you do if somebody took away a hundred thousand dollars you worked ten years for?"

"You're through Schaun." Murcheson snapped a drawer of his desk closed. "You'll never run another race."

"Just because I had a drink or two? Are you crazy?"

"Not because of the drinking. I can't blame you for that." The Chief of Operations rose.

"Why, then?"

"Because the issue will forever be in doubt. Don't you see that?" Murcheson's glance was half pitying. "They couldn't give you the prize because of that doubt. Maybe you didn't ram McAllister, but the doubt is there. And that's what has ruined your career."

"It's not ruined," Bert said doggedly. "I'll race again next year. I'll clip off another five minutes."

Murcheson shook his head. "There'll be no more racing for you. At least not in the World Classic."

Bert looked at him dazedly.

"As I said," Murcheson went on, "I know what it all means to you, but it's just—just one of those things."

"What am I supposed to do then, just drop dead?"

"You'll have plenty to do. You'll be pretty busy."

"Doing what, for example?"

"Appearing in court, Bert. I shouldn't be telling you this, but McAllister's saying he's going to start suit against you. He wants damages for the death of his son."

"I should pay *him?*" Bert started to laugh. It was a hysterical laugh. "I should pay McAllister!"

Murcheson stared at the laughing man. Then he shook his head and walked away. Half way across the room he turned. "How much money do you have, Bert?"

"Why?"

"McAllister's got to keep you in court for a year. I just hope you have enough to get out of sitting around in jails waiting for the next trial. McAllister—he'll never give up, you know. He's convinced you rammed the *Mac IV* and he's a determined man."

Damn McAllister! *Both* McAllisters.

September 5, 2025

When Bert awakened, he wasn't in his own room in the pilot's barracks. He couldn't recall how he got there, but from what he saw around him he knew he hadn't been alone. Empty bottles on the dresser; some still standing, others on their sides. One was half full of cigarette butts. Spots on the mirror. A drink had cascaded down the dresser front. He imagined if he touched the stain it would still be wet and sticky.

The bedclothes were disarranged, the windows were

blinded, the bathroom door open, and he could see sodden towels on the floor. The light was still on.

He moved—and groaned.

With an effort he sat up on the edge of the bed, found himself still in his clothes. He punched the blind control for open. The windows blazed with light. He covered his eyes and quickly reversed the process.

What time of day was it?

He fell gently back to bed again, this time face down, the service dial within reach. He dialed for menu. With something to eat . . . well, at least coffee. . . .

"Service has been discontinued," a voice said mechanically.

He groaned again.

After he dragged himself into the bathroom, ran cold water over his head, he felt a little better. He began to collect himself. There had been the race. And then. . . .

That part of yesterday the liquor had successfully hidden, that he had wanted hidden, suddenly ran free of its hiding place and slammed against his aching head.

He sat down hard on the edge of the bathtub, dumb with the knowledge of it.

Through.

I can't be. But I am. I'm finished. Washed up. Just as if I never began.

What to do?

Maybe a job in some other classification, some other category with the Classic. But he shuddered at the thought of watching others take off for other races in other years. No, that wasn't the answer. Besides, Murcheson said he'd be tied up in legal action for a while. Well, I have some money. But, of course, not as much as McAllister.

Fighter pilot? Okay for a war. But there hadn't been a war for fifty years. Any other kind of pilot? Probably not. The word would get around. McAllister would see to that.

"I'd still like to punch the old man's face in," he said out loud.

But that would only make matters worse.

No, there was another answer somewhere, some lucrative profession, maybe one requiring an investment. There would be any number of jobs, jobs with salaries. Pitifully small salaries. He didn't want one of those. He had gambled ten years of his life for a hundred thousand dollars and had lost. He was ready to gamble again for high stakes. The higher the better. But how? Where?

I'm thirty-one, he said to himself. I've got to make up for lost time. I've got to turn this disadvantage into an advantage somehow. How to do it?

Maybe you should just thank your lucky stars you're still alive and Roger McAllister didn't knock a hole in your ship.

He snorted, remembered how the approaching *Mac IV* filled all the rear windows.

Roger McAllister's the lucky one in this case. He can thank *his* lucky stars. . . .

Stars!

No, not stars, really, but shiny dots in the sky just the same. . . . The answer was there!

The knock on the door couldn't have been louder if his head had been the door.

"Come in!" he yelled from the bathroom, trying to summon up enough energy to hoist himself to his feet.

The door opened. Shoes. They went one way, then another. They finally came to the bathroom. Lovell Gardner was in them. He stood looking down at Bert.

"I wondered if you'd come out of it yet."

"This is a difficult stage," Bert said. "I haven't fully emerged from my cocoon yet. Whose room is this?"

"Evans's."

"Evans's? He won the race, didn't he?"

"Yeah. He took off already."

"I don't remember much, Lovell."

"It's just as well."

"I was that bad, eh?"

"You were plenty bad."

"Made a regular fool of myself, huh? That's me, all right."

"I never saw a man who felt more sorry for himself."

"Maybe you better not tell me any more. Give me a hand. I've got to get up off this bathtub. I'm stuck."

"You don't look bad," Lovell said, coming over to help him.

"It's only protective coloration that comes from years of this sort of thing."

"You don't have to be funny. I know how you feel."

Bert moaned. "Let's not go through that routine again. You and Murcheson both know more about how I feel than I do." He sat down on the bed, reached for a cigar, withdrew shreds of tobacco leaf from a breast pocket.

"Here," Lovell said, offering a package. "Have a cigarette."

"Only because I'm desperate will I accept."

"I'm all packed, ready to go. You're the last one here."

"That's me," Bert said, lighting up. "Always staying around until the last dog is hanged. Only this time I'm the dog."

"I haven't got much time. Due in Columbus shortly. What are you going to do?"

"I'm not going back to L.A., Lovell."

"Great. Great. Where, then?"

Bert squinted at the man. "I'm going to Mars."

"Mars!"

"Yes, Mars."

Lovell was bewildered. "What's on Mars?"

"Not really Mars, Lovell. That's just the first step."

"Anybody's crazy who wants to go to Mars. Ask anybody who's been there. Desert, cold, wind, dry. . . ."

"And the Stinkers. Don't forget the Stinkers."

"I never believed that stuff about the Stinkers. Sounds like a story somebody dreamed up."

"There's money out there, Lovell."

Gardner shrugged. "Maybe. But I never met anybody who made any. I can't see you as a prospector, though, if that's what you have in mind."

"That's it," Bert said. "I've just decided. Just thought about it while I was sitting in there on the bathub. Where do you suppose our reactor fuel comes from? From the asteroids, that's where. And a guy who can make a real strike out there is set for life."

Lovell laughed hollowly. "That's why everybody's so anxious to leave Earth. Thousands every day."

"Okay," Bert said. "So not very many people take off for prospecting. Can you blame them? It's a tough life. You've got to live on a tiny, clumsy ship for weeks at a time looking for the stuff. Then when you find it you've got to haul it back to Mars for processing. Then you've got to go back out there and start all over. It's not an easy life. But once you've made a rich haul, you're in."

"I'm not," Lovell said. "Too many uncertainties."

"What's more uncertain than racing? Where did you end up this time?"

Lovell studied Bert's face. "You know, Bert, it may be just the thing for you, considering what's happened."

"This guy McAllister," Bert confided, "is going to sue me for damages. If I stayed here on Earth he'd tie me up for years. But if I take off for Mars, I'll be out of Earth jurisdiction."

"Say, I forgot about that. Once in space you're free of legal processes. That and taxes. No income tax, no sales tax.

But it must be pretty rugged if they waive things like that in order to get you to go."

"I know it's no bed of roses. But I figured I'd better do something while I still have some money. Once McAllister gets at me I'll start using it up fast. Might even end up in jail without any."

Lovell nodded. "I've heard it's pretty much of a frontier."

"It's *the* frontier, son," Bert said.

"But you'll never be able to come back. At least, if you do you'll still have to face McAllister and court action."

"Maybe I'll have more dough than McAllister by that time."

"It's a thought. Well, I've got to go, Bert." He moved to the door.

"Glad to have met you, Mr. Gardner. See you around. If I get any calls from any cute blondes, tell them they can reach me on Asteroid Thirteen Eighty-Three Limburgia."

FOUR

1950 - 2025

"URANIUM is a thousand times more plentiful than gold," said nuclear engineers back in the late 1950's. "There is no reason to think we'll exhaust Earth's supply before two thousand years, even at the expected rate of consumption of the year 2000."

The engineers were right on the first count, wrong on the second.

Uranium *was* plentiful in the Earth's crust. It was especially rich in the Shinkolobwe Mine deep in the Katanga Province of the Congo, in the diggings around Canada's Great Bear Lake, in many of the layers of sandstone on the Colorado Plateau.

So men scratched away at Earth, probing canyon walls, boring with diamond drills, seeking the elusive treasure in almost inaccessible pockets on tablelands, on deserts, on the top of mesas. They flew over vast areas with radioactivity-detection equipment in an endless search for a metal that was, as engineers had pointed out, plentiful enough, but deeply hidden in many different places.

But as the years passed, the need for nuclear fuel became increasingly acute, for extrapolating engineers had misjudged man's ability and eagerness to embrace the atom. They had not visualized the sudden dissatisfaction with gasoline, oil and coal that came with the manufacture of economical nuclear reactors in the late 1970's, and the resultant re-tooling for atomic energy in almost every field of human endeavor.

Engineers who had once thought nuclear reactors for homes were impractical and who had shaken their heads over reactors for aircraft lived to see these things become commonplace. They had not imagined using nuclear energy to move or restrict great masses of air and thereby control the weather.

They were, in fact, just as short-sighted as their fathers had been before them.

And thereby hangs the ukase of 1990, the order from all governments for scientists to work at cracking the more plentiful atoms, for researchers to study the extraction of uranium from sea water again.

For time was running out on the nuclear assets which once wasted by a slow clock.

Man had speeded up that clock.

So it was that the eyes of engineers turned spaceward while their brothers frantically sought to wrest further secrets from the atom in laboratories. Out among the planets somewhere, they said, lay a fuel, plenty of it, waiting to be taken, to be brought back to Earth to feed the ever-hungry nuclear reactors.

The exploration of space, which had been undertaken by various governments under federal appropriations, and by astronomical societies, now became a necessity. The sterile mountainous wastes of the Moon were revisited and re-examined. More ambitious expeditions set off to probe the twilight zones of Mercury, the storm-battered surface of Venus, the arid plains of Mars.

But nowhere did men find a rich source of radioactive ore.

Undaunted, men set out for more distant vistas: the asteroids and the eleven moons of Jupiter and the planets beyond, if necessary.

But further travel was not necessary. Engineers had hardly got into the problem of interstellar travel when word came that excellent sources of uranium had been found in the asteroid belt, that great, broad zone of barren, airless worlds between Mars and Jupiter.

And so the Great Search ended.

Immediately eight great refining companies of Earth set up processing plants on Mars—Why ship back to Earth that which could be processed on Mars?—and commenced operations. And at once there was a rush of prospectors to the asteroid belt to compete with the refinery people's own search parties. A few become wealthy in an incredibly short time and returned to Earth, but many more never returned and were forgotten. At first, large work parties left Earth for employment in the refineries, but word drifted back that life there was hard and dull and the pay not extraordinary. Still, many of the hardy and adventuresome set out for a year or two of life on another planet just to see what it was like.

But for the average man, the first steady flow of fuel from Mars ended another great quest and an interest in the planet, and he turned his eyes and mind to other things.

It didn't take long for magazine and newspaper stories about life on Mars to become passé. People lost interest in pictures stories on prospecting for uranium in the asteroid belt or life in refinery communities. Even a series on the Stinkers, the Martian natives—those long-eared, red-eyed creatures with that horrible smell—failed to titillate readers any longer. There grew, in fact, a disbelief in the existence of such creatures in some quarters. This was due to the many conflicting stories that were written about them.

People became more interested in what men would find on the moons of Jupiter. And there was pressure to complete a star ship so an expedition could leave the solar system entirely. That *would* be something.

But if there was a scarcity of uranium for processing on Earth, there was uranium to be had on the asteroids—if you could find it. And governments, having just gone through a time of fearful uncertainty about nuclear fuel, did not discourage a search for it. The United States Government Printing Office, for example, published a thick booklet entitled "Prospecting Among the Asteroids," which they sent to anyone interested. It emphasized the fact that there were hundreds and thousands of asteroids that had not yet been explored. And good luck to you.

The adventure of hunting for uranium was made even more alluring by legislation which rendered prospectors free of income tax and the regular processes of law.

As a result, men who might never have turned their eyes away from Earth found it suddenly attractive.

Or found it the lesser of two evils.

Men like Bert Schaun, for example.

FIVE

January 3, 2026

HE COULD have made a better landing. He hovered too long, as if he were uncertain and afraid of dropping too hard, and he used too much fuel as a consequence. Bert knew he should have trusted the gauges; he made the mistake of looking at the terrain below and found it impossible to think of it as different from Earth terrain. That's when the speaker overhead blasted at him.

"For God's sake, man, you're not a butterfly. Let her down. Let her down!"

So he turned away from viewing the ground below and guided the *Fern* straight down the landing pattern fix, running the descent controls along the scale revised for Mars gravitation.

He hardly felt a jar when the spacer met support and the engines stopped automatically.

"That's better," the speaker blared. "Now one more thing before you open the lock and pop out like a cork: adjust for atmosphere."

Bert had already done so, was on the point of telling the speaker he wasn't as stupid as all that, but refrained from comment. Instead, he opened the lock and ran the ladder down.

It was cold and the air was thin. He zipped his jacket, went down the ladder, and stood on the apron of Seven, fishing in his pocket for a match for his cigar.

It had been a long, confining trip. Even if he had stepped out of his ship into a good-sized room, the room would have looked immense to him at that moment. As it was, the landing port seemed gigantic. Still, he knew it was not as large as an average landing area on Earth. What he saw might have been Earth, but it would have been a more desolate Earth than he had ever known. Looking between other ships on the landing area to his left, he could see a monotonous expanse of brown that stretched uninterrupted to the horizon. Above, the sky was different, a deeper blue, and the clouds had more color than they had on Earth. There were almost luminescent ones high overhead, while angry-looking orange ones scudded much lower. As for gravity, he felt unencumbered by weight, but he had been in space so long he had lost his ability to compare it with Earth gravitation.

A whine far away on his right made him turn. High in the sky over Seven, breaking through lower clouds, dropped two spacers carrying a line of gondolas between them. A little while ago, he knew, those gondolas and one of the work ships had been circling Mars in an orbit. A second ship had been sent up to assist in the unloading.

And those gondolas carried uranium ore.

Now, beyond the immediate buildings of the flight area, he could see the tops of other brown structures: chimneys, bright silver shafts, and a network of shining pipes. Somewhere among them the ships would settle, the gondolas would be emptied and perhaps one of the spacers would be outward bound again soon, collecting empty ore boats from orbit.

Well, this is it, Schaun, he told himself. This is why you sold the sleek, trim *Skysweep* you labored so many years over. This is why you bought the *Fern*, that short, stubby, lumbering work ship you just got out of. Yes, this is why you crossed those millions of miles of space. What do you think of it?

Not much, he answered himself, clamping teeth down on his cigar. But I'll make the best of it just as others have. And maybe I can do better than if I had won the Classic. That took me ten years to work up to. Maybe I can do it in less time here. But I'll have to be lucky, I realize that.

At least there won't be any McAllister trying to put me out of the race here.

Or any old man out to get my skin.

Bert gave a final glance around at the few other ships on the apron, then walked to the Operations hut. The cold penetrated his jacket and he felt curiously light-headed. Well, he'd get used to it, he supposed.

He had expected a bustling Operations office: a few radio-men and flight engineers sitting around talking and maybe even arguing, their voices filling the air above the clack of machines, the whir of tapers, and the crackle of communications receivers. But there was only one man in the small office—a makeshift office by Earth standards—a sour-faced, hollow-eyed man with a spike beard, and he sat in the midst of the mutterings, squeaks, and tweetings of a bank of speakers on the wall to the right of his desk. A bank of controls faced him at the rear of it. There were no tapers or clacking machines.

The man made a few adjustments on the control panel and then waved to him. "Welcome to Mars, Mr. Schaun. My name's Hotchkiss. Be with you in a minute." He spoke a few low words into a speaker and then turned to him. "You're a few days early."

"I didn't waste any time getting here."

"Really pushed your spacer, eh? You weren't due until three days from now."

"I guess I did push the *Fern* a little. But it's a good ship."

"It looks good from here," Hotchkiss said, squinting out the broad window at it. Then he grinned. "That landing fooled you a little, didn't it? It does everybody the first time. You'll get used to it, though. Have a chair."

"Thanks, but it feels good to stand up and move around for a change."

"I know how it is. I used to enjoy walking around myself.

Now I have to use this." With a grimance he gestured to a crutch.

Bert saw with a start most of the man's right leg was missing.

"Lost it in diffusion. Took a spill with a load of slugs."

Bert looked at him blankly.

"I was where you are now two years ago, Schaun. Came down in a burst of glory and nearly cracked up." He laughed a bit ruefully. "At least you had sense enough to give up trying to get down manually."

Bert was shocked. "You mean you were a prospector two years ago?"

The man nodded wryly. "I was standing where you are, eager for work with the Sully Refining Company just as you are. Of course we didn't have a building as nice as this then. Things were a little rough in those days. But I didn't care. I couldn't wait to get out to the belt. But I might as well have stayed home for all the good it did me."

"You weren't lucky, is that it? Or is it really that tough out there?"

"I didn't find a thing," Hotchkiss said bitterly, casting an eye over the control panel. "I was one of those guys dead set on making a big haul, too. Maybe I'd have made it if I had a little more time, a little more money. But I ran out of both. Had to come back and work for Sully and they put me in crushing and grinding for a while, but it was too damn hot. I thought I was lucky when I got over in the diffuser unit, but that was really worse than before. Too much steam and heat." He shrugged jerkily, as if to shake off unpleasantness, saying, "But I don't want to tell you the story of my life."

"I'm interested," Bert said. "You were a prospector and a pilot, still they put you to work in the refinery. It doesn't make sense!"

Hotchkiss laughed. "It does when you know the refinery people. Prospectors and would-be prospectors are a dime a dozen. But somebody to work in the refineries? They're hard to come by. Nobody wants a job like that. The truth about the work in the processing units has found its way to Earth. It must have, because fewer and fewer people sign up for processing work these days. The work's hard, the environment's bad, and the pay is nothing to write home about in spite of the hazards and hardships.

"And prospecting, too. You never hear about the unlucky ones, just the ones who struck it rich out there. And they're the ones who can afford to go back to Earth to spend what they made and spread the word where they got it. Nobody hears our story or there wouldn't be so many ore hunters probing those rocks."

"You make it sound plenty bad," Bert said, lighting his cigar again and wondering how much of what he was hearing was true. Hotchkiss didn't look as if he'd be much of a pilot.

"It *is* bad if you go in for straight prospecting. If you get a chance, you ought to work on assignment for Sully. That way you won't go broke and end up where I am. Or worse."

"I don't see why you had to end up broke. You had your ship, didn't you?"

"Sure, but I couldn't sell it. I had to mortgage it for my last run. It belongs to Sully now. I've seen a lot of ships go that way."

"But you're working now. Couldn't you buy it back?"

Hotchkiss shook his head. "Sully won't sell. They never sell a ship once they get their hands on it. Besides, they'd rather have me right here. They're shorthanded all around."

"Sounds like a guy had better watch his step around here or Sully makes a refinery worker out of him," Bert said.

"They'll do it if they get half a chance." Then Hotchkiss brightened. "But tell me about Earth. It's still there, isn't it?"

"It's still there, Hotchkiss, and in much the same condition as when you left it, I'd say. I don't think you'd be able to see any difference."

"I suppose not. Things don't change there as they do here. New buildings all the time, new faces, saying good-bye to the old ones, the lucky ones whose contracts have run out, that is. But in spite of the changes it's still a hell of a place to be, if you ask me."

"I suppose," Bert said, suddenly tiring of the small talk. "I'm supposed to see a guy named Lem Osborne."

"He's over at the head office: Building One. But you can't go there yet. You have to see Babcock first."

"Babcock? Who's he?"

"He's the reception committee for all the centers. He's flying over from Four. That's the Schlenker Company and Babcock's headquarters. Remember, you came in a few days early. Otherwise he'd have been here waiting for you when you came in. I was talking with him just a few minutes ago. He'll be around as soon as he can."

"But why do I have to wait for him?"

"You have to be cleared, Schaun. It's the policy. Babcock clears everybody."

"Who does he work for?"

"Himself. He heads up security, has a small police force over at Four, but there's not much trouble around here. Of course if it weren't for the refineries, he wouldn't be working at all, so naturally he works pretty close with them." Seeing the annoyed look on Bert's face, he hastened to say, "But you don't have anything to worry about. He'll pass you. It's easy getting in. Finding a way to get out is the hard part."

"How long do you think it will be before he gets here?"

Hotchkiss glanced at the wall clock. "It's just two. He should be on his way now. It'll be less than an hour."

Suddenly the small Operations office seemed more confining than his ship had ever been.

"Where can a man get a drink around here, Hotchkiss?"

"Emma Klein's—that's building twenty-nine—is open right now. But you'd better wait for your clearance first."

"Don't tell me I have to have clearance before I can get a drink!"

"Mr. Babcock wouldn't like your not being here when he gets here."

"You can tell this Babcock where he can find me."

The air, tenuous as it was, felt better than the hot, dry air of the Operations office, even though the effort of walking left him panting and a little dizzy. He made his way in the direction Hotchkiss had reluctantly pointed out, passing small, squat buildings on the way, noticing they were all made of the same brown buildings blocks and assuming they were constructed of a substance indigenous to Mars. He wondered if all the planet's architecture was so utilitarian.

He walked in silence and alone, his boots kicking up a little sepia dust, the sound of his heels sometimes echoing from the ugly structures, Hotchkiss's depressing talk lingering with him. Had he been a fool to come to Mars to try to wrest from the asteroid belt the riches that were there? Of course not. That's why the refinery companies were on Mars. Merely because things didn't turn out for some prospectors didn't mean things wouldn't turn out for Bert Schaun. Remembering Hotchkiss now as he walked along, he concluded the man failed because some people are destined to fail. In fact, Hotchkiss looked and talked pretty much as if he enjoyed failing.

Having made this conclusion, he felt better and soon came up to building twenty-nine.

What caught Bert's eye when he opened the door was not Mrs. Klein, who looked up at him from behind the bar with an expression close to surprise, or the heads that turned toward him at every table, but the three pictures on the

back bar. They were enlarged color photographs of Earth
scenes: a cool, quiet mountain stream, a view of rolling New
England hills in summer, and the New York City harbor
at midday.

While these scenes evoked in him a momentary surge of
nostalgia for things of Earth, it was Mrs. Klein, when Bert
finally managed to tear his eyes away from the pictures,
who inspired the stronger emotion. She was a head shorter
than he, blue-eyed, round-faced, and her shiny, black hair
was drawn into a knot at the back of her head. She was not
beautiful, but her countenance was one of cheer, and the way
she held her full, red lips made Bert feel she was about
ready to laugh.

"I see now where everybody is," he said, drawing up a
stool at the bar. "They're all at building twenty-nine."

"I get my share, I guess," Emma said, smiling and swab-
bing the countertop before him. "I never saw you before."

"Just checked in at Operations. I'll take a little bourbon on
the rocks, if there is such a thing on Mars."

"There is. And more." Seeing him glance at the filled
tables, she said, "These men just got off the morning shift."

He looked around at the faces of the men, most of them
lean, bearded faces, the faces of men who seemed to be
trying hard to capture a fleeting moment's pleasure. He
sensed a weariness about them, catching it in their eyes, in
their manner and in their laugh. Was Mars a planet of
Hotchkisses?

"Since you just got in," Emma said, setting the drink in
front of him, "I think it only fair to warn you this will hit you
pretty hard. Difference in air pressure, you know."

"I want it to hit hard," he said, looking her square in the
eye. "It's been a long time."

She flushed and turned away, her eyes bright and busy.
He was in a position to see more of her than he had been at
the door and he liked what he saw. He was pleased with

her well-rounded figure, having no use for the thin, gangling women of the advertisements. She was aware of his inspection and he was further pleased to note it didn't seem to bother her. He could see she knew just what to say to these men: a little firmness here, a little lightness there, a smile, a frown. . . .

"So you're from Earth, eh?"

Bert turned to the voice and looked into the face of an older man sitting next to him.

"My name's Sam Streeper. I heard you tell Emma you was just in." Sam had a gray beard, bloodshot eyes, and his heavy jacket seemed a little too big for him.

"Yeah, just got in. I'm Bert Schaun."

Sam offered a hand and Bert clasped and shook it.

"How'd the Classic do this year?"

Bet narrowed his eyes and studied the face. But there was nothing in it to read. "Why do you ask that?"

"Oh, I always used to follow it. Even was on Simmons Field a couple times for the start and finish. I miss it up here. You see it this year?"

"Yes," Bert said, not wanting to look him in the eye when he said it. "I watched it." It was conceivable the man would not connect him with the big race, but it would be something to remember in case someone did. "It was a good race."

"Understand somebody got killed."

"That's right." Bert gripped his glass firmly in his fist. If it was coming, it would come soon and he wanted to be ready for it.

"Too bad." Sam drained his glass and signaled for more. "Heard you tell Emma you ain't been cleared yet. That right?"

Bert relaxed. "That's right, too. The man at Operations wanted me to stay there until I was, but I got thirsty."

"Already you're thirsty, eh? Well, you're goin' to be thirsty from now on. That's about all this place is good for—

I mean this whole planet and all the ports in it—a place to raise a thirst. A mean thirst." He watched glumly as Emma poured them another drink. "You got any idea why that guy at Op tried to keep you there?"

"He said a man named Babcock was supposed to show up soon."

"He wanted you to see Babcock first. Didn't want you talkin' to anybody else and find out what a lousy setup this is."

"He didn't talk that way. He seemed pretty unhappy with it himself."

Sam nodded. "He's been unhappy since he got here. But what I said about it still goes. They want to hook you first, name on that dotted line. Then you're stuck and they don't give a damn any more."

"The refinery people, you mean."

"None other. Of course with you it ain't goin' to be so bad. I guess you'll get away on your hauls. But you won't like it even then. Just remember, you'll be lucky you ain't workin' in the refinery. That's where a lot of them end up if they can't handle their money, gamble it away, or let the processors talk them into givin' up lookin' for ore."

"Now don't tell me you're a broken down prospector like Hotchkiss."

"Nope. I don't know nothin' else but refinery work. Came up to do nothin' but that and I'm sorry I started."

"What did you do on Earth?"

"Mechanic. Worked on spacers. Up here I work on machines in the refinery. Thought I was smart to come up. I'll take the spacer work though."

"Can't you do that here?"

"Then who'd do the machinery work?"

"You sound as if you don't like it around here either."

"Who does?" He swung around to face Bert. "You want

some advice? If I was you, I'd turn around and hightail it back home."

"Why?"

"Because Mars ain't a fit place for human bein's, that's why. They ought to give it back to the Stinkers."

"Stinkers? I've heard about them."

"Who hasn't?" Sam laughed. "Everybody always wants to know about the Stinkers the minute they land. They don't know how scarce they are. We must have scared hell out of 'em when we took over. I never saw but one and I'll tell you he sure raised a hell of a stink."

"What do they look like? I've seen picture and drawings, but I couldn't tell much from them."

"Well, I'll tell you," Sam said, chuckling, "if you was to see one in a poor light, I don't think you'd see much difference between one of them and one of us. Except maybe they're smaller."

"What about this one you saw? Where did you see him?"

"Oh, somebody caught one that came too close to Seven. They brought him in and . . . well, they made him run the gauntlet and a lot of other things."

"What happened to him?"

"Somebody hit him too hard. They had to cremate him. Afraid maybe if they buried him as he was, he'd stink the place up."

"That was a dirty thing to do, drag the thing into town, wasn't it?"

"Weren't my idea. It was awful."

"Why should they do a thing like that?"

Sam shook his head. "You got me. I guess maybe it was because he was different. Mars don't seem to bring out the best in people."

"From what I've heard so far, I'll go along with that."

Sam sighed. "I got another whole year of it. When that

year is up, Brother, I'm takin' the first freighter home. I've stayed longer than most anyhow."

"Does everybody feel as you do about it?"

"Most everybody. It's the work, maybe. It's not like a factory at home. You never get far enough away from it here. And you don't get near enough money for what you got to put up with."

"Didn't you know how much you were going to be paid before you left Earth?"

Sam smiled wryly. "I hate to admit it. I thought I was gettin' away from somethin'. Just like everybody else. Buyin' a pig in a poke. I liked the idea of evadin' what was comin' back there. But now I'm goin' back and face the music. I'd rather have that than this."

Bert knew better than to ask what it was.

"Then there's nothin' to do around here, unless you call drinkin' somethin'. And you can use up your whole pay check doin' that. And that's fine for the refineries, because the profits go right back to them. Then there's no place to go. And for some that's the worst thing of all, not bein' able to get away from everybody else. And last, and mighty important, there ain't many women around, only a few wives of prospectors, like Emma here."

Sam leaned a little closer. "Incidentally, her old man was killed about six months ago. I don't know why she don't go home instead of workin' here."

"You mean she just works here?"

"Nobody owns nothin' around here but the refinery people. I guess nobody has enough money to start anythin' 'cept the successful prospectors and they're anxious to get the hell back to Earth to spend it. No, Emma works just like the rest of us. Funny thing, too. They say she has scads of dough. Klein was one of the lucky hunters. Made a rich haul before he . . . died. The story is"—and here he assumed a low, confidential tone—"that he made too big a strike and Sully didn't like it, so they took it away from him."

"Just rumor, though, isn't it?"

"You'll hear the story if you're here long enough. The way I heard it, Klein went out on a three month trek—a month and a half each way—with provisions for only that long. He never came back. They say some of Sully's men met his ship out in space, boarded it, jammed the controls and set his course for infinity. So he's still out there some'eres. But dead."

"Nobody's proved it, I suppose."

"Pretty hard to prove a thing like that, Mister."

Bert drank the last few drops in his glass, not liking what he had seen and heard so far, with an exception or two. "How about this strike of his? How do you know Sully took it over?"

Sam shrugged. "I don't know. But why else should they get rid of Klein?"

"*If* they got rid of him."

Sam eyed him coldly. "Let me know what you think in a couple months, Schaun." Then he brightened. "Say, wasn't there a man named Schaun in the Classic this year?"

Bert nodded.

"That wouldn't be you by any chance, would it?"

"No. That was my grandfather."

Sam's eyes had a wary look.

"And," Bert added firmly, "I'd prefer your forgetting all about it."

"Yeah," Sam said slowly. "I see what you mean. Well, I've got to go." He got off the stool. "I'll see you, Schaun."

The crowd was thinning now; the tavern was not half full. He managed to catch Emma's eye.

"If you think I can stand it, I'll have another."

"Unless I counted wrong, that will be three."

"Three to get ready, they say. Always keep track of what your customers drink?"

She surveyed him critically. "You seem to be standing them all right. That's a bit unusual."

"Maybe I'm an unusual man."

"And maybe you think a lot of yourself." She didn't say it disparagingly.

"Somebody's got to, nobody else seems to."

"I don't see why. You seem to have good points."

She looked away under his steady gaze and a spot of pink grew on her cheek. Bert found himself wishing there was no one else in the bar.

"I'd like to talk to you," he said.

"Aren't you talking to me?"

"I don't mean like this."

Emma regarded him seriously, to the exclusion of all else, the bantering manner gone, the blue eyes intense.

"I have a rule—"

"Rules are made to be broken," he said, almost before she had the words out of her mouth.

"Who are you?" she asked, eyes narrowing.

"My name's Bert Schaun."

"What do you want to talk to me about?"

"I'm not sure . . . yet."

Her eyes went beyond him to the door. They brightened. "Someone who wants to see you has just walked in, Mr. Schaun."

Bert turned to see a tall man, a wide-shouldered blond man with curious blue eyes, looking at him from the doorway.

"That's Steve Babcock," she said.

SIX

"You must be Schaun," Steve said as he came up to the bar in a long, easy stride. "You're the only one I don't know." "I'm Steve Babcock."

Bert took the hand. Steve Babcock did not seem to be a petty man, as he had expected from Hotchkiss's description; he had expected someone not so big, someone not so friendly, a man with an obvious fetish for obeying rules and giving admonitions. This man was relaxed, confident and unassuming.

"In Steve Babcock's head," Emma said, flashing Steve a warm smile, "there's a photographic record of every face and name on Mars."

Steve grinned. "I wish you were one hundred per cent right. A great kidder, Emma. You'll find that out, Schaun."

"I kid everybody but you," Emma said. "Your usual?"

Steve nodded, then turned to Bert. "You're early, Schaun. I was over at Four doing a little work when I got word you were here. Sorry to keep you waiting. But then, I see you made good use of the time. Have another on me?"

"Thanks, I will."

"You haven't been around, Steve," Emma said. "What's the matter? Do they have better-looking bartenders over at Four?"

"You know better than that, Emma. I've been busy, that's all. And I've got to get back as soon as I check Schaun in." He raised his glass. "Well, here's good luck to you, Schaun."

"And from what I hear, I'll need it."

Steve grinned again, but this time the eyes were not really amused. "It's an unhappy place to everybody who doesn't like it. Me, I like it. And it does take a little luck to work the asteroids. But I saw that ship of yours on the landing pattern. I'd say you stand a little better chance than most. You know how to buy a ship. And you look as if you could stand the gaff."

"Thanks. Then the only thing standing in my way seems to be that clearance Hotchkiss mentioned up at Operations."

"The clearance is just a formality," Steve said. "Have to register your ship if it's going to be working around here. From there we go to your physical—that's a formality, too, believe me—and then we'll talk to Mr. Osborne."

"We? I think I'd rather do my own talking, Babcock."

"I always take the new men over, Schaun. Besides, for the record, I'll have to know how you sign on."

"Got a finger on everybody, eh? And a memory picture, too, as Emma said. That must be quite a few people to remember."

"About five thousand. It's my job."

"Much crime?"

"Quarrels, a few fights. Nobody has time to think up anything elaborate. We've got a jail over at Four but we've had only a few drunks in it this past year."

Quite a contrast between the picture Sam Streeper had painted and the one Steve Babcock was presenting. Of course there was a difference in occupations and a difference in men.

"I hear," Bert said testily, "that Emma's husband died out in space." He watched the man for reaction.

Steve's shoulders merely moved in a shrug. "He was a hell of a good man. And he's not the first, won't be the last. Going out there alone is like going in swimming by yourself. If something happens to you, there's nobody around to help you. But how did you know about that? Did Emma tell you?"

"No, just a guy at the bar."

"Who was it?" The blue eyes were cool and bright.

"I didn't catch the name."

"Oh." The eyes lost their interest. "There's a lot of fancy stories about Hank Klein going the rounds. And I don't like them. Officially, he just never came back. We've been expecting to find his wrecked ship out there some place. We've been looking for it a long time."

Now Bert had two views of Klein's death. One view was given by a man whose business it was to investigate a thing like that, the other by a man who received his information from others. Of the two, Bert believed Steve Babcock. Truth becomes a warped, misshapen thing when it travels through too many heads.

"This guy also said something else."

"He was quite a talkative guy, wasn't he? What else did he have to say?"

"He said a Stinker was killed here in Seven."

Steve laughed. "You did hear things, didn't you? Well, they did just that. They shouldn't have done it, of course. Our attitude toward the Stinkers is live and let live, but here was a crowd and you know how a crowd can be, and those Stinkers don't have that name for nothing. A few drinks and one thing led to another."

"Did you ever find out who did it?"

"I could have picked the two or three responsible ones out of the crowd, but that would have meant two or three less men reporting for work the next day and we need every man on the job. Maybe you don't know about the manpower shortage on Mars. Besides, it's just as well. The incident will serve as a warning to other Stinkers to stay away."

"I take it you don't care much for the Stinkers."

Steve looked at him with pained amusement. "Are you kidding? Nobody cares much for Stinkers. Do you suppose they did what they did because they liked them?"

"Still, it seems pretty rash. . . ."

"You just don't know, Schaun, that's all. Maybe you'll meet one some day. Then let me know what you think."

He glanced at his wristwatch. "We'd better move. I've got to get back to Four."

Lem Osborne jumped up when they entered, came a-round his desk and reached for Bert's hand.

"Glad to see you, Schaun," he said warmly. "Glad to see you. Sit down. Have a good trip?"

"So-so," Bert said, sitting in one of the folding chairs before the metal desk and wondering why the general manager of the Sully Refining Company should be so effusive.

Steve sat in one of the other chairs, and Osborne took the papers he offered, returned to his desk, withdrew glasses from his jacket breast pocket, and started to read the results of Steve's perfunctory examination of the *Fern* and Bert's physical, his lips moving silently as he did so. He was a round-faced, harried-looking, balding man with heavy worry lines on his forehead and shadows under his eyes.

"You've got a good ship," Osborne said, laying one paper aside. "I'm glad to see that."

"It cost me plenty," Bert said.

"He keeps it in good shape, too," Steve offered.

"Mmm." And Osborne was immersed in the physical report.

Osborne's office was large for Mars, about twenty feet square, with plastic walls and a black plastic floor. It contained only the one metal desk, half a dozen folding chairs similar to the ones they were sitting in, a viewphone, intercom, filing cabinet, and a faded world calendar. The only spot of color was the bouquet of artificial flowers on Osborne's desk. And they looked out of place there.

The office itself occupied a small area in the largest building in Seven, and from beyond the walls came a low humming and clicking that Bert guessed was part of the refining operation deep within the plant. Maybe that continuous hum and clicking helped etch lines in the man's face.

"Well," the general manager said, looking up, "everything appears to be in order. You can start working for Sully right now as far as I'm concerned."

"I'm glad to hear that," Steve said. "I thought we had that all straightened out with those wires."

"We didn't go into one detail though," Osborne said. "And that's your assignment." He opened a drawer and drew out a sheaf of papers. "A ship like yours ought to be assigned a good strike. You will get five dollars a ton for all the ore you haul, and fifteen dollars a day expense money."

Now Bert new why Osborne had been so glad to see him.

"I think you've got that wrong, Mr. Osborne," he said. "I didn't come here to haul ore. I just want to sign up with Sully to sell what I find."

"You're already signed up with Sully," Osborne said. "You did that on Earth. I just naturally assumed you wanted to work on assignment. As a matter of fact, I'd advise you to do just that. That way you get a place to sleep, your meals while you're in port, and you get unloading assistance and your ship will be serviced whenever you think it needs it, all without charge."

"It's none of my business, but I'd recommend your taking the assignment job, Schaun," Steve said. "Then you don't have to worry about looking for ore. All you do is load up and bring it in. And the more you bring in, the more you earn. It's as simple as that."

"That's very nice of Sully," Bert said evenly, "but I think I'll be finding my own ore."

"Of course in that case you'll get whatever the ore's assayed," Osborne said quickly. "But I may as well tell you, the belt is big and most of the rocks don't bear a trace of anything."

"They must bear something or you wouldn't be in business."

"Oh," Osborne said, laughing a little, "don't get me wrong. I'm not saying there's no uranium out there. I just say it's pretty hard to find."

"Most men fresh from Earth want to be prospectors," Steve explained. "But they usually turn to mining before it's all over Too many guys are going broke out there trying to line up a good strike. The companies would rather have them bringing in what is alread uncovered out there."

"At five dollars a ton? Tell me, Mr. Osborne, is that Earth tons or Mars tons?"

"Please," Osborne said, affronted. "What do you think we are? Earth tons, of course."

"I just wanted to get it straight, that's all. Isn't anybody doing any prospecting? Or does everybody work for Sully on assignment?"

Osborne got up, ran a hand over nonexistent hair. "There's no need for prospecting, Schaun. That's the word I'd like to get back to Earth. But still they come, wanting to look for ore. We've got more veins uncovered now than we can work. What we lack is manpower to bring it in and manpower to process it." He started to walk, talking and gesturing. "We have a lot invested out here. We have a big job to do, feeding energy to Earth, the eight of us: eight companies all working toward the same goal and finding we can't do the job we'd like because we don't have enough men to do it with. The trouble isn't so much with the processing—we have barely enough men for that—but the hauling. Too many men are looking for ore and not enough are bringing it in."

"Five dollars a ton is hardly what I expected to make, and it doesn't seem enough for all the risks you're talking about. I could make money like that back on Earth."

"It's better than making nothing at all," Steve reminded. "You've got to remember there are a lot of unlucky prospectors working in the plants."

"I know," Bert said. "I talked to Hotchkiss. But I'm ready to take that chance."

Osborne gave him an owlish look. "Optimism's all right, but do you realize the costs if you want to operate your own way?"

"I'm ready to pay."

"Ten dollars a night for lodging?"

"I'll sleep in the ship."

"Ten dollars a night for occupying a space on the landing pattern?"

"I'll keep my ship in orbit and come down with somebody else."

"Think so? Maybe everybody else will be too busy. We work together pretty well around here."

"So I've seen," Bert said knowingly, glancing at Steve.

"And," Osborne added, "there's the matter of ten dollars a gondola, and they carry only eight tons of ore each. How many are you going to take along on your first trip?"

"Ten dollars each? Why, that's robbery! You ought to furnish them!"

"And fifty dollars for an assist," Osborne added. "Fifty dollars for one of our ships to come up and help you bring your load down. If you have a load, that is."

"That's not fair!"

"Not fair?" Osborne's eyes glittered and he leaned forward on the desk. "Why isn't it fair? It cost a pretty penny to set this place up. Why shouldn't people who make use of it pay? Why shouldn't you pay for a place to sleep, for your meals, for a ship to help you unload?"

"It's not that I don't see what you are trying to do," Bert said, "but that seems out of line."

"Everything," Steve said dryly, "is expensive on Mars."

"So I'm discovering," Bert said bitingly, "and the most expensive thing of all seems to be having your own way."

"Then why don't you see things my way?" Osborne

asked, seating himself behind the desk again. "You work for Sully and none of those things cost you anything."

"And I'm just a truck for hire."

"There's security in that. And fifteen dollars expense money each day." Osborne picked up the papers again. "I can give you your first assignment right now."

Bet reached for and found a new cigar. Savagely he unskinned it and bit off the end of it. "Sorry," he said. "I'm not buying it."

Osborne dropped the papers back to his desk. "You're just like all the rest, aren't you, Schaun? You come up here expecting to walk right in and tell us how to manage things, what you will do and what you won't do, and all you're interested in is what you can make out of it."

"I suppose," Bert said incisively, "you're not interested in what you can make out of me."

Osborne slapped the papers down. "I wish you had the pressures I have. They're screaming for power on Earth. We still haven't got over the hump, still haven't caught up with the demand. And you want to go out galavanting around with a fine ship like that looking for a new lode."

"When I find it, you'll have plenty of ore."

"If you find it," Osborne said coldly.

"Why don't you sleep on it, Schaun?" Steve suggested cheerfully. "Maybe you'll think differently about it in the morning."

Bert got up. "I intend to be gone by morning. Where do I pay for the time I've already used up on the landing pattern? And for the ten gondolas I'm going to need tomorrow morning?"

"Ten gondolas?"

"At least ten. And I'll pay in advance for my first assist."

Osborne put the papers in a drawer and slammed the

drawer shut, hard. "I think you are being a fool, Schaun."

"Maybe. But I'll have a try at it my way first."

SEVEN

"WELL!" Emma said in surprise when she found Bert's face among those at the bar. "I didn't expect you back. I thought you'd be halfway to the belt by this time."

"I told you I wanted to talk to you," Bert said. "And I meant it."

"And I told you I had a rule about things like that," she said firmly. "And I meant that."

"Two purposeful people. We ought to get along."

She ignored him, went to serve others at the bar.

Three hours later, he and another man, an older, bespectacled man who sat staring at his drink and mumbling to it, were the only ones remaining in building twenty-nine.

"Time to close," Emma said, looking at Bert and saying it loud enough for the other man to hear. "You will have to go."

The man down the bar continued his private conversation with the glass. Bert made no move to get up.

"Come on, Mr. Gates," Emma said, going over and shaking the gray-haired man's arm. "Closing time."

"Eh? Wha's'at?" He looked up at her dully through thick lenses.

"Need some help?" Bert offered.

"I won't need any help with Mr. Gates," she said. "This is a nightly affair." She went around the bar and helped the old man off his bar stool, zipped his jacket for him while he grinned at her foolishly. Then she moved to the door and opened it, the bitter chill of the Martian night sweeping in and sucking the warmth from the room. "Out you go, Mr. Gates."

The old man toddled to the door and as he passed through he managed to mumble, "Thanks, Emma." She closed the door quickly.

"Will he make it?" Bert asked. "It's pretty cold out there."

"The cold will take him out of it," she said, not moving from the door. "He's never failed to make it yet."

For a moment they looked at each other across the room, she leaning against the door, he on the stool, his elbows on the bar. Even in the harsh light of the fluoro over the doorway, Bert found the soft curve of cheek and jaw and breast attractive. He said, "I've listened to a lot of stuff the past three hours."

"Think of me," she said. "I've listened to it all day."

"Pretty dull, isn't it?"

"Not always. But today it was. I'm tired."

"You don't look tired."

"I am. . . . And I don't want to play."

"I didn't stay for games."

"What did you stay for then?"

"I want to talk with you, that's all."

"I wish I could believe that."

"Why shouldn't you?"

"Because I'm one of the few women in Seven and because you have a predatory look in your eye."

"Nobody ever told me that before," Bert said grinning. "It must be the Martian air."

She continued to stand for a moment. Then she turned, snapped the lock on the door, saying, "You say you only want to talk. I'll take your word for that."

He watched her as she came across the floor and around the bar, liking her figure, her poise, her forthrightness.

"You're an odd man," she said when she started preparing drinks for them. "You have your clearance and you're still here. Most men wouldn't waste a minute getting out to the belt. Time is money when you're hauling ore, you know."

He shook his head. "I'm not hauling ore."

She looked up in surprise. "Not hauling ore?"

"I'm not working on assignment."

"How did you ever convince Osborne of that?"

"I didn't convince him; I told him."

She gave him an admiring glance. "I believe you did. Osborne doesn't like to be told."

"I gathered that."

Emma carried their drinks to a table. "Let's sit out here. I'm dead from standing all day."

He dropped off the stool and pulled out a scraping chair and sat opposite her. She pushed his drink toward him, lifted her own glass in the slim white fingers of both hands and held it.

"I hope you have plenty of money."

"Why?"

"They'll drain a small fortune out of you if you don't hit, charging you for every little thing."

"This has happened before?"

"Many times. Unless you can pay indefinitely, they'll finally get your ship and you won't be able to go out any more. Then after they've bled you white they'll put one of their own men in it and use it for hauling, paying you next to nothing for the use of it and work you for less than that in the refinery. That's what happens to prospectors who don't see it their way."

"I'd sell the ship before I'd let them do that."

"Sell it?" She laughed a little. "To whom?"

"I see. They've got me coming or going, haven't they?"

"They run things. No question about that."

"Even you?"

"I could get out. So could you . . . now."

"So I better find a good strike, eh?"

She nodded. "It's the only way to have your own way around here."

He drank a little. It was quiet in the tavern, almost eerie, the single fluoro burning over the door, the empty chairs, the long shadows on the floors and walls.

Emma felt it and shivered a little.

"Cold?" he asked.

"No. This place gives me a chill when there's nobody in it."

"We're in it."

"I mean except you and me."

"You've never been out in space alone or you'd know what real loneliness is."

She shivered again, took a sip of her drink. Bert brought out a new cigar, undressed it, and lighted it.

"Who are you, really?" Emma asked suddenly.

He stared at her in surprise.

"I can't believe you're just a prospector. You're different from the others."

"How am I different?"

"I can't describe it."

"I'm nothing special," he said, blowing a plume of smoke and watching it billow. "I'm just a guy." He was glad she had said that. It showed she had looked beyond his appearance, that she might be seeing in him the very thing he saw in her. And that's what he had wanted to know. "What's it like out there in the belt, Emma?"

She lifted her eyebrows. "Why ask me? I've never been out there."

"Your husband was. What did he have to say about it?"

She lowered her drink a little unsteadily. "What do you know about my husband?"

"Only what I heard while sitting at the bar."

"What do they say about him?"

He shrugged. "A lot of things. I didn't believe most of them."

"I suppose . . . I suppose they told you what happened to him."

"They say he never came back from his last trip."

She nodded, eyes sober. "He's gone, all right."

"They also said somebody jammed the controls and sent him sailing off to nowhere."

"Who told you that?"

"Several of them."

She looked beyond him, as if to see through the walls and out to space, her fingers white around her glass. "It doesn't make any difference how it happened. I just know I'll never see him again. I'd rather think of it that way. 'Dead' is an ugly word."

"Do you think somebody did jam his controls?"

"Why do you keep asking that?"

"I just want to know what you think."

She gazed at him for a moment before answering. "I can't see why Sully'd do a thing like that just to get a rich asteroid."

"They seem pretty grasping."

"I won't deny that. But to kill?" She shook her head. "I don't want to think that."

"Was your husband a good pilot?"

"Hank was one of the best." Her eyes glowed in remembrance. Then she darted a glance at him. "In a way you remind me of him, the color of your hair, your build. In fact, you gave me a start when you walked in this afternoon. And then what you did today, telling Osborne what you were going to do instead of the other way around—Hank did the same thing three years ago. I'll bet you're a good pilot, too, aren't you?"

"One of the best," Bert said. "What else can I say?"

"What were you before you came to Mars? I mean, what did you do?"

"I was a pilot," Bert said carefully.

"That's to your credit. Hank was only a minor executive in Hastings Arcars. He had to start from scratch with ships. But he learned quickly."

"Whatever made you two come to Mars?"

"We were both restless. Hank's work kept him busy day and night and I was working, too. We saw little of each other. One night we decided to have one last fling, do something exciting, maybe take a long chance to make a pile or lose our shirts. After that, we said to each other, we'd have a family and settled down. Coming to Mars was Hank's idea. He wanted to go and make his strike and come back. But I vetoed that. I told him wherever he went I was going, too. You know, it took me a whole year to convince him I was serious.

"We set out—it wasn't quite three years ago—and at first it was like a holiday, being together all the time. We didn't mind the potato flakes, the dehydrated milk, the powdered everything, the fact there was no place to go and nothing to do. We were going to get in and get out and live gloriously ever after."

Emma smiled ruefully. " 'Get in and get out.' That was a laugh. I wish it had been that easy. We'd be back there now, living on easy street. You know how long it took Hank to make his strike? A year and a half. We were almost broke by that time, fearing we'd have to go to work in the refinery, for everybody mortgages everything for a last run, you know. But he made a rich strike. One of the richest. Maybe it would have ended differently if it hadn't been such a wonderful discovery."

She looked up and her eyes were bright. "He once told me the refinery people offered to buy his mine, but he refused to sell. Now it doesn't make any difference. He never told me where it is and I wouldn't know if Sully knows or not."

Emma laughed. "I was going to sit and listen to you and here I am telling you my life story. Let's hear about you for a change."

"You said you could get out of here," Bert said. "Why don't you?"

She avoided his eyes, looked through what remained of her drink to the bottom of her glass. "Maybe I like it here."

"I can't believe that. And I can't see why you stay, every day facing the men who knew your husband. It's not like a woman to want to do that."

"Isn't it?" she said tartly. "May I have a reason."

"Maybe," Bert said testily, "you like someone here."

She met his look now. "Yes," she said, "maybe I do." She sipped a little more of her drink.

"Steve Babcock, for example."

"What makes you think that?" she asked quickly.

Bert laughed. "So it's true, eh?"

She flushed. "What do you mean, it's true?"

"Your face gives you away, Emma."

"Does it?" she was angry now, downed her drink and put the glass down heavily on the table. "I think you'd better go." She rose, her eyes cool.

"I suppose I'd better." Bert got up and stretched. "It's been nice."

"Hasn't it," Emma said acidly, starting to pass him.

"What"s got into you?" he asked, taking her arm and turning her toward him.

"You seem to know everything," she said hotly, "suppose you explain that."

"I hit a tender spot, didn't I? What did I say—that business about Steve Babcock? Why should that upset you?"

"I'm still waiting for your analysis," she said challengingly, not moving away.

He still held her arm, was suddenly conscious of her nearness. She sensed it, too, started to pull away.

"Don't—" she protested as he swept her to him.

She was warm and soft and she struggled in his arms, saying, "You promised. . . ."

He found her lips. They were soft, too, and for a moment she answered his kiss.

Then she tore herself from him, eyes bright with fury.

"I knew I shouldn't have let you stay."

"I'm glad you did, though," Bert said, grinning and reaching for her again.

She ducked away toward the door. "No more of that. You've got to go now."

"O.K." Bert zipped his heavy jacket, donned his thick hat.

At the door she said, "How long will you be gone?" She tried to make it sound disinterested.

He grinned again, pleased to see her not really angry. "Two months to begin with," he said coming to her and taking in the wide, blue eyes, the fine nose, the sheen of swept-back hair. He'd want to take the memory of that along with him.

"Come back," she said softly, and as he moved toward her she opened the door and the frigid air rushed in between them.

There was nothing he could do but go through the door. She was not dressed for the cold and he didn't want her standing there bearing the full force of it.

"Good luck, Bert," she said as he went outside.

He heard the door close behind him.

EIGHT

January 19, 2026

COMPARED to galaxies, the asteroid belt is no more than a pinch of dust strewn casually between two planets, insignificant pebbles circling a small sun. From the standpoint of planets, the ring of dust is enormous and forbidding, measuring nearly a half billion miles from inner to outer edge, its fragments varied and erratic, each of them too small to attract or hold an atmosphere, too far from the sun to be warm; they are barren worlds without water or life.

But to Bert Schaun the giant ellipse into which he sent the *Fern* was a challenge every bit as big as that of the Classic, with a possibility of its being even more rewarding. He was glad to leave behind the emptiness of the long way to Mars, eager to have done with the days of doing nothing but reading, sleeping and thinking. Here was what he had come for. Here was the new life, for somewhere among these rocks that spun endlessly around the sun was the treasure he was seeking.

The alarm bell, silent so long, rang with such sudden insistence that he jerked his arm over to shut it off, noting, as he did so, the foreign body's position on the indicator. With the eager anticipation of a child opening a Christmas package, Bert enlarged the view of his first rock on the screen, accommodated the *Fern's* velocity to it, and measured. A good three miles across, taking it from crag to crag, the sun glinting pink from its illuminated side. He'd have whooped with joy if he had seen a splash of yellow, but he knew carnotite wouldn't be that easily available.

Bert steadied the ship, keeping the rock in the center of the screen, swung the scintillometer into action, ran in the

66

photomultiplier output and turned to see the resultant figure in the oscilloscope. There was a small hump. The energy level of the gamma radiation was almost nonexistent.

He grinned. It was a nice rock and if there had been ore on it, it would have made his job easy. But what did he expect? Certainly not a hit the first time at bat.

He jabbed the accelerator, shot away from the rock, snapping the alarm system on again. Ten minutes later it went off and he located the new rock on the viewscope, trained the scintillometer on it. This time the scope showed a more gratifying level of radiation—at least high in comparison with the first rock. The resulting figure: three.

He turned the *Fern* toward the rock and circled it, the claim color chart in his hand. He did not see the magenta of Sully, the red of Schlenker, or any of the sprayed colors of the remaining six processors. Neither was there a pastel hue of a private prospector.

Bert stopped the *Fern*, idly watched the rock on the screen as he brought out a new cigar and lighted it. Who said uranium was hard to find? But he'd have to decide now. Should he be satisfied with three pounds per ton? He could fill the ten gondolas and go back and sell it and make a profit, but it would not be anywhere near the profit he was reaching for. There were rocks out there with ten and twelve pounds of uranium per ton. And that was profit with a capital letter.

Two tries—one failure and one fair pickings. He grunted, shoved the ship around, and headed into the stream. There would be other rocks, other chances. Osborne would only be amused if he brought in ore like this after all he had said.

The ship hummed along, the compressor hissing, the rock he had just inspected hardly distinguishable now from the stars on the aft screen he had activated. Bert chewed on his cigar, toying with the idea of readying his space suit. But no, he'd have plenty of time for that when he found the rock he was looking for. Just to pass the time he manipulated the grapples, the endless belt of buckets, the diamond drills, blasting cones, eroders, gimlets and saws. Everything was ready to go. He' sat back to relax, but he felt more like a fighter trying to relax before the next bell.

It was half an hour later when the alarm sounded again. A magenta rock, this one, and when he turned his scintillometer on it, the wave was peaked high. There must have been eight pounds per ton on that one! Lucky Sully!

An hour passed. Another alarm. A rock as big as Simmons Field—and not even a hint of a bump on the scope. All that rock and not a smell of radiation! He snorted and turned the ship away.

The fifth alarm. The blue of a processor. The color chart showed it belonged to Gianetti, the Italian refinery at Three. Only five pounds per ton. They hadn't done as well as Sully.

Then twenty-three rocks passed with no trace of radiation.

The twenty-fourth was an anomaly. The alarm sounded, the detector showed very little mass, and Bert turned the screen pickup in its direction. There, in the viewing area, was an effulgent rock, an asteroid completely unlike any others he had seen, one that glowed in the dark like a luminous-dialed clock.

It was ghostly. He decided it might be dangerous, pulled away, trained the scintillometer on it and watched for the inevitable reaction, guessing the rock was so highly charged it would be impossible to mine.

But the scintillometer showed nothing. Not a trace of energy. Not even the remotest suggestion of a hump. Just a flat line.

Bert stared at the pale, radiant rock for a long time, wondering what it could be if it weren't radioactive, watching it revolve slowly. . . . And suddenly he found his head nodding. He looked at his chronometer and realized he had been chasing asteroids for the better part of a day. He matched the spin of the asteroid, went to bed, slept fitfully.

"Where did you hear that story, Gar?" Emma asked, half angry, giving him the benefit of her undivided attention.

The man with the pock-marked face stirred uneasily on his stool. "Why?"

"Because I've heard it so many times."

"Really? You mean somebody else already told you?" Gar was troubled. "I didn't think anybody else'd have the nerve. I only told you because you've been so nice to me and I thought you ought to know. I thought somebody ought to tell you." He frowned into his drink. "You've got lots of friends. I should've known somebody'd beat me to it."

"It was nice of you to think of me, Gar. I like that."

He looked up, bright-eyed. "Really?"

"Yes."

He leaned forward on the bar. "I'm sure the story's true."

She leaned toward him. "What makes you so sure, Gar?"

"I've heard it so much. Everybody knows it."

"Do they ever say who did it?"

"No," he said, shaking his head. "Come to think of it, Mrs. Klein, they don't say."

She smiled. "Would you do something for me, Gar?"

He looked up, only half believing. "Me?"

She nodded.

"Sure. Anything."

"You go back to the man you heard that from and tell him I'd pay a lot of money to know who it was."

"Sure. I'll tell him. You leave that to me. Maybe he knows who did it.'

"Maybe he does, Gar."

January 20, 2026

The second day in the field Bert found two asteroids with ore, one with too small a reading to bother with, and the second with only a two-pound reading. But this second one had been sprayed with the pastel yellow of a prospector! Why, Bert had passed up a three-pounder the very first day! Maybe I shouldn't have been so hasty, he thought.

January 21, 2026

The third day in the belt he found an asteroid, one a little larger than any others he had seen, and he saw two ships on its surface. Enlarging his view, he could see tiny figures nearby. He decided not to stop the *Fern*. He needed every hour to search for ore, didn't want to waste time exchanging pleasantries. Plenty of time to do that on Mars.

January 22—January 29, 2026

The fourth day passed, as did the fifth, each day little different from the preceding one, and soon ten of them stretched out in a row, ten precious days without his finding a single worthwhile rock that was not claimed!

Maybe Osborne is right after all, he thought. Maybe all the good rocks are taken. But he knew it was only his discouragement talking. There were thousands of asteroids. Tens of thousands. And so far—he checked his figures—he had inspected one hundred and seventy-three.

Maybe I should have dug into the second one, the one that measured three pounds, he told himself. Maybe I ought to go back there now. But then he knew he couldn't do that. He had marked down no co-ordinates for it. He decided then and there to register any promising ones in the future.

January 30—February 8, 2026

The days marched by in single file; but quickly the ten days stretching out to two weeks. Then three weeks.

February 14, 2026

On the twenty-seventh day of his hunt, weary and sick at heart because he had sighted no rock with any detectable radiation for five days, Bert turned his ship toward Mars. He wanted to continue his search, but he could not because he had no more provisions.

Next time, he thought, I'll stock up more. I'll load all the way, every inch of her. And I'll go deeper into the belt.

March 6, 2026

"It was bad out there," Bert said, slumping in the chair and fingering the glass before him.

"I know," Emma said softly from the other side of the kitchen table.

"It's not the nothingness of space; I'm used to that. And it's not the distance or the time it takes getting there or coming back, although I wish it were nearer. It's going through it all for nothing."

They sat in the little kitchen behind the back bar, only the hum of the heating system for company, Emma with her shoes off, her feet propped up on another chair and still managing to look lady-like, and Bert conscious of the hard back of his chair after two months of the cushioned couch of the *Fern*. He was dog tired and distraught.

"Next time," he said, "I'm going farther. Maybe farther than anybody else has been. I ran into too many colored rocks on this round. Everybody and his brother color-sprayed every worthwhile hunk of anything."

"I suppose you wouldn't consider giving it up."

"Give up?" He snorted. "Not while I can still breathe."

"And you still own your ship, remember that."

"I'd blow her to bits before I'd let Osborne have her."

"Oh, you're a hard man, aren't you?"

"Sure, I'm a hard man when it comes to guys like Osborne."

"And you think you'd really blow up the *Fern?*"

"Damn right I would."

"You and Hank Klein. So much alike. Bluster and brag and never-say-die. Only he didn't have to blow up his ship."

"I don't like this, Emma. This whole setup."

"Neither did Hank," she said, memory lurking behind her eyes. "He'd rant about it every time he came back. But all his ravings—what did they get him?"

"You have never really said."

"He's gone, isn't he?" She moved in her chair, pulled her feet off the other one, turned to him. "Why can't men be satisfied to make their money just hauling ore? There's money in it, maybe not as much as there is in finding your own, but it could grow."

"Wait a minute, Emma," he said, surprised at this change in her. "That doesn't sound like the girl who came to Mars with her husband to make a fortune."

"Of course it doesn't," she said a little harshly. "And do you know why? Because she's not the same girl any more. She doesn't have her husband now. And why doesn't she? I'll tell you: Because her husband felt just as you do, because he was going to buck the big refinery combine and go out on his own, and go farther than anybody else, and make the biggest strike ever."

"And what's wrong with that?"

"What's wrong with that?" She stared at him.

"Yes," he said irritably. "He made his strike, didn't he?"

"Yes, he made his strike, the thing he was working for, and do you know what kind of a strike? A thirteen-pounder, that's what kind!"

Bert whistled. "I had no idea it was that big. Well, he earned it, I'd say."

"Of course he earned it. He always came back here

gloomy and dejected, and then, like a dutiful wife, I'd fire his spirit again. 'We'll show those boys,' I'd say. 'We'll beat 'em yet, Hank!' And then he'd look at me and he'd get all fired up again and he'd get that glow in his eyes and say, 'Yes, Baby, I think we will,' and then he'd be off again."

Bert grinned. "You were pretty good on the inspirational end, weren't you, Emma?"

"Oh, yes, wasn't I," she said and Bert was surprised to see her eyes tear-rimmed. "I inspired him all right. I sent him out there each time, patted him on the head and kissed him and told him, 'Baby needs a new pair of shoes.'"

"Sure," Bert said comfortingly. "Why, if it hadn't been for you—"

"Must you say it?" she cried shrilly, rising.

He started, seeing now what she meant. "I didn't mean—"

"I know what you meant!" she cried, leaning on the table toward him. "And it's all I have thought about since. You and Hank, yes, and me, too, all of us alike, all thinking of the treasure at the end of the rainbow, but never thinking of what also might lie there. And you want to go, so I help and push you toward it. I pushed him, can't you see that? I pushed him a little to far, farther than anybody else, pushed him to his death as if I had killed him myself!"

Bert stared at this woman leaning over him, not knowing what to say to her.

Slowly Emma sat down again, saying, "If he had never found what he was looking for we'd still be together."

"What really happened to him, Emma?"

She glared at him. "You're a fool, Bert Schaun."

"Now you're talking like Osborne. Why?"

"You have no idea? You don't know?"

"Can't say that I do," he said gruffly, uncomfortable.

"Well, I'll tell you then. It's because when you sit there and talk like that you might as well be my husband."

"I should think you'd like that."

"My God, do I have to draw pictures? Bert, can't you see I don't want you to go out there? Or maybe you don't know what's happened to me."

He said nothing.

"Look," she said, planting elbows on the table and leaning toward him. "You came in here last time and I let you talk to me. I don't know why. You angered me, too. It was right then that something happened, just as it did when I first knew Hank. When you left here last time, I liked you. Again I didn't know why. I thought you'd be gone a few days and I'd forget all about you. I hoped that's the way it would be. But it didn't work out that way. I found it was like having Hank back, like having him out there again. And I found myself worrying about you and hating it. It's easy for you to be out there in a ship millions of miles away because you know what's happening to you, but for me sitting back here at building twenty-nine, it's no picnic, wondering what's with you. I only wish it hadn't happened, but it has. Now does that make it clear?"

"Why, Emma!" He grinned in surprise.

"Oh, hell, you have the thickest skull. Almost as thick as Hank's. Sometimes I'd have to draw pictures for him, too."

"I thought a lot about you out there," he confided.

"That's not the point," she continued. "The point is: the minute the bar closes and we get back here all you want to do is talk about going out there again and making the big strike. I went through that once, remember? I don't want to go through it again. There, now I've even colored the picture for you. Is that plain enough or do I have to project it in three dimensions on a wide screen for you?"

He watched her lift her drink to her lips quickly, and he saw what Hank Klein must have seen, the firmness, the resolve, the understanding and tenderness in her face. And he knew then why Hank Klein had never given up. And sud denly he didn't like the emptiness of his own life, and the emptiness of his personal singleness of purpose, and his longing to find a rich lode for her became a physical ache despite the fact that she didn't want him to go out there again.

"All right," he said, "I've seen the picture, color and all. Let's say I know how you feel. I'm still not giving up." He added firmly, so there'd be no question, "I can't quit now that I've set my course. That's what Osborne and the rest of them want."

"Oh, hell, I should have gone to the party," she said, looking away as if she couldn't stand the sight of him.

"Party?"

"Yes. I was supposed to go over to Four for a party Steve Babcock and his boys are throwing. I gave it up when you called from Op."

"I'm sorry," he said coolly.

"Steve ordered a live lamb from Earth. God only knows how much it cost him to get it here. They're having roast lamb tonight."

"Roast lamb?" His mouth watered at the thought. "Maybe you should have gone."

"I'm convinced of it now."

"Well," he said, looking at his watch, "maybe there's still time."

"But I don't *want* to go," she said. Then she added stiffly, "I wouldn't go now anyway. I'll just keep sitting here hearing about how you're going out there again."

He pushed his chair back violently, went around the table to her, pulled her up savagely, held her tightly to him, looked into her hostile eyes.

He bent to kiss her; she turned her head away. He tightened his hold, at last found her lips. She struggled, and then, trembling a little, she answered him.

"I've got to go out there," he whispered in her ear, later, the warmth of her in his arms.

She stiffened.

"If I've never done anything else in my life, I've got to go out there, Emma. I couldn't face myself if I didn't. Can't you understand that?"

Her fine white teeth were pressed into her full lower lip as she looked up at him, her constrained face a dim shape.

"I know," she murmured at last.

NINE

March 8–April 19 2026

BERT SCHAUN plunged the *Fern* into the belt with undiminished speed, relying on the detection system to automatically change his course to miss any asteroids in his flight path. He caught glimpses of them as they sped past: A large bright sphere nearly three miles through, a small, irregular-shaped mass resembling something torn from the Grand Canyon, a series of tiny objects, some smooth, some crooked and black or shiny, gathering the sun's weak rays and reflecting them like a microscope's mirror, a myriad path of stone and metal looking like a swarm of bees on the screen, a few larger asteroids again.

He noticed with satisfaction that most of the larger bodies were colored, giving evidence of ownership. The others must have held no radioactive ore. Occassionally he managed to catch one in the scintillometer sights as it went by, just to prove his assumption.

Days passed and at length he tired of the continual speculation and turned his attention to other things: testing the machinery, picking up a few signals on the receiver, recalling Emma's face, Osborne's office, the monotony of Mars architecture, but all the same noting less evidence of man's work as he moved deeper among the planetoids.

April 20—May 2, 2026

One day, when twenty-fours had passed without sighting a single colored asteroid, he slowed the *Fern* and carefully marked his position. Then, grim and determined, he started to weight every uneven hunk of rock he saw. The first day he found none that even budged the energy meter. On the second day he encountered a three, carefully marking the co-ordinates for future reference. Then three days passed with nothing. On the sixth day he found two-two-pounders, and he recorded these, though they would hardly have paid him to mine since he was so far away from Mars.

A week later he had examined exactly seventy-three other likely-looking asteroids, found only one that contained any uranium and it was a one-pounder. Still not worried, he renewed his search, working around the clock, impatient with the time it took him to get from one rock to the next.

May 3, 2026

The heavy-set man at the end of the bar bothered Emma. He drank, but he didn't talk, didn't seem to fit in with the rest of the crowd in the tavern. She knew who he was. They called him Will and they said he worked with the grinders and crushers in one of the early steps of the refinery process. His last name was Abrahamson, she remembered. But he was on a different shift and she saw him only when he was moved for a day or two to the shift her patrons worked.

There was clearly something on his mind. She caught him looking at her covertly. He would bear watching.

He stayed for a long time, seemed to be waiting for the crowd to thin out.

She made business for herself at his end of the bar. "Another drink?" she asked, as if she had just thought of it.

"No thanks," he said, his gray eyes finding hers. His eyes were cold and unflinching.

"You drink like a man waiting for someone," she said, trying t o draw him out.

"I am."

"I see. Well," she looked at the clock, "we close up pretty soon. I don't think anybody else is coming in."

"I'm waiting to see you."

"Oh?" A pulse throbbed in her neck. She looked at him squarely. "Why?"

He managed a smile. It seemed difficult for him. "You don't need to be scared," he said softly. "I just want to ask a question. I didn't want to ask it in front of everybody."

"It's that kind of a question?"

He nodded. "Somebody told me you're offering money to find out a certain fact."

"Is it a fact?" she countered.

"I think so."

"Suppose you tell me what it is."

"Suppose you tell me what you're offering."

"Are we talking about the same thing?"

"You want to know who killed Hank Klein, don't you?"

"Yes," she said quickly. "Do you know who did?"

Will shook his head. "No, but I know a man who was in on it."

" 'In' on it?" She was shocked. "You mean there was more than one?"

"Not so loud." He looked around at the scattered drinkers. She hadn't realized her voice had become shrill.

"As I said, I don't know anyqthing about it, but I know a man who might be willing to talk if there's money in it."

"There is."

"How much?"

She told him.

He gave a low whistle. "I'll tell him."

He drank what remained in his glass and left.
She stared at the door for a long time afterward.

May 5, 2026

It was on his fifty-ninth day out of Mars that Bert found it.
He had just about given up, was on the point of returning to
the three-pounder he had catalogued on his second day in the
belt, when he sighted the big egg-shaped, striated asteroid,
unsullied by prospectors' or processors' marks. He swung the
scintillometer toward it, aimed and triggered the release,
and looked at the scope's screen.

The hump jumped clear off the graph!

With trembling fingers he reduced his reference lines and
tested it again. The energy level registered at twelve and a
half pounds!

He sank back exhausted, and stared at the hunk of mineral
he had sought for so long. He called it an unprintable name,
but he added, "I love you just the same." Then he broke out
the bottle he had brought aboard for just such an occasion,
toasted the rock, the *Fern*, Emma, Steve and everybody else
he could think of—even Osborne, after several toasts. Then,
feeling glorious, he fell into a deep and restful sleep.

June 11, 2026

Thirty miles above Mars, swinging in a wide arc that
would put him into orbit, he alerted Seven Operations.

"Hotchkiss," the dry voice came back.

"Schaun on the *Fern*," Bert said bouyantly. "Got a load of
twelve pound stuff I want to get rid of."

He could hear Hotchkiss's sharp intake of breath. "Twelve
pound, did you say, Schaun?"

"As a matter of fact, it's a little better than that. Twelve
and a half, to be exact."

"You're a lucky stiff," Hotchkiss said enviously, his voice tinny through the grill.

"Send me up an assist and I'll buy everybody in Seven a drink."

There was no immediate answer and Bert thought for a moment he had lost contact.

"You still there, Hotchkiss?"

"Yeah. Listen, Schaun, I forgot to tell you: you're supposed to put anything you have in orbit and come down. Osborne wants to see you."

"Osborne can go to hell," Bert said heatedly. "I've been out three months and I'm sick of being a nursemaid to ten freight cars."

"I bet you are," Hotchkiss said respectfully, "but those are the orders I got. Had 'em for about a month now."

"Look," Bert said, "I'll buy you a dozen drinks if you send an assist up here first."

"Sorry. No can do, Schaun. You got to come down first."

"Okay." Bert snapped off the communicator. Angry, he pushed his acceleration hard to get the gondolas in orbit, then detached the hitch. Damn Osborne! What did he want, anyway? Some technicality, or more probably, some deal to get the ore cheaper than the assayed price. Well, there'll be some haggling over that. They weren't going to cheat him out of what he had found.

He deliberately dropped the ship like a plummet, stalling it a few hundred feet above the field in a fiery show of exhaust, then floating gently down on the fix. He banged open the lock, dropped to the ground without benefit of ladder, and stalked off for Osborne's office, ignoring Operations.

"Oh, there you are, Schaun," Osborne said affably, getting to his feet as soon as Bert stomped into the office. "Hotchkiss called only a few minutes ago."

"Yes, here I am," Bert said sharply. "What's the idea of not letting me have an assist first? Now I'll have to go back up and get the stuff."

"Hotchkiss tells me you made a good strike. Sit down, Schaun."

"I'm tired of sitting. I want to get up there and bring that ore down. Why the delay?"

Osborne tried to smile. He cleared his throat. "I can understand your feelings, Schaun. Especially with that find you have."

"What is it? Get to the point, will you? I've got things to do. I'm buying everybody in this whole place a drink over at Emma Klein's as soon as I get the ore disposed of."

"Very generous of you, I'm sure," Osborne said, sitting at his desk and avoiding Bert's eyes. "The fact is, though . . ." His voice trailed off.

A foreboding swept over Bert. He could see Osborne was disturbed, that he was having difficulty bringing himself to say something. Surely, this couldn't be haggling. Still . . .

"What is it?" Bert asked with less insistence, sinking into the offered chair.

"The fact of the matter is we can't buy that ore of yours." Osborne looked at him squarely.

"Can't buy my ore!" Bert grabbed the seat of his chair and leaned forward. "Why not? You need it, you admitted that yourself. You said you were crying for ore. Now I've got it and you say you don't want it. What the hell!"

Osborne nodded. "I know it doesn't make sense, but you'll have to understand I'm just working for the Sully Company. I have to take orders, too. And they are not to buy your ore. The other companies won't buy it either, in case you're wondering."

Bert looked at the man in amazement. This was clearly something he had never expected. Haggling, yes, but this— it was unthinkable.

"Why?" Bert finally managed to ask.

"I can't tell you that."

"Wait a minute, Osborne. It's one thing not to buy my ore, but it's another thing not to let me know why."

"I'm sorry, Schaun. Truly sorry."

"Your company signed a contract with me, remember?"

Osborne shrugged. "Evidently they're willing to let you contest that if you wish. But you'll have to go to Earth to do it. Do you have enough fuel to get back there?"

"I'm not leaving Mars. You're not chasing me out of here."

"Nobody's chasing you," Osborne said, producing a handkerchief and mopping his forehead with it, "but since we can't buy what you haul, I'd think there'd be little reason to stay."

"Maybe I could work in the refinery," Bert said, wondering what kind of reaction this would get.

"We need men desperately, Schaun, believe me. But there's no place for you there either."

"Sully wants me out of the way real bad. Why?"

"You're a good man," Osborne said earnestly. "We need good men like you on this godforsaken planet."

"What am I supposed to do with all that ore in the gondolas?"

"Nothing. I can't buy it, so it will have to stay in orbit until I get further instructions."

"I've got a good mind to dump the whole works on Seven."

Osborne sighed. "I couldn't blame you if you did. I only hope you don't."

Even Emma's squeal of delight when she saw him failed to lift Bert out of his depression.

"I heard you were back," she said, eyes glowing, "and I heard you hit a twelve-pounder."

There were only three men at a table in the tavern. One of them waved, saying, "We heard you was buying drinks for everybody."

"Give them a drink, Emma," Bert said, moving to the bar.

Her face darkened when she saw his. "What's the matter? You don't look very happy."

"The good news traveled fast, didn't it? But you haven't heard the bad news."

"Bad news?" She looked at him anxiously.

He nodded. "Sully won't buy my ore."

"Won't buy your ore!"

"That's what I said when Osborne told me." He recounted his conversation with the general manager.

"But why? *Why?*"

"I don't know. Better let me have a double one on the rocks."

"You gotta watch the refinery boys," the same man at the table said. "You can't tell what they're gonna do next." Others at the table muttered their agreement.

"I just don't understand it, Bert," Emma said, preparing drinks. "You go out there and risk your life and find a good source like that, and then they won't buy it."

Bert downed his drink quickly to ease the agony of frustration that held him, a thousand doubts and uncertainties hammering at him. Something he did wrong? An error somewhere in signing up? How could there be! A legal mistake? And as he thought of things legal he remembered the court procedure he escaped by his leaving Earth and at once recalled Thornton McAllister, a big man with the Classic. Could he be as big a man with the refinery people? He decided not, though it was the only reason that made sense to him. Would a man go that far? Maybe, if it was a man like McAllister.

"Hell," said the talkative man at the table, "if I was you, Schaun, I'd go back and get in the Classic again. I'd show these damn processors."

"Shut up, Orph," one of the other men said.

"Why?" Orph demanded to know. "I used to follow the

Classic. Always thought Schaun was a good man. Came up a little higher every year, didn't he?"

"Who says I'm that Schaun?" Bert asked angrily from his stool at the bar. The news was out, that much was clear. Now he wanted to know where it started.

"Everybody knows it," Orph said sulkily.

"He's right," the second man said.

"He didn't mean any offense, Mr. Schaun," the third man said.

"I heard it, too," Emma said at his elbow and he turned to her. "Steve was talking about it. Could it—could it have anything to do with their refusing to buy your ore?"

"I don't know."

"Why didn't you tell me about yourself, Bert?"

"I told you I was a pilot."

"But you didn't say what kind."

"Would it have made any difference?"

"No." He liked the firm answer. She went on, "But I felt a little left out when I heard about it."

"I suppose the last race came in for a lot of comment around here?"

"Don't sound so bitter, Bert. Of course everybody talked about it when it was brought up."

"And how do you vote? Guilty or not guilty?"

"Not guilty, if it makes you feel any better to hear me say it. You didn't have to ask, you know."

The tavern door opened and heads swiveled to see who it was. Steve Babcock came across the floor, saying, "Bert! I heard you were back." He drew up a stool. "I just came over from Four to tell you what a rotten deal I think you're getting."

"Thanks, Steve. Let me buy you a drink. Emma?"

"Just because his son was killed in the race!" Steve said heatedly, shaking his head. "Never heard anything like it."

Bert stared at him. "So, it *was* McAllister!"

"Of course it was."

"Why didn't Osborne tell me?"

Steve fingered his drink. "Maybe he doesn't know. Or maybe he thinks it better not to tell you. Sometimes I don't understand that man. I was curious myself when I heard you were through, so I went into action to find out for you. A few long distance inquiries was all it took; McAllister's the man."

"But how can McAllister have anything to do with the refinery people? How can he tell them what to do?"

"Don't you know?" Steve asked in surprise. "Hell, Thornton McAllister controls the purse strings for all the credit operations on Mars. You knew he was president of the Allied Banking Company, didn't you? And ABC's the world's biggest lending outfit. Not only that, he's a member of the international committee set up to arrange the finances for the whole Martian venture. He just exerted a little influence, that's all."

Well, he didn't have to worry about why any more. McAllister's powerful influence had even sought him out on Mars. The man was obviously dedicated to the task of getting Bert Schaun back to Earth. So he could sue him for everything he had. Well, the way things were going, he wouldn't get much. But maybe with all the power he seemed to throw around, he'd do something more than that.

"Anything I can do to help?" Steve asked.

"Can't think of anything right now, thanks, Steve. If I go back, McAllister will start his legal wheels rolling. If I stay here . . . Maybe if I stay here McAllister will come up after me. Then I could give him a nice ride in the *Fern*, take him out some place and dump him. I know just the asteroid."

"If you need fuel or anything to get back . . ."

"I'm not broke yet, Steve. Not quite. Besides, I have ten cars of twelve-pound ore out in orbit."

"Osborne can't buy it."

"I know. But it's mine. Maybe I ought to set up my own refinery."

"The Schaun Company," Emma said. "I like the sound of it."

"Yeah," Steve said dryly. "Maybe you could get McAllister to finance it."

"Maybe I ought to take the ore back and dump it in McAllister's back yard."

"Maybe he'd buy it."

"Say," Emma said suddenly. She looked at Bert brightly. "I think I have an idea."

"Shoot. The Schaun Company needs stockholders with ideas."

"No, listen, I'm not fooling," she said with an intensity that demanded attention. "Why can't somebody buy that ore?"

"Are you kidding?" Steve said.

"The other companies won't buy it either, Osborne said."

"No, you don't get it. I mean *me*. There's nothing says I can't buy it, is there, Steve?"

Steve shrugged. "I suppose not, but—"

"So I buy it, then I sell it to Sully, don't you see? Then Sully gets the ore, which it needs, Osborne's happy and out of his dilemma, and Bert gets money for the ore. What's wrong with that?"

"It makes sense at that," Bert said, warming to it. "That way Sully won't be buying it from me." A grin grew on his face. "Emma, I think maybe you've solved the problem."

"I think she has. Emma," Steve said, "I'm proud of you. You not only have looks, you have brains, too."

"And that way," Bert went on, "I can still go out there, mine that ore, come back and sell it, McAllister be damned."

"You can do that until McAllister hears about it," Steve warned. "Then they'll be unable to buy from Emma either."

"Who's going to tell him"

"It will get around."

"Then I'll sell the ore to you, Steve."

Steve laughed. "You can always be just one jump ahead of Osborne that way. You know, Schaun, I think Emma's got this thing licked."

"Let's drink on it."

"Let's have several drinks on it."

"Come on in for a nightcap, Steve, it's early. Really now, Steve, ol' boy, it is."

Steve's a good boy, no doubt of that. Bet he's feeling as good as I am, too. What an evening!

"No. Can't do 'er, Bert. Gotta get back to ol' Four." Steve lurched away from the ladder of the *Fern*.

Bert leaned back heavily against the ladder and watched him go, a black figure a little unsteady on the landing area, headed for his ship. Maybe, Bert said to himself, I ought to help him get back to Four. Don't want him to get picked up for drunk driving. He chuckled to himself, looked up at the bright stars, so much brighter than Earth stars! Still the same stars, though, eh?

Damn, it's cold!

He hadn't noticed the cold before, could feel the sting of it through his thick jacket. It sobered him considerably. He knew he should be getting into the ship before his extremities became numb.

Bert started up the ladder, punched the lock stud, entered the *Fern*, and shivered inside the warm lock. Now why, he asked himself, does a person shiver when he comes in out of the cold?

Suddenly he stiffened. Something was wrong. He shook his head to get rid of the haze and came instantly alert.

Something was wrong!

You can't ride a ship night and day for months at a time without knowing when something's not right.

What was it?

That hum . . . what was it? What did he leave on? What was working? He tried to recall his actions before he let the ship down. He'd been excited then. Had he forgotten something?

He entered the inner part of the ship, a feeling of numbness centering around his heart. Things were not right. The smell of the air, the sounds of the ship itself. The feeling—

A step.

He whirled in time to see a figure lunge at him, threw up an arm to ward off the blow, something shiny whizzing past his ear and striking his shoulder hard.

He went down. His assailant—he saw the dark eyes, the wild, black hair—came at him. He lifted a knee and the man went over him.

They were both on their feet then, closing in tight, punching, feinting, and—

The man was reaching for the lock stud to go out. Bert jumped him, clawed him away from it, his fingers tightening around his throat. The man pressed away from the wall and they fell again.

The man did not get up.

Schaun rose, weary and breathless, stood looking down at the man, a heavy-set, mustached man. Why had he tried to get out of the ship?

The answer came in an explosion of sound and fire that threw Bert to the floor and pinned him there with the acceleration. He tried to move, found he could not. He was a helpless thing in the clutch of the *Fern's* mounting power.

Somebody had set the controls—

A second blast ripped the *Fern* from one end to the other. Bert caught a glimpse of the flash of sparks and fire and the roar of it that was like a sudden weight on his ears.

Then he saw nothing.

TEN

June 12, 2026

BERT SCHAUN woke with a start, the deafening thunder of the crash still echoing in his ears. His sudden movement shot needles of pain into protesting muscles.

He lay still then, staring at the metal ceiling above him and thinking how quiet everything was and wondering where the light was coming from, for it was not the light of the ship's own system.

Gingerly he moved his head, felt stabs of pain as his neck bones snapped and cracked. Next he tried his arms. It was agony to move them, but they responded. He held each hand in front of his eyes in turn. They were whole, though his left hand was caked with dried blood.

He tried his feet and legs. They moved. Now his heart labored with his effort and he could hear himself puffing and wheezing. The reflected light on the ceiling was getting brighter. It hurt his eyes.

Then he remembered the previous evening, the long session of drinking with Steve and Emma, the saying good-bye to Steve, and he moaned at the recollection of how drunk he had been at the time. He licked his dry lips with a sudden giant thirst.

The man! His attacker—where was he?

With torturous effort he lifted his head, propped himself on his elbows, and looked around. The ship was a shambles, a tangle of twisted wires and wrenched plates, and he thought: How did I ever survive this?

Then he saw him. The mustached man was slumped at a grotesque angle in a high corner to his left, and from beneath the man's jacket ran a rivulet of blood long since hardened.

It was this blood, Bert realized now, that had stained his hand.

Summoning all his strength, Bert pushed himself to his feet, stood there dizzy and weak, leaning against a slanting bulkhead for support, his feet sliding along the sloping floor. With difficulty he made his way to the stranger. One touch of the cold flesh proved him long dead.

Who was he? Why did he wait for him? Why had he set the controls? Bert grunted. The man had tried to knock him out, but before he could escape the doomed ship Bert had attacked him, caused him to go along with it to his death. But why had the man tried such a thing?

Bert hobbled along the tilted floor, aching in every muscle, made it to the dark kitchen where he groped for and found water. Afterward he lay on the cold metal floor to recapture his strength. Then he struggled out to the room he had vacated, saw that the source of light was the open lock. The inner door had been jerked open, the outer door evidently torn off by the crash.

He squinted through the opening, saw red dunes in the early morning sunlight.

With one last look at the dead man, Bert went through the lock and dropped to the ground. The morning light was touching eroded hills and bringing them to life with brilliant yellows and reds and browns. He walked from the ship through ankle-deep sands, looked back at the *Fern* and saw that it had come down out of the sky almost head first, burying itself a good ten feet in the sand. It would not be worth salvaging.

He stopped on a tufted hillock and looked all around. Beneath the navy blue sky and its iridescent clouds was a silent land in every direction, a never-ending stretch of lonely, drifting sands and hills. Which way Seven?

He looked at the *Fern* again and, judging from the angle at which she had plowed into the red-tinged sands, assumed she had come from the north. The trip had been incredibly short; Seven must be just beyond the rise of the weathered ridge in that direction.

He started off, the mounting sun and his activity warming him. He took off his jacket and carried it, feeling the stiffness and soreness leaving his legs and arms. Finally he came to the hill, an outcropping of windswept rock, and stood there. In that direction he was going he saw nothing new, only a far distant hill similar to the one he was standing on.

Bert looked back. How small the *Fern* looked! Just like a toy spacer, a plaything thrown there by a child.

He shrugged and stepped north off the stone ridge, sinking at once in the sand again. It was warmer now. Maybe he should have brought along a jug of water. But no, Seven must be beyond the next rise. It had to be!

What seemed an eternity later he came to the next rocky crag, found it to be higher than it had looked from a distance, and had to climb. He was a weary man by the time he got to the top.

His heart sank with his first view of the new scene.

Nothing to see. Not even another ridge.

But surely . . . In despair he sat down on the summit, exhausted. Maybe he should go back to the ship. At least there was water there. How foolish of me not to bring some along, he chided himself. But perhaps there was something beyond the horizon. . . .

He forced himself to his feet, clambered down the steep rock, trudged through the sand, foot after foot, head down now, the sun hot on his back, the dry wind cutting into his eyes and lips. If only he hadn't been so stupid about water!

It seemed hours before he noticed a change in the terrain before him. A hill actually rose there! And this one—this one, he told himself exultantly—had vegetation. A little, anyway. He hurried up the smooth rise to the top, looked beyond it, saw nothing but more sand, then turned his attention to the plants about his feet. Where there were plants there must be water. He found a sharp rock, started to dig and in so doing cut the stems of several of the plants. They oozed a liquid.

He stooped, fingered a tubelike shoot with dust-covered, leathery leaves, nicked the stem with a fingernail. A watery substance squeezed out. It looked quite palatable. He plucked another plant, held the stem so none of the liquid would drip out, brought it to his lips. The sap was sweet and cool. He pulled up another plant, let more of it run into his mouth. He yanked out another, drank its juice, still another, and more, until the ground around him was littered with green.

Suddenly he stopped. The stuff didn't taste good any more. He spat out the last of it, eyed the distant hill, walked off the rise, one foot sinking in the sand, then the other, the sand gluey and his feet resisting his efforts to pull them out, and the day was getting darker. . . . Darker? That was strange, the sun was still overhead! Mars was a peculiar place! And there was the hill ahead, a green hill, with fountains and trees and girls in the forest—there *were* girls there, weren't there? Good-looking ones, running here and there, clad in only the filmiest of cloth, and beckoning. Funny to find a place like that here! He hoped he'd make it before the sun refused to shine any longer. And maybe Emma would be right there, too. Maybe she came there often when she tired of working at the bar. Sure, she'd be there, right over there by that hill with the rest of the girls around the next corner across the street. Hurry, hurry, now, or you'll be late. Late? I was never late to school in my life! Where *is* everybody? How long have I been in bed? I shall go back to sleep. Too early to get up, girls or no. Too early to bed . . . early to rise . . . wealthy . . . and . . .

He fell in a heap, a crumpled figure on the lonely, endless sand

"Why did you come here?" Will Abrahamson shouted irritably above the roar of the crushers and grinders. "Nobody's supposed to come in here."

Only Will's eyes were clean and gray. The rest of him was dirt-streaked: His face, his hairy chest and his thin work pants. The way he stood glaring at her he looked like some enraged primordial animal, his body glistening with sweat caused half by his work and half by the neighboring percolators and ovens.

"You never came back," she yelled at him.

"I didn't expect to."

She read the words his lips formed rather than heard him because of the incessant squeal and screech of the grinders.

"Did you see the man you were supposed to?"

"What?"

She repeated the question, louder.

He nodded. "He'll be around. Time's not right, he said."

June 13, 2026

Out of the dark world of misty shapes and out-of-proportion things, Bert's mind came groping, knowing there was reality beyond this because he had seen the glimmerings of it, the sparks, the dancing flames of life, and in one last desperate leap from the depths of terrifying dream images, he reached reality and clung there by a slim hold.

He could see the fire plainly now. It was warm. As he moved still farther toward consciousness, his other senses were alerted and responded. He smelled the burning wood and leaves, saw the jiggling lights and shadows of the fire on the vault of the cave he was in, felt the pain in his throat and stomach, and he knew a weakness he had never felt before.

He managed to turn his head. There, to one side, was a *something*, a gray shape, a hairless thing, and as he looked at it, it moved. Slowly it turned its head and Bert saw the twisted face and fiery red eyes that glowed in the firelight.

He moaned and lost consciousness.

When he awoke again, it was day. He twisted his head quickly, senses cringing at what he expected to see. But the gray shape was gone. The fire was smouldering.

Bert moved, heard and felt twigs snap beneath him. Was there no bone, no muscles in his body that did not ache? He sat up, finding even this position dizzying. Looking around, he saw the cave was not large and opened out to a view of the omnipresent barren waste of Mars. The heat from the shining red sand was actually oppressive.

As his gaze returned to the cave, he was surprised to see two clay plates, two cups and several metal utensils nearby. The plates, he found when he had them in his hands, were thin, light and beautifully decorated with a ring of flowers around the edge. There must be flowers on Mars then, he concluded, though he had never seen any. The metal kitchenware was well made, too, he discovered. An intricate design had been worked into the handles. The metal was light and strong and untarnished, and it set him to wondering what it was.

Then he saw the book. It was hardly bigger than his hand, had a soft, flexible black cover inscribed with much scroll work, and inside, obviously written by pen, were symbols he did not understand. The pages were thicker than the pages of books he had known, and there were illustrations by an artist with a fine hand and an eye for detail. The creatures pictured were identical to the one he had seen when he had awakened so briefly during the night.

Had it been a Stinker?

He sniffed but could detect no offensive odor. Maybe that stuff about the Stinkers was just so much hogwash. He turned his back to the entrance light, the better to see the book, and immersed himself in it, turning the pages slowly and examining the pictures. They were peopled by things with long ears, gray faces, hairless bodies and red eyes, and he could not help but admire the artistry of the weave of the cloth they used like a blanket around them. The figures were engaged in a number of familiar pursuits: planting, hoeing, weaving, reading, love-making, playing games. Why, they must be quite highly developed, he thought. What's the matter with Earthmen? I thought they were supposed to be monkeys or hardly more than vegetables, or at best, primitive men.

A shadow fell on the page. Something was in the entranceway. He turned quickly and saw him. It was the creature who had lain at his side.

My Good, he thought, he's smaller than I imagined. Barely five feet tall. And not very pretty.

And then as they eyed each other, Bert caught the alien's scent and then he understood why Earthmen had stayed away from them. The longer they stared at each other, the stronger the smell became, eddying and flowing around Bert.

He turned away to hide his thought: Stinker is the right name for them all right. He wished he had strength enough to get up and run out to the fresh air.

And suddenly the stench was worse, sickening him, making him retch. It was almost a tangible thing that filled his nose and mouth and lungs and made his eyes water.

Bert struggled to control himself, to rise above the fetid odor the alien exuded. He nodded a greeting, smiling weakly. He'd show the Martian he held nothing against him. After all, the little guy saved his life.

"Hi!" Bert said cheerily, waving a friendly hand.

The Martian's red eyes went wide, his long ears trembled, and he came into the cave carrying a bowl, yammering in an excited voice, his movements washing along a wave of smell Bert could hardly stand. As Bert watched, the alien set the bowl on the floor, dipped the cup in it and handed it to him.

It was almost an effeminate gesture. Bert grinned and accepted the cup. It was water, cool and refreshing. Where did he get it?

Then the creature with the ridiculous ears drew from an inner fold of his blanket several pieces of what looked like rope and offered them to him. Bert took them. They were black and gummy and looked like licorice. The alien pointed to his own mouth, so Bert followed the suggestion and tried them. They were salty but palatable.

The Martian was pleased, twisted his face in a lopsided smile, showing toothless black gums, and Bert found himself answering with a grin. Then the alien pointed to the book Bert still held in his hand and muttered something unintelligible.

Bert held up the book, saying, "Book."

"Book," the alien said in his whistling voice. Then his ears jerked violently and his face darkened perceptibly.

Hell, Bert thought, if this guy can say "Book," he can say anything. He pointed to himself and said "Bert." The alien pointed to himself and said it. Bert shook his head, pointed to himself again, said the word. The ears wriggled, the face wrinkled and grew darker with pleasure, and the alien pushed a finger at Bert and pronounced his name.

"Good going," Bert said. "Now what's *your* name?"

The alien could not have understood, still he must have sensed the question. He pointed to himself and said, "Greckle."

"Greckle, eh?" He laughed. "Stinker would be more like it."

"Stinker?" the little man gave the Martian equivalent of a laugh, a strident piping, like the trill of a bird. "Stinker, stinker, stinker!" He laughed again.

"It's not funny," Bert said, but he couldn't help laughing with him, Greckle looked so ridiculous. "Where you from, Greckle?" And when the alien looked at him blankly, he said, "Hell, Friday, I'll be damned if I'll undertake your education. I really want to get out of here. Where's Seven, boy? Do you know?"

The blank look was frozen on the face.

Bert sighed, used a twig from his bed to draw a picture on the dirt of the cave floor, a picture of Seven's landing area complete with several ships, the refinery, the low-slung buildings.

Greckle's red eyes snapped, he nodded and pointed through a wall of the cave.

"You're not so dumb, eh?" Bert said. "Well, try to understand this, chum: I've got to get back there." He started to get to his feet.

"Bert!" Greckle hissed, pushing him down gently.

Either the Martian was stronger than he looked or Bert was so weak he couldn't resist him. He went down. Well, it was just as well. He obviously was going nowhere in his present condition.

"Book," Greckle said, holding out a five-fingered hand. Except it was gray, it could have been an Earth girl's hand and Bert looked at the alien suspiciously. But no, he remembered the breasts much in evidence in the drawings in the book. Well, you had to give the alien credit: He remembers. Bert handed the book to him.

Grackle sat down, leaned against a wall of the cave, turned several pages, found what he was looking for, and started to read in a lilting, liquid voice full of sibilant sounds. For some reason Bert found it calming and satisfying even though he couldn't understand a word of it. Every once in a while the alien would glance at him and Bert would nod his encouragement.

With a start Bert realized Greckle was no longer emitting an odor. Either that or the initial stench had burned out his olfactory centers. Still, Bert could smell the remains of he fire, so that couldn't be true. Could Stinkers turn it on and off?

He went to sleep thinking about it.

June 14—21, 2026

Bert's weakness prevailed for several days, though he was impatient to be off for Seven, so he had to be content to stay in the cave, conserve his strength and let the little Martian serve him, a thing the alien seemed to enjoy doing. He ate the things Greckle brought him, drank the juices, and enlarged the little guy's vocabulary at the same time. The Martian's aptitude amazed him. All he needed to do was mention a word once and it was forever Greckle's.

On the fourth day Greckle did not push him down when he tried to get up, and Bert walked around the cave and out through the entranceway several times. On the fifth day Greckle brought him a long stick which Bert used to lean on while they walked around in the vicinity of the cave, the alien pointing out some of the green things growing nearby. Once they came upon the plant Bert had drunk the juice of and, by his action and a few of the words he had learned, Greckle managed to convey its dangers. The walk exhausted Bert far more than he cared to admit, so when Greckle brought out his book to read again, he was only too glad to lie down and listen. The reading was an odd thing. He always felt so calm and rested when the alien did it. He could not imagine why this was so.

As to the alien's odor, there was more of it at some times than others, and Bert finally gave up wondering why. But it never sseemed as offensive as it had at that first meeting in the entranceway.

When the alien was gone foraging for food, Bert's mind turned to many things, the strangeness of Martian culture— it *was* a culture because of the book and artifacts, though it seemed a rather primitive one—the dilemma he would be in when he returned to Seven, and the puzzle of the attack upon him in the *Fern*.

He spent more time thinking of the attack than he did the other things, weighing and considering and viewing it from every angle. It seemed plain to him now that Osborne's kindness was only superficial, that the Sully Company, once he had made his rich strike, had plans for his demise so they could take it over. And what a rotten business it was! But then, what about McAllister? Well, that was only coincidence, that's all, and Osborne made surface noises to make it seem as if he were more concerned with that than anything else.

I make a good strike, he told himself. So I'm a marked man. Even Emma must have feared this, the way she was talking. She was afraid I'd go just like her husband. And how right she was! They send a guy out to my ship. He gets the controls set, waits for me to come in to put them into operation, plans to knock me out and jump out himself and let the ship take off and crash. But his plan goes haywire.

In Klein's case there were two ships. It was simple. Somebody puts him out of the way, gathers up all his records and transfers them to the second ship, letting Klein and his ship go sailing off to oblivion. Sully—Osborne, really—has all the charts to go over at his leisure.

Damn you, Osborne! Did you come out yourself and get the records from the crashed *Fern?* Maybe you hadn't counted on my being so drunk I could survive a crash like that. Does it worry you that you didn't find me there? But then you've probably got a ship or two on the way to my asteroid right now and you've probably given me up for dead, for what could survive a night on the Martian desert? Only an ice cube. Or certain growing things indigenous to the planet.

What about Steve Babcock? How much of this does he know about? Surely he'll be trying to solve the mystery of the crash of the *Fern*, perhaps has already reached the inevitable conclusion. What does he do then? Run to Osborne and accuse him of it? How does one accuse his boss of a thing like that? He knew Steve had to co-operate with the processor overlords, but he also knew Steve ought not to countenance murder. Steve and I better have a long talk, he told himself. I've got to find out which side you're on, and if you're on the right side, I've got to work with you.

Bert shook his head as he lay there hearing Greckle coming up the slope to the entrance. A lot of things were going to have to be settled when he got back to Seven. And it wasn't going to be easy.

June 25, 2026

A few days later, at last fit to make the trek in the direction Greckle indicated Seven was, Bert announced: "Greckle, I've got to be on my way. Got to get back to Seven." He grinned. "But it's been fun, don't think it hasn't."

A shadow crossed Greckle's face. "Home?" he asked.

"Not exactly," Bert said. "But it's where I'm going. Seven. That's what it's called."

"Sev-en," Greckle hissed. "Seven. Bert live there."

"Right. Greckle, the way you pick up speech makes you a pretty amazing fellow, you know that, don't you?"

Greckle's black gums were exposed in a twisted grin as he nodded his head. "You wait," he said. He put out the fire, gathered up the plates and cups and utensils and put them away in blanket pockets Bert hadn't noticed before. Then he moved out of the cave, beckoning with his arm and saying, "Come."

Bert followed, curious to know what Greckle was up to. They walked several miles along a high ridge and it became evident to Bert as they did so that this was the way the Martians traveled from place to place. Why cross a desert when you could always take one of Nature's roads where you were going? This was not the way to Seven, but it was bringing him nearer it in a roundabout way as that.

Finally they came to a point where several ridges ran together, and Greckle pointed to an arrangement of structures on an adjacent plateau.

"Home," Greckle said simply.

"Your home, perhaps," Bert said. The houses were constructed of building blocks much as Seven's were, but the shade was a little lighter brown. And none was more than a single story high. But the thing that impressed Bert most was their pleasing arrangement, their balance, the fine sense of design used in laying them out with the curving paths among them. It put Seven to shame. The aliens were definitely artistic. But did they heat their homes? Had they light? Water? He wondered about these.

"Come," Greckle said again, stepping off the ridge.

"No," Bert said, suddenly envisioning what it would be like to be exposed to so many aliens at once. The result of their collective sudatory activities might be more than one human being could stand.

Instantly Greckle's face wrinkled and lost color, and his ears dropped with disappointment. And there was that smell again.

"I can't go, Greckle," Bert said gently, not wishing to tell him the real reason, for he would like to know more about the aliens, "I've got to get back to Seven. Can't you understand?"

The odor was more pronounced now and Bert was eager to be on his way.

"Greckle come," the alien said brightly, moving toward Bert.

Bert shook his head. "I wouldn't advise it," he said. "You stay here. Go home." He pointed to the village below.

The alien was again crestfallen. Then he brightened. "Here," he said withdrawing a number of the licorice-like sticks from the folds of his wrap-around. "Food." Then he produced a small clay canteen. "Water."

Bert took them, moved by the alien's generosity. Then, before it would show, he moved toward a ridge that ran in the direction he wanted to go. "Thanks for everything, Greckle," he said. "Goodbye, fella." He walked on, turned to wave without stopping.

The figure he left behind was a crushed one. An arm lifted. The hand gave a feeble wave.

"Good-bye, Bert," the alien said, the words hardly audible across the intervening space.

Bert did not look back again.

ELEVEN

June 25, 2026

THE SUN was low in the sky when Bert entered Seven. He was tempted to stop at Emma Klein's before he confronted Osborne, but though the pull of her was strong, he resisted it. He wanted to face Osborne with a clear head and without Emma's dissuasion ringing in his ears. He looked for no one, saw no one as he strode determinedly through the empty, dusty streets to the Sully building.

Osborne would be sitting behind his desk when he opened the door, and Bert fancied the man would look up in horror when he saw him. And his face, Bert chuckled, would be a rewarding thing to see, for the answer to everything would be there, and in what he would say.

But Bert was not prepared for what he did see when he pushed Osborne's office door, for it opened on a smoke-filled room, a room filled with faces, and for a moment he couldn't find Osborne's among them.

Then Bert saw the man, saw his eyes go wide. But there was, strangely enough, no horror there.

"My God, it's Schaun!" The mouth hung opened, then snapped shut. "We thought you were dead!"

Bert watched the man rise, saw the worry-shadowed eyes looking more worried than ever, saw the bald head rise from those around it, and he suddenly knew Osborne was going to be pleasant, and this infuriated him. Wasn't this the man who had blocked his every move, the man who had made him the unwilling object of violence?

"I'm not quite dead," Bert said coldly. "No thanks to you."

"Who is this guy?" a dark, heavy-set man asked Osborne, glowering at Bert.

"He's Bert Schaun," Osborne said. "His ship crashed south of here. We thought he was a goner."

"Surprised you though, didn't I?"

A hand was on his shoulder and Bert swung around at the pressure and looked square into the eyes of Steve Babcock, who said, "We did think you were dead, Bert. Whatever happened?"

"For details before the crash, I refer you to Osborne here. He planned it."

"You don't know what you're saying, Schaun," Osborne said, affronted.

"Don't I? Suppose you tell them how you tried to get me to haul ore instead of going out on my own, how you refused to buy ore when I made that good strike, and finally, how you tried to wreck my ship so you could go through my records."

"That's preposterous," Osborne snapped. He brought out a handkerchief and swabbed his forehead. "You've got everything all wrong from beginning to end. As Sam Ferrara here —he's with Gianetti—and Tom Wagner—he's general manager over at Schlenker—"

"I didn't come here to ask them anything," Bert answered. "It's you I'm asking."

"I'm only trying to point out that they operate exactly as the Sully Company does," Osborne said patiently. "As for wrecking your ship—"

"We always try to discourage private prospecting," Ferrara said. "And why shouldn't we? It's too uncertain and a waste of time when there are all those claims already established out there."

"If a man comes to Mars to do prospecting," Bert said, "he ought to be allowed to do just that."

"I don't recall that anyone stopped you," Osborne said dryly.

"No," Bert said, "nobody stopped me from going out. But what about when I came back with that twelve-pound ore?"

"That was unfortunate," Osborne said. "You remember that, gentlemen. The directive from the central office asking all companies to boycott Schaun."

"A nice move by Thornton McAllister," Bert said. "Don't forget to add that. Or didn't you know?"

"I knew," Osborne said. "I didn't think it wise to say. But how did you find out?"

"I remember it," Wagner said. "I didn't like it, but there wasn't any question about complying. We had no choice, Schaun."

"As long as he brought it up," Osborne said in quiet anger, polishing his glasses vigorously and looking squarely at him, "you might as well know McAllister wants him for what he did to his boy during the Classic."

"It so happened," Bert said icily, "his boy tried to ram my ship and killed himself doing it, regardless of what his father tries to make everybody believe. It seems his word carries a lot more weight than mine, though he was thousands of miles away when it happened."

"I remember you," Ferrara said. "I've seen you race in the Classic. You were a damn fine pilot."

"Thanks," Bert said. "It so happens I still am."

"Schaun's guilt or innocence doesn't make any difference," Wagner said. "We still can't do business with him."

"What's supposed to happen to that ore I've got in orbit then?" Bert asked.

Osborne colored. "It's not in orbit any more, Schaun."

"I see. You waited, then, until I was out of the way—"

"You've got to understand we thought you were dead, man!"

Bert whirled to Steve. "All right, Steve. There you have it. They took my ore. My property. As law enforcement officer, what do you intend to do about that? Or are you in on this, too?"

Steve flushed. "Bert," he said not unkindly, "I wish you'd try to be reasonable. Put yourself in Mr. Osborne's place. If you thought someone was dead, what would you do?"

"It was impounded, Schaun," Osborne said. "We need those cars. You had ten of them, remember? We couldn't let them sail around Mars forever."

"Of course you couldn't. You just send a guy out to my ship to set the controls so I'd crash, and then you'd have them."

Osborne snorted with fury. "Damn it, Schaun! I didn't send anybody to your ship. I don't know what happened. All I know is Hotchkiss reported your erratic takeoff and I notified Steve and told him to try to find out what happened. He went out, found your ship and asked for a search party to find you. We even organized that."

"It's as big a mystery to us as it must be to you, Bert," Steve said. "I can see how you figured Sully had something to do with it, but you're way off base thinking that way."

"Oh, I am, eh? Well then maybe you could tell me what that guy was doing on the *Fern*."

"His name was Gregg," Osborne said. "Alonzo Gregg. From Two. God only knows what he had in mind. Steve knew him."

"I didn't know him too well," Steve said, "but from what I've been able to piece together, I think Gregg went berserk. It's happened before on Mars. A guy seems perfectly normal one minute, and then the next he goes off the deep end. Gregg was a man like that, as good a refinery man as you'll find, an expert on the ovens over at Two. Why he tried to do what he did we'll never know. The people he worked with said he seemed perfectly normal the day before."

"That's the way we figured it," Osborne said. "The crash knocked you out and you walked away from the ship in a dazed condition."

"What *did* happen to you?" Wagner wanted to know.

"I survived. An alien named Greckle saved my life after I drank the juice of a poisonous plant."

"A Stinker?" Wagner asked incredulously. "You mean a Stinker saved your life?"

"An alien," Bert corrected, noticing with annoyance how they all seemed to cringe at the thought. "They're not so bad."

"Oh, come now," Osborne said. "You ought to know better than that."

"How did you ever stand it?" Ferrara wanted to know.

"How did I ever stand having my life saved?"

"That's not what I mean—"

"I know what you mean," Bert snapped, looking around at them contemptuously, "you and the rest of the people here. You don't know anything about the aliens, do you? You don't know that they can be real people, do you? Why, the answers to all your problems rest with those people!"

"I think we've wasted enough time talking to a madman," Wagner said wearily.

Osborne coughed self-consciously. "We were in the middle of an important matter here, Schaun. . . ."

"I think you'd better go," Steve said gently.

"Yeah," Ferrara added. "Maybe you'd better go back and live with the Stinkers since you like them so much."

There was laughter at this. It only added to the cold fury around Bert's heart. He left before he lost his head completely.

"That was a mistake," Steve said when the office door closed behind them, "busting in there like that."

"Maybe it was," Bert admitted, "but I still wouldn't put it past Osborne to pull a stunt like wrecking my ship."

"You killed whatever career you might have had on Mars, Bert. You know that, don't you?"

"Osborne nearly ended it for me the way it was."

"Now you'll have to go back to Earth."

"Earth?" Bert looked at him. Steve was serious. "I came here to make a fortune, Steve. I'm still going to make it one way or another."

"Selling your ore to somebody else first is out, too, Bert. They're just following orders, Bert. What are you going to do now?"

"I don't know. You're pretty thick with those boys back there, aren't you, Steve?"

"I suppose it looks that way, but remember they're my bosses. I hate these damn meetings, actually. I just sit there and they seldom ask me a thing. But they insist I come. Sometimes I think I'm just a whipping boy."

"What about the crash? Don't you think Osborne could have engineered the whole thing?"

Steve frowned, rubbed his chin with his knuckles. "Frankly, I don't know what to think. Sometimes I wonder if I'm being told everything."

"And what about Hank Klein's death?" Bert persisted. "What ever did you really find out about that?"

"Bert, I've followed every rumor on that thing. I've got my men pumping everybody. And I'm forced to conclude that it's one of those wild things that somebody starts. But don't think I've given up. I've still got a couple promising leads. Maybe they'll develop into something. I only hope I don't find out Osborne did it. Then I don't know what I'll do."

"I see your point. Well, if you ever find out he did, I'll give you what help I can."

"I'd better get back in before they think I've deserted them," Steve said, smiling. "Thanks for your offer, though. And if there's anything I can do, let me know, hear?"

Fortunately Emma Klein's was deserted. He had to talk to Emma and he didn't want everybody and his brother listening in.

She went white when she saw him, but she didn't drop the glass she was washing. She just stood there watching him approach the bar, looking as if she were seeing him in a vision.

"Hi, Emma," he said, grinning and glad to see her at last.

"It *is* you," she said softly. "They said you were dead, Bert, that you'd never survive out there on the desert." She carefully put down the glass. Color was coming back to her cheeks.

"Yeah, but they underestimated me, didn't they? A Martian rescued me, Emma. A cute Martian. One with rabbit ears."

"You don't know how glad I am to see you, Bert."

"That goes for me, too, Emma. How've you been?"

"How've *I* been?" It was a little shrill. "Should I say 'fine'? I've done nothing but worry about you."

"You shouldn't have. I could stand a drink."

"I'll bet you could." Her fingers flew at the task. And after she handed him the glass and he felt the warmth of it spread through him, he sat there looking at her, drinking in the gladness in her eyes, their brightness, the wonderful smile she wore, and on impulse he raised up from his stool, pulled her head to him and kissed her, over the bar. Her lips were warm and soft, as he knew they would be, and he felt her hands pulling his head to her, and the move put them sliding sidewise so that he had to put out his hand to prevent his falling on the bar. They broke away, laughing.

"Thanks, Emma," he said, settling back on the stool. "I needed that."

"No worse than I did," she said, brushing hair back in place, her cheeks red now, her breasts rising and falling perceptibly. "I'm just glad we didn't have an audience."

"I wish you could close up now, Emma. I've got to talk to you."

"It's only a few more hours, Bert. Then I want to hear everything."

"I don't think I can keep it that long. I just came from a talk with Osborne. He had a lot of boys over from the other places. Steve was there, too. They seem to agree there's nothing left for me around here. They tell me I ought to head back to Earth."

"You're not going, are you?" she asked fearfully.

"You know what John Paul Jones said about just beginning to fight? That's me."

"I'm glad to hear that."

"Yeah, but what am I going to fight with? I don't have a ship and even if I did, what could I do with it? How can you lick a combination like that?"

"Maybe you could start that refinery."

"I was joking. What do I know about processing ore?"

"Maybe you could get some of the dissatisfied men to go in with you."

"No." He shook his head and eyed the scenes of Earth on the back bar. Maybe I ought to go back, he thought. Earth looks mighty inviting. "Nice pictures."

"Don't let them give you any ideas, Bert Schaun," she said, putting a warm hand over his.

"I'll go back some day. No, Emma, running a refinery isn't in my line. Piloting ships is. But I can't even do that now."

"Too bad Sully runs everything in Seven. Otherwise you could open a spacer repair station or something along that line. But they wouldn't let you repair their ships, would they?"

"Not Sully. Not old Osborne. You know something? This is the first time in years I haven't had a ship of my own. It makes me feel lost."

"Why don't you buy one?"

"It would take everything I've got and then some. *If* I could buy one on Mars."

"I could help you with the difference."

"Where would I buy one? Sully's taken those from the down-and-out prospectors and put them on ore runs. And the prospectors let them get away with it!"

"I've seen a lot of ships end up that way."

"If only I could find a prospector willing to sell me his ship! That would be a way to get one."

She studied his face. "A ship means a lot to you, doesn't it?"

"I'm afraid so. Even if I can't use it."

"Well, why don't you buy one, fix it up and then sell it, if you feel that way? That will give you something to do."

He stared at her. "You know, you may have something there, Emma. I could start a used spacer lot just like they have on Earth. Bert Schaun, Spacer Dealer. Like that?" He laughed.

"I don't think it's funny," she said earnestly. "That way you'd be getting back at Sully and all the rest. Instead of having to mortgage their ships and work in the refinery, the unlucky prospectors would have a chance to get back to Earth if they wanted to, or hire themselves out to Sully at a decent wage, threatening to go to Earth if they don't get it."

"Say, I like that!" The idea was beginning to send prickles down his spine. What was wrong with it? He'd buy every spacer he could and—"How many prospectors do you suppose there are, Emma?"

"From what I hear there must be several hundred, counting all eight ports. Somebody's always giving up, it seems."

"And I could sell ships back to anybody who massed enough money," he said eagerly. "Maybe two prospectors now working in the refinery could pool their resources and buy a single ship." Then he sobered. "But I can't do that," he said.

"Why not, Bert? Why not?"

"I don't have enough money."

"Don't let that worry you. I have."

"And don't you be ridiculous. I couldn't take money from a woman."

She gave him a withering look. "Maybe pride. You'd let a little thing like that stand in the way?"

"It's just not right, Emma. You're a widow. You're going to need your money. Suppose I were a flop?"

"You won't be, Bert. I know it."

They had been quiet a long time, losing themselves in the darkness of her room, reaching for and touching each other occasionally to make sure they were there, or lighting cigarettes and seeing each other's faces in the momentary flash of light.

"I still don't like it," Bert said.

"Stop grumbling. You've been saying that over and over. I say: don't think about it. You let me do the worrying."

"I don't want you to."

"And I want to."

"But why should you want to set me up in business?"

"Oh, Bert, can't you see why?"

Yes, he could see why. He felt her need for him as much as he felt his need for her, and it was this that had made him quiet, waiting for that moment, re-examining his heart and mind. He had gone through the rest of the day from the moment he had entered the tavern after his incident with Osborne, telling her about the crash, about his experience with the alien, and knowing all the time what he was going to do and never finding a proper moment for it. But now it seemed at hand.

"Emma," he said, finding his voice husky and wishing it wasn't. And when she didn't answer, he said her name again.

"Yes."

"Will you marry me?"

And again when there was no answer, he felt his face crimson, his pulse pounding. Damn it! Why didn't she say something? She knew how he felt.

""I can't do that," she said finally, and he heard her sit up. "And not because of the money." She was at his side, her hand in his. "I just can't right now."

"Why?"

He felt her turn away, felt her fingers tighten, her body tense.

"Is it because of Steve Babcock?"

"No, of course not."

"You've been awfully nice to Steve."

She pulled away. "What a thing to say!"

"I didn't mean it the way it sounded!" Damn it, he thought, I'm always putting my foot in my mouth with her.

"Why shouldn't I be nice to him? You just don't know what that man has done for me." She settled back again. "When Hank and I first came to Mars, Steve often asked me to go out with him when Hank was gone. I refused, but not because I didn't want to go, but because I didn't know what Hank would think. But it was hideous with nothing to do, no one to talk to. Finally Steve talked to Hank about it, told him

I was mooning my days away alone; that I was losing weight and composure worrying so; that I ought to do something to take my mind off the waiting, told him I'd turned down a few parties he'd held so some of the people around here could get acquainted. Hank told me I was silly, that I ought to go out once in a while, that he trusted me and Steve, too, that he didn't want me tearing my heart out. In fact, he ordered me to do things while he was gone.

"So I went with Steve a few times. Oh, he was pretty amorous; I don't deny that. I'll even go so far as to say I was attracted to him and maybe even that was the reason he asked Hank in the first place. But we never did anything out of line. I managed to keep him in his place. And then the time came when Hank didn't come back. Nobody was more solicitous than Steve. He stayed by my side all the time and my loss seemed to be his, for he liked Hank a lot, and vice versa. I even think he was afraid I was going to do something rash, you know, like taking a bottle of sleeping pills or something. He was more than a gentleman, Bert, and has been since. When Hank didn't come back it was Steve who sent out half a dozen ships to try to find him—he even went over the refinery people's heads and nearly got fired for it. And he's kept me posted on all the rumors he's run down on it. He's done all he can and if I'm nice to him, well, that's the way I feel, I guess."

"Are you—are you in love with him?"

She laughed a little. "I thought I was once. Before you came, Bert."

"That doesn't tell me why you won't marry me, Emma. Is it because of Hank then?"

"In a way, yes, Bert."

She got up, turned on a light, looked at him, squinting in the brightness.

"You didn't tell me at first who you are and why you came to Mars," she said. "And I haven't been quite fair with you.

So I'll tell you why I'm staying and why you must accept my money."

He rose and sat on the bed to watch her.

"I'm sure Hank was murdered," she said. "He was too good a pilot ever to lose his way or forget to do something or have an accident. I think I know who did it and I've got money working to find out for sure. And when I do . . ."

Here was an Emma he had never seen, a militant Emma, a woman with the light of deadly purpose in her eyes.

"Don't you see, Bert? I can't really live like an unencumbered woman until I know the truth. I must know if he was murdered or not. Sometimes I think perhaps he'll turn up yet, like when you walked in the first day."

"Who do you think is responsible? Osborne?"

She shook her head slowly. "If it's Osborne you can be sure he didn't do it himself. No, I don't even want to try to guess. And I don't want you to either. This is my battle, my own personal one, the thing I've got to do for Hank—the last thing. So please don't be angry, Bert, but that's the way I feel."

TWELVE

August 10, 2026

BERT stepped off the ladder, moved back the better to observe the sign he had painted. A little crude, the lettering, but then he was no professional, and it was in keeping with the spirit of Mars. Besides, a used spacer lot needed signs. Many of them. Advertising was the soul of the business. It was just too bad, he thought, that he couldn't advertise in the little weekly paper they put out over at Four. But it was refinery-run and consisted mostly of gossip about who was doing what, who was coming and who was going, changes in positions and occupations, the arrival and departure of space craft. But for all of that, the *Mars News* was well read.

He looked beyond the red, white and blue sign that spanned the entranceway overhead, to the small, bright yellow office building—what was a used spacer lot without one?—and chuckled. At least there was one building on Mars that wasn't a dull, monotonous brown. The yellow paint had set him back plenty, but it was worth it.

And beyond the office, arranged in a neat row, were five spacers, neat, shining and tidy. The merchandise. The first was bought of a prospector down to his last nickel, a man only too glad to find a way to get back to Earth without having to work in the refinery and add this pay to what little money his ship would earn at the hands of the Schlenker Company. The second was from a potential uranium hunter who had become ill his first day on Mars and had thought better of poking around among asteroids for hauling for Gianetti. The third, fourth and fifth were purchased from former prospectors who had demanded the return of their ships from the processors. There had been seven ships, but a customer had already purchased the seventh one—he was a man who had been exceptionally lucky in one of the many games of chance always going on in the living quarters. He was out prospecting again and Bert silently prayed for his good fortune.

Business, Bert decided, was going to be good. Word would get around, and there was plenty of room behind the office for the ships the word would bring in. He and Emma had figured the refinery companies were using more than a hundred borrowed ships, which meant there were that many men working in the plants who would rather be out looking for ore, or who wished they had started out hauling ore instead of looking for it. And where there were men there were always ways and means of combining forces, raising

funds, forming a little corporation and selecting one of them
to work the ship bought collectively.

Schaun's Used Spacers was apt to change the economy of
life on Mars. And it was about time somebody did, Bert
thought.

He picked up his ladder, paint bucket and brush, and
started for his office, happy in his resolve and eager for
action. He had only seated himself comfortably behind the
desk, had skinned a cigar he had recently acquired several
boxes of on a special order to Earth, when he spied a figure
turning in at the entranceway. A customer already? No, it
was only Steve Babcock.

Bert didn't get out of his chair when the man came in. He
let him stand there, leaning against the jamb.

'Long time, no see, Steve. Where've you been keeping
yourself?"

"Busy. Nine's going to open soon. Been screening men.
They're having a tough time getting them over there. You
need chairs."

- "Yeah. Keep forgetting to get some."

"In business for good, eh?" Steve looked around the office,
his eyes settling on the spacers he could see through the window behind Bert. "I see you didn't have any trouble getting
a ship or two."

"Haven't had any trouble so far."

"Way over at Nine I've been hearing how Bert Schaun's
the friend of the unlucky prospector."

"We unlucky fellows have to stick together. It's a lot better than being stuck separately."

Steve laughed. "Feeling good, aren't you? Well, I don't
blame you. This is quite a layout you've got."

"Never felt better and it has been fixed up nice, hasn't
it? I've been pretty busy myself, Steve."

Steve moved away from the door, crossed the room and

stood looking out the rear windows. "Room for lots of ships out there."

"As far as the eye can see," Bert said, turning toward him in the swivel chair. "Of course I don't have a landing pattern or a fix yet, but that will come later."

"I suppose." Steve turned from the window, leaned against it. "You know what, Bert?"

"What?"

"Hell, I don't know how to tell you this. I've been putting off coming over here because of it." He pressed his lips together firmly and looked at Bert squarely. "The refinery people don't like it. They asked me to come over and tell you that."

Bert made clucking noises. "Too bad."

"They don't like it at all, Bert."

"They object to the whole thing or just part of it?"

"Well, they don't like it especially that you've made an offer to Sam Streeper."

"Sam's a good man; a little sour, maybe. Can't blame them though. He used to be a spacer mechanic back on Earth. I need a man like that, Steve. If business gets rolling we'll have a lot of repairs to make; we'll have to make the old ships run like new."

"Sam is a good man in his line, Bert. I know for a fact Sully hates like the devil to lose him."

"Sam knows how they feel. But he says the salary isn't the important thing. He says he feels it's time to make a change."

"Also," Steve said, coming now to sit on the desk, "they've heard you talked to Tracy and Klyborne.'

"By golly," Bert said, grinning, "word does get around, doesn't it? Well, I didn't make any definite proposal. I just sounded them out, that's all."

Steve ground his cigarette in Bert's ash tray. "They want to know what you're trying to do."

"Just trying to make a living, tell them. I figure it's about the only thing left for me to do on Mars."

"I can understand. Hell, I even sympathize. But they're put out because you've taken seven ships out of circulation, robbed the processors of the services of several men, and it looks as if they're going to lose a good man in Streeper. He's given his notice."

Bert knew he had, realized then that this, more than anything else, was the reason Steve had come around. But he said only, "Really? Well, in that case I'll have to line up something for him to do."

"Bert, the processors don't want to lose any more men. There aren't enough to go around as it is. And now there's Nine to consider."

"They might try working the Martians."

"The Stinkers? Are you serious? Those jobs require a little something in the upper story, not goops who live like mice on the desert."

"You're wrong there, Steve. They have brains. Did you know they can read and write? Have you seen how they've laid out their villages?"

"Oh, come off it, Bert. How many men do you think they'd have left after the first Stinker walked in? They'd have to issue gas masks to everybody. They wouldn't hear of it."

"Well, they might try getting more men from Earth then." He smiled. "Or do you suppose the word's got around about living conditions and pay?"

"There were men at first, but the novelty's gone and the men who've gone back haven't been very enthusiastic. Even the government's special immunity inducements haven't helped."

"Whose fault is that?"

"You'd lay it on the processors, Bert. I know that. But they're not entirely to blame. The trouble's with the men.

Take a look at them. Frontier type? Hell, no. Misfits, mostly. Guys who want somebody to hold their hand."

"The processors might try putting a little more money in it."

"You might try telling them that."

"I'm not likely to tell them anything."

"I know you got a rotten deal, Bert. The processors aren't denying it either, but their hands are tied. McAllister's got too much influence."

"If they had any guts at all they'd tell McAllister to go soak his head."

"They've been thinking along that line, Bert."

"Oh?" Bert eyed the big man on his desk with renewed interest. He hadn't expected them to be hurting this much quite yet. Still, the lot represented the shape of things to come and they were as capable as he in figuring out what would happen if business got good. "What have they been thinking, Steve?"

"Bert, I've been asked to make an offer to you." He looked up from the ash tray he'd been moving about the desk like a chess piece.

"Yeah?"

"The refinery bunch will buy all your ships at the price you paid for them, plus ten per cent for profit, and give you a job supervising the hauling of ore for Nine. They feel they can do that without violating any directives from the central office."

Bert grinned up at him. "That's mighty nice of them, Steve," he said. "Mighty nice. I'm glad to see they've had a change of heart. You think they'd sign a contract on that?"

"I know damn well they would."

"A non-cancellable contract?"

"I'm sure of it."

"My, my!"

"Well, what do you say? What shall I tell them?"

Bert pursed his lips thoughtfully and studied the opposite wall. "I know what you can tell them," he said.

"What?"

"You can tell them to go to hell."

August 21, 2026

For a man so thin Sam Streeper was indefatigable, matching Bert stride for stride, insisting on carrying more alarm posts than Bert, the load resting easily on his wiry frame. His hammer blows were harder and louder than Bert's, his wind was still good after a dozen plantings, and he wasted no time marveling at the progress they had made, moving quickly on to the next site, leaving Bert only to pick up his share and tag along.

"Wait a minute," Bert said at last, fighting for breath after driving an obstinate radio past half-way into the hard-baked red plain at the far edge of the landing area he had staked out. "Let's rest a minute."

Bert sat on the warm, flat land and swabbed his face with a handkerchief. Sam, still holding his hammer, leaned on the metal post and grinned at him, showing his crooked teeth.

"You ain't in condition, Bert, that's all."

"Maybe not. I never did like field work though. Where did you get all your energy, Sam?"

Sam looked up at the variegated late afternoon sky. "Guess I'm just glad to get out in the open, glad to get a chance to stretch my muscles. I'll feel it tomorrow, though, don't you worry. You know, Mars ain't a bad place, lookin' at it from here. Sure the air's thin, it gets cold in a hurry, but you can see a long ways. Course I admit there ain't much to see. But look at that sky! That's enough to make a man want to write poetry, you know that?"

"Some people on Mars do just that, Sam. The aliens."

"I heard you was with them quite a spell."

"I was with just one. A little guy named Greckle. Used to read to me out of a book. Of course I didn't understand any of it since it was Martian, but it was—well, I guess you'd call it pretty."

Sam laughed. "I'm glad it was you and not me. I had a smell of a Stinker once. I hope I never smell one again."

"If you force yourself not to think about it, it's not as bad as you think. And they don't have an odor all the time."

"Maybe so," Sam said, not wanting to disagree. "Look how low that sun is, Bert. It's about to turn cool. We'll never get this thing up if we sit around chewin' the fat."

Bert got up, groaning. "You're a hard taskmaster, Sam. But you're so right. How many more posts?"

"If we stagger 'em we got five more. If you want to settle for straight row plantin', it'll take three anyway before we tie into the other arm."

"All right," Bert said wearily, picking up his hammer. "Let's knock them in staggered."

If Bert had known it was going to be this much trouble, he'd have thought twice about putting in an alarm system. But he guessed he'd have put one in anyway. After Steve's visit to tell him of the refinery companies' proposal and his rejection of it, and the subsequent drafting of Sam Streeper from right out of the Sully plant, he realized he was in for trouble and decided not to take any more chances. He didn't want any spacers taking off at an angle to be wrecked on the desert somewhere. The alarm posts would be insurance against that and any inquisitive visitors, for they offered protection in an area two hundred feet in every direction, flashing an alarm to the office if anything of sufficient mass should venture into the detector net.

They hammered the post in the rest of the way. On Earth, even in hard clay, it wouldn't have taken them half as long as it did here in the tightly compressed ground of Mars.

"What do you suppose this ground's got in it that makes it so hard, Sam?"

"Sand, I reckon. Come on, let's get to the next one."

They picked up their posts and tools and moved on.

"You think this is ridiculous, Sam?" Bert asked. "Unnecessary, maybe?"

"I dunno," Sam said honestly. "I guess you ain't the most popular man on Mars though."

"The radio alarm posts will set off a relay in the office," Bert said. "Once I get the trouble pinpointed I've got a high-powered rifle with an infrascope to finish the job, day or night. I ought to be able to pick anything off within half a mile."

"I won't deny you might have to use it. I know Sully don't like what you're doin' and I suppose they got it in for me now, too. You should have heard Osborne before I left."

Bert chuckled. "I'd have liked to have been there."

"He told me I'd never work for them again, and he told me you'd fold before long. 'Sam,' he said, 'Sam, you'll be a derelict when that happens.' But he didn't scare me none. Mechanics are scarce people on Mars. He'd take me back if I wanted to go back. Yeah, you should have seen him. Never saw him so mad."

"I imagine they're all angry. Wait till I get Tracy and Klyborne. They'll blow their tops then."

"You'll be gettin' two good men."

"There'll be plenty to do, Sam, if I've got this thing figured right. Lots of spacer work. The ships can stand it, too. Most men don't keep their machines up. Take the *Martha Q.* for example. She's going to need a complete overhaul. She's got to be in A Number One shape before I'll show her."

Sam laughed. "I saw that fancy sign of yours out there. 'Guaranteed OK Used Spacers.' Reminds me of Earth. You know, Bert, I never thought of it before, but I miss all that

Earth advertisin', all those signs everywhere you look. There's hardly a sign around here, you notice that?"

"Don't need them. Everything is owned by the refinery people. Everything but what we've got."

"And we'll make it somethin' big, maybe we could even get a blinkin' sign or a depthy like they got along Broadway. And we'll have spacer to match. Clean 'em up good, make 'em shine and really run. Don't you worry, Bert, you won't have anythin' to be ashamed of when we get through."

The sun was much lower in the sky when they drove the last post, the cool evening breeze chilling them, tugging at their jackets and trouser legs.

"Sure don't take long to cool off, does it" Sam observed.

"I'd hate to spend the night out here," Bert said, picking up his tools. He raised up, stood looking at the post tips that dotted the area in a long, straggly curve. "I'm sure glad we got them all in."

"And no time to spare," Sam said, joining him for a last look at the accomplishment.

Suddenly a sharp *crack* made them turn their heads in the direction of the sound. Immediately there was a *spat* and Sam's hammer flew from his hand.

Sam danced on one foot, holding his hand and grimacing in pain, crying, "Damn! Damn! Damn!"

"You get hit?" Bert asked.

"In the hand," Sam said.

The shot had come from behind a rise far to the right and as Bert looked along the brown ridge, there was another flash of light and a *crack.*

Bert fell to the ground, barely beating Sam there.

The bullet soughed overhead, kicking up a little dust beyond them where it hit the ground, twanged as it ricocheted.

"Damn poor shot," Sam said. "I wish I knew which one of us he was aimin' at."

"Just warning shots, I think," Bert said, hugging the

ground. "They want us to know they're still thinking about us."

"I didn't guess wrong about our popularity then. I wonder who's behind that gun."

"You can bet it's not Osborne," Bert said. "He'd send a small boy for a job like this."

Another shot and another bullet threw a handful of dirt in their faces. There was no doubt in Bert's mind the man with the gun was either the same man who had put Gregg up to the wrecking of the *Fern,* or another hired one, just as Gregg had been, for he would never believe Gregg had just gone batty.

"I think we'd better make a run for it," Bert said. "I'd rather be a moving target. That guy might et the range if we stay here."

"I'm game if you are. Lead off."

Then they were on their feet, their tools forgotten, their fatigue evaporating in the danger, as they raced for their lives over the bare, dry ground for the office. Even as they ran, fearing the gunshot that could end their lives, Bert was amazed at the stamina of the sinewy older man, for he kept abreast of him all the way. There were several shots but none of them came close.

"I think," Sam panted as they reached the building, "that we're goin' to need that alarm system after all."

"Glad you said 'we'," Bert said, breathing hard, rushing to his locked desk, fumbling for and finding the key in his pocket, inserting it and jerking open the drawer with the rifle and scope in it. "I thought maybe the shots would scare you out. And maybe that's what the man wants." He jammed the scope in place, ran to the window, heaved up the sash, and poked the gun through, sighting in the scope.

"They won't scare me," Sam said, joining him at the window, "It'll take more than a couple pot shots to make me quit. See anythin'?"

"Not a thing," Bert said, taking a last look along the vacant ridge before lowering the gun. "For an old man you've got a lot of speed, Sam."

"Grew up in Chicago," Sam said, grinning. "Was always on the run there. Not from choice either."

"Here, let's see that hand."

"It's nothin'," Sam said, showing him his hand. Remnants of the splattering bullet had scratched the knuckle of his forefinger, bit a hunk of skin out of the fleshy part of the thumb.

"They drew a little blood, didn't they?"

"Sure did. And you know what? I don't think we've seen the last of the guy with the gun."

THIRTEEN

October 10, 2026

BERT SCHAUN watched Thornton McAllister's daughter and her new husband, Spencer Dean, walk out of his line of sight, and he was filled with the memory of the day of the Classic, shuddering with the remembered horror of the exploding ship and the events that followed.

He knew he had not been wise to say he'd keep the yacht, for it would be a bother to watch over, although there had been no alarming incidents recently, but something about the girl and the couple's predicament touched him. Perhaps the yacht would have advertising value. It would be there on the lot and everybody'd see it and they'd talk about it. It wouldn't look bad out there with those twenty-three ships. In fact, it might even give the place a little class.

The alien! He had almost forgotten about him! Sam had called even before the Deans had come. Was the creature still out on the lot somewhere?

He switched on the intercom, called the station Sam had talked from.

"Tracy," the voice came back.

"Is Sam around there somewhere?"

"He's up by the *Martha Q.* He's got a Stinker cornered up there."

"I'll be right down. I got tied up."

He found Sam Streeper at the ladder to the *Martha Q.*

"Take a smell of that," Sam said, nodding toward the ship's lock and wrinkling his nose. "He's inside."

"You see him go in?"

"Didn't have to."

Bert started for the ladder.

"Hey, you going in there?" Sam was aghast.

"Sure."

"I wouldn't go in there for a million dollars."

"Nobody's asking you to," Bert said a little stiffly, mounting the ladder.

He found the Martian in the control room simply by following his nose. And when he entered the room, the Martian heard him and whirled away from the instruments, cringing in a corner, his eyes wide, his face light gray with fear. The stench was nauseating.

Then the alien's face brightened. "Bert!" he said, ears trembling, gray face darkening as he came out of the corner.

"I'll be damned!" Bert said.

The rabbit ears were jumping, the eyes were a bright red, the black gums much in evidence in the toothless smile.

"What in God's name are you doing here, Greckle?"

Greckle just grinned shyly.

"You look like an idiot child, Greckle, you know that?" Bert said, finding the grin contagious. He was surprised to find the smell less offensive now. But he'd have to get the alien out of there before it got bad again.

"Sheep," Greckle said, not losing the lopsided grin.

For a moment Bert did not understand. Then the Martian said it again and gestured to include the whole vessel.

"Ship, you mean," Bert said.

"Ship," the Martian said.

"How did you get by the alarm system? And how did you get in here?"

"Walk. Walk in. Walk by yellow box, see sheep—ship. Like ship. Walk in. I like Bert."

Bert had been on the point of gruffly ordering him off the ship and hustling him off the lot, but his disarming manner, his genuine affection and the memory of what the little fellow had done for him and the care he had taken of him in the cave suddenly made it impossible for him to hurt him. It was, in its way, an affection of sorts. The odd part of it was that he found it a pleasant affection, a warming thing. The aliens were strange creatures—formidable if you had never seen one and listened only to others who had, repulsive if you came near one, and likable after you got to know one. Why couldn't the rest of them see that?

"You've stirred things up around here," Bert said. "And your odor hasn't helped."

"Stink," Greckle said, losing his grin. "I know. Stinker. That bad."

"Well, we can't stay in here. Come on."

Bert led the way to the lock and the ladder to the ground. Sam Streeper must have heard them coming. He was nowhere near when they stepped to the ground.

"You can't come barging in on the lot like that," Bert said, walking him toward the office. "People don't like it. They don't understand."

"Ship," Greckle said, stopping and turning to look at it. "Had to see ship."

Bert saw the red glow of his eyes. Damn if he isn't taken with it, he thought. Very few people look at ships that way, and those that do are usually pilots or engineers or mechanics.

"I see you haven't forgotten the words I taught you."

"Never forget," Greckle said, turning to him. "You speak. I listen. Never forget."

"I don't believe you do forget," Bert said, marveling anew at the alien's retentive powers, and watching his eyes go lovingly to the ship again.

"Learn. Quickly."

"Yes, you do," Bert said. "You should learn more."

Greckle turned and understood. His face wrinkled in the twisted grin and his ears jiggled. "Good. Want to learn. Want to learn big."

"Much," Bert corrected.

"Want to learn things. Much. Many things."

The lot was at the edge of Seven, which accounted for the alien's being able to venture into it without notice of Seven residents. If he came there undetected once, why couldn't he come there again? Or often? Bert felt he owed him something for saving his life, so wouldn't giving him what knowledge he could, be payment in kind? He'd have the time, for there weren't customers every minute of the day, and besides, he was curious to put the alien to the test. How much could he learn? Was there a limit? He could hold class in the *Martha Q*, or perhaps that might not be such a good idea. Perhaps a far corner of the lot would be better.

"Could you come every day?" Bert asked. "Every day at a certain time?"

"I can come," Greckle said firmly. "Learn about ship."

"Good. We'll start your lessons tomorrow."

October 11—November 15, 2026

The primary education of Greckle was accomplished on a far corner of the lot in the early morning hours, Bert taking along his rifle for protection, though he never had any use for it. The schooling was simple and uneventful—until it became necessary to move to a spacer for more advanced phases of learning.

The alien's mind was like a sponge, all-absorbent and retentive, and it sometimes demanded things of Bert that Bert could not give, such as a decent explanation of the vagaries of English pronunciation, the need for laws governing human behavior, differences in man's religious concepts, and a case in point: why he carried the weapon with him each morning.

The teacher sometimes became an inquiring pupil and, as such, Bert learned of the Martians' reverence for life, form, substance and balance; the fact that they had no need for law enforcement, and that their food consisted solely of the plants each one cultivated. Their stories, always a true measure of a people, were never ones of violence but of a search for truth and beauty, a oneness with nature and each other. They were simple tales of love of alien-male and alien-female, but they were always on an ethereal plane and appealed to the heart and mind rather than the physical.

Why, then, Bert kept asking himself, was an alien like Greckle drawn to the spacers, the people who had invaded his planet, and to the things the people had brought with them? The answer, he discovered, was simply that this was an area not developed among them, a new branch of knowledge that would be embraced. The fact of its existence, not hitherto dreamed of, made the assimilation of it a necessity, and Bert was the catalyst for this, for without Bert the alien would have returned to his orderly community to be further ignored by men.

Bert started with elementary language, figures, and some simple scientific facts. The language presented no difficulty whatever, the alien was interested in the arithmetical and algebraic concepts and easily learned them, but he was fascinated by and had a little trouble with the science. In a few weeks Bert had exhausted every fact about social ethics, had already gone far into logarithms, differential equations and tensor notation, but was still at a rather primary level in levers, pulleys, electricity and chemical reaction. The reason was, Bert discovered, that the alien's culture had long passed his own in social ethics. Their abstruse thinking had quickly made working with figures a facile thing, an interesting game and diversion. But the hard, basic facts of science were so new the alien seemed a little in awe of them. It was in this area that Bert concentrated his efforts.

It was at the end of the first month, in between selling and buying spacers and expecting trouble with the processors that never came, that Emma discovered what he was doing. There was no need to try to conceal it, Bert decided, so he told her. Though she was, as were all people from Earth, unwilling at first to meet the alien, and was sickened by her initial visit (both, to Bert's amusement, proved to be shy), she soon grew to like him. Many was the time she stayed the night at the office, to go out with Bert for the class in the field. On occasion she even managed to provide information Bert lacked.

"He's like a magnet, Bert," she said once. "He draws everything you know out of you and then probes for more."

The alien never changed, even with his new wisdom. He was still "the grinning brain," as Emma called him—grateful, obedient, and cheerful. His odor, though manifesting itself during a difficult time or two, was not apparent on the breeze-swept plain.

Several days Greckle absented himself, explaining he had duties to perform at his village, but from force of habit Emma and Bert made their way to the spot to exchange pleasantries for an hour or two and to confess to each other they'd never been happier.

It was on such a morning as this, as he was holding her

close to him, that he asked her again if she wouldn't change
her mind right then and say she'd marry him.

"No," she said, kissing him. "But soon, darling."

November 29, 2026

And it was on a morning many days later, after Bert had
transferred his class with Greckle to the *Martha Q.*, that the
trouble started.

It was Sam Streeper.

Sam came into the office one afternoon, wiping his grimy
hands on a cloth, and standing in embarrassed silence.

"What's on your mind?" Bert asked cheerily, though he
could see the storm warnings clearly in Sam's face.

"It's that Stinker," he said, looking down at his fingernails
and starting to pick at them. "We—Tracy, Klyborne and I—
we know you met him out in the field. That was O.K. But—
well, it don't make no difference to me, but Tracy and Klyborne. . . . They are real put out."

"I don't see why they should be, Sam. You fellows don't
have anything to do with him. He's my responsibility."

"But just havin' him around, Bert, he's apt to cause
trouble."

"Not Greckle. He's as peaceful a guy as I've ever seen."

"He's still a Stinker."

"But he never did anything to you, did he, Sam? Now be
honest with me, man."

"No, can't say that he has, but—" Sam's face reddened.

"But what?"

"Look, Bert," Sam said, looking up fiercely, "the three
of us will work ourselves to a frazzle for you because we don't
like working for the refineries. We know what they are, what
they pay."

"Business has been good," Bert said. "We've sold three
ships this past week. If it's money—"

"It's not money." Sam took a deep breath. "It's showin' that Stinker around on the spacer, showin' him how the engines work and how the ships are operated and—" His shoulders sagged. "We just don't want to work with him, that's all. Why, it's as if you were trainin' him for one of our jobs."

"You know better than that, Sam. He'd never be able to do what you do." But he said it reservedly, for Greckle had shown tremendous strides in the past few days. It wouldn't be long, he knew, before the alien could operate and repair a ship.

"Maybe he won't ever take over, Bert," Sam said, "but I just thought you ought to know how things stand."

"I appreciate what you're telling me, Sam. And I want you fellows to know you're welcome here as long as you want to stay. As for the alien, you don't have to worry about him. He's been curious and he's learning, but he'll never replace anybody."

That night he went to Emma Klein's. He needed a drink. Several of them. The Martian was nearing the most interesting part of his education, impatient to learn everything there was about spacers and it wouldn't be fair to stop it now just to please three workmen, no matter how badly he needed them. If only they would forget about Greckle and let him finish! Who could tell, perhaps the alien might be able to go on from where man had stopped in his development of interstellar ships. Or in any one of the fields man had excelled in.

He felt it when he walked in, felt the sudden lull in conversation, saw the avoided eyes of those seated at the tables. It was a small thing, but it was significant.

And there was Emma. An Emma without her usual smile. There was worry there where the smile should have been, and her face was pale.

"Bert," she said, when he seated himself at the bar, "I've got to talk to you." She looked around furtively.

"What's wrong, Emma?"

"That's what I want to talk to you about."

"Is it about these people? I noticed—"

"The word's got around you have an alien out on the lot and they don't like it."

"It seems," Bert said, taking his drink and swallowing it quickly and putting the glass down for a refill, "that nobody likes it."

"Somebody's stirring them up," she said.

"Guess who," he said. "Osborne will stop at nothing."

"Bert," she said desperately, ignoring several customers who were signaling frantically for service, "you've got to get rid of Greckle." And, seeing the look on his face, she added, "For a while at least."

"Nobody's got to come out to the lot if he doesn't want to," he said firmly. "The alien's not going to hurt them."

"Don't be stubborn, Bert. Don't be!"

"Greckle's not hurting anybody. He can stay as long as he wants to. He's learning about the spacers now."

"I know how you feel about him," she said, eyes welling with tears, "and I feel the same way. But—"

"But what?" He looked at her severely. "I don't like the way people refuse to understand them, Emma. I'm not going to be pressured into it." And he added gently, "And I don't want you to be either."

"All right," she said, resigned. "I only hope nothing happens."

FOURTEEN

November 30, 2026

EMMA heard the tapping, sat up instantly in bed, wondering who it could be. She reached under her pillow, withdrew her pistol, put her feet in her slippers and went through the kitchen to the tavern.

There was a figure on the other side of the door.

Bert? Was he in trouble?

She unlatched the door quickly. The man stepped in and as the frigid air washed around her, she stepped back, snapped on the light.

It was a stranger, a big man who cast a big shadow under the light, and his eyes went at once to the gun.

"What do you want?" she asked calmly.

"You're Emma Klein, aren't you?"

"Yes."

"I want to talk to you."

"Just keep standing there. And keep talking." She had seen him somewhere, but she couldn't recall just where.

He smiled thinly. "O.K. Maybe you know me, maybe not. My name's Brant Huygens. I work for Steve Babcock over at Four. Police work."

"I remember you." His face was clear now. She had seen him at several of Steve's parties. "Does Steve have a message for me?"

"I didn't come here for him, Lady. I came on business of my own." His eyes went to the bar. "How about a drink?"

"After hours."

"Stop kidding. It's cold out there."

She served him a drink, watched him. He was under tension, all right. Even the drink failed to dispel the white around the eyes. And his hand on the bar left a moist imprint. Hands in out of the cold seldom did that. She waited.

Finally he wet his lips and said, "I suppose you can guess why I'm here."

"That's a poor beginning," she said coolly. "I'm not playing guessing games. What do you want?"

He swallowed and looked at her steadily. "You want to know who killed your husband?"

"Yes."

"You offered money."

"Yes." She repeated the amount.

He licked his lips. "Where's the money? Do you have it?"

"I have it."

"I've got to see it first."

She shook her head. "Not the way I play it. How do I know you know who killed my husband?"

"I know."

"Have you told Steve?"

"Listen," he said, exasperated, "I came to tell you some names—"

"Names? You could name anybody. How would I know you just heard about my offer and dreamed them up? No, Mr. Huygens, it's got to be better than that. You've got to have proof. Have you proof?"

"Proof? What do you mean 'proof'? Hell, there isn't any proof!"

"How do you know there isn't?"

"I—I just know there isn't."

"I don't pay until there is," she said firmly.

"Lady, you don't know what you're asking. You want the impossible. Where'll I ever find proof?"

"That's up to you."

His face clouded, his eyes grew small. "I made a long trip over here," he said. "I came over without anybody knowing, planning it that way. I don't like to go away disappointed."

Emma moved away from the bar, her pistol before her. You'd better walk straight out that door," she said, "and make the long trip back where you came from."

He paused at the door. "I know you and Steve are pretty thick. If you tell him I was here, you'll never find out what I know. He wouldn't like it if he knew I came over here like this. You don't tell him and I'll start to work on the proof. Is that a deal?"

She studied his eyes for a long time, found them as untrustworthy as any she'd ever seen, but decided to go along in spite of it. "All right," she said.

"I'll give you a call one of these days.".

December 2, 2026—January 4, 2027

Bert continued his instruction of Greckle in space ship operation and maintenance, ever alert for a sign of trouble. The alien noticed the change in him.

"You are not the same, Bert," Greckle said. "Something has happened to you. Inside. I can tell. What is it?"

"Nothing," Bert snapped, angry that his tenseness should be obvious even to a Martian. Then he relented. "I guess maybe I've been working too hard. I suppose I am a little jumpy."

"Jumpy?" The alien grinned. "I know what you mean and I guess you have not been. But the word draws a picture in my mind that makes me want to laugh. I have never seen you jump."

As a relief from instruction in theory, they took the *Martha Q* into space for a little practical experience in navigation, and for a few moments Bert let the alien take the controls. The look in Greckle's eyes when he took the ship was enough to make the whole project worthwhile, Bert thought. And the Martian was silent for once in this new experience of being one with the ship, and Bert could see his joy in the feel of the power at his fingertips, the joy that only a man with the love of spacers can fully enjoy.

During the rest of the flight the alien was a question mark, a creature of inexhaustible queries and requests for information, letting no action by Bert go unnoticed or unexplained.

The alien was even curious when Bert withdrew the fuel pellets from the office safe.

"It's probably ridiculous," Bert explained, "but it's an old-fashioned custom and standard practice on used spacer lots not to leave a full tank of fuel. It invites theft, either of the fuel itself or of the ship."

Greckle shook his head and Bert said wearily, "Don't say it, Greckle. I know. There is no such thing as theft among your kind. Well, we've had a different rearing, I guess. It's something that will be with the human race forever, I'm afraid."

The teaching of Greckle now became an obsession, a counterattack against the scorn of objectors and a violation of it, an insistence that he show everyone how he stood on the matter; rushing the alien through training that should have taken weeks, Greckle never faltering and not aware of the accelerated pace. Bert didn't know what would happen when he taught him everything he could, but rather than think about that he returned to the lessons with renewed vigor, expanding the teaching time from an hour or two in the early morning to most of the morning and a few hours in the late afternoon.

It wasn't long before the alien made his first flight of the *Martha Q* unassisted, though Bert rode in the control room with him. Greckle piloted the ship with the hands of an expert, made a perfect takeoff and landing. Both teacher and pupil were mighty pleased with themselves.

January 5, 2027

The morning of the epic flight, Streeper, Tracy and Klyborne, three stern-faced mechanics, presented themselves at Bert's office. They stood self-consciously at the doorway exchanging glances.

"What's on your minds?" Bert asked, feeling already the tension they had brought with them.

"We want to talk to you," Tracy said. A big, beefy man not given to much talk, Tracy's position as spokesman, with Streeper just standing by, made the move an ominous one.

"Go ahead," Bert said coolly.

"You've been a good boss," Tracy said. He stopped, reddened.

"Thanks. But I know that's not what you came to say."

"No, it isn't," Tracy admitted. "But we want you to know we ain't got nothing against you personally."

"I know. It's about the alien, I suppose."

"Yes, sir, it is."

"What about him?"

"Well . . ." Tracy was unable to go on.

"It's either him or us, Mr. Schaun," Klyborne put in. "Either he goes or we do."

Bert wanted to lash out at them, to tell them how stupid they were, feeling his anger flash hot and demanding. But he only sat unmoving, looking at Sam Streeper now and saying, "Is that the way you feel, Sam?"

"When we were out there and they were takin' shots at us, I was with you a hundred per cent, Bert."

"And now?"

Sam would not say. He only looked at Bert challengingly.

"We stood it as long as we could," Tracy said. "Everybody's laughing at us."

"They say you've gone crazy," Sam said. "Crazy over that Stinker. They're tellin' jokes about you."

"Is that so? And the jokes—are they any good?"

"Nobody's ever palled around with a Stinker before," Klyborne said. "People don't like it."

"It ain't natural," Tracy said. "That's what they're saying."

"And they've been callin' us 'the Stinker's helpers,'" Sam said. "That is, when they talk to us."

"We thought we'd come and see you," Tracy said. "We thought we'd let you know."

"And maybe you'd do something."

Bert examined their faces, strained, rigid, inflexible faces, faces that were pushing him hard to do what he knew he must not do, what he would not do, and behind them he saw the faces of others, the glee in Osborne's face at this turn of events, and the sullen faces of those in the tavern, and he made a silent vow he'd not do what they wanted—not because he wanted to oppose them, but because what they wanted was not right. The fantasy about the Stinkers had lived long enough. It was high time they were recognized for what they were and their capabilities utilized; for their talents, if Greckle was any example, far outweighed the disadvantage of their scent.

"And what," Bert asked, "do you want me to do?"

"We already told you," Klyborne said. "Get rid of the Stinker."

"Do you suggest I kill him, perhaps? Would that do? But then we'd have to burn him, wouldn't we, as the other alien was burned so he wouldn't smell up the area."

"That's not what they mean—" Sam started to say.

"Or," Bert said, voice rising in anger, "perhaps you'd like to have him so you could take care of him yourself or give him to your friends in the refinery. It would give you all something to do."

"Bert, I—" Then Sam snapped his mouth shut and glared.

"Did you know that the alien's name is Greckle? Did you know he can speak English? Did you ever talk to him? Or did you just watch him walk around and mutter under your breath?"

"I ain't talking to no Stinker," Klyborne said belligerently. And looking Bert square in the eye, he said, "And I ain't about to and nobody's going to make me."

"Nobody's going to make you is right," Bert said heatedly. "It isn't something you ought to be made to do. It's something you ought to make yourself do. Did you see the flight he made yesterday? Do you know he knows almost as much as I do about spacers?" And when they didn't answer, he said, "I suppose you're afraid he'll take your jobs."

"It ain't that," Sam said.

"What is it then?" Bert snapped.

"He's got to go or we do," Klyborne said.

"It's trouble," Sam said. "You don't know what they're saying. There'll be trouble."

"Well, trouble is nothing new to me."

"But *we* don't want trouble," Tracy said.

"That's right, Mr. Schaun," Klyborne said. "Now, if you'd get rid of that Stinker—"

"I'm not going to get rid of him," Bert said without emotion. "Is that clear?"

"Clear enough for me," Klyborne said, face darkening. "I've heard all I want to hear." He edged toward the door.

Sam gave Bert a pleading look, stood his ground until the other two had gone out, then turned. He paused at the door and looked back. "Bert—"

"Yeah."

"I think you're makin' a big mistake."

"And I think you are, Sam."

Then Sam slipped through the door and was gone.

Bert reached for a cigar, sat with it unlighted in his mouth for a long time, eyes still on the door the three men had walked through.

He met Greckle in the control room of the *Martha Q*.

"What do we do today, Bert?" Greckle asked, moving his hands lovingly over the control knobs.

"School's out today," Bert said. "You'd better go home. You can come back tomorrow. Maybe we can do something then."

"Is something wrong?"

"In a way. Now you run along. I've got some important things to do." He would overhaul the *Martha Q*. That would take a good eight hours, give him a chance to work off some of the steam he had suddenly accumulated, and let him have time to think things out.

"I will stay out of your way," Greckle said. "Shall I polish the *Pamela?*"

"The yacht? It needs it. O.K." Bert went to the tool compartment and opened it, started laying things out he'd need.

"What is wrong?"

Bert started throwing tools around. "You still here?" The alien's incessant questioning was something he couldn't stand today. "I thought I told you to go home."

"Polish the yacht. You told me it would be all right if I did that."

"Well," he roared, "why the hell aren't you doing it then?"

The alien's scent filled the control room. For some reason it seemed worse than usual.

"Bert, you are angry."

"Damn right I am. My three mechanics walked out on me. And do you know why? Because of you. There, now you know. So hightail it somewhere so I don't have to look at you."

"I will, Bert. I will." The alien's face brightened. "Maybe I can help. *Really* help."

Bert stood and faced him, smiling wryly. "I wish you could. But I don't see how." He picked up a rag and threw it at him. "Here, get out and start polishing. A good job for you, Rabbit Ears. Ought to take you a week."

The Martian left the control room and Bert settled down to dismantling the *Martha Q's* engine, giving himself up to the work, grunting and sweating and relishing the feel of dirt and grease and metal. It was good to get into an engine again.

The afternoon was warmer than usual, so he opened the lock and felt a faint breeze once in a while, even in the control room, shifting his lights here and there, spraying this part, greasing that part, washing another, replacing worn pieces from stock, lost in his job, a man apart and alone with an engine, doing what he knew and doing it well.

Then he heard a number of whistling voices, hardly more than whispers above the breeze, a great number of them, and he stopped his work to listen and heard them more clearly.

Puzzled, he left the control room, went through the lock and down the ladder. The murmuring voices were coming from the direction of the *Pamela*. He walked that way.

He stopped in amazement when he saw them, a dozen Martians, each one the image of Greckle, and each one equipped with a polishing cloth and polish, climbing ladders to reach parts of the yacht and rubbing the areas briskly. The metal gleamed.

And when they saw him they stopped, staring at him with round red eyes. The murmuring ceased.

Greckle detached himself from the group, came over to Bert with the biggest lopsided grin Bert had ever seen on his face.

"These are some of my relatives," Greckle said. "I hope you do not mind. I have taught them all you have taught me. They can polish the *Pamela* quickly, as you can see. They like ships, too, and will do any work you have for them."

Bert groaned and sat on a large rock nearby.

"Is it wrong to bring them here? I wanted to ask, but I was afraid you would be angry again."

"Send them home, Greckle," Bert said, not knowing whether to laugh or cry. "Send them home right away."

The alien was offended. "Home?"

Bert caught a whiff of his scent. That, multiplied by twelve . . . And it was suddenly worse. "Yes, Greckle, send them home. It will only be more trouble if they stay. Thanks, though. Thanks for thinking of me."

"I am sorry, Bert. I shall tell them to go home at once."

And I need a drink, Bert told himself, heading for his office.

FIFTEEN

January 6, 2027

BERT lifted his head from his desk, a dry taste in his mouth. He looked out the window and saw it was morning. Then he spied the empty bottle on his desk and knew why he had a bad taste.

"A hell of a way for a proprietor of a used spacer lot to act," he chided himself.

He rose from the desk, weary in every joint and muscle. The drinking hadn't accomplished but one thing: It had put what seemed a longer distance between yesterday and today. And maybe, because of that, it was worth it.

He went to the small lavatory in the corner and looked at his face in the mirror. Beard popping out all over. Bloodshot eyes. I look like a Martian, myself, this morning, he told himself.

He sighed, opened the larder, extracted a few cans, pressed their tops and waited for the exothermic reaction that would heat their contents. Breakfast would settle his stomach, if nothing else. While he waited for the cans to warm he walked to the rear window and looked out over the lot. Greckle, he saw, was atop the *Pamela*, polishing cloth in hand, hard at work. The morning sun glinted from the gleaming metal sides.

"You little son of a gun," he said affectionately, "you're really on the ball, aren't you?"

When he had finished his breakfast and shaved, he felt half human again. Now all there was left to do was solve all his problems. Could he exist without his three mechanics? Perhaps, if Greckle could really do the work. And he might. After all, the little guy was even more indefatigable than Streeper. But would anyone buy any of his ships? That was

143

another question. The alien on the lot wouldn't help in that category, and the news about Tracy, Klyborne and Streeper would be whispered around, and he grimaced to think of how the truth would be twisted before it made the complete circle of ears and mouths. But if he played a waiting game, biding his time, using patient firmness, perhaps they would come around to his way of thinking.

That is, unless Osborne pushed things, unless he started whipping up reactions against him. Bert was certain Osborne had initiated the talk against Greckle, would follow it up now that he had the advantage. No need to fire bullets any more; there was a better weapon, wasn't there, Osborne?

How to combat it Bert shook his head. That would require some thinking. And it demanded a clear head. He knocked the empty bottle in the waste basket. No more of that.

He went to the door to open it for the day, saw Steve Babcock coming up the walk. Steve waved. Bert waved in return and wondered what Steve had on his mind. On another errand for Osborne?

"I see you've gone and solved the problem of cheap help," Steve said, smiling and coming through the door past Bert. He went to the rear window. "Seems to be doing a good job, too."

"Greckle is very conscientious," Bert said. "Intelligent, too."

Steve turned from the window, the smile still on his face. He sat in the swivel chair and looked at Bert.

"What brings you here?" Bert said, not wanting to parry, taking a customer's chair.

"Business."

"Yeah? What kind of business?"

"Oh," Steve said archly, "I'll get to it. How've things been going?"

"Suppose you tell me." He didn't like the way Steve was acting. It didn't seem to be the same old Steve.

"Not good, have they? You've lost three good mechanics, I hear."

"I'd expect you to know about them. They walked out yesterday."

"Why?"

"Don't make me laugh. You know. Come on, let's have it. What did you come for? What do you want?"

"I don't want anything, Bert," Steve said soberly. "I've just come to tell you something."

"Well, tell it and get it over with."

"I hate to have to tell you, Bert, but your Stinker friend will have to go."

"Is that so?" Bert said, bristling.

"Yes, that's so. He's a bad influence around here. I'm speaking as law enforcement man now, not as a representative of the refinery people. You saw how Tracy, Klyborne and Streeper reacted. That's a good sample. For the best interests of everybody concerned, you've got to get rid of him."

"For the best interests of the refinery people, you mean. Then that would put me out of business."

"There's nothing personal in it on the part of the refinery people, Bert. Or on my part either. The Stinkers just haven't worked out, that's all. They cause trouble all along the line."

"The aliens don't start trouble, Steve."

"Stinkers, you mean."

"I mean *aliens*. Martians. Whoever hung that monicker on them did them an injustice."

"Whatever you call him doesn't matter, but if you don't get him out of Seven and back to the stinkhole he lives in, we'll have to do the job for you, Bert."

"You and how many, Steve?" Bert said quietly.

Steve leaned forward. "What's the matter with you, Bert? Have you gone batty? Everybody thinks you're nuts for taking up with one of those skunks. I used to think you were a nice guy."

"That's how much everybody knows about them—you included, Steve. Let me ask you: what's come over you? They're not so bad once you get used to them and try to understand them."

Steve snorted. "I suppose the next thing you're going to tell me is they don't stink."

"The next thing I'm going to tell you is to stop using that word. It's been overworked."

"They still stink, the word notwithstanding."

"They have an odor at times. Especially when their feelings are hurt. I used to think it was worse than it actually is."

"Then your nose is wearing out being so close to one. I could tell there was one around here as soon as I turned in at the lot."

Bert eyed the big man stonily. "It's your imagination. It doesn't carry that far. It doesn't rub off and it doesn't stay. That much I know."

"I tell you, Bert, I could smell him clear out at the entrance."

"You saw him and then imagined the rest."

"The hell I did!"

"You don't give them a chance!"

Steve smacked the desk with a fist. "Who *wants* to give a damn Stinker a chance? That's your trouble right there in a nutshell."

Bert gripped his chair tightly, stared at the man, wondering how he managed to be so twisted so suddenly. "Steve," he said, "did you ever wonder what you must smell like to a Martian?"

"That's a filthy thing to say," Steve cried, balling his fists and rising from the swivel chair, glaring at Bert, "I ought to punch you right in the nose for that."

"*Is* it so filthy?" Bert retorted, rising and kicking the chair away, sending it crashing into the desk. "Suppose they had come to Earth and started to build factories and never asked us a damn thing?"

"Don't be an ass. We're way ahead of them. They'd never do that. This is different."

"Oh, it's all right to ignore the natives, even though you take half their planet away from them, eh?"

"Anybody with any sense would ignore creatures like they are. Hell, they smell and they're stupid."

"Is that so? Well, let me tell you, Mister, you're way wrong. They wear clothes, fancy clothes with fine needlework. You wouldn't know. You never got that close. They have a language. It's probably as pretty to them as ours is to us. You'd never learn it, Steve, and neither would I. We're not bright enough. Oh, maybe we would in time, but we'd never learn it as fast as that alien out there on the *Pamela* has learned ours."

"Who wants to learn their language? I'm sure I don't."

"And they are simple, co-operative people interested in our ways and our thoughts and our accomplishments. And another thing maybe you'll never understand: They like us. Even after all we've done to them, they still like us. They want us to help them. Only we won't let them."

"You're crazy," Steve said, staring at him. "That's what they're saying all over Seven. 'Bert Schaun's gone completely nuts. Stark, raving nuts.' I didn't believe them, until just now."

"I'm not crazy," Bert said. "All I've done is take the logical step we should have taken when we first landed on this planet. The aliens are our friends. They want to help us. And they have potentialities nobody's ever realized. Potentialities useful to Sully and the rest of the refineries."

"I don't believe it. Nobody thinks so but you, and that's why you're so out of step and different from everybody else."

"You just don't know them, Steve."

"Go ahead and love the Stinkers if you want to sink that

low, but that doesn't mean the rest of us have to get down there with you."

"Who's being filthy now?"

"You're impossible," Steve said, moving away from behind the desk. "I'm through trying to protect you, through trying to see things your way, sympathizing with you. The Stinker has to go. Nothing can change that. As the law enforcement chief, I'm telling you that. Now, are you going to see to it that he goes, or do we have to tend to it ourselves?"

"The Stinker stays," Bert said slowly and evenly. "Over my dead body he leaves here."

"Have it your own way, then," Steve said.

Bert looked up from the shining retractable ground support stems, up the smooth sides of the yacht to the top where the ship's hull curved inward. All was spotless, polished. And at the top, working furiously with polish and rag, was Greckle, perched there, unmindful of his precarious position.

"How am I doing?" Greckle called down.

"Fine, Greckle. It's a fine job."

Bert saw the ears jiggle, the face darken and the eyes shine, and instantly he shared the alien's joy as it washed over him. What was there about the aliens frightened people? Even Steve now. He couldn't understand it.

"Come on down," he called. "I want to talk to you."

Greckle worked his way to the ladder and climbed down it.

"Are we going to start the lessons again?" Greckle asked when he stood on the ground.

"No," Bert said. "I just want to ask you a question."

"A question? What is the question?"

"Greckle," he said. "Tell me: do I stink?"

"Stink?" The eyes were suddenly wild and the voice was a shrill whistle. Now there were waves of scent and warmth and cold and the gray flesh of the Martian was mottled light and dark.

"I do not know what the word means," Greckle said. "But I know it is your word for us. Not *your* word, but the word of others. I have listened. I have heard."

"You have a nose, Greckle. Can you smell? Can you detect cigar smoke, for example? Do you know it's there if you can't see it? Or food—can you smell food?"

The Martian shook his head. "I'm afraid we have no sense of smell as you have."

"Maybe you've lost it on this arid planet then. But tell me something else. Is there anything at all offensive about us?"

The Martian's color deepened and his exudation was strong. "Only your moods. Anger is the worst."

"You mean you sense these things?"

"Yes. When that man was in your office just now and you both were angry, I could feel it out here. It is—unnerving, I think the word is."

"And when we're happy?"

"We feel happy, too."

Bert scratched his head. "But when I compliment you, I feel good. So your feelings are contagious, too."

"It is—how do you say it?—reversible. We can project our love for others." The Martian's face darkened further. He looked away. "It is how we find our friends, by their feelings about us. And we return it and it mingles and works and builds up and makes us all very much happier."

"Greckle, look at me."

The alien lifted his eyes to meet his.

"Now think something good, something happy."

"You mean like the love I have for you, Bert Schaun, I, whom you let polish your ship and whom you teach and I am very grateful to?"

Bert felt the flush of embarrassment, fought it down. "Yes, Greckle."

The eyes went wide, the ears jiggled frantically, and at first the air was redolent with the Martian's characteristic scent. Then it was suddenly gone and Bert felt the surge of well being and happiness within him . . . and a love for this creature before him, this oddly-shaped gray alien with the rabbit ears and the bleary red eyes. Now he understood why he felt so good when the alien had read to him in the cave, and hundreds of other times when their spirits had met briefly in an exchange of joy.

Bert sat down on a nearby box, dazed, still looking in wonder at the alien.

"It's a wonderful thing," he said. "A wonderful thing, Greckle. But why have you been keeping it a secret? Why don't you do what you do to me to all Earthmen? Then there'd be no question of their acceptance of you."

Greckle shook his head sadly. "They never let us get close enough, Bert. Every time we are, we sense this—this rejection?"

"That's the word."

"And it unnerves us and makes it all the worse. We did not know what it was that caused Earthmen to become so angry when we were around until you told me. We did not know of this sense of smell of yours. We did not know you were sensitive to this thing called scent, that it disturbed your olfactory centers. We thought Earthmen were the way they were naturally. Until you came. And now that we know what it is, we are trying to control it, and I think we shall triumph. We shall triumph if we of Mars can lock our minds when we are near Earthmen and convey our love of them to them. But so far there have never been enough of us around an Earthman to show him when we all project our love together. They always run away. Or become angry and ask us to leave. And it is hard to control it when the Earthmen are in numbers around us and very angry."

"I see. I think your scent-making must be something organic, a vestigial thing, a carry-over from primitive days, as is our appendix. It is still with you, the scent driving away Earthmen, where it used to drive off animals long extinct, who would otherwise have attacked you."

"I think that is true, Bert. I have asked the elders and they think that is what has happened. They say we should all have good thoughts and not let the Earthmen frighten or unnerve us. Then there is no scent." Greckle grinned. "It is easy to have no scent around you, Bert."

Again that feeling of happiness and love and friendship. Now it was easy to feel, now that he knew what it was, now that he could expect it. It was like a friend putting his hand in yours. And Greckle was right. Embracing its glow only made it all the more warm and real and overpowering.

And there was no scent at all.

"Why are you so different from the others, Bert?"

"I don't think I am, Greckle."

"We were so happy when we saw your ships come. And we were so unhappy when you turned away from us."

Bert turned to the alien and saw instead a fellow being with much the same problems as he, the same yearnings, the same ambitions perhaps, separated now only by a thin fabric of organic difference.

The folly of Earthmen!

"You people never had a chance, did you, Greckle?"

"A chance for what, Bert?"

Bert rose. "Come on, let's take the *Martha Q* out for a spin." He waved to infinity. "I've got to get up where it's clean and quiet. And I want you to pilot the ship, Greckle."

The happiness was almost overwhelming.

And completely free of scent.

SIXTEEN

Seven A.M., January 7, 2027

BERT was awakened by the sound of shattering glass.

He jerked upright in the cot in his office, his mind snapping alert. What the devil! He looked around, saw that a pane of the window facing the street had been broken.

He stood up. About twenty men were gathered beneath the entrance sign, laughing and talking. One pointed to the window. Another threw a new rock. It hit the building with a dull thud.

Bert threw on his clothes quickly, went to the door, jerked it open.

"There he is!" a man shouted, pointing.

"Stinker lover!" another called.

The crowd was growing, men streaming toward the lot from the center of Seven. There were a few women among them. Bert spotted several small children.

"Hiya, Stinky!" a man jeered. "How's your friend?"

"Yeah, where's your Stinker pal? Did you sleep with him?"

"Ain't Beautiful up yet, Schaun?"

There was more laughter now because there were more people and they milled around the entranceway.

"What do you people want?" Bert asked, seething. Osborne never missed a trick, did he? Now he was inciting a riot, goading these people on to do something.

"Come on, Schaun, let's see the Stinker. We ain't got all day."

"Where you hiding him, lover boy?"

"You and him are great pals, ain't you? G-r-e-a-t pals."

The crowd roared. There were fifty people out front now, jostling each other, the ones in back pushing the ones in front past the entranceway arch.

"Bert Schaun, Guaranteed OK Used Spacers. You got an OK Used Stinker by any chance?"

"Let's see the Stinker."

The crowd took it up, chanted, "Let's see the Stinker" over and over.

From somewhere another rock came sailing, missing Bert's head by inches.

They pushed against the board holding up the entrance-way sign. It swayed. This gave several of the husky men an idea. They moved to the supports and started working them back and forth in the ground. There was the sound of splintering wood as the sign tottered and feel resoundingly to the ground.

"Hey!" Bert cried, springing forward. He was met with a barrage of stones, rocks, pieces of metal, chunks of clay and pieces of wood. He threw his arms up to shield himself, fell back. He could hear the sound of crashing glass behind him. There, he thought, go the rest of the front windows.

Bert ignored the rocks, went back into the office. He snatched his rifle from off the wall, opened the rear window, crawled through it, climbed the ladder to the roof.

When he reached the front part of the building the crowd had already grown to more than a hundred. They were crowded halfway to the office. When he appeared, there rose a great cry.

"There he is!"

"On top of the building!"

"I see him!"

"Come on down. We want to give you a bath."

"Want to buy a case of deodorant soap, Schaun?"

Again the chant.

"Where's the Stinker?"

"We came for the Stinker!"

Bert brought the rifle out from behind him, pointed it at the men in front. That quieted the crowd.

"You all better get back where you came from," he warned. "While you're still able."

The crowd fell back, grumbling.

"Not without the Stinker," someone yelled.

Bert spied Steve Babcock at the rear of the crowd, leaning against what was left of the entranceway sign support, a smirk on his face. What had happened to that man?

"Steve!" Bert shouted. "Steve Babcock, you're the law enforcement officer. Are you going to let this happen?"

"Looks like they're making their own laws this morning," Steve sang back.

The people laughed and were encouraged by this, edging closer to the office. They started to fan out, to go around and surround the office.

Bert fired a warning shot on one side. "Keep out there in front," he shouted.

"Better watch that shooting," Steve cried. "You might hit somebody. And that would be the end of you."

"Tell them to keep back then or I'll take some of them with me."

Bert heard a step behind him, whirled, his finger ready on the trigger.

It was Greckle, wide-eyed and pale.

"You shouldn't have come here," Bert hissed. "Get back! Get back! Go back while you can!"

"No," Greckle said. "This may be the chance to explain."

"There's no chance to explain," Bert said. "Not now. They're after you."

A great roar went up from the crowd.

"There he is!"

"It's him!"

"The Stinker!"

There were howls, boos, screams, shrieks, hoots and cat-calls.

Greckle was curious. He stepped to see the crowd better.

"Get back!" Bert cried, pushing him toward the rear of the roof. "You'll be killed!"

"Let him go!" the crowd yelled.

"Don't send him back!"

"Let's see what a Stinker looks like!"

Then the rocks came. They both ducked them as best they could.

The crowd inched closer.

"Let's get 'em!"

"Let's tear the place down!"

"Let's kill the Stinker!"

"Schaun, too!"

The mass of people was agitated now and excitement rippled everywhere, eyes were wide, teeth bared, obscenities were shouted.

Suddenly there was a sharp *crack* of another rifle.

Bert heard the bullet in the air, heard it hit.

Greckle cried out, clutched at his head.

The people jerked to a stop, gasped.

Greckle, with a low moan, sank to the rooftop, lay there, a pitifully small, solitary, crumpled figure.

Bert stared at him, unwilling to believe this.

Then he slowly turned to the crowd and shared for a moment their stunned disbelief.

Bert was calm now. His blood was like ice, his grip never more certain, his nerves never more sure.

The rifle came up, the safety snapped off.

Once again the crowd gasped, watching this man on the roof, this man with the terrible look in his eyes.

"Who fired that shot?" he said coldly, sweeping the crowd with his gun. And when they started to edge away, he cried, "Stand where you are! All of you! The first one of you who moves is dead!"

They stood, a people afraid, a people who knew better than to disobey the voice they heard now.

"Now, Bert," Steve said, starting toward the office.

"You stay where you are!" Bert ordered, moving to the edge of the roof.

Steve stopped.

Bert jumped from the roof, landing like a cat on his feet, his rifle at the ready, his finger on the trigger.

He moved now among the assembly, a gaunt, determined man.

Suddenly there was a shout and the crowd spilled over itself, and Bert was left alone in an ever-widening circle as the people fled in every direction. He could see no one with a rifle now, could risk no shot, could not be heard if he shouted.

And when the crowd was gone he saw, a few feet from him, the rifle he was looking for. But the man who had fired it was gone.

Bert picked it up, examined it for a name or a serial number, found neither, looked up into the mocking eyes of Steve Babcock who still stood by the broken post.

"Whose rifle is this?" Bert asked him in a raspy voice.

"I haven't the faintest idea," Steve said.

"It's your duty to find out."

"Suppose *you* find out, Schaun. You won't have anything to do now that your business is ruined."

Steve turned and walked away.

Seven-thirty A.M., January 7, 2027

One whole section of Four consisted of nothing but warehouses, row on row, places where processors stored the final product of the toil and sweat of the refineries, places where supplies and consumer goods were stored until parties from each of the other seven—and soon to be eight—communities came to pick them up, for it was only at Four, by agreement, that the freighters landed.

There was nothing to distinguish warehouse twenty-three

from its fellows, except in the number painted black on brown. That and the fact that two people who didn't belong in it were there.

"Cripes, I thought you were never coming," the man said.

"I came as soon as I could, came with Gus Werner. I'll take the mail ship back later this morning."

"You got the money?" Brant Huygens rubbed his bristly jaw with yellow-stained fingers.

"If you've got what you say you have," Emma said. "I couldn't understand you very well on the viewphone."

"I couldn't come out and spill everything that way." He zipped his jacket open, pulled the inside lining apart and jerked out a piece of paper. "Here." And when she reached for it, he drew back. "The money, first?"

"Oh, all right." Emma fumbled with her purse, opened it, withdrew a small packet from beside the pistol.

He snatched it with eager, shaking hands.

Instantly she had the pistol in her hand. "The proof, if you please!"

He shoved the paper at her. She unfolded it with nervous hands, keeping a wary eye on Huygens.

And then she saw. There, in Hank's bold scrawl, was a page from the log of his ship. As she read it, she saw it was the record of the location of his claim, written with an exactness typical of him. It ended with these words: "Baby'll get more than a new pair of shoes out of this one." She remembered the way his face looked each time he said it, the way his lips moved when he uttered the words.

"Who did it?" she asked coldly.

"Eh?" he said, startled, looking up from the bills. Then he smiled, put the packet where the paper had been. "Sure you want to know? You won't like it."

"Who?" she asked, her voice shrill.

"Steve Babcock."

Steve! She took an involuntary step backward, felt herself coming apart at the joints, her blood congealing.

And then she knew it was true. Those nights he talked to her in the tavern when Hank was out on a run, how he'd been a gentleman at first, then become bolder and she had to tell him to go. And then suddenly he was the gentleman again and she marveled at the change in him and accepted him again. And now she knew that's when he had planned it.

And then Hank didn't come back. And how comforting Steve had been! The things he did for her! Telling her of the ships he had sent out for Hank! And all the time . . .

"How—how did it happen?" she managed to ask Huygens.

"He made them do it. Chad Jenks, Paul Ernst and Tom Seeley. They left me behind."

"Did they?" Her eyes glittered coldly.

"Honest they did. You don't think I could tell you this if I'd been in on it, do you?"

"Yes, I do."

"Well, I wasn't. They met his ship out a couple days. Gave the distress signal and he tied up to them. I don't know the details. All I know is Steve made Chad jam the controls with a torch. Then they transferred over to this other ship."

"Where's Steve now?"

"Over at Seven."

"Seven! What's he doing over there?"

Brant looked at his wristwatch. "Oh, he's got business. How do you think I got that paper? Hell, I had to wait for a day when they'd all be gone, when they'd leave me behind. So they left me in charge of the office today; I asked Steve if I could stay, see? Told him I wasn't feeling so good." He laughed. "That's rich, isn't it? Leaving me over here? I'll be gone on a freighter by the time they get back. That'll bo quite a while." He lit a cigarette, confident now, offered her one. She declined. "That paper what you want?"

"Yes," she said almost inaudibly.

"Steve never used the location. He was planning to some day, though. I couldn't figure him out. If it'd been me—"

"Steve's an odd man."

"Yeah, sure is. He did a lot of things I never could figure out." He looked at his wristwatch again. "Hell, I got time. You want to hear about it?"

Seven forty-five A.M., January 7, 2027

When Bert viewed Greckle's body on the roof again, his throat tightened and his vision blurred with wetness, and he thought: Steve was right, Greckle, you and I are alone on this planet, different from anyone else. And he couldn't have felt worse if his best friend had been shot down.

He went over to the fallen figure, turned the alien over, saw that blood—a grayish, white, sticky blood—was issuing from a point above the juncture of ear and head.

He was still alive then! There was hope!

He upbraided himself for spending so much time on the ground, handling the rifle, and speaking to Steve. He had a problem: How to get the alien off the roof. There was no one to help him now. And no one would help him should he ask. But the alien's chances for life must be the same as a human, he thought, and his life depends on my getting that wound closed. He looked closer, swabbed away some of the gray blood and saw that the bullet had but grazed his head. He hoped it had not injured the skull.

Bert made a carry out of rope, brought the figure in his arms to the edge of the roof and lowered him slowly to the ground. Then he carried him into the office and lay him on the cot.

Water to clean the wound, an astringent to coagulate the blood—what would it be?—plenty of bandages. Hot water?

Bert busied himself tending the wound, wrapping it with bandages from the first aid kit of the *Martha Q*. He was certain then that he had done all he could, that if there was no permanent injury beneath, the Martian would recover.

He sat for hours watching the alien breathe, the steady rise and fall of his chest nearly putting him to sleep. When would he awaken?

And the big question: What happens then?

The crowd was certain the alien was dead, so they would not be back. But what would happen when they learned he was not dead after all? Would they return in renewed frenzy, to wreak the havoc they had set out to do in the first place?

There was no more business. Steve had that correct. The word would go far and wide that Bert Schaun's place was off-limits. Business with him was verboten. Oh, perhaps a desperate prospector might try to sell him a ship, but who would buy? The taint that existed in the minds of the people would be an insurmountable barrier for would-be purchasers. They would not risk it. He knew that.

So, business was kaput. What then? He sighed, not knowing, not even wanting to think about it. It was enough to worry about Greckle, to wait and see if he would recover, and if he did, to beg his pardon, to try to excuse the action of his fellows. How to explain a thing like that?

In comparison with the unsullied ethics of the natives of Mars, the ways of the people of Earth were dark ways. There could be no excuse, no explanation, no forgiveness.

He dozed, and when he awakened the sun was nearly overhead. He stirred and tended to Greckle again, changing the bandages and seeing the matted blood of the wound now and hoping it was a good sign.

The alien did not awaken.

Where was Emma?

The sudden thought struck him as he was sitting down to continue his vigil: she had not been with the crowd. He would have seen her if she had.

She was probably sleeping.

But she would have heard about what happened by this time, wouldn't she? And wouldn't she have come to him? Wouldn't she have offered to do something? It troubled him. It wasn't right. Then a new thought stirred him. Had she deserted him, too?

No, he told himself, that can't be. She is above all this. It is not just Greckle and I, as I thought, it is Greckle, Emma and I. There are three of us, and one of us is not here, did not come.

He heard a sound outside. A step on the walk. He picked up his rifle, stood up and waited.

A knock on the door.

"Who is it?"

"Sam. Sam Streeper, Bert."

"What do you want?"

"I want to talk."

"Is anybody with you?"

"No."

"All right. Just a minute." Bert looked out of the windows before he moved to the door. It would be just like them to work out a trick of some sort to make him move out into the open. He saw no one, unlocked the door and stepped to one side, rifle ready.

Sam came in, took off his hat, didn't see Bert until Bert started to move around in front of him with the rifle.

"Bert," Sam said lamely, "you can put that thing down."

"Can I?"

"I'm sorry about what happened, Bert. I just want you to know we ain't all against you. Some of us don't like what went on around here."

"Didn't you? Then why didn't you do something about it?"

Sam shrugged his thin shoulders. "What could we do? Some of them were half drunk."

"It was rotten, Sam."

"I know. I'd like to sit down."

"Sit down then." Bert shoved the door shut with his foot, locked it again, moved to Greckle's side.

"How is the little guy?" Sam said, coming over.

"You're getting awfuly concerned for a man who walked out because of him."

"I was wrong, Bert. I knew it the minute I walked out of here. But I was too proud to come back. Until now. Until I saw what they did to him up on the roof."

"He'll live, I think."

"I'm glad to hear that. Is there anything I can do?"

"I don't think so."

Sam coughed a little embarrassedly. "I brought something along," he said, and he fumbled inside his jacket, bringing out a pistol. "I thought maybe you might need some help." He laid the pistol on the desk. "They're all gettin' loaded at Emma's. I figured maybe they'd head back this way."

"At Emma's, eh?"

"Some of them. Steve's got a party goin' in another place."

"And Emma is waiting on those at the tavern?"

"No, she ain't. They say she ain't been around all day. They broke in the place early this morning when they couldn't get an answer. And nobody's workin' in the refinery and Osborne's hoppin' mad."

"He's angry?" This he could hardly believe.

"Yep. It's a mess, I tell you."

"But you say Emma's not there?"

"Right. I forgot how you feel about her."

"I didn't see her out there this morning. Where—does anybody know where she is?"

"Don't think so. Leastwise, I ain't heard nobody say."

Bert looked at him earnestly. "Sam," he said, "do you really mean what you say? Do you really want to do something?"

"Sure thing, Bert. What can I do?"

"Will you stay here with Greckle?"

"Sure, but—"

"I've got to get down there. I've got to find out what happened to Emma."

"You can't go down there! They'll kill you for sure! Why, you ain't got a chance."

"I don't care. If they've done something to her, I've got to help her. She probably said something or did something —she felt the way I do about Greckle here—"

"It's your funeral," Sam said firmly. "I hate to see you goin' to it."

SEVENTEEN

Eleven-thirty A.M., January 7, 2027

"HEY, EMMA, where'd you come from?"

"Where've you been hidin', Emma?"

"Well, I'll be damned!"

"We been lookin' for you."

"We was here bright and early, ain't that right, boys?"

"Busted the door down, we did."

Emma moved through the drinkers and their laughter, a person apart, a pale woman, not understanding, not appreciating, and when she finally came to a grizzled face she knew well, she addressed it.

"Gar," she said, "what's happening?"

"You shoulda been here," he said thickly. "Shoulda been." He smiled foolishly. " 'S all over now."

"You wanna know?" Will Abrahamson spoke up from a neighboring table. "I'll tell you wa' we done. We got that Stinker, we did." Haltingly, he told her.

And as she listened, her resolve grew. An ugly thing was on the face of the land. A thing that had to be erased, destroyed. The tragedy of it was that it seemed to be up to her to do it. What kind of men were these? Couldn't they see? Didn't they know?

"Where is Steve?" she asked at last.

"Him?" Will snorted. "He's too good to drink with us, he is. Him and his boys'r over at thirty-nine. Throwin' a li'l party for theirselves." He belched, gave her an owly stare, went back to his drink. "Hope they're havin' as good a time as we are."

Eleven forty-five A.M., January 7, 2027

Bert Schaun slogged through the yellow dust of the street, unmindful of the way it was filling his shoes. His rifle was cradled in his arms, his eyes were straight ahead straining for his first glimpse of the tavern. They'd tell him there where she was. Somebody would know, he didn't care who. And if they wouldn't tell him he'd make them tell.

He didn't want to think what he'd do if they refused.

He stepped a little more lightly now. Instincts dulled by what had happened at the office now were sharpened and his pulse quickened in the face of the impending action. There was no real law here. And for the first time he saw Mars for what it really was: a frontier, rugged, unpolished, and raw. And it remained for the abused to strike back in their interests and for what they thought was right.

Bert saw the tavern now, and he hurried his stride. Then he saw a figure come through the door.

It was Emma!

"Emma!" he cried, running toward her.

She appeared not to have heard as she crossed the street and vanished from sight.

He hurried to the corner, turned it and saw her halfway down the block.

"Emma!" he shouted again.

Again she failed to pay heed. What was wrong with her?

Then she turned into a building.

He ran fast, came up panting to the place she had entered, reached over, savagely grasped the knob, twisted it and yanked the door open.

He stopped on the threshold.

Four men were there at a table—three men and Steve Babcock. Emma stood almost in front of Bert at the door.

Bert could see the gun in her hands.

Steve Babcock, his face strained and pasty white, did not even see Bert as he slowly rose. His eyes were on Emma, his mouth open in surprise.

Cr-r-ack!

The sound exploded with thunderous force, and Bert saw several things at once: Emma's shoulders jerking back from the force of the pistol she had fired with her two hands, the figure of Steve still standing by his chair, his face uncomprehending, the three men who erupted suddenly in a frenzy of action, sending their chairs sailing.

In a moment it was all over.

One of the men wrenched the gun from her hands and she fell in a heap on the floor, head in hands, sobbing. Steve still stood, his face still white, staring at her.

"She tried to kill you, Steve," one of the men said.

Bert was as stunned as Steve. Why had she tried to kill him. Had all Mars gone mad?

"Emma!" Bert cried then, moving toward her.

Her head whipped up and she saw him.

"Go back!" she cried. "Go back!"

He halted, confused.

"Don't you see? It's Steve! He's the one."

As he stared at her, his rifle was suddenly yanked from his grasp. Recovering, he reached for it, found it just beyond his reach in the hands of one of the men.

"Take it easy, Mister," the man said menacingly, backing and bringing the rifle to bear on Bert's stomach.

The gun became unimportant, and Bert was at Emma's side. "Are you all right?"

"I'm all right," she said, leaning against his shoulder as he crouched. "But I'm a lousy shot. I should have killed him. I should have killed him for all he's done."

Bert looked up at Steve who still stood like a man in a stupor, his glazed eyes still on Emma.

"He killed Hank, Bert, and he was ruining everything for you."

"What are we going to do with these two?" the man with Bert's rifle asked Steve.

But Steve did not answer.

"I knew it was him," Emma said. "I should have known he was responsible for the other, too."

Now Steve sank to his chair. "Huygens," he said dazedly. "It was Huygens."

"Steve," the same man asked again. "Steve—"

"I should never have left him there at the office," Steve went on in a voice barely audible. "I knew he was breaking. And I know now why he wanted to stay in Four today."

"Steve!"

"Shut up, Chad!" Steve cried, turning on the man angrily. "Your goddam weak sister Brant Huygens is responsible for this, wanted to stay over at Four. Ha!" He pounded the table with a flat hand. "Wait till I catch up with him! Wait till I get him." His fingers curled to a tight fist. Then his eyes found Emma's again. "Emma," he said beseechingly, "Emma —I—" His face contorted grotesquely.

"It's no use, Steve," Emma said coldly. "I know all about you now."

"Huygens," Steve said hoarsely. "He hated me. He lied, Emma. He lied. You've got to believe that."

"He gave me a page from Hank's log, Steve."

Steve winced as if from a body blow, and once again the color drained from his face. "I—I'll make it up to you, Emma," he whispered. "Honest I will."

"You're a sick man," Emma said. "You've ruined Mars for everyone, ruling it more like a dictator than a law enforcement man, you managed to make the refinery people think you were doing a fine job for them, and you've turned the people against the race that could help them."

"You don't know what you're talking about," Steve said thickly.

"Don't I?" Emma smiled thinly. "You're the kind who takes what he wants. You couldn't have me because I was married, so you fix that. You just get rid of my husband. Simple, wasn't it But it didn't work out right."

"It's true I wanted you," Steve said, "but—"

"Why don't you tell Bert what you did for him? You saw him as a rival and I suppose it's my fault I saw so much of him and gave you that impression. So you were going to put him out of the way. But he wouldn't have to be killed. You had fancier plans. You'd drive him back to Earth. You found out about the Classic and what happened there, so you got in touch with Thornton McAllister. And then when I was about to buy his ore, you managed to get McAllister to revise his order because Bert was going to slip through a loophole."

"You're imagining things!" Steve said vehemently.

"Why would Huygens imagine a thing like that? And what about Gregg? You sent him out to do away with Bert because the other devices didn't work. And you promised Gregg you'd finance his way home to his wife and family if he did the job for you, poor guy. You, always you, messing people's lives, pushing them around like pawns, and always giving the impression it's the processors who are to blame!"

"I don't want to hear any more," Steve said darkly.

"Is it because I'm striking so close to home, Steve? Is that it? Well, then let me go on. I paid Huygens plenty and he bared his soul. Let me tell about how you came with the generous refinery offer to buy Bert out at a hundred per cent profit and then quoted a bare ten per cent, knowing he'd refuse. And then how you went back and told them Bert ranted and raved and cussed them out. Sticking pins in both sides, you were, for you were going to really get rid of Bert and then the way would be clear for you!"

"You better shut up," Steve said, rising, his eyes narrow, a white line along his jaw.

"Oh, no, I won't shut up. Not until I tell about how you sent Chad out to fire on Bert and Sam Streeper while they were putting up alarm posts, knowing they'd figure it was the refinery people. And then when that didn't work, you waited until the alien came along. That was tailor-made, wasn't it, Steve? The people were all ready for it, needed just a little pushing. It was what you were waiting for, wasn't it!"

"I'm warning you," Steve said, face flushed.

"So what did you do? You started stirring everybody up into a froth. You really got them thinking of nothing but that alien out there. They didn't like the alien to begin with, but you made them hate him. You sent your men around among them and told lies, filthy things about them. And when you were ready you worked them up, broke into the tavern and gave them all drinks before you sent them out there to the lot. 'Let's not work today!' you made them say. 'Let's get the Stinker and Bert Schaun, too, while we're at it so we can have peace around here!' That's what you cried. Oh, not you, yourself. Your hirelings and the poor, deluded, bored people who believed you because you were the law, you and your acolytes, your worse-than-thugs."

"Are you through?" Steve asked icily.

"Yes, I'm through," Emma said huskily, shuddering and turning away to the protection of Bert's shoulder.

"I didn't know, Emma," Bert said softly. "I just didn't know, did I?"

"You can't be blamed," she murmured.

"The two lovers," Steve rasped, scraping his chair back and glaring. "Aren't they a sight!"

"Steve," Chad said, "I think we better get out of here."

"Out of here?" Steve asked in surprise. "You're going to let what a woman says worry you?"

"She may have told somebody," Chad said. "Suppose they turn on us?"

"You are a fool, Chad Jenks. A stupid, ignorant man. People don't turn on the law."

"Just the same," Chad said, "I don't like it."

"It isn't up to you, whether you like it or not," Steve said. "I'm still running things."

Chad frowned, said nothing.

Finally one of the other men spoke up. "What are we going to do, Steve?"

"That's better, Tom. Now let me ask you a question: What do you do with a festering sore?"

"Why, treat it. Isn't that right?"

"That's right," Steve said almost gaily. "You show more sense than Chad here. You root it out, cut it out, kill it."

"Are you thinking—"

"Yes, I am, Chad. But it won't be right here. It's got to be clean and neat and no bloodshed. I don't want bloodshed."

"I still don't like it," Chad grumbled.

"You're going to have to come along, though," Steve said. "You're going to use that torch of yours again."

"I tell you I don't like it!"

"Will you shut up! Next thing you know you'll be asking to be left behind like Huygens was. And I don't want that to happen again, is that clear?"

To Bert the rest was a nightmare; Steve, like a crazy man,

his eyes lighted by some mad hilarity, his face flushed, sometimes shouting at his men, sometime cajoling, sometimes joking, but telling them what must be done, and leering at Bert
and Emma and strutting before them and laughing and taunt-
ing them.

"We want to make it comfortable for them, don't we,
Tom?" Steve said, fists on hips and delighted with himself.
"Isn't that right, Paul? Chad?" And then he laughed.

The other two men laughed with less conviction, but Chad
did not laugh at all. He shook his head and spat on the floor.

"But we'd better move," Steve said. "We wouldn't want to
be late for the date. A far-away date." And then his laugh
was louder and more shrill.

Finally, when Steve tired of his ridicule, he ordered them
out of the building.

"You lead the way, Chad, and you two," he said to the dedicated Tom Seeley and Paul Ernest, "take care of our lovers
here. I'll bring up the rear." He added significantly, "And
remember, I have the rifle."

"Where are we going?" Chad wanted to know.

"The spacer lot, ignoramus. Now move!"

"The lot?"

"Of course. You don't think I'd use one of our ships, do
you? It's got to look as if they took off in one of his own
ships."

"But Steve—!"

Tom averted another outburst by saying, "Come on, Chad.
Let's get it over with."

And so they left the building, walking a circuitous route
to the lot, unseen and unheard, unmolested and unques-
tioned. And when they stood in the shadows of the ships,
Steve said, "Tom, run back to the office there and make
sure there's nobody in it. We'll wait for you. Paul, when he
comes back, you and Tom get into that ship there"—he
squinted to make out the name in the bright afternoon sun—

"the *Betty June*. You'd better pilot her. You're the better man. And you, Chad, lead the way into the *Martha Q*."

Tom left for the office and Bert wondered what kind of reception Sam Streeper would give him there. If it was what he expected, if Sam—and perhaps Greckle, if he had regained consciousness—had been watching the strange procession, there would be one less of them to worry about, for Sam wouldn't let him get out alive.

"Look, Steve," Chad protested, "we can't just walk into a ship like this and take off."

"Are you telling me what I can or can't do?" Steve asked indignantly.

"But we don't even know if these ships will operate. They ought to be checked out first. And what about emergency batteries."

"Not time for that. Besides, Bert Schaun wouldn't have a bad ship on his lot. And we won't need any emergency batteries."

"I tell you, it's the most dangerous thing you can do, Steve."

"You'll do what I say, Chad," Steve seethed. "You'll get in there and pilot that thing as if it were your own and you had all the confidence in the world in it."

"You'll never get away with a thing like this," Bert said. "Think not?"

"You'll have to pay some day."

"A true believer in poetic justice, aren't you, Bert? But you may be right at that. And I don't care. Do you know why? Because by that time both of you will be dead. And that's all I care about right now."

"You *are* insane," Emma said softly. "You're a child. You can't have what you want, so you destroy it in a fit of temper."

The sight of Tom running back filled Bert with a new despair. "There's nobody in the office," Tom said.

"I didn't think there was," Steve said. "Well, let's get on our way."

EIGHTEEN

Afternoon, January 7, 2027

THEY sat in the control room a few feet from each other, Steve covering them with the rifle and Chad working quietly in the pilot's couch as the ship slipped out of the thin envelope of air. In a few moments they were in the blackness of space and Bert could see the stars in the forward window.

Ten minutes later Steve said, "All right, Chad, now you can cover while I do a little knot tying. Just enough to keep them busy while we get out of here. See the *Betty June?*"

"She's not far on the starboard," Chad said, catching the rifle Steve tossed him. He took the position Steve had kept on the way out while Steve rummaged through an equipment locker until he found the kind of rope he wanted.

"You don't like this, do you, Chad?" Bert said. "It will be your neck as much as Steve's you know. Why do you stand for it?"

Chad glowered, said nothing.

Steve, busy with the ropes, said, "Don't let Bert rile you, Chad."

"You've already shown what you think of all this," Emma said. "Chad, it just comes down to whether you're a man or a mouse."

"And that will be enough out of you," Steve said.

"One shot," Bert said. "That's all, Chad. You could get him from where you are."

Chad's eyes grew wider at the thought. His face paled as he looked at Steve. Sweat dotted his forehead.

"Chad knows when he's well off," Steve said, not noticing the change in him.

"It's the only chance you'll get," Bert said evenly. "It's either now or never."

"Let me have that gun," Steve said, seeing his face and striding forward.

The gun wavered from Bert and Emma, was pointed now at Steve's midsection. Chad's face was filmed with sweat, his nostrils flared. He ran his tongue over dry lips.

Steve darted a hand out, hit the gun to one side and took it. "Get hold of yourself, Chad. Tie those knots." He was breathing hard. "You're just stupid enough to do something ridiculous with a gun."

Chad blew his breath out, came over to Bert and Emma and continued tying their hands to a protruding metal loop.

"Add plenty of knots," Steve said. "Just to keep them busy for a while. And when you get through with that, nail this spacer down."

The knots tied, Chad got a torch from the locker, pushed the throttle in as far as it would go. The acceleration was heavy, providing a gravity in excess of that of Mars. Then he played the end of the bright orange flame on the lever, welding it to the ship's frame.

That will do it, Bert thought. That will carry the *Martha Q* to God knows where. And there's no way to stop her now.

"Don't forget and leave the torch here," Steve reminded. "Now get out of here."

Chad drew one of the bulky, flexible suits from its storage compartment. A few minutes later the outer lock closed after him.

"There he goes," Steve said, watching him from the window.

Bert worked furiously with the rope. Chad hadn't tied the knots too tightly; Bert had several loossened already.

"Well, dears," Steve said, putting the rifle on the pilot's

cushion, "I really must be going." He went to the compartment, withdrew another suit, put it on. Before he clamped the helmet in place, he said, "Bon voyage."

Bert and Emma could only watch, helpless.

He walked to the corridor and in a few moments Bert heard the inner lock slam shut.

Just then he loosened the last of the large knots, had one hand free, worked feverishly to loosen his other hand.

There!

He rushed to the control panel. What to do? He wished there were some way to actuate or cut out the lock mechanism, but there was none. Once a person had gone through it from this side, the initiative rested with him, not with anyone in the control room. He could come back in or go on through. That would complete the cycle. And finding the wires that controlled the lock would be a half day's job.

The clang of the outer lock had a ring of finality.

He could not get Steve back now.

Bert turned, came to Emma and unloosened her hands, avoiding her eyes.

"This is it, isn't it?" she said.

He nodded.

Together they went to the window, saw Steve out in space, a brilliant white figure against a deep black, star-strewn sky, half-way to the *Betty June*, propelling himself with blasts on his reactor pistol.

"He'll get aboard," Bert said, "then the *Betty June* will alter course, swerve away and start back for Mars."

"And us?" Emma said. "What happens to us"

"I don't know," he said honestly. "I can stop the power. I can cut it. But then what? I can't change direction. We'll sail along. Sail until we hit something."

"And we'll be a handful of dust by then," she said quietly.

They watched the figure in the space suit so near the *Betty June* now.

And then they saw a strange thing happen.

The lights aboard the *Betty June* winked out.

Bert pressed his face close to the glass, the better to see the ship. Now why did the lights go out? What was it? And then he saw, with a start, that there was no exhaust trail from the other ship.

"What's happened on the *Betty June?*" Emma asked. "Why did they do that?"

"I don't know. I can't figure it out."

They were watching Steve at the ship's lock when the lights of their own ship flickered and died. Then all power ceased aboard the *Martha Q*, the hum of the drive running down a descending scale and sighing to a stop.

And it was terribly quiet.

In the reflected light from the *Betty June* they looked at each other in wonder.

And then the truth smashed home to him! *The fuel was gone.*

"Of course!" he cried.

"What?"

"I always empty the fuel chambers when I get the ships," he told her. "The fuel for both ships is back in the safe in the office. They've been operating on residual fuel, whatever little remained in the tanks at takeoff time!"

"So that's it."

"Yes," he said, chuckling. "It's a wonder it lasted as long as it did."

He started to laugh then, a loud, long, rolling laugh that smashed back at him from all around.

NINETEEN

January 8, 2027

THE TWO SHIPS hung in the void, two dots on the face of the

infinite, apparently motionless, still and dark. Over one crawled an insect searching for an entry, a bee returned to the hive and unable to find his way in, and the insect was Steve Babcock, an infinitesimal hunk of protoplasm on an infinitesimal metal thing, and, like an ephemeral insect, his life would soon ebb away, only his shell remaining, a mute reminder of the life that had once quickened it.

As for the lives of the living things within the ships, the peas in the pod, they too would die soon, living for this brief movement between galaxies, a mere fraction of time in the endless run of things in the universe. Then they, too, would be unmoving and non-living.

"Afraid?" he whispered.

"No. Not as long as I'm with you."

They lay close on the pilot's couch, viewing the panorama of world and stars and other galaxies stretched out before them beyond the control room window, loose straps holding them down so slight movements would not send them floating away.

"You know," Emma said, "I feel as if I were back on my uncle's farm in Iowa. There's a hill there and I used to lie on it on summer nights and watch the stars go by and I'd wonder what they were and how far away."

"I never knew you ever lived on a farm."

"I did part of the time. There are lots of things about me you don't know."

"We'll never know each other, Emma. There's too little time."

"It doesn't matter. Nothing matters except that we're here and we're together. . . . You know? There's peace here. It makes you wonder why there is so much hustle and bustle."

"I wonder how they're making out over on the *Betty June*."

"I don't want to think about it, Bert."

This was the end result, this sitting and talking and whispering, sometimes laughing and sometimes sad. They had become observers of life, of this universe so soon to be left behind, and as such observers, they viewed it with true objectivity, admitting its wonders, telling each other of its perils, judging its good things and its bad. Where some people measure their lives by years of being together, they were measuring theirs by the hours that remained.

The *Martha Q* was without fuel, the precious commodity refined in such abundance on the planet they had left, the power for the heating system and the air freshener as well as the ship itself. If there had been emergency batteries, it would have been another matter. Heat, light and radio. But all they had were emergency heaters, those tanks of chemical substances that, when intermingled, provided heat during electrical crises. If it hadn't been for these there would have been a chill first, then cold, and then the slow dip to absolute zero.

Bert had activated them. He had also opened a valve of one of the oxygen tanks.

And figured they had a week of life.

Those on the *Betty June* would not fare quite as well. There were three of them inside the ship, three people breathing and using up precious oxygen, to two on the *Martha Q*. The thing at the lock of the *Betty June* did not count, for the lock would never open without power.

The hours passed. They slept and hated to sleep, knowing it robbed them of precious last moments together.

The panorama, the vista of stars, did not change. It was as if they were suspended between galaxies, a tiny island of their own, and they brought their meals to the control room, the better to observe their domain.

They talked quietly, keeping their vigil with the stars, trying to forget the days that passed, their voices growing shriller, their speech a little faster, their smiles a little too frequent, concealing from each other what they felt of their approaching dissolution.

January 10, 2027

It was on the third day that Bert's gaze became fixed on a point in space.

"What is it?" Emma asked, rising a little to see, too.

"That star," he said. "Do you see it there to one side of the *Betty June?*" He pointed. "Behind the aft jets there. It moved —it *is* moving."

"I see it," Emma said excitedly. "It *did* move."

"It's not a star!" he cried. "It's a ship!"

Bert moved so violently toward the control panel he soared up and hit his head hard on a protruding metal arm, swore and guided himself to the instrument panel, then said, "Damn! I forgot. No power. I can't fire a single signal rocket."

"Don't all ships keep a lookout for others?"

"They have a detector system. We might get caught in it if the ship drifts close enough. Otherwise it will pass us by. It might pass us by anyway. Especially if it's a one-man ship and he's in a hurry or happens to be sleeping."

"Wouldn't the alarm ring and wake him?"

"Not if he turned it off. The ship would just change its course automatically to pass us by. I don't think it will come anywhere near us, though. Space is infinite, Emma. He won't see us unless he's keeping awfully close watch on things."

Together they watched the ship move until it was eclipsed by the *Betty June*. They waited impatiently for it to appear again, finally saw it slip out of the nose of the other ship.

"It's not coming this way at all," Bert said, trying hard to keep the disappointment out of his voice. "It's bound for somewhere and it's moving fast."

"Wait, Bert," Emma said, "isn't it getting larger?"

It could be, Bert said to himself, but he knew that in watching a single object in the sky one's vision often plays tricks.

But it *was* getting larger!

"Bert!"

"I see it, Emma! It's sighted us!"

The ship had changed its course radically and soon had grown from a faint white dot to the brightest star in the sky. And then they saw the afterglow trail hangling like a long curved curtain in the sky.

"It's a big ship, Emma."

"Yes, it is. Why, Bert—!"

"Emma, it's the yacht! The *Pamela!*"

They watched in rapturous silence as the ship grew as it neared, a beautiful, sleek vessel, and they saw it hover over the *Betty June* and then head for the *Martha Q*. In a short time its immensity filled all the windows and obstructed the view.

Then they heard the welcome clang of metal and the scraping sounds and poundings as the ships came together, and suddenly the ship was filled with light.

"They've connected with the outside electrical terminals," Bert explained.

And then there was the clang of the outer lock, the click of the inner and the hiss of air pressure being equalized. Their ears popped.

They floated to the corridor to see the figure soaring toward them.

They saw the bandaged head and lopsided grin of Greckle.

"Hello, Bert," he said simply, ears jiggling violently, using the wall supports to halt.

And then they saw another figure behind him.

Sam Streeper.

No reunion was ever happier.

And when it was over, Greckle and Sam told them how Greckle had regained consciousness in the office just before Sam sighted the group headed, it seemed, for the office itself.

"We got out of there," Sam said.

"We did not know it was you until too late," Greckle said. "We saw the ships leave and then I remembered about the fuel. We knew you would not get far."

"I was all for goin' right after you," Sam said, "but Greckle here had a better idea."

"Come," Greckle said. "I will show you what I have brought with me."

They turned and led the way to the yacht.

"I collected all my relatives and friends," Greckle said when they entered the main lounge of the big ship. He indicated the assembly of Martians there.

There was no scent, only waves of happiness, and Bert counted twenty-three Martians, all with grins, only some of their grins were even more lopsided than Greckle's. And their ridiculous ears trembled with the abundance of joy.

"I thought they might be needed to influence anyone we might meet," Greckle explained. "All of us thinking of happiness would make any Earthman see that we mean no harm."

"I didn't know about this," Sam said. "I sure think it's great. The little guy's told me all about it."

"Oh," Greckle said, "I have forgotten a most necessary Earth custom." And he was not content until he had introduced every last one of the Martians present and told of any blood connection in Earth terms.

"We thought we'd never lay eyes on you again," Sam said.

"We hunted and hunted," Greckle added. "But we finally saw you and we are sublimely happy."

"We saw you pause at the *Betty June*," Bert said. "I'm glad you didn't stop there first."

"The man in the space suit. We wondered who it was."

"That's Steve Babcock," Emma explained. "He didn't quite make it inside the ship before the power failed."

"I am sorry, truly sorry," Greckle said. "I am sure we could have convinced even him. Now shall we take the *Martha Q* in tow and rescue the men in the other ship?"

Bert darted a look at Sam.

Sam grinned, jerked a thumb at the alien. "He's the captain."

Greckle looked at him, something of pride showing in his homely face. Then he turned to the others, saying, "All right, at your posts, everyone, as I have explained. We shall tow the *Martha Q* and pull up to the *Betty June* as we did here. Does everyone understand?"

There were replies of assent.

"Why, they're all talking and understanding English," Emma exclaimed in surprise."

"Of course," Greckle said. "Did not Bert tell you? They have learned everything Bert taught me. If we are going to work with Earthmen, we shall use English."

"I think it's wonderful," Emma said.

"It is that," Bert said. "They're a wonderful people."

"They will let us work for them, will they not, Bert?"

"I think they'll be glad to have you work for them, Greckle. In fact, they ought to be honored."

TWENTY

January 31, 2027

THEY made the strangest procession ever seen on Mars.

They started from the lot, Chad Jenks in the lead, followed by the two other Earthmen who had been on the doomed *Betty June*. Then came the twenty-three aliens, grinning, elfish-like creatures who scurried along like children.

And then came Greckle, Bert and Emma, and Sam Streeper.

It was a straggly march on Seven, but it could not have been more epic making if it had been an army a thousand times as strong.

As they walked along, faces appeared at windows and people came out of the brown buildings and stared and the Martians grinned back and the four men in the lead waved.

And the spirit that moved with the group, the happiness that they made within themselves spread out and engulfed the curious and they silently joined the parade, the victory march toward the heart of Seven.

As Bert walked along, arm in arm with Emma and Greckle, he remembered the amazed look on Chad's face when he came through the lock to the rescuing vessel, expecting to see—what?—and seeing instead, the aliens. And he chuckled even now as he recalled his hesitation, his realization that he could not go back into the *Betty June*, that he had to come forward, had to meet and mingle with the aliens, had to admit it was the Martians who had saved him from what might have been.

And then Chad's puzzled face as he advanced, nose wrinkling, expecting the worst, and seeing only the grinning faces and feeling the overpowering force of the happy thoughts. . . . And smelling nothing.

And his words, his first words, words that Bert would never forget: "My God, they're Stinkers. Only they don't stink!"

And the knowledge then that the battle had been won.

That had broken it. That moment. For Chad was the biggest of the three Earthmen on the *Betty June*. And when Tom and Paul put their heads through and saw Chad standing there, the bewilderment in his eyes, the strange, soft look on his face, the rest was easy.

The explanations had been simple and easy for even Chad to understand, and he not only understood, he was chagrined to think that nobody had known about it before, that something he had so firmly believed in wasn't true after all.

That's why they were glad to lead the parade, not even caring that what they had done for Steve would mean punishment, for this suddenly was bigger than themselves, and they felt it and understood it, even as the people who joined the marchers now understood it.

The greatest thing that had ever happened on Mars was happening.

There were no shouts, no boos or catcalls or words or yells. There were only the silent people, the sound of steps, the moving along of men and aliens and an occasional whispered comment.

And at length they reached the Sully Refining Company building and the door to it opened and Osborne came out to see the strangest sight of his life.

What happened there is history.

January 14, 2027, and afterward. . . .

There aren't many Earthmen on Mars any more, but Bert and Emma are still there. And so is Osborne.

They like it there.

Bert isn't handling ore. And he isn't handling spacers. He's the business agent for the Martian Union of Workers. He was elected such by the Martians. And he's making more money than he ever did before.

He's paid by the refinery people, a grateful group of processors no longer facing a manpower problem.

And Emma isn't tending bar.

She's tending three children.

And sometimes the children ask her why they don't have rabbit ears so they could wriggle them like their Martian playmates can.

HIS LIFE WAS THE WORLD'S DEAREST POSSESSION — HERS THE PRICE OF IT!

What terrors were performed in Laboratory One, that its very name could cause strong men and innocent children to tremble with fear? Only the Master knew that it was not terror that was housed behind those impregnable walls but the most precious secret of the ages—the secret of immortality.

The safety of all humanity lay in the Master's silence —yet the life of the one woman he loved hung in the balance. He could buy a new lease on her precious life at the price of the world's security. Only a god can resist temptation—and the Master, though he had lived a thousand years, was still a man.

Turn this book over for second complete novel

CAST OF CHARACTERS

THE MASTER
The safety of planets lay on his shoulders—but he was just a man—doing a god's job.

ELLORA
She would willingly die for the Master—but how could she stay alive for him?

TARMA
Her world was a wild garden of Eden—until she tasted the bitter fruit of renunciation.

KORSON
He found a reason for living—too late.

DR. RONDING
He was fighting hard—but a virus gives no quarter.

DR. EVERLING
Like all too many of his predecessors, he had the lust for power.

The Man
Who Lived
Forever

R. DeWITT MILLER
and
ANNA HUNGER

ACE BOOKS

A Division of A. A. Wyn, Inc.

23 West 47th Street, New York 36, N. Y.

CHAPTER ONE

TERRA CITY was saffron-dusted by a combination of haze and afternoon sunlight. It had an unreal quality, as if it were about to become some sort of elf land.

In the room atop the telecast tower, stillness and isolation had become so intense that the Master's quiet voice sounded loud.

"What have I gained by living a thousand years?"

Varden, the Master's chief assistant, did not answer for a moment. Finally he said:

"You should know better than I'"

"Answer the question."

Varden turned, and as he did so, the ebbing sunlight flicked across his shoulders, on each of which gleamed the single silver star of a World Scientist.

"Very well, I'll answer it." The lightness in Varden's tone was forced. "That the Master could live so long and learn so little is one of the reasons I don't believe in a Supreme Spirit. Every other man on earth—except you—is too young for women part of his brief life, and too old for them during another distressing period. *You* never really grow old, and become young again every thirty years. And *you* are the one who complains."

"We are not discussing theology."

"I am. Do you expect me to believe in an *intelligent* Supreme Spirit who would allow one man and only one man to remain immortal—and then choose an idiot? No, this universe was designed by some lunatic deity escaped from the fool house of the gods."

5

The Master pushed aside the stack of papers on his desk, and lit his pipe.

"Of what use is eternal life if the only woman you ever loved is dying and you can do nothing to save her?" There it was, the Master thought. He had said it, the truth everyone had known but he had never admitted, even to Varden.

"That the Master's lady, Ellora," Varden said gently, "has *the sickness* is tragedy. But it is also fate. If there is anything I could do which would in the smallest degree help either of you, I would do it. You know that."

The Master unhooked his blue cape, and dropped it on the back of his chair. Beneath the cape, he wore the conventional dress of a World Scientist—a loose-fitting maroon tunic and trousers bloused into low, soft boots. On each shoulder was the single silver star. Only the cape designated him as the Master.

He rested his elbows on the desk and stared through the swirl of tobacco smoke. "Must I accept this, then?"

"One does not struggle against destiny."

"Perhaps it is because I have so often altered destiny that I find it hard to accept what I cannot change."

"I know it is presumptuous, Master, to suggest that you are illogical, but it is obvious that whether the Lady Ellora dies of the sickness or not, she would eventually die of old age—which would be unpleasant for you to witness. Fifteen, or perhaps twenty years more together . . . what is that brief instant to a man who has lived ten centuries and will never die?"

The unusual formality and earnestness of Varden's words impressed the Master. Not often did the casual, somewhat ribald man show a different side of his nature. "You are lucky, Varden," he said. "You will live only one lifetime. And you have never fallen in love."

Varden looked at the Master and the conversation dwindled away. The Master was silent a long time. Then he said,

"Downstairs in conference room C, a meeting is going on. The most outstanding physicians and scientists of Earth are gathered there for only one purpose,—a great, concerted effort to discover a cure for the sickness. They may find it."

"Yes, Master, they *may*." Varden sat on the corner of the desk. He was a short, fat, balding man, with brown eyes that were usually laughing. They were now. "Master, you need something new to worry about."

"I do?"

"Yes, and I've got it for you."

"What is it?"

A committee of the Arborean Tree Protection Society is waiting downstairs with a slab of redwood. They have traveled many weary miles for the opportunity to present it to you."

"No!"

"You agreed to the appointment two months ago. They paid to have that damned thing hauled by Continental-Cargo-Sphere all the way from the West Coast. The presentation is the climax of the five hundredth anniversary of the founding of the Society. You can't back out now."

The Master looked steadily at Varden. "You suggested this to keep my mind off—"

"Even *you* have to keep appointments sometimes!"

"Very well. However, if the honorable Society has succeeded in transporting their monumental slab this far, they can certainly bring it up here. I will not go down to the Audience Hall."

"They plan to make the presentation in this room. Of course they want a telerecord of the ceremony, and the recording equipment is up here. I will send for the technicians."

"And you will pour me a double brandy."

Varden poured the drink and went out.

The Master's long, powerful fingers gripped the glass,

and once more his thoughts went back to the woman who was dying in the blue-walled, sunlit bedroom. The old irony stabbed at him. Ellora would die, and there was nothing he could do about it. With all the power in the world at his disposal, he could not keep one heart beating an hour longer.

In an effort to pull his thoughts away, he tried to visualize the committee of the Arborean Tree Protection Society. They would be insignificant, ordinary people, not scientists or even political emissaries. Yet they had a right to meet The Master and present him with a silly slab of redwood. They had as much right as anyone else. Much more, he thought, than most of the pompous statesmen and long-winded professors to whom he must talk.

The Master had just finished his brandy when he saw the procession coming across the bridge which connected the Telecast Tower with the main block of World Center buildings. Varden was in the lead. Behind him, four men struggled with the gigantic slab. At the rear of the group marched a young woman.

The slab stuck in the doorway but finally, with some adroit coaching by Varden, they pushed it through. When the committee members had assumed their stance beside the slab and the Master knew the speech was almost upon him, he rose and signalled the telerecord technicians.

Standing behind the desk, the Master looked even taller than the six feet three inches that the world knew so well. His age might have been anywhere from fifty to sixty. His body was spare, almost gaunt, as if the clothing of flesh were too small for his big frame. But the body of the man was only an out-of-focus background for the eyes; the flow of time itself seemed to exist in their grey depths.

"Good afternoon. May I welcome your Society to World Center." There could be no doubt that it was the voice of the Master of the world. "This presentation by your organization is an honor which I deeply appreciate."

The young woman stepped forward and whisked a man-uscript from somewhere beneath her green robe. Her hands shook violently and she had difficulty in reading.

"This slab was cut from a giant Sequoia which died in the present year, the year 3097. Science has proven that each ring of such a tree represents one year of growth. Thus it was ascertained that this tree began its life in the year 100. As you can see, we have carefully marked certain rings which indicate important dates since that year."

The young woman extracted a telescopic pointer from some other sanctuary beneath her robe, and began extending the rod to its full length. The Master had trouble keeping his face composed. The pointer stuck halfway, and one of the committee stepped briskly forward and helped the girl unjam it. With the end of the pointer, she indicated a date printed on a ring near the center of the slab.

"On this date the Matriarchy of Rome is said to have fallen." She moved the pointer. "On this date a religious document, the Magna Charta, was signed." She moved the rod again. "On this date in the year 1776, America was founded by a group of Tea Men who revolted against the Czar."

The Master's mind drifted off. Muddling of history was the unalienable right of educators. Suddenly the young woman's voice changed tone.

"On this date the office of the Master was created, and you, the immortal one, came among our race. We do not know who you are, or why you never die. Your beginning is known to the Council of World Scientists, and that is enough for us.

"We know that without you men could not control science and the machine. It is impossible for anyone in the brief span of a human lifetime to acquire enough knowledge to coordinate the complexities of our civilization.

"We realize too, that the organization of World Scientists,

through its control of weapons and sources of power, has forever banished the madness of which we read in our history books, the madness of War. It is obvious that the World Scientists must have for a leader a man who can live forever.

"Therefore, we, as representatives of the Arborean Tree Protection Society present to you this slab as a symbol of the incredible truth that even the oldest living things on earth can die, but the Master cannot."

The Master looked away a moment before he bowed slightly and answered, "I accept your gift with a deep sense of appreciation. The telerecord of this meeting will be ready in ten minutes, but I wish to express my thanks with something less cold and formal. Varden, what are the arrangements?"

"The committee dines tonight at the Pavilion. I hope the entertainment will be up to their expectations. Tomorrow I have placed at their disposal a guide who will show them through Terra City and World Center. The following day they will leave on a special ship for an overnight trip to Moon Base."

The Master saw that the girl, surprised and without benefit of a prepared script, was wordless. He stepped from behind his desk and held out his hand.

As the slim, trembling fingers closed around his, he wondered, as he sometimes did on these occasions, if it were startling to discover that his were normal human hands, things of flesh and blood. The girl tried to speak and could not.

"I hope your stay here will be pleasant."

As she mumbled a reply, she became calmer.

He shook hands with the other members of the committee, and chatted a few minutes. Then Varden called one of the Master's guards who escorted the group out.

The Master returned to his desk. The telerecord tech-

nicians left their plastic-enclosed booth, and the Master and Varden remained alone with the slab of redwood.

Varden poured himself a brandy, sipped it and carefully placed the glass on the slab. It stood on a ring which was marked *America Discovered By Eric, A Red Man.*

"What shall we do with the firewood?"

The Master looked up. "Have it mounted somewhere—anywhere. Possibly in the little patio by the pool. But take it out of here at once."

"Always complaining."

"Varden, I have listened to your insults and alleged humor for a good many years. I have often speculated as to what action I should take. If there were only some way that you could be made immortal. . . ."

"Isn't there?"

The Master did not answer.

"Incidently, how *did* you become the Master? Why does the world need a Master?"

"You will find complete data in the archives of World Scientists."

"Why should I waste my time and eyesight when I can ask you?"

"To put it briefly, if there were no Master, there would be no civilization on this planet."

"With all respect to your unmitigated egotism, Master, that isn't an answer."

The Master refilled his pipe. "For some reason that lies hidden behind the cosmic scheme of things, the highest form of life on this planet, Earth, is afflicted with two principal faults. All creatures in the universe have faults, but mankind's two faults are *basic.*"

"The first is an insatiable desire to build endless machinery which soon becomes so complex that it requires more than one human lifetime to understand it. Also, man seems

blinded to the fact that the machine is not an end in itself, but only a means to mankind's happiness.

"The second fault is mankind's uncontrollable urge to kill its own species."

Seating himself on the redwood slab, Varden lit a cigarette. "I asked for a simple answer, not a speech."

"You asked for enlightenment, and enlightment you shall have. To continue:

"Besides the Earth there is—as you well know—one other planet which is inhabited by intelligent creatures. Our relations with them are part of your daily work. You also know that at least one other planet within this solar system was once inhabited. Our archaeological expeditions have proven this. Then, of course, there are the creatures from other solar systems, who occasionally visit the earth.

"For some reason—which is also hidden behind the scheme of things—all of the creatures who have visited here are very similar to ourselves, and yet" —The Master leaned forward—"No where—either in the creatures whom we know in life or those known only through the ruins which mark their death throes—do we find the slightest evidence of any desire to be slaves to a machine, or to kill each other. We and we alone are afflicted with such idiotic tendencies."

Varden was standing before the great window. Outside, darkness had fallen over Terra City. He spoke without turning. "Go on."

"Our planet was in chaos. War followed war. Civilization seemed doomed to destruction. What we needed was an organization of scientists who would use their knowledge for the fostering of human happiness; who understood that man gains nothing by killing man and that the machine should free man as an individual, not enslave him as a necessary part of the machine."

The Master paused and gestured toward a large copy of

the *Oath of a World Scientist* which glowed with soft fluorescence on the wall of the room.

"Read that again. The man who wrote it—he died almost ten centuries ago—was perhaps more of a poet than a law maker, but time seems to have proven that he caught the essence of the idea."

The Chief Assistant looked at his watch and glanced up at the oath.

> *I will guard mankind from the weapons mankind has invented, but I myself will not carry a weapon. I will not engage in politics. Although I may hold any religious belief I choose, or may hold none, I will not engage in any religious controversy or use any power given me as a World Scientist to promote any religion. I will be kindly, considerate and, to the best of my power, understanding to the inhabitants of this earth and those of any other world. I will not own property, but will hold the property of mankind as a trust. On the order of the Master, or the council of World Scientists, or on my own discretion if a major war should break out, I will destroy all Final Weapons, even if it results in the destruction of the Earth. In accepting these silver stars and with them the power and honor they confer, I freely state that my life shall be of no consequence in relation to this oath.*

Varden turned back to the Master. "What does that oath prove? I took it, and I've administered it more times than I can remember. But that still doesn't answer my question. Why should there be a Master?"

"World Scientists, like other men and women, have a habit of dying. Therefore, the organization must have at its head someone immortal, to form the line of continuity over the ages. Only such a person can be sufficiently un-

believable to command mankind's belief. Ask the girl from the Arborean Society."

"Perhaps I—" Varden glanced again at his watch and stopped. He dropped his hand lightly on the Master's shoulder. "The committee in conference room C will be ready to report now," he said.

The Master stood up. "Very well."

As they left the room in the Telecast Tower, Varden said, "Master, if the scientists and physicians have found no solution, there is one other chance."

The Master turned. "Yes?"

"This morning I received a letter from a man named Everling. I have briefly checked his record. At one time he did some brilliant scientific work. He claims to have cured the sickness, and wants an appointment with you. He stated that he would arrive in Terra City tomorrow on the afternoon magno-rocket from Asia."

"Have an exhaustive check made of his record."

"I have already given an order for it."

"Thank you, Varden."

"I have also arranged for your meeting with the scientists and physicians to be held in the living room. I thought it would be better."

The Master looked down at the balastrade of the bridge they were now crossing.

"Yes," he said.

CHAPTER TWO

THE LONG, low-ceilinged living room was quiet as the Master and Varden entered it. The men standing around the block crystal coffee table should have been talking.

Obviously, they had heard his footsteps. This silence, thought the Master, was his answer.

He knew these men well, as he had known thousands of others like them, but he was too tired to greet each one. They would understand. He went to the fireplace and stood with his back to the flames, watching the firelight create magic as it reflected in the crystal block.

After a moment he said, "Gentlemen?"

Irascible old Dr. Ronding, biochemist, spoke first.

"Master, there is only one answer. The sickness is caused by a virus!" He jerked out his cigar, tossed it in the fireplace and pointed his beard at the other men. "These eggheads have been talking nonsense."

"Ronding," the quiet voice was that of Dr. Venton, Director of Disease Control. "It is you who speak nonsense. Obviously the sickness cannot be caused by a virus. My theory is that it is caused by minute, invisible spores which float freely in space. We know these spores exist, but we do not know their origin. From time to time the earth travels through a concentration of spores, and one of them must be the cause of the sickness."

"Ridiculous!" shouted Ronding.

"I must agree with Dr. Ronding." It was Dr. Twining of Electronics Research. "The spore theory in untenable. I am convinced that the cause of this disease will never be found in the fields of chemistry, biology or physiology. I believe it is a disturbance of the body's electro-magnetic balance."

No one seemed to have anything more to say. They stood silently watching the Master, Finally, he said, "In other words, gentlemen, the theories are many but the cure is not."

Still no one spoke.

"You come from all parts of the earth," the Master went on. "The disease is world-wide. I had hopes that a general discussion of your individual experiences with it would pro-

duce a cure." He could not resist the irony. " I even provided a patient."

"Don't you think, Master, that we realized your hopes?" someone asked softly.

"Yes," he said. "I know this and appreciate it. And I also know that all of you are wondering why, if a cure for the sickness is possible, it would not be the Master who would find it. I will explain.

"There are a hundred other problems with which I am daily concerned. The sickness has not yet become so widespread as to command my full attention. If, out of selfish motives, I should devote my entire time to this work, I would cease to function as the Master, and thereby betray my trust to humanity. In any case, this problem is one for a specialist, not a coordinator. Before this conference began, I outlined to you the lines of research which my long experience suggested."

"We have done our best, Master." Ronding's voice was no longer strident. It was flat, defeated.

"Yet the mark of the sickness still remains on my wife's throat." And, as he said the words, the room vanished and he saw only her white, graceful throat, blemished now by the horrible blue mark of the sickness.

A voice, which he did not recognize, came from that void where the room had been.

"Otherwise, the Lady Ellora is as beautiful as ever."

The Master forced the void to once more become a room. Such things must never happen again. This was extreme weakness, and he could not allow himself such luxuries. His tone was that of the Master, or at least he hoped it was.

"Thank you, gentlemen. You have done your very best. No man can do more. I know that you are anxious to return to your homes and your work. The conference is over." He bowed slightly. "Goodnight."

Turning from the group he stood before the fire, his tall

figure blocking out the flames. As they passed him each man murmured a word or two, which he did not hear.

Ronding was the last to go. He paused a moment beside the Master, and this time the Master heard the words.

"We did do our best, Master. Sometimes—"

"I know."

"Damn it, we will win! But it will take time."

"Yes, Dr. Ronding. But there is little time—for her!" The Master drew the folds of his cloak about him, until it covered him like a blue shroud, screening him from the outside world, from the room and anyone in it.

Ronding went out quietly.

There was no sound in the room now, except for the fire, crackling and blazing. The Master loosened his cloak and let it slide from his shoulders. He sat down and his eyes moved absently from item to item of the furnishings he had collected through the centuries.

There were curiosities from everywhere: the mysterious blue of a small statue carved out of aqualite, that baffling mineral with its eleven-sided crystals, from Venus; a child-sized chair brought him by an expedition who had found it in an almost obliterated city on the central canal of Mars; a bit of an asteroid in which was an impression that he believed to be a fingerprint; a table whose top was a single piece of garnet which had been cut from a gigantic blood red mass found in a fissure on the moon; an ash tray supported by a segment of dinosaur thigh bone; a seemingly indestructible rug from Asia; a long, low divan, fashioned the year before by the finest craftsman of Terra City, and selected by him for the Lady Ellora.

Cold, inanimate treasures of the world. There was small comfort in them, now.

Around the edge of the door which Ronding had left ajar, a black button of a nose considered matters. Slowly, big shoulders wriggled the door open. A large shepherd slipped

into the room. On silent paws he crossed to the Master, and the black button sought and found a hand.

The Master's fingers followed along the dog's nose and began to scratch him behind the ears. "Flim," he asked, "do you have a theory about the sickness?"

The dog's tail expressed ecstasy, due to the scratching behind the ears. After a moment the Master rose.

"Shall we go and see her now?"

The dog led the way as they left the room.

The woman who was The Master's Lady, and therefore the second greatest enigma of mankind, was in bed, although dusk had just deepened into night. She lay propped up by an assortment of gayly colored satin pillows, staring at a book which she was too tired to read.

Her pale gold hair fell loosely around features whose purity of line made them seem almost unreal, as if a supreme sculptor had moulded them out of living flesh. Her wide-spaced, luminous gray eyes, dark circled by the ravages of disease, lifted from the book and stared into the night. On the smooth, curving throat was a small, roundish mark, dark blue in color—the fatal insignia of the sickness.

Outside the huge pane of glass which formed one end of the room she could see the black dome of the night. The evening wind carried the perfume of the jasmine which twined around a small balcony. An early night-bird was singing furiously somewhere close by.

She let the book drop from her hands. He would be coming soon. She always knew when he would come, and he would never believe that she did. How long, she thought, must she exist only between the bed and the lounge by the window. The few steps from one to the other had become a daily lifespan.

Pushing back the covers, she slowly swung her feet to the floor, then rested a moment until her strength returned.

The hideous, unpredictable weakness was upon her again.

After a moment she stood up, steadying herself with one hand on the night table beside her bed. The slim beauty of her figure had wasted to thin fragility. Her erect dignity was gone and her shoulders drooped.

Once more she faced that terrible trip from the bed to the dressing table. She had sent her maid away; she must be alone when he came. Step by staggering step she made the perilous journey that four months before had been only three swift strides, and sank down on the deep-cushioned stool.

She picked up a comb and began to arrange her hair. With each motion of the comb, she told herself that he must not see her suffer. She must always remember that it is more terrible to watch another's agony, and be unable to help, than to bear your own. There must be no tears, no discouragement, no hopelessness. He must not see.

She finished her hair, slipped into a bed jacket of cobweb lace and once more made the long journey back to bed. A touch of perfume from a translucent jade bottle and she was ready.

It was only a moment until her gay, "Come in!" answered his knock.

Flim came first, crossing to her bed with the dignity which is the right of large dogs. She was leaning over to pet him, when she felt the Master's arms tighten around her.

For a long while he held her until she laughed and pushed him away. She tilted her head a little, frowning at him.

"What have you been doing that I won't like? Such overwhelming ardor calls for an explanation."

He followed her light mood. "I thought you would hear about it in spite of my strict orders. No one pays any attention to my orders, anyway. I have been to an auction."

"You bought another musical instrument you know you can't learn to play."

He shook his head. "I purchased a complete, well-trained harem with the best references and credentials."

"Where are you going to keep the girls?"

"I shall refurnish and redecorate the International Council Room."

"This will give world politics a new twist."

He had been moving around restlessly while he spoke. Now he dropped into a chair at her bedside. Her face, her body were like familiar, haunting music; her movements were a constant rhythm, and her love the swelling crescendo of a great orchestra. And as he was thinking, his eyes, following the line of her throat, came to the blue mark.

Quickly she pulled her bedjacket over the mark. "You must not look at it."

"You are my wife—your agony is my agony." His lips twisted in a bitterly ironic smile. "I have only to give an order and World Scientists would destroy the moon. Yet the mark of the sickness remains, and I can do nothing to remove it."

"You have accomplished great things, incredible things."

"Perhaps. I have all the power that Earth has to give. Men think of me as a cosmic benefactor. But do they ever think of the loneliness beyond loneliness?"

She took his hand. "Please . . . don't."

After a moment she said, "What—what did they say, those men at the conference?"

The crushing of his hopes bowed his head a little, and he could not look at her nor speak. A quick, indrawn breath like a stab of pain was all the sign she gave before she reached out to touch his lowered head.

"I understand."

He met her eyes. "They can't help you." Fury and frus-

tration brought him to his feet, once more to pace the room
that was her prison.

"No one can help you. I cannot." He was near the
breaking point now.

"Remember, darling, Remember our wonderful hours
together!"

"Most of them spent here, within the walls of World
Center. You were twenty five when I married you—that
was one of the times when I was young. For twenty years
you have lived in this place. The Master's Lady! Cursed as
I am to play a role so that bungling humanity does not
bring upon itself the misery and horror it so richly deserves."

For an instant her voice had the old, calm strength.

"That is unworthy of the Master."

"It is worthy of your husband. There is a word from long
ago which is still used every day. Did we ever have a
'honeymoon'?"

"We've always had a honeymoon. My world is you,
dearest."

"Thank you for the banality."

"Thank me for the truth."

Pausing beside the dressing table, he glanced down at
the frivolities laid out with such care—jewels, perfumes,
other trifles that meant Ellora. "Years without end. I am
tired of the whole stupid mockery, tired of saying goodby
to every human being I learn to understand and care for.
To the only woman I ever loved."

"You have had many wives before me. You loved them.
You will love again."

"Ellora, my Lady, I have had more experience than you.
I have found during our time together that there really is
only one most beloved. Why this should be so, I do not
understand. It is. I accept it in its wonder."

The ceaseless gnawing of the pain was too much. His
eyes fell upon a low table that had been built by some

long dead Martian craftsman. On the table was a plate of peaches, fresh and round. Beside the plate lay a knife. The Master picked it up.

"I am tired, Ellora, incredibly tired." His voice had the quietness of finality. "I have said my last goodby. I believe that there is something beyond death. The day you go to that something, I go with you."

"Master!"

He ignored her cry.

"I have the emotions of a man, not a god." He ran his finger along the blade of the knife, then made a light, quick cut. A thin line of red appeared on the flesh. "I have the desires, the hopes, the pain of a man."

Red drops fell from his finger onto the table.

From some unknown reserve of energy, strength came to her. In an instant she got out of bed, crossed the room and flung herself upon him, seizing the hand that held the knife.

"Your life does not belong to you! It belongs to humanity, Master!"

The fingers that held the knife relaxed slowly, lingeringly. It had been a foolish, childish gesture. The release of death was not for him. As he put his arm around her waist and helped her back to bed, he said, "Forgive me, sweetheart. It was cruel of me to have upset you."

For a while he stood looking down at the white, exhausted face. Then, going to the World Center Intercom-Visaphone on its stand in the corner of a room, he pressed a button. The face of the central operator appeared on the small round screen.

The Master spoke softly. "Varden, please."

The screen went blank and a moment later Varden's face appeared.

"Have you completed your check on this man Everling?"

"It will be done in an hour."

"Meet me in my study at eight o'clock. You said Everling was arriving tomorrow. I wish to confer with him as soon as possible."

CHAPTER THREE

THE THIRD-CLASS magno-rocket from Asia carried the usual polyglot. Rows of battered couches were filled with laborers, heavy-booted and wide-belted, with tunics and jackets in the bright, iridescent colors that they loved. Some of the laborers' women were aboard; the younger ones in trim skirts and low-cut bodices, the older ones in the shapeless sort of garments that merely cover a body. Most of the men were asleep. The women chattered together or flirted casually with men who appeared to be alone.

A pale young man, who was reading, wore the graduation ribbons of the Asian University. He was obviously dreaming of becoming a World Scientist. In the couch beside him was an aging woman wearing the long robe and carefully selected jewels of Terra City Society.

On the two front couches reclined a pair who were startling, even for the third-class rocket from Asia. The man, strongly built and about forty, was dressed in what appeared to be a religious costume—but it was not the garb of any religion known on Earth. His robe, of rough, dark green material was tied with a gold sash. The leather sandals on his bare feet were fastened with gold cords, the knot of each one held in place by a single red jewel. Attached to his robe was a cowl, which was now pulled tightly about his face. Deep in the shadow his dark eyes were half closed, perhaps in meditation.

The girl wore a simple robe that was neither elegant

nor plain. It was the same dark green but the sheen of the synthetic fabric created a shimmering, constantly changing pattern of radiance. The body covered by the robe was that of a young woman, but the face was that of a child. Her hands were clenched about the handle of a small cage in which a tiny yellow bird trembled.

Occasionally the girl spoke soothingly to the bird. Her soft voice did not follow the pattern of any language, not even the lilting cadence of Venusian speech. But the bird seemed to understand and gradually stopped its shivering.

The man and the girl had not spoken since boarding the rocket. Now, as the eerie stillness of magno-flight was suddenly broken by the snarl of the landing jets, the man said, "We are almost there, my child."

His quiet voice had the quality of solemnity and peace of soul. The girl nodded, but did not answer.

The needle of the speed indicator at the front of the cabin dropped from two thousand miles per hour to three hundred, and the rocket began to circle. The man looked out the window, and pointed to something below.

"Terra City."

"Yes, Everling."

"Tarmo, we are here at last!"

"Why did we come? Why did we leave our peace in the old tower? Why did we leave the animals we love? Why could we bring only this one with us?"

"You do not understand, my child. It will take a little time."

Terra City rushed up from beneath the ship. The landing jets roared a final blast and were still. Number forty-nine, third-class out of Asia for Terra City, came in for a perfect landing.

They walked together in the bright sunlight. Everling had disragarded the raucous cries of the jet car drivers,

and had quietly picked up the two plain traveling cases which were their only luggage. Tarmo carried the bird cage. As they approached the center of the city, the needle-like shaft of the telecast tower took shape against a background of endlessly changing cloud patterns.

Because of the Master's final order for decentralization, Terra City was not large, but its beauty and ceaseless activity first awed, then frightened the girl. The life with Everling in the crumbling tower in Cheenwa had prepared her for nothing like this. Her long dead mother and father were faint images; only Everling and the tower were real to her.

The bird, Tarmo thought, is safe in its cage. It does not wonder about these streets that lead like the spokes of a wheel to something unknown in the center. But it may be hungry. She touched Everling's arm.

"He is hungry. Can you buy him some seed?"

"Of course, my child."

They stopped before a shop in the window of which a large Klynadon from a Venusian swamp was prominently displayed. Tarmo watched the slate-gray creature pace back and forth in its atmosphere-conditioned cage, while Everling purchased a package of seeds.

As she fed the bird, Tarmo said, "He must be sad. All creatures in cages must be sad. They are not free."

"I do not think so. Most people prefer to be slaves, safe in a protected, routine life. It is probably the same with birds."

They walked on, past the great marble slabs which enclosed the public baths. Near the entrance to the baths, a fountain sent plumes of clear water arching against the sky. The spray fell in a curtain of mist about an exquisitely carved nude in the center of the pool. Beside the pool stood a huge statue of the President of the Union of South America who had presented the fountain to Terra City in

2542. A small bird was asleep on the statue's nose, and a man selling lottery tickets leaned against the pedestal.

Cubes and triangles, curving lines and sharp angles had been subtly blended by the superb designers who had planned the city, built in the twenty-fourth century. Everywhere there were trees and grass, whose fresh greeness surrounded and formed a background for the magenta, coral, aquamarine, and white of the buildings.

Everling paused before a rack of free booklets which stood at the entrance of the Terra City Historical Society. He glanced through one of the pamphlets which described how the city had been built on the site of a slum-ridden horror which had been destroyed by order of the Master. He seemed especially interested in a particular sentence: *The Master exercised extreme care in evacuating the inhabitants of the original city and in finding comfortable temporary homes for them elsewhere.*

They walked on. Ahead of them, the television tower at World Center became more sharply defined against the eternally moving clouds.

Tarmo's feet dragged as if she were very tired. She had lagged several yards behind Everling when he turned and said, "Why do you walk so slowly? We have some distance to go."

She came up beside him. Her face, with its wide cheekbones and delicately slanted green eyes, was sullen.

"I don't like this place. Let's go home."

"Nonsense."

"The buildings are too big and the streets are too long. They make me afraid."

"Terra City is the most beautiful, the most important city on Earth."

She shook her head, and the dark waves of hair tossed, then settled back on her shoulders. "I don't like it here.

I don't like the voices. There are too many of them. The light hurts my eyes. It is a place that cuts."

"You must grow up, Tarmo, and forget your fancies."

She looked far past him.

"I want the stillness. I want my animals, my birds. And I want them free."

She had gone back with her thoughts to Cheenwa and the old tower of gray stone, half covered with moss and vines, the only human habitation in miles of primitive isolation. Around the tower the forest crowded in, the intricate patterns of branches and leaves filtering the harshness out of the light.

It was that soft, all-encompassing light that she could not find here. She loved the light as she loved the animals who had been her only companions. Once she had met two other children near a cold, clear pool in the forest. Later they came to the tower, making a pleasurably frightening game out of their visits to this strange place.

Everling had been kind to the children. He had been sad when they ceased to visit her. Then he had said, "Do not be unhappy. Life is made up of greetings and leave-takings. Learn from the animals. It is they that you love most deeply." She had answered, "Yes." She had really believed she did.

Someone was speaking to her. Everling's voice, in Terra City.

'You are in need of food, Tarmo. Let us rest here a moment.

They stopped at a sidewalk cafe, and Everling seated her at a table. As he sat down opposite her, he said, "The way of life is different here. You will soon become accustomed to it."

When she had finished eating, he ordered a glass of Zylute for her and wine for himself. The ruby redness in his glass contrasted with the green of her synthetic drink. Everling wrapped himself in his long robe and his thoughts.

The afternoon sunlight slanted across the cafe and Tarmo's eyes idly followed the golden bars and rays until loud voices from an adjoining table attracted her attention.

"He comes from another planet where people live longer than we do."

"You are a fool, my friend. But there is no reason to demonstrate the obvious. Any jet pusher on a clunker run knows that the Master is the only survivor of the lost continent. You can't explain him any other way."

The first voice answered quickly, "You'll never learn anything, Gondek, with your mouth open. When the great floods came and Atlantis sank, a whole civilization, a whole way of life, was gone. They had the secret of eternal life—and the Master was the only survivor."

The tramp of heavy boots sounded on the pavement and a jolly voice called out, "Sorry I'm late. Don't try to explain anything to Gondek. Waste of breath. I'll buy the drinks and call the points of discussion. One drink— life in general. Two drinks—the Master. Three drinks—love."

Tarmo turned slightly and saw a glass in a rough, powerful hand.

"A thousand years!"

"That is your ultimate. Did you ever think how much weariness, how many partings, how much agony that many years of life would make possible? An ordinary lifetime has enough of them. Would you really want to live forever?"

"Say, that's a funny idea. Never thought of it."

"I suppose you don't know there's trouble at the Center right now. I haven't been able to find out what it is, but the rumor is too strong not to have some foundation."

"And you don't know what the trouble's about?" asked the first man. "It's the sickness that's causing the worry at the Center. I'll bet ten to one that someone close to the Master has it!"

"Could it be the Master who—"

"Of course not. People who have the sickness die."

Tarmo turned to Everling. "Is he—the Master—a man like you?"

"I do not know."

"Do people love him or hate him?"

"They wonder about his eternal life. A few adore him. Some envy him. Most people merely accept him, as they accept life."

Tarmo was silent for a moment, then continued, "If the Master created this city, he is not a good man. There are too many people here. Who knows what they are thinking? Who knows what they will do?"

Everling answered indifferently. "What all men and women do. To many Terra City is their whole life. Others are here on business. Some come in hope of making their fortunes."

"There is no fortune here for us."

"Tarmo," Everling was suddenly grave. "I thought you understood my purpose in coming to Terra City was my belief that it was here I could best aid mankind. To do what one considers his duty is not to seek a fortune."

"Yes, Everling."

He paid the waiter and they once more walked on. In half an hour they had reached one of the high, delicately tapered walls which surrounded the World Center. The wall, with its single line of carving, seemed almost fragile; something built to enhance, not to protect. But a hundred unseen devices gave protection that walls cannot give.

The most intangible of all safety measures were the words from the *Oath of a World Scientist:* . . . *I will destroy all Final Weapons, even if it results in the destruction of the Earth.*

Only the rain and the sunlight, the wind and the fragrance of flowers, the sickness, death and tomorrow could cross that wall freely.

Behind the wall, and the three others like it, were the

Master's private library, containing the best of human thought since people began to think, and his small museum. There were, also, the larger library and museum which all persons could freely visit. Within that vital rectangle were the central offices of the Committee of the World Scientists, the Master's quarters, the telecast tower and Laboratory I.

Everling and Tarmo paused before the main gate and watched a small boy who was bouncing a resilent monoloid crystal sphere. The tremendous resilence of the ball carried it high, and a flick of afternoon breeze dropped it on top of the wall where it hesitated a moment, then bounced over.

The boy approached one of the Master's guards standing beside the gate and gravely surveyed him.

"Are you going to keep my ball?"

The guard grinned. "Just a minute."

The gate was open only an instant, but Everling and Tarmo had a glimpse of great banks of flowers, a small fountain, and everywhere the green of eternal springtime. The guard returned with the ball, and the small boy bounced it on down the street.

Everling turned to Tarmo. "Come, we are going into the Center."

He started forward, but Tarmo would not move. Everling looked at her. "Come, Tarmo."

"I won't go into that place. I won't!" Terror, stark and uncontrolled, was in her voice. "If we go there they can send us to Laboratory I. Everybody knows that. Even the children in Cheenwa. When you go into Laboratory I, you never come out!"

Everling's dark eyes beneath his cowl met hers steadily. He held out his hand.

"You have nothing to fear, my child. I have protected you always."

With Tarmo clutching his hand, Everling went to the

guard and presented a small packet of papers. The guard appraised them swiftly.

"These credentials are sufficient only for admission to the anteroom. You and the girl follow me."

In the long, low-ceilinged room the guard handed the papers to a clerk at the desk. The clerk glanced at the credentials and then at the daily check list. With a quick, decisive gesture he reached for the visaphone, saying, "Be seated, sir. There will be a short delay."

The bird can be free in this room, thought Tarmo. It is quiet here. He will not be frightened. There is nothing to harm him.

She opened the cage and the bird darted into the free air which was the only environment it understood. As it circled the room, its wings brushed the far wall. It shivered an instant, hung suspended as if supported by some unseen hand, and died as it fell to the floor.

Neither the bird nor Tarmo had knowledge of the concealed, highly charged panels which recorded, both fluoroscopically and photographically, the images of all those who entered World Center. The image of the bird had appeared on the fluorescent screen. The photographic circuit had been made. And the technicians would curse a burned out circuit.

The clerk stepped quickly from behind his desk and stooped to pick up the bird. But Tarmo, pushing him aside, gently closed her hands around the fragile thing on the floor.

CHAPTER FOUR

WHEN VARDEN entered the anteroom, he was confronted by a somber, cowled man and a girl who was crying softly as she talked to a dead bird held in her lap.

Varden considered the scene. Handling unusual affairs was his business. He remembered the day he had walked into the same room and found the superintendent of Moon Base trying to strangle a Venusian pilot because of some protocol about the proper registry of a ship. He crossed the room and stood before the cowled man.

"You are Dr. Everling?"

"Yes, I am Everling. And you—I see that you are a World Scientist—"

"I am Varden, the Master's chief assistant. The girl?"

"She is my ward. She traveled here with me from Cheenwa. Her name is Tarmo."

Varden knelt and picked up the small golden cage with the door swinging open. He carefully closed the door and snapped the catch.

"You will not need this now. What happened?"

"He is dead. I wanted him to be free, just for a few minutes. He flew against that—"

"The photo-fluorescent panel. I'm sorry. But it isn't anyone's fault. We do not expect pet birds to fly around this room."

"It is dead."

"Death is something none of us can avoid."

"One man has avoided it," Everling said quietly.

Varden rose from his stooping position before the girl. "That is why I am here. The Master wishes to meet you at once. If you and your ward will follow me . . ."

They walked silently through courts and corridors; the tall, cowled man, the Master's chief assistant, and the girl carrying the dead bird.

As they were entering a passageway whose curved ceiling was only dimly visible, Tarmo suddenly stopped. She stood immobile, clutching the bird.

"Tarmo," Everling spoke with firmness. "You must not lag behind. Come quickly."

"No! He's taking us to Laboratory I!"

In an instant she was running back down the passage. Everling had started after her, when Varden caught his arm.

"No, Dr. Everling, that is not the way. She will not go far." He stepped to a recess in the wall and pressed a button. In the dimness of the passage a tiny red light appeared. Varden turned to Everling. "She is quite safe—have no fears for her. Come, the Master is waiting."

As they emerged from the passageway the telecast tower stood before them. Varden led the way across the rose-colored bridge of marble.

The Master's eyes showed no surprise as he extended his hand to the man from Cheenwà. He had the facts before him on his desk.

"Good afternoon, Dr. Everling. Have you been in Terra City before?"

"Almost ten years ago, Master. But I do not think it will have changed greatly."

The Master touched the control that slid back the converging panel which covered the great window. The incredible gray eyes did not leave Everling's face as the stranger studied the magnificent city.

After a moment Everling said. "No, Master, I cannot see any changes. It is eternal, as you are. Naturally, I have never seen the city from this tower which seems hung in the sky."

"I find this room a most pleasant place. Perhaps you will understand, Dr. Everling, as I have heard that you, too, are accustomed to working in a tower."

"Mine is somewhat different, Master. It is overgrown with primordial wilderness. But, as you point out, all towers are essentially the same."

The Master glanced at the file folder which lay on the desk. "That file contains the pertinent data concerning you.

Will you correct me if any of my information is in error?"

The cowled head bowed slightly.

"Ten years ago," the Master went on, "you were an obscure but apparently brilliant biochemist. Then, for some personal reason, you left Terra City and isolated yourself in the wilderness of Cheenwa. There you lived in an ancient tower. The archaeologists are uncertain as to the structure's date, but it certainly predates me. Concerning what type of work you carried on in the tower I have, of course, no knowledge.

"I notice that your dress is peculiar. However, I do not associate it with any religious order."

"All that you have is correct, Master. I do not belong to any religious organization. I consider my style of dress desirable—that is all."

"Very well. The important point is that you wrote me stating that you had discovered a cure for the sickness."

"I have." He spoke quietly, without emphasis.

Returning to his desk, the Master sat down and rested his clasped hands on the file folder. "If you have done so, you deserve humanity's thanks—and mine. However, as you well realize, there remains the matter of proof."

"The diagnosis of the sickness is certain because of the bluish mark. No one has ever recovered from this disease. My ward, Tarmo, had the sickness. I treated her. She recovered."

"Where is she?"

"I brought her with me to Terra City. Unfortunately—"

"The girl was frightened," Varden interrupted. "Some fool had told her an old wives' tale about Laboratory I. She bolted. I know the guards must have long since found her. Shall I have her conducted up here?"

The Master shook his head. "I will see her later." Staring at his folded hands, he was silent a moment. "Dr. Everling, there is a fact concerning my personal life which it is vital

that you know. However, I must ask you to use discretion in speaking of it to others."

"I understand, Master."

"My wife has the sickness."

"This was already known to me."

"In that forsaken jungle of Cheenwa? My wife's illness is known only to a trusted few."

"There are other channels of knowledge besides the normal senses. It was through such means that I discovered I might be of use to you."

"Most interesting. I, too, have thought along such lines. We will discuss these matters at another time. What is important now is your method of cure."

"First, Master, I must examine my patient."

"How much time will you require?"

"My examination should last only a few minutes."

The Master turned to Varden. "Conduct Dr. Everling to the Lady Ellora's bedroom. Remain there during the examination. My wife will be less disturbed if I am not present. I will follow you in ten minutes."

Varden led the way out of the room.

Alone, the Master considered whether it would be wise to send for this girl whom Everling claimed to have cured. She was certainly young and naive. Her actions were sufficient indication of that. Moreover, she was frightened, possibly hysterical. Everling was a brilliant man, and he would know more about him in half an hour. Surely he could do without cross-questioning a child.

It was too soon yet to speculate as to Everling's merits, or lack of them. The greatest of all intellectual blunders was to reason without sufficient data. He had learned that lesson many lifetimes ago.

The Master opened the door quietly. Varden and Everling were standing by the bed. Ellora's white, emaciated face

was very still among the bright silken pillows. He went to the bed and kissed her, but her lips could not return the pressure of his.

As he straightened up, he wished that he could sit on the bed, but that would be an unseeming gesture, something he would have done before Varden but not before a stranger.

"Dr. Everling," he said, "what is your conclusion?"

"The disease is obviously far advanced. The weakness is extreme, the color of the mark deep and its outline well defined. You will note that the reflexes are already partially lost, and—"

"I appreciate your thoroughness, but I do not wish to prolong this discussion. It will only tire her. There is only one essential point. Do you believe that you can cure her?"

"Master, I *know* I can."

From the white drawn face on the pillows came a cry, "I must not die, Dr. Everling. I must not! The Master wants me to live."

Exhaustion quenched the fire in her eyes and slowly closed the lids. Quickly, Varden picked up a glass of violet liquid and held it to her lips.

"This stimulant will help you."

The Master watched as Ellora swallowed a little of the violet fluid. Then, with a motion of his expressive fingers, he indicated that Everling should follow him.

They stepped into a small alcove where a single curved glass window created the illusion that the room was floating above the moonlit gardens below.

"Her words are significant," Everling said. "She wishes to live only because you desire it. This indicates a noble spirit— but also a great lack of vitality. It is this draining away of vitality which is the true cause of the sickness."

"A symptom, Doctor, is not a cause. Proceed, but be brief and be specific."

"I have spent many years far from civilization. In those

years I have come closer to the basic truths of reality than your science has or ever will. But you asked me to be specific. I have found a science above and beyond the data, methods and discoveries which are symbolized by the organization of World Scientists."

"Do you speak of a philosophy, or a proven cure for the sickness?"

"Both, Master. To understand what I have discovered, you must realize that the cure is based on the philosophy. Vitality is the result of the will to live, and the will to live is the result of struggle. Men are designed for struggle. Do they struggle now?"

The Master made no answer.

"The mathematical setting up of population quotas for each region," Everling continued, "has taken from men the basic incentive to contend for natural resources. The great plagues and epidemics have been conquered—and with them something against which men's bodies were designed to fight. Yet the sickness, which is increasing every day, has become mankind's doom. What, then, has been gained by the elimination of daily struggle and of war?"

The Master looked at the full moon and wondered what the men and women who died during the final atomic shelling of Moon Base would have thought of such an argument.

Everling continued. "The sickness is merely the physical manifestation of pampered mankind's loss of the fundemental will to live, the fundamental ability to struggle. Man was not designed—"

"You have stated that you are able to cure the sickness. Can you cure my wife?"

"Yes."

"How?"

"Long before even your time, Master, men in the countries of the East developed certain methods of training their

bodies and minds. These men discovered the secret of charging themselves with that strange, but real force which science dismisses under the term vitality. Moreover, these men of long ago gained such mental control over this force that they could cause it to flow into another person.

"World histories mention such men, but they are treated as ignorant primitives or charlatans. The last of them died, along with most of the population of Asia, when that continent was deluged with atomic dust during one of the great wars. As you recall, ninety-five percent of the people of Asia died because they had no protection from the dust."

The Master nodded.

"From my early researches, I felt sure that a description of their methods existed. I followed a hundred false clues, but finally I discovered the ancient record in the country of Cheenwa. For ten years I lived alone, except for my ward, Tarmo, in the old tower.

"I perfected myself in the ascetic discipline. At last I became so adept in turning my vitality into another that I was able to cure Tarmo of the sickness. In the same way, I will cure your wife."

"What is your exact procedure."

"I inject a drug which I have compounded. This drug temporarily lulls the patient's mind and allows me to work directly with the subconscious. Then, by an act of will, I pass some of my vitality into the patient. This gives immediate relief from the terrible weariness and depression of the sickness, and it stimulates the patient's own dormant will to fight and live. It is this second reaction which makes the cure permanent."

"How long would your treatment be necessary?"

"I would expect a cure within the month."

"You may attempt the cure," the Master said, turning away toward the bedroom.

Everling's calm voice followed him. "There is one condition."

"What is it?"

"No other scientist or physician must be allowed to watch my treatment, nor be in consultation with me. I must work entirely alone."

The Master forced himself to answer calmly. "I cannot allow that."

With a backward step, Everling spread his hands apart, palms turned out in a gesture which might have been resignation or defeat. "Then I can do nothing."

Suddenly, the Master's voice was biting.

"Let us presume that you actually have discovered a cure for the sickness. Then your last statement could only mean that you intend to keep the cure as your secret. In order to glory in your own power, you will allow others to die in agony. If that is the case, you are neither a great scientist nor a decent man."

"You misunderstand me, Master. The reasons for my request are just and necessary—as I shall explain to you."

Abruptly, the Master swung about and led the way back to the bedside of the Lady Ellora. She was sitting up, hope bright in her eyes.

"I cannot permit this man to treat you."

"Dearest, you can't mean—"

"Dr. Everling has spoken a great many interesting generalities. However, he has just stated that he will not allow any other scientist or physician to observe or check his methods. Such an approach leaves me no choice."

The man in the strange robe said quietly, "Master, you do not understand me. Another physician would confuse the patient, and make the cure doubtful. No World Scientist would comprehend my approach to the problem. The very nature of the cure prohibits complexity. That is why I came directly to you."

With her eyes fixed on the Master, Lady Ellora said softly, "If he cures me, does it matter how?"

Her words disturbed the Master. Would he ever forgive himself if he did not take this last gamble?

"It will take me several years," Everling said, "to train men in my methods. Until I have proven my case, I would certainly not expect the Master to provide me with the opportunities for such a training program."

"If there is a chance of helping others . . ." The Lady Ellora's voice trailed away into a whisper.

"It is only common justice," Everling said, "to allow every man a chance to prove his case."

"You are a practically unknown scientist," the Master said.

The old fire flamed briefly in Lady Ellora's voice. "Every scientist was unknown *once*."

"You propose to use my wife as a guinea pig."

"Your wife before anyone else!" she cried hoarsely.

The Master stared at her, puzzled.

"I have never been able to help you in your work in any fashion. Let me have my one chance to really *be* the Master's Lady."

He watched her for a long moment. Then he turned to Everling and nodded.

Everling bowed. "I shall begin my treatment at once."

With a deep sigh, the Lady Ellora's head sank back among the pillows.

The Master took Varden's arm and they left the blue bedroom.

At the passageway to the telecast tower bridge they separated, and Varden turned down the corridor which led to his office. The corridor was dimly lit and he almost crashed into a guard who was carrying Tarmo. The girl was fast asleep.

Varden found the situation amusing. "Rylek," he said, I

wouldn't have believed it of you. But I suppose still waters do run deep."

The guard stood very erect, the girl balanced in his arms. "You do not understand, sir."

"All I have heard all day is, 'You do not understand.' Doesn't anybody understand anything?"

"No, sir."

"I'm glad to hear it. Get on with your story—and make it good."

"Well, sir, I was assigned to stay with her. She had this dead bird, you see. She wanted to bury it."

"Was this accomplished?"

"We buried it in the garden by the little pool."

"And the funeral?"

The guard hesitated. "We . . . we put a stick in the ground to mark the grave. It was impressive, sir."

Varden realized the joke was played out and smiled. "I've got to have a laugh sometimes, Rylek. Forget it. Now carry the girl to E guest bedroom in the Master's quarters. Inform the chief maid of the situation."

A voice spoke from behind Varden. "I will carry her."

Everling took the sleeping girl from the arms of the guard. With the guard leading the way, they entered a side corridor.

Varden silently watched them go.

CHAPTER FIVE

"When the Master will ask the Council for a donor, and which of you chance will choose, is unknown. Nevertheless, during the coming year one of you may be called upon to go to Laboratory I and give his life that the Master shall not die.

"Or, to put it another way, the one life you possess may be required by the people of this world. You understood this two months ago when you accepted the oath of a World Scientist."

Varden paused and looked at the young men in the lecture hall. Row after row of silver stars. Approximately a hundred and fifty men this year at a guess.

He realized that the men were impatient and went on: "As you know, the normal period between donations is thirty years. However, it may vary considerably. The decision as to the exact time for a donation is made by the Master.

"The basis of your selection as possible donors was your physical fitness in relation to a simple medical fact, a fact which you could not control. The final choice will be made by pure chance. You were informed of all this after you passed the World Scientist examinations, but before you took the oath. However, at that time you did not know that you would be members of the group of potential donors.

"The purpose of this meeting is to inform you of that fact. Also, to impress upon you that you must consider this as something real—not a legend. A donor may be called for this year, and if this occurs, one of you will be selected.

"I have no intention of frightening you. If you become frightened of the inevitable, you are not worthy of being World Scientists. An intelligent human being adjusts his life by taking into account all known possibilities.

"You can calculate the chance—which is small—that any of you will be called this year. Now that I have made that speech, let me say that I don't expect any of you to be much concerned. But it is my duty, according to custom, to brief you on this matter. Perhaps I am closer than most to the reality of the donor. A donor was called during my first year as a World Scientist—and I was one of the selected group."

A wave of uneasiness hung over the room. Earnestly,

almost grimly, the men fastened their attention upon Varden.

"I am here to answer any questions which you may have. So, gentlemen, begin."

A man in the back row stood up. "If I were called as donor, how long would I have between notification and . . ."

"Two weeks."

"Many World Scientists are women," said another. "Why is a woman not allowed to be a donor?"

"It is not a matter of sex, as such. However, there is a reason having to do with—as I understand it—the very nature of life itself, which makes it impossible for a woman to be a donor. The technical background behind that point is known only to the Master."

A third young man rose. "If I should be called, how would my dependents be taken care of?"

"To your wife, ten thousand villars for life. To your children, five thousand villars until they reach twenty-one. Beyond that, unlimited free education. Your wife and any dependent over twenty-one may build a house of his design at the expense of the World Scientists. For all dependents —free medical care for life."

"What if I should refuse to be the donor?"

"The violation of the oath of a World Scientist is lifetime banishment—probably to Mars or Moon Base. The man's name and the reason for banishment would be publicly announced."

After a pause, Varden added, "Are there any further questions?"

There was an eloquent scuffling of feet.

Varden smiled. "You will now have the immense privilege of shaking hands with me as you leave. If it seems to waste your time, remember I did not establish the custom. Good afternoon, gentlemen—and good luck."

Varden's search for the Master led him to a cool patio. The sky was a pale amber from a mist veiling the sunlight,

a mist which gathered in smoke-colored clouds among the branches of the gnarled old olive trees and caressed the flower starred shrubbery.

At one end of the patio was a small pool set into flag-stones. Water lilies and intricately patterned magenta marzons, grown from long dormant seeds found in the labyrinth of a Martian underground city, floated on the still water.

It was a secluded spot, a scene designed for peace. But when Varden entered the patio he saw that the design had evidently gone wrong; the dove had long since grabbed an olive twig and departed.

Tarmo, half concealed by the shrubbery, was gobbling a large piece of pie. Koom, the chief cook, was screeching something unintelligible from the shadow of an archway. The girl took a final bite, and tossed the last of the crust into the pool where a large, iridescent fish snapped it up. Koom ran lumberingly from the archway. With long, easy strides Tarmo reached the pool and leaped across it. Koom, attempting to follow her, tripped and splashed among the water lillies and marzons.

As he scrambled out, he screamed, "Stupid little female! That pie was especially ordered by the Master. I'll tell him what you've done. He'll send you to Laboratory I!"

Instantly, unbridled terror shone from her green eyes. The old specter, haunting her from childhood, formless but awe-some, was at hand.

Before she could move, the quiet voice that the world knew so well spoke from the dimness of another archway. "Do not be afraid, Tarmo."

The Master stepped out into the eerie light of the patio. Tarmo stared at the vapor-shrouded figure, then darted to a nearby wall. The wall was covered with vines whose tendrils were locked to the masonry by centuries. Frantically the girl sought for a foothold, found one and began to climb.

The Master turned to Koom. "I will attend to this. I am sorry about the pie, but I doubt if some other dessert will kill me." With a gesture he dismissed the cook.

Tarmo paused a moment for breath and again began to climb. However, her long robe, already torn, caught in the vines and she was trapped, clinging there, half suspended, helpless. Seen through the mist, her hair disheveled and her face covered with dust from the ancient vines, she seemed to Varden more like a trapped wild creature than a young girl.

The Master's voice was gentle. "Come here, Tarmo."

She had been facing the wall as her hands gripped the stout vines; now, turning towards him her robe ripped loose and she slid to the ground. There she crouched, her back against the wall, alert, watching him. After a moment, the Master spoke.

"No one will harm you. Do not believe foolish stories about me or Laboratory I." At the mention of the Laboratory she cringed, but as the Master's calm voice went on she became quieter. "You are safe, Tarmo. But I want you to be happy, also. Now, come to me."

Reluctantly she took a step forward.

"You believe me, do you not?"

She nodded.

While the Master had been speaking, Flim had joined the group. He sat on the grass and watched, motionless except for the tip of his tail which undulated in a slow rhythm.

"You are my guest, Tarmo. That means we are friends—and friends do not run away from each other."

She came a little closer, staring at him.

"Do I seem so strange to you."

"No," she whispered. "It's your eyes that are strange."

"Why?"

"Because they tell me that you know so many things. Perhaps as many as Everling. But I don't want you to know me—to hear what I think before I speak. To know what I

dream. I will be alone with myself." ·

He smiled. "I am not a conqueror, my dear. Nor an invader of your spirit. You have my word."

Holding out his hand, he waited. She came to him slowly, with sliding, tentative steps. Hesitantly, she put out her hand and took his.

"Now we are friends, Tarmo. You will never again be frightened by the terrible Master. You can see that he is only a man."

"Yes, Master," she nodded.

"But," he went on, "you must tell Koom that you are sorry. When you are hungry, ask him for something. He will give it to you."

"I wasn't hungry." There was laughter now in her voice. "It was a kind of game."

The third member of the group made his presence known by rubbing against the Master's knee. The Master glanced down. As he scratched the dog's head he said to Tarmo, "This is Flim. He needs someone to play his kind of games. Will you?"

Dropping down on her knees, the girl stretched out her hands to the dog. Flim came eagerly to them and her arms encircled the big head. She began to talk into his ear, using a language that only he could understand.

Varden decided that the show was over and crossed the patio, saying, "I looked for you, Master, for half an hour. I find you trying to promote yourself as god-father, when you're supposed to spend your time solving the problems of humanity. The only kind of pie you should know anything about is spelled pi."

"Who was wasting whose time by eavesdropping? Well, what is it? Moon Base again?"

"No, thank God. But I've been talking to Ronding. He's screaming for better assistants."

"You know Ronding is always screaming about something.

I will go over the list of available men in the morning. Meanwhile, I shall go back to solving the problems of humanity." He looked at the girl, who was playing with the dog. "We are friends, now, Tarmo?"

She smiled up at him and he started slowly toward the nearest archway. As he watched the tall figure, Varden realized that the Master stooped a little, and that he looked very tired.

Varden dropped into a chair beside the pool and lit a cigar. Tarmo lay flat on her stomach, drinking from the pool.

"Do you go back into a tree trunk at night to sleep?" Varden inquired.

Tarmo looked up from the water, the curly ends of her hair dripping. "What?"

"Forget it. I pity any man but the Master who tries to tame you."

Her eyes were wide. "Tame?"

"The dog there was wild once. Now he's your companion. He's been tamed."

Her small, firm hand rubbed Flim's nose. "He could turn wild again, couldn't he?"

Varden wondered if she hoped he would. "Tarmo," he said, "would you like to hunt? To kill?"

"Maybe—if somebody hurt me."

Varden laughed. "You don't look as if anyone could hurt you very easily. A young she-tiger couldn't look any healthier. But Everling told me that you were very sick once."

The sea-green eyes, flecked with amber, stared past him, into something he could not see. There was no way by which he could enter the room in the old tower into which the mist often drifted, as it was drifting around them now. Nor could he see remnants of bread and bits of cake carefully laid out for the birds. Or understand the games

she had invented out of the pattern of the bedcover; games which had filled endless long hours.

"The sun went away." she said at last. "I stayed in the dark . . . in my room. The birds came to the window ledge and sang for me. . . ."

"Didn't your playmates come to see you?"

"I had two playmates once. But they went away before I was sick. They never came back."

"Of course it's a wilderness out there, but Dr. Everling must have had some friends. Didn't he bring them to see you?"

"I don't remember."

"How did you feel, Tarmo?"

"Sick."

Varden laughed. "Did you like it there, in the—"

Tarmo was no longer listening. She had turned her head and Varden could see only her profile. As he watched her chin lifted inch by inch. As her eyes came into line with the second floor balcony she became still. The balcony was covered with jasmine, and beyond it was the blue bedroom of the Master's Lady.

Everling was leaning on the balustrade. He spoke no words nor made any gesture, yet Tarmo began to run across the patio. Everling was standing outside the door of the Lady Ellora's room when she reached the second floor. He smiled and carefully smoothed the dark hair which had fallen across her forehead.

"You wanted me?"

"Yes," he said. "It is time to dress for dinner. And, my child, it appears that you need to dress."

Putting his arm around her shoulders, he walked with her along the corridor. It was so safe here, she thought. All that she had ever known of home, parents, friends, were within the crook of his arm.

CHAPTER SIX

THE MASTER chalked his cue and looked down at the three ivory billiard balls. It was one of those inexplicable days when his game was bad. For more than an hour he had been practicing and the ivory balls remained lifeless.

Perhaps it was the weather. He glanced at the sky outside the window. The veil of cirrus clouds over Terra City had taken on a leaden hue. It would be raining in an hour.

The Master turned back to the table. He missed a three cushion carom around the corner, racked his cue, and left the billiard room.

He entered a long slanting gallery in which his footsteps followed him with persistent echoes, and emerged into afternoon grayness.

The scene before him was relentlessly harsh. High walls surrounded a courtyard surfaced with sandstone slabs, precisely fitted. In the center of the court was a squat, rectangular, windowless building. The low clouds seemed to be pressing the building into the earth, trying, the Master thought, to bury it once and for all, so that soft, green grass could grow where it had stood.

He crossed the court and stopped before the single entrance to the building. The doorway was indicated only by the almost imperceptible cracks which outlined it, and the simple inscription engraved above it—*Laboratory I*.

The Master pressed the button which opened the combination cubicle. As he carefully set the dials, his thoughts drifted to what the technician who designed the combination lock almost nine hundred years before, had said:

"Master, there are one billion, four hundred million, seven

hundred and nineteen thousand, six hundred and forty-seven possible combinations. As the code cannot be deciphered by any known method, as the combination cannot be ascertained by any physical analyses, and as the use of force will automatically seal the lock, I doubt if anyone will pass through this door unless you wish them to do so."

No one ever had. He had changed the combination every week. And he had forgotten it only once. That was around 2700 when Zelt had been his chief assistant. It had been his own fault for telling Zelt that he had forgotten the combination. For three weeks Zelt's jokes had made his life intolerable. Then he had remembered the combination.

The massive nitron door, more than a meter thick, was swinging slowly inward. He followed it into the dimness beyond. The door, in response to the timing mechanism, silently swung back into its original position and, as it did so, soft lighting flooded the room before him.

With the closing of the door, the last physical contact between the Master and mankind was severed. Except for the visaphone, which he could turn off at will, he was completely isolated.

The Master walked slowly through the maze of equipment. He could have found his way in his sleep; every magnetron, every calculator, each piece of biological or harmonic apparatus was embedded in his mind, a basic part of his consciousness.

Only the North wall of Laboratory I was starkly bare of instruments. The Master touched a button and the metal panels which formed the wall began to descend into recesses. They dropped individually—starting from the right and continuing to the left. As each panel slipped noiselessly into the floor, it revealed a metal cabinet. The cabinets were identical and obviously designed to contain a normal human being, standing erect. They were sealed with thick panes of transparent, unbreakable plastic.

Within each cabinet, a nude young man stood in an attitude of dignity and pride. For some reason, which even the Master had been unable to fathom, all of the young men's faces had the same expression—a quiet smile. Destiny was over for them and they were satisfied.

Around each young man there swirled a thin, sparkling nebula. The nebula seemed almost a living thing; iridescent, rainbow-hued.

Beside each young man—and also bathed in the shimmering mist—was an urn. On the upper metal framework of every cabinet was stamped a date.

There were thirty-three cabinets. The Master walked down the long row, pausing occasionally before one of the motionless figures. After he had reached the last cabinet, he stepped back, leaned against an atomic integrator, and looked for a long time at the vista of men and dates. Once more he touched the button and the panels began to rise from the floor, progressively, obliterating the faces with their quiet smiles.

He walked, a shadowy figure, between the great stolid machines. In the short passage that led to the door which separated him from other men, he picked up an atomic torch from a small niche and pointed the beam at an opalescent disk set into the wall.

Instantly, the invisible radiation, matching exactly the radiation of the disk, unlocked the great door. As it moved outward, the Master replaced the torch in its niche, and went outside. Behind him the slab swung back into place. Laboratory I was sealed to ordinary men.

A great weight of unmeasurable fatigue, which he knew so well, settled upon him. But that was tomorrow's problem. He must not think of that. He had not thought about it for hours. Now he realized who was responsible for the relief. Varden. It was he who had suggested that a little billiard practice might freshen him up.

Enmeshed in his thoughts, he was startled to come suddenly upon the robed figure of Everling.

Equally startled by the Master's abrupt appearance, Everling averted his eyes and became deeply interested in a single, nondescript flower which was perched on the end of a long stem.

The flower, the Master observed, was growing out of a crack in the sandstone blocks of the courtyard. Superbly cut, there had remained one little flaw. A wind, a single seed, time—and a flower. Amusing to consider the flaw in perfect craftsmanship. More amusing to watch the man.

"Good afternoon, Dr. Everling."

"Good afternoon, Master." Neither the face looking out from the cowl nor the tone conveyed any emotion except slight surprise.

The Master walked past him without pausing. As he continued across the court he thought, "A little knowledge is a dangerous thing, but too much knowledge is equally dangerous, and makes for doubt of one's fellow man."

CHAPTER SEVEN

THE MASTER'S desk was a mound of documents and reports. He decided on a frontal assault rather than meticulous efficiency. The frontal assault was beginning to produce results when Varden came in.

"Moon Base called again."

The Master did not look up. "Oxygen plant?"

"Of course. They're living up there on the stored supply —which won't last forever."

The Master wrote *More information needed* on a request from the Genetics Committee for a cut in the South American

birth rate, signed a grant of one thousand villars to a young scientist, and looked up.

"That Moon Base oxygen plant was built almost four hundred years ago. We now have far better methods of extracting oxygen from oxidized ore. Write an urgent order to the Council for a requisition to build a modern plant. Send up whatever technicians are necessary to repair the old plant. Dr. Bolton should head the group. Tell him to have the old plant operating in two days—if he needs string and baling wire, I will send it by special magno-ship."

The Master turned back to his desk. As he worked fatigue began to wash over him like an implacable wave. Somehow he could not bring his mind into sharp focus. It ran off on endless tangents. After a moment, he folded his arms on the pile of papers. Was there never any end to paper work? Slowly, his head fell forward drowsily, until it rested on his folded arms.

"Master!"

The Master's head snapped up. He had thought Varden was gone from the room.

"You must call for a donor—"

"It is not yet time!"

"Master, it *is* time!" Varden went out.

As the Master worked, he became conscious of the sound of rain against the windows. He glanced up. Lightning flashed across the Sky of Terra City. This, he thought, would be a great storm.

Wind rattled the windows in their heavy metal frames. Those old fashioned windows were an idiosyncrasy of the Master. For some reason, he had never learned to appreciate windows whose plastic panes slid noiselessly into wall recesses at the touch of a button. To him they symbolized a completely synthetic existence.

He was making a notation to change the location of two Austro-Asia magno-rocket bases, when the wind won a

brief victory in its battle with the windows. A latch gave way and a pane crashed open. The wind cleared the Master's desk with efficiency, blowing the papers in all directions. Behind it came a flood of rain.

The Master's mind commanded his body to dive for the window and close it. But his body obeyed slowly and awkwardly. As he rose, the wind almost toppled him backwards. He stumbled to the window, groping in the rain that blurred his sight. Leaning far out, he fumbled for the metal sash.

As he did so, he glanced downward. Below him the sheer wall fell, a rain-gleaming precipice, to the courtyard a hundred feet below. For an instant the world dimmed and whirled. Then his will drove his eyes back to the corner of the sash.

It was a fight now—his numbed, outstretched fingers a-gainst wind, rain and slippery metal. Twice the wind jerked the sash loose from his grip. At last his fingers found a slightly roughened spot on the metal and held. Slowly he tugged, pulling the pane inward until he could reach the latch and jam it shut.

Swaying on his way back to his chair, he dropped into it heavily. The room suddenly filled with a gray mist. Perhaps, he thought, fog had come in with the rain. Yet fog did not come with rain . . . Perhaps . . .

He slumped over the desk, arms outstretched. Rain water, dripping from his hair and clothes, formed a little pool on the polished wood where he rested his head and he spoke without moving. "Some brandy—quickly."

As Varden poured the drink, he watched the Master slowly sit up and lean back in the chair.

"Window blew open. Storm—very sudden."

Varden handed him the brandy. The Master spilled part of it.

"It will help," Varden said gently. "But you need more than that."

"It is thirty-seven years," Varden continued, "since you asked the Council for a donor."

"When I need one, I will tell you. I am merely a bit tired."

"If this were the first time, I would agree with you. But during the last general conference of the Planning Committee you twice lost the thread of the conversation. Some of your work is months behind schedule. I've been with you daily for a long time—at least by my standard of time—and I think I can judge the point when you cease to be the Master and degenerate into an old man. You know what will happen then."

"Yes, I know."

"Then you must—"

"No, Varden. I refuse to face another young man now."

Varden refilled the Master's glass and handed it to him.

The Master sipped the warming, strengthening liquid and when he spoke, his voice seemed to Varden an echo of the relentless rain beating against the windows.

"You do not understand. Every thirty years for a millennium I have forced myself to face a strong, intelligent young man at the door of Laboratory I. The scene is always the same.

"I stand there and formally tell him what he already knows—that once he walks into that laboratory, he will die. I can say nothing else. Then I ask him if his affairs are in order, and if he has said his goodbyes. Usually, he merely nods. Then I say, 'Or haven't you told anybody that you are the donor? Do you want me to do it for you afterwards?'

"Then he says, 'Forget it. But can I have a smoke and a drink before . . .' He smiles. They always smile, Varden. Why don't they ever do anything but smile!"

Varden was staring at one of the papers which had been blown to the floor. It was a formal letter, and began: *To the office of the Master: The third commission from the Venusian*

Interplanetary Travel Authority wishes to point out that . . .

Without looking up, Varden said, "What is the loss of one young man, compared with the destiny of a planet? Perhaps a solar system?"

The roar of the storm surrounded and compressed the silence of the room. The papers made a great crackling noise as Varden collected them. He placed them on the Master's desk and waited.

At last the Master looked directly at his chief assistant. "Call the Council in session tomorrow. Tell them that I want a new donor. Now, hand me that Moon Base order so I can sign it." He picked up his glass and drained it.

A young World Scientist was tapping out the rhythm of a melody played by the dance orchestra at the Pavilion. Halfway through the song, the musicians stopped abruptly. The curtains were drawn back from the huge telecast screen.

"Special announcement. On request of the Master, the Council has chosen a new donor. The donor is, of course, a World Scientist. The names of all those who were acceptable have been placed in a mechanical selector, and fate has chosen one."

The men and women at the tables reacted only with a dull undertone of startled conversation. To them the news meant everything—and nothing. It meant an enigma greater than life or death, or even the meaning of existence. It was the final enigma of the Master. But it also meant something that did not personally concern them.

"As has been the custom in the past," the announcer's voice was heavy with solemnity, "there will be a pause for a few moments in honor of the man who will give his life for the Master and civilization."

The people were silent as the screen went blank, but from the speaker poured out the opening bars of *The Green*

Hills of Earth. As the planet's hymn blended with the moonlight and shadow of the Pavilion, a young World scientist picked up his glass and finished his drink.

He signalled a waiter and indicated another round. The waiter handed him the check which he signed *Korson*.

When the hymn was over and the orchestra resumed its music, he turned to the man across the table. "I'm sorry that you didn't pass the examinations, Lorg. Perhaps next year."

"So you won't lose your galley slave at the Clinic. I'll never be a World Scientist. Remember, I'm older than you."

"You can always try again. You can have a go at the exam for five alternate years between the ages of twenty-seven and thirty-seven. You've only used one try."

As the waiter poured their drinks the men's eyes wandered about the room. The tables were scattered around the dance floor. A dimmed eterno-light gleamed here and there.

Beyond the Pavilion's cafes, lounges, cool recreation rooms, gardens, and open air dance floors, the largest park in Terra City stretched for miles. Outdoor and indoor swimming pools, playgrounds for children, the great stadium, groves of old olive trees, banks of colorful flowers, amphitheatres for impassioned orations and glens for whispered words; all these were within the huge park.

Two girls walking ahead of their escorts, passed the table at which the young men sat. One of the girls spoke over her shoulder, "Don't forget the party tonight, Korson."

"I'll be there."

Lorg's big head seemed to waver on his long, fragile neck. "How do you do it? I can never take time off. Maybe a few days once or twice a year—unually when I'm sick. You know, I work longer than anyone else at the Clinic."

"There's more than simply a steady grind to becoming a World Scientist," Korson answered.

"Meaning what?"

"Experimentation in any science is something like a sculptor tentatively hacking at a block of stone. Or an artist dabbing at a fresh piece of canvas. Or a musician. Part of it is inspiration. You can't force it to come. There's no use hacking or painting, until the idea is there. Even so, you may throw out the first idea, and the second. But you can't work until you have something to work on."

"I've lots of ideas," Lorg said.

"Sketch them out in notes—and then forget them. While you're busy with one thing, you'll get an answer to something else."

Lorg's tense fingers dug sweaty wrinkles into the table cloth. "I'll do just what you said. I'll do anything. I must pass the exam next time."

The meal was placed before them. Lorg picked idly at the food. "Next time," he said. "I must make it next time."

Korson, shoveling his dinner down lustily, spoke with his mouth full. "There's plenty of time for everything." He swallowed his food and continued, "What you need—"

A hand lightly touched his shoulder.

He turned. A man in the uniform of the Master's Guard was standing behind him.

"You are Korson?"

"Yes."

"I was informed at the Clinic that you could be found here."

A paper with an official seal was held out to him. Breaking the seal, Korson read:

> *Korson, donor for the Master, will*
> *present himself two weeks from*
> *this date at the World Center.*

His mind would not accept the fact. It couldn't happen to me. Not to *me!*

The guard saluted and, turning, began to thread his way past the tables toward the exit. Involuntarily Korson's hand went out in protest, in appeal. "It's too soon. . . ." he whispered, staring at the man's back as he went away.

Korson was on his feet, although he did not realize it. From a long way off he heard a faint little voice piping, "Korson, what is it? It—it can't be—*you*—"

CHAPTER EIGHT

OUTSIDE the Pavilion Korson hailed a jet car, crossed the park, and stepped out at the entrance to Terra City Clinic.

Cool, pungent dampness rose from the wide strip of grass which surrounded the clinic. A delicate scent drifted from the flowers in the two gigantic limestone urns that flanked the entrance. Above the doorway glowed a single eterno-light, around which a large moth was circling. Again and again, the moth beat with futile, disintegrating wings against the globe.

Korson entered the Clinic, walked to his laboratory and opened the door. He was home, now. It was familiar here, safe. The chemical solution he had been filtering was dripping steadily, exactly as he had left it. The drops were falling in the same precise rhythm. Nothing had changed. Nothing had happened.

With meticulous care he put on his white smock. Then he crossed to the scarred laboratory table. On the table was an old pewter mug, battered, with the single word *Pavilion* engraved on it. But there was no beer in the mug, now. It was filled with those tools around which his life revolved: solution thermometers, pipettes, test tubes, indicators.

Slowly, automatically, he seated himself before the neutron microscope. From the rack of stained and mounted cultures, he selected the third from the right and placed it in the microscope. His sure fingers made the primary adjustments, locked them, and began the precise alignment. The image was in position. It was only necessary to focus.

Somehow, he could not sharpen the image. It blurred and faded. He realized that the core of his mind had withdrawn from visual sensation and had concentrated on the purely auditory—the sound of the filtered drops falling into the beaker. One every ten seconds. Hourglass of science. Light and steady was the beat of the drops, while time raced faster and faster.

He turned from the microscope and picked up a letter he had received that morning. It was from his brother, Kenler.

Kor, do you remember the day we spent
together a couple of months ago? We swam
in the river above the dam . . .

Plunging deep into the water. Korson's muscular, wide-shouldered body moved gracefully down to the flat bottom of soft mud. Spires of grass waved gently; a lazy fish passed close to Korson's face, and darted away in fright. Water closed round him, softly touching his eyes and lips.

Coming to the surface, his honey-colored hair plastered wetly against his head, he saw the water moving faster as it neared the rapids. He swam in that direction and soon his powerful shoulders were fighting the flood of white-crested water which poured between narrow banks. The roar was deafening; he could not see past the green and white froth filling his eyes. One leg scraped a sharp rock.

When at last he reached the bank, dragged himself up

and lay panting, his brother, watching him, shook his head. "You'll try that once too often."

Kenler's grave, lean face was calm as always. He looks more like a scientist than I do, thought Korson.

Later, in the cabin over mugs of ale, Korson lay flat on the floor, a long, thin cheroot in the corner of his mouth.

"Funny," said Kenler. "we're so different. I'm happy living the good life—"

"Hermit stuff."

"You in the city with your test tubes. Walking the straight and narrow past of ambition."

"Ambition's path, yes." answered Korson. "But my idea is balance. Plenty of fun and plenty of work. Concentration is the secret. I practiced early. Trained myself to bring one idea into my mind and keep it there for five or ten minutes. Dropped it. Picked up another. That's proper channeling. It's worked."

Kenler sighed, feeling ineffectual beside the brother who was older than himself but whom everyone thought was the younger. "Nothing can distuurb that calm self-sufficiency . . . Sometimes I worry. You and I, since Mother and Father died —we've only got each other. Soon I'll be married. When that happens, you—"

Korson sat up, staring at Kenler. "You have a peculiarly nauseating expression on your face. Did you say you were getting married? That you're madly in love?"

Kenler nodded. "It happened suddenly."

"It always happens suddenly!" Korson said. Then he rose and clapped his brother on the back heartily. "Good luck. Be happy." Going to the stove he began rattling pans, preparatory to cooking the trout they had caught that morning.

Kenler eyed him gravely. "I hope you don't become too sleek and sharp in the city, with every little cog and wheel working perfectly. All made up of nice little sanitary com-

partments, hermetically sealed." His smile was crooked. "You'd be better off for a few bits of earth and bugs to annoy you. . . ."

The chemical solution was still dripping slowly, steadily.

Once more Korson's eyes focused upon the letter lying on the lab table. The little sealed compartments did him no good now. Should he write Kenler and tell him?

A World Scientist who had sworn to guard the property of mankind hurled a battered mug at a neutron microscope worth fifty thousand villars.

Korson was stopped at the gate of the World Center by a guard.

"I do not recognize you, sir. May I be of any assistance?"

"Take me to the Master at once."

"It is impossible. If you will leave your name . . ."

Without answering, Korson reached into the pocket of his carefully pressed tunic and took out the donor's summons. There was a faint smile on his face as he handed it to the guard.

The guard read the first line, and stiffened. Folding the paper he returned it to Korson. "Sorry, sir. Please follow me."

Erect, rather arrogantly, Korson strode behind him into the anteroom.

The guard spoke to the desk clerk and at once the clerk switched on the visaphone. "Varden—urgent."

In the dimness of his great library the Master turned around at the sound of a footstep. "Good afternoon, Varden. Moon Base?"

"Of course. Bolton just asked for you to send up the 'string and baling wire.' I hope you know what that phrase means. I don't."

"I do. Prepare an order."

"There's another little matter. You have a peculiar visitor.

This time he doesn't wear a weird costume. He's just out of place—in time. To be exact, he's seven days out of place. Korson, the donor."

In the cone of light from the single source of illumination above the desk, the Master's mouth twitched nervously and his voice was strained. "Never before has a donor presented himself before the appointed hour!"

He closed the book he had been reading. "Have Korson brought here at once. I'll outline the Moon Base order later."

As Korson stood in the doorway of the library, the Master wondered if it had finally come—the first appeal for life? The appeal even he could not grant. Well, it had to come sometime. He stepped from behind the desk, his blue cape swinging with his movements.

Korson came a few steps into the room. Among the shadows of the library, the figure of the Master was lost. Korson stood waiting, poised and challenging.

A figure emerged from the darkness of a corner. There was the click of a switch and the room was filled with rich, mellow radiance.

"I am sorry. I did not realize how dark it was."

"I am Korson, the donor."

"Obviously. And I, obviously, am the Master. Now will you come a little nearer?"

Korson took two halting steps.

"Much nearer, please. We are not on a duelling ground."

The Master turned to a cabinet and took from it a bottle and two glasses. Slowly he filled the glasses with a rich liqueur, aromatic with strange spices. He extended one to Korson, who took it in silence.

"It is only natural," the Master said, "that you regard me as an enemy. But shall we not drink to the possibility of our becoming friends?"

Korson drank with the Master and said quietly, "I have

no enemies, or friends, now. I have only a destiny— and I'm rotten at histrionics. I am no longer awed by anything, including you."

He turned his back to the Master and dropped into a deep leather chair.

"Why did you come here before your appointed time?"

"Have I embarrassed you?"

"Yes," the Master said simply.

The calm directness bothered Korson a little. He looked at the Master. The eyes bothered him, so he glanced away.

"I want to get this business over with," he said. "This afternoon if possible. At the latest, tonight."

"Your approach is certainly different from all the others. Remember, you have seven days left. If you are a profound young man, you will use them to make peace with your soul."

The authority in this unusual cloaked figure made Korson assert himself. "Aren't you being a trifle dull about this little affair, Master?" He went to the cabinet and poured himself another drink. "I've left my laboratory." For an instant his voice almost got out of control. "It's up to you to find someone to finish my job. I don't say farewells. As for my soul—if I have one—what could I do in seven days?"

The words hung in the air between them, for the Master did not answer.

After a moment Korson said roughly, "I could spend my time polishing my stars."

"That remark, Korson, is unworthy of you."

He felt a wave of shame pass over him such as he had never known before, and the blood came up in his cheeks. Yet he told himself persistently that the Master was only a figurehead, who did not have to do the dying.

"Seven days. It is death, isn't it?"

The Master did not answer.

"Finish the job now!"

"It is out of my hands. The Council sets the hour."

Putting down his glass, Korson wandered about the library. Most of the books on the banks of shelves before him dealt with philosophy. Parchments in long forgotten languages were stored in racks. Tablets which bore strange inscriptions were encased in clear, protective plastic.

Here, and here alone on Earth, were assembled the finest, most profound thoughts of men. This was the ultimate treasure house of human wisdom—and before him stood the man who should be the wisest of men. Perhaps he *could* find an answer in seven days. It was also the way to exact payment from the man for whom he must die.

"Master, you have about you the work of the most brilliant minds of all ages. The greatest teachers and philosophers. You have studied all of them, and weighed their arguments. Many of their discussions deal with death, and what—if anything—comes afterwards. I might learn a great deal even in seven days—with *you* as my instructor!"

Korson saw the blow had found its mark. The face before him became the face of a tired old man, and the voice halting.

"Force me . . . to see you . . . every day?"

"Yes." Korson's face was hard with victory.

"The young are cruel."

"You will have plenty of time to recover."

Silently, the Master turned away for a moment. At last he murmured, "That is true."

As Korson continued, he knew that he was beaten. "You offer me nothing but death. The least you can do is give me the wisdom to meet it as I should."

There was no help for it, the Master realized. For seven days he must accept the torment this young man demanded of him.

"You cannot expect me," he said slowly, "to solve the final riddle in seven days or seven lifetimes. However, you may stay. A room will be assigned to you in my private

quarters." He paused and added quietly, "I ask that you look within your own innermost being and answer one question. Do you honestly believe that I am happy when I meet a donor at the door of Laboratory I?"

CHAPTER NINE

THE FIRST DAY was ebbing. Korson and the Master had been talking during the late afternoon. Now, Korson rose and stood beside the desk.

"If it won't inconvenience you, Master, I would prefer that my status here be that of a protege. It may sound odd and cause some rumors, but I would rather no one knew I was the donor."

"I understand."

"Thanks."

"Our discussion has been most interesting, Korson. I wish we could continue. But that sublimely cursed Moon Base is still in trouble."

"Can I be of any help?" Instantly, Korson realized what he had said.

The Master smiled. "I'm afraid not. I suggest you wander around the gardens and try to be happy, but if you are still determined to solve the final mystery, you might read the passages I have marked in those volumes."

Korson picked up the stack of books."

"The evening meal is at seven-thirty," the Master added. "Will you join us?"

"Of course."

Korson walked through the gardens until he reached a grove of pines that towered like grounded lances in the fading light. Laying the pile of books on the thick pad of

fallen needles, he dropped down on the ground. For a moment he stared through shafts of hazy amber sunlight, upward to the sky with its eternally restless clouds. Then, settling himself comfortably, his back against a tree, he opened a book.

Concentration was difficult. The strangeness of this tiny world dominated his thoughts. That morning, as he had passed through another part of the grounds, he had seen, through the pale mist, the swiftly moving figure of a girl. Her movements had an unearthly quality. Dancing lightly, arms moving like willows in the wind, lithe young body clothed only in an iridescent gossamer robe, she had disappeared behind the coral trumpets of a Xalpan tree.

He pulled his thoughts back and flipped over the pages of another book. Again he tossed it aside, and listened to the sound of birds twittering, calling to each other in soft, excited notes. For a moment he thought that he heard a human voice join the conversation, speaking not in the language of man, but in rhythmic half-tones, resembling Chinese music.

Curious, he stood up and walked in the direction of the sounds. Threading his way among the pines, his footsteps muffled by the needles, he came to a small patio in the center of which was a tiny pool.

Standing beside the pool was a girl, the same girl he had seen that morning. Her back was to Korson. A bird was perched on each of her shoulders, another on her wrist. Korson had taken a few steps toward her when his heel clicked on a stone.

There was a fluttering of wings and the birds were gone. Tarmo whirled around.

"You frightened them away! They come every day to talk to me. They are my only friends here!"

"I'm sorry."

She darted past him, but he caught her arm.

"Do you live here? What's your name?"

Tarmo tried to free herself, but could not. Puzzled, she looked up at him. "You're stronger than the others."

"Am I?"

He released her arm but, not moving, she continued to study his face.

"You're younger, too." Her eyes slid away from his face, sideways, searching the grass. One small foot took a hesitant step, and paused. A few of the birds returned, to hover over her.

He smiled. "Funny child."

"First Varden calls me a female, now you call me a child."

"You're both, aren't you? And beautiful. You've been told that, haven't you?"

What was strange about him, about his voice? Everling had never spoken to her like this, nor Varden, nor even the Master. It must mean something, she thought, but it is something I do not understand. And it is something I do not want to run away from.

Korson came close to her. He slipped his hand beneath her chin, lifting her head. She stiffened, instinctively bracing against his wordless challenge. "Now you're somebody else. I don't like the somebody else."

"You will."

Gently she raised his hand to her lips. Then, deliberately her small teeth clamped hard of his fingers. He jerked his hand away and sucked the fingers.

She went back to the pool, dropped into one of the chairs beside it, and curled her feet under her. Korson stretched out in the grass and lit a cigarette.

"Do you live here?" she asked.

"I'm here on business with the Master."

"You shouldn't have come. You might have to stay inside these walls, like I do."

"Who are you? Why are you here?"

"I'm Tarmo. The Lady Ellora is sick. Everling is curing her. And I must be with Everling. He has always taken care of me."

"He must be a fine man. Your father?"

"No. I don't remember my father—or my mother. . . ."

"Guardian?"

"No. He doesn't guard me."

A mass of purple cloud trapped the last bit of gold from the setting sun and sent a shaft of light into the grove. Tarmo's hair was blue-black as Korson leaned closer to her, his boldness gone, and his tone gentler. "It's the light on your hair . . ." He could not take his eyes from her. "Shining on your hair . . ."

She raised her head suddenly, as if she were listening.

"Yes," she said, but she was not speaking to Korson.

The rustle of a long robe caused Korson to turn as a quiet voice spoke.

"Go to your room, my child. Do not spend so much time dreaming by the pool. Read the lessons I have given you, then dress for dinner."

Cowl and sparkling ruby. Certainly this was a haunted grove, thought Korson, as he studied the powerfully built man.

When Tarmo had gone, Everling looked at Korson steadily. "I understand that no one is allowed here except on special business."

"I *am* on special business."

"Important enough to permit you the freedom of the Master's private gardens?"

"Yes."

Everling's voice carried no trace of anger. It merely stated a fact. "My ward is very charming—and very young. If you have followed her here—"

Korson's patience ran out. "I don't know who the hell *you* are with your head hidden inside that damn sack, but

I will not be called a liar—even in fancy words. I'm here because *I am the donor!*"

Twilight, silence, a haunted grove. Everling's hoarse tones seemed loud.

"Please forget what I've said. I am Dr. Everling. At present I am treating the Master's wife."

"I'm Korson.".

The eyes deep within the shadow of the cowl caught the glint of silver on the young man's shoulder. "World Scientist?"

Korson nodded.

"Sorrow is part of life, but the giving of a life before it is fully consummated is more than sorrowful. It is tragedy, and therefore noble."

The man was harmless, but boring, Korson thought. He was searching for an easy method of breaking off the conversation, when Everling continued:

"This particular tragedy is part of our governmental system. We have accepted it as a lesser evil to others we have known. Curious. Similar to primitive tribes who flung victims over a cliff to propitiate their gods . . . or burned human sacrifices alive on an altar. I understand that all World Scientists know exactly the role the donor must play?"

"They don't."

"Then, all you know is that you are the donor? That your friends and family will never see you again? That no one has any idea what will become of your body, even of your ashes?"

"Do you specialize in psychiatry, Doctor? If you do, let me say— for whatever the data may be worth—that my mind is at peace. I'll admit I was afraid once, but the time for that is past."

"Yes, it is past. Still, it is natural for me, as a physician, to wonder whether the Master is ever troubled by the memory of all the brave young men who have died for him. What,

indeed, passes through his mind as he goes about his work in Laboratory I?"

Impatiently, Korson gathered up his books. "I'm sorry I told you I was the donor. The Master has been kind enough to allow me to live here during my last few days. I don't know whether he'll appreciate anyone realizing who I am."

Musing, seeming to not look at the young man but to be gazing into the future, or the past, Everling answered slowly, "It is strange that you should say that. Viewed in a certain light, your position here is the same as that of Tarmo and myself."

"All that matters to me, is that no one besides yourself knows the truth—particularly that funny kid who is your ward."

"Shall we all consider ourselves part of the Master's family?"

"That's as good a way of putting it as any." Korson nodded and walked away through the evening dusk.

CHAPTER TEN

THE MASTER opened the door of a small room in a corner of Laboratory I. In that tiny area, which seemed lost in the great laboratory, were the apparatus and files he used in what was to him his most important work—the creation of a machine through which he could communicate with the dead.

He was firmly convinced that at death human beings simply entered a new type of existence which was, at first, similar to life on earth. He conceived of this new life as infinitely expanding. It was vaster and more interesting than the one type of life he had known. He also believed that

the dead sometimes talked to the living; that they used the living as their method of communication.

Statesmen, rulers, prophets and teachers had used such a means of communication between existences. But for the Master it was impossible. Should he associate himself, even remotely, with anything that might appear unusual or religious, whispers would become more powerful than the long ago wars, and soon there would be no Master.

The only solution for him was to devise a machine through which he could talk with the dead in the lonely isolation of Laboratory I. He had constructed device after device, and always the result had been the same—failure. Hopelessness had dropped a shroud over the whole project. It had been a long time since he had entered the little room.

Ellora was dying. Even if this strange Everling had actually conquered the sickness, she would die eventually. Then she would be *there* and he would be *here*. Trapped. The only link between them would be memory—unless he could devise a machine.

It was vital, now. He must try again.

His last attempt had been an effort to modulate an isolated segment of visual radiation, a beam of lavender light. He concentrated on his notes and diagrams, seeking desperately for some clue.

The visaphone in the laboratory had a one-way visual circuit. There must be no chance of the outside world glimpsing the laboratory's interior. The Master kept the sound circuit turned off, except when he wished to speak to someone. Nothing and no one from outside could reach him unless he desired it.

It was this isolation and timelessness of Laboratory I that caused the Master so often to forget the routines which dominated the world outside. Now, when he glanced up to rest his eyes, he was startled to see that the time indicator showed it was long past the hour of the evening meal.

He rose, switching off the small, intense working light. Tomorrow he might solve the final problem. Or the day after. Or any day. Eventually he must succeed.

Suddenly, the stark isolation of the room closed in on him. She might die while he was here. Neither weird machines, which did not work, nor philosophy could save him. He must remember to tell her. He must.

He closed the door of the little room and left Laboratory I.

Finishing the last amber drops in his glass of Vintage 3085 —a good year for the white grapes—the Master glanced down the long table. For days he had been dining alone or with Korson. Tonight he wanted to talk to Everling, so he had invited him and Tarmo. But where was Varden? Just as the Master was about to make inquiries, his chief assistant came in, apologizing.

"Those damn lessons ran overtime. And Moon Base—"

"Varden," the Master said, "if you use that excuse again . . . What's this about lessons?" He turned to Everling. "Varden is our social butterfly."

"Butterfly, hell. This is hard work. Dancing lessons."

In answer to the Master's stare of incredulity, Varden continued doggedly. "I don't intend to get out of touch with everything. It's good exercise, too.

Varden sat down and turned to Korson. "I understand that you are here to study with the Master."

Korson nodded.

The Master added, "My first protege. What are the rules for a patron?"

"The first rule is to break rules," Everling said lightly.

The Master looked at him. "You should know."

Everling offered a dish of the crisp, paper-thin rolls to Korson. As he was about to take one, Tarmo reached for the plate.

Shoving it under her nose, Korson said, "Try them. They're better than human fingers."

"You're still angry," Tarmo said as she filled her mouth.

Korson, watching the unlovely gesture, wondered why it seemed so delightful to him. There was magic in this primitive child—at least, for the moment. "Do you like dolls, my dear? Or do you love only wild things like your birds?"

Her green eyes narrowed. "I think *you* are the one to play with dolls, to fondle and caress them. I think you put them back on a shelf and forget them. Unless you are careless and break one. Then you run away and hide."

What was this girl in the saffron robe? Was she child or woman? Or perhaps a sort of human chameleon who changed personality with her moods? Baffled, Korson turned his attention to the conversation between the other men.

"Those who feel they must roam the world for experience and understanding are deluded," Everling was saying. "For, by intensive observation, a man whose boundaries are the four walls of a small area can travel twice as far and learn infinitely more."

"You in your tower," Varden said. "And the Master in World Center."

The Master smiled. "The Doctor's statement is perhaps an over-simplification. My thought is that if a man could come to know a single person completely, he would have encompassed a good part of the wisdom of the world."

"Human vivisection—of the heart and brain," Varden broke in. "A very nasty proposal."

"A psychic intrusion, I grant you," the Master laughed.

The great carved ruby glowed on Everling's hand as he reached for his wine. "And yet a clear view of the human spirit in its entirety would be the most illuminating, exciting experience in the world!"

The Master signaled a servant to refill the wine glasses. Then he glanced at Everling. "One would need to make a

chart of the soul," he said. "Like an unknown sea, full of depths and currents. Swarming with marine life."

"The two of you," Varden interrupted, "are inventing a lot of trouble. What if you soul scavengers chose the wrong person?"

The Master decided it was time to come to the point. "Dr. Everling, let us discuss this another time. I want to know how the Lady Ellora is progressing?"

"She is improving."

."I intend to have a talk with her tonight. I hope there *is* improvement. If not, I shall call in other physicians for consultation tomorrow."

A sudden sharp sound attracted the Master's attention. At the opposite end of the table a servant was arranging the coffee service meticulously in front of the one chair that directly faced him. The Master's voice was curt. "You know the Lady Ellora does not dine with us."

She stood in the doorway, tall lithe, radiant. Her low-cut robe was almost the shade of lavendar that he had struggled with in the little room in the laboratory. Around her throat was a piece of jewelry he had never seen before; a collar of matched sapphires from which hung a single diamond star that nestled between the curves of her breasts. The star patterned after the insignia of the World Scientists.

She bowed, very slightly; a gesture of double meaning. It seemed intended for the entire group but was meant only for the man at the head of the table. As she came forward, her steps gliding smoothly over the polished floor, she said, "Good evening." And, to him alone, "I am sorry Master, that I am late."

Without sitting down, she took a cup and began to pour the coffee. "Will you have brandy in your coffee?" Raising her eyes she looked directly at him.

Suddenly, the realization of one small fact stopped the flood of joy that was rising within him. The collar. She had made

a gallant gesture, but the collar remained, an obvious concealment of the blue mark. Hopelessness clutched at him.

She did not wait for him to reply. Pouring brandy into the cup, she handed it to a servant. Then she turned to Tarmo.

"I've neglected you since you arrived." The rich, vibrant voice flowed like a limpid stream talking in the sunlight. "Let me make up for it, my dear." Her hands went swiftly to her throat. The impish smile he knew so well lurked in the corners of her lips. With a quick movement, she unfastened the collar and tossed the jewels, a cascade of gleaming loveliness, to Tarmo.

The throat was bare now, smooth, unmarked. No blue stigma of the sickness showed on the velvet skin.

As the Master rose to his feet, the scene before him was out of focus and blurred—except for one face.

After dinner, Korson suggested a walk to Tarmo. She led the way, across wide lawns, through formal gardens, past the grove of pines, to a glen where a small stream gurgled and splashed.

Sinking to her knees in the moss she looked into the dark, moving water. "Do you like it here?" she asked. "I found this place the day after they put me behind these walls."

"It's beautiful."

"You're not angry anymore?"

"I never was," he laughed.

"And you believe now that Everling will cure Lady Ellora?"

"Yes."

She dipped her hand into the water. Moonlight caught the ripples as they raced over her fingers. Korson lay down beside her.

"Do you know," she said, "why I had to find this place?"

"Do you *have* to find any place?"

"You must search for the place you want. This was most like it. So I found it."

"Where do you want to be?"

"Back in Cheenwa. In the old tower."

"Tarmo," he said, "listen to me. You are no longer a child. You must learn to live with other people and not shut yourself away in a desolate country. Everling knows that. You can't go back—you can only go forward."

"I know where I want to be!"

He sat up, took her slender shoulders between his hands, giving her a gentle shake. "Wake up, Tarmo! You must make a place for yourself in the everyday world. Find friends. You can't live in isolation forever."

"There is Everling."

"He won't be with you always."

Wide, clear eyes stared up at him, puzzling, musing.

Korson stood up. "Let's go back. I have a great deal to learn—and very little time."

How tall he is, she thought. How strong. His skin is smooth in the moonlight and he moves like a big animal, powerfully, silently.

Returning through the magic of early night, Tarmo stayed close at his side. Sometimes their shoulders brushed. Once she held his hand lightly. The touch of him is good, she thought, and he is my friend. But tonight he will go into the library and I will not see him again until tomorrow.

It was late when the Master entered the Lady Ellora's bedroom. Sitting on the edge of the lounge, he took her in his arms, his eyes searching her throat for the slightest sign of the blue mark. There was none.

"Scientists—myself particularly—are not allowed to believe in miracles. But if this is a miracle, of what importance is science?"

"Don't thank miracles," she laughed. "Thank Dr. Everling."

"Tomorrow he will be duly honored."

He pulled up a chair near the lounge. "Dearest, please listen carefully. I have long been disturbed by the thought that you might want to reach me in Laboratory I, and be unable to do so."

"Don't be silly. Leave the sound circuit turned on."

"It has been my custom to turn it off, except when I want two-way communication with someone outside the laboratory. Until I met you, I could conceive of nothing urgent enough. . . ."

The devil of her half smile found its way into her voice. "Now that you've learned better, leave the switch turned on."

"It is an old habit. I might forget."

"Not *you*."

"I've forgotten many things."

"Surely the incredible Master can write. Put a note on the switch."

"I might not see it," he said impatiently. "Besides, the circuit might be broken, the power might fail. Such things happened before. Three times in—"

"A thousand years," she smiled.

There was no answering lightness in his voice. He was giving an order. "I shall tell you the combination which opens the door of Laboratory I. Memorize it. If you ever need me, and cannot reach me, give the combination to Varden—or even one of the guards."

She could not believe she had heard him correctly. "You've never given the combination to any one else!"

"Nor did I expect to. As you know, I change it every week." He hesitated. "I have thought the matter over carefully. No harm can come of this act. I will give you the combination now."

He made her repeat it after him many times over. At last he relaxed, satisfied that she knew it.

She said softly as she kissed him, "Don't you understand that the tragedies of life are not its happenings, but its fears?"

When the Master left the blue bedroom and descended the curving staircase, his mind was quieter than it had been for a long time.

He opened the door of his study, and tobacco smoke billowed out into the corridor. From the amount of smoke and the half empty wine bottle on the table beside his chair, it was obvious that Varden had prepared himself for a long wait.

"This grape grease is fairly decent." Varden held up the bottle. "How is she?"

"She was sleeping when I left," the Master said, pouring himself a glass of wine. "It has been months since I have seen her doze off so naturally."

"She was beautiful tonight." Varden stared at a plume of smoke which spiraled upward from the end of his cigar. "Now what?"

"Tomorrow I will make a world-wide, special telecast from the tower. I shall announce that Dr. Everling has developed a cure for the sickness."

Varden watched his smoke phantom disintegrate. When the last wisp had vanished, he said, "Master, there is reason now to hope—but isn't it, perhaps, too soon for such an announcement? *I* can take chances and make mistakes. You can't."

The thin stem of the Master's wine glass gleamed as he turned it between his fingers and smiled. "You sometimes play the ancient game of poker, which seems immune to time. There is a phrase connected with it, 'calling a bluff'.

If Dr. Everling is anything less than an honest man, we shall soon know it."

Yes, Varden thought, he would always be the Master.

CHAPTER ELEVEN

THE MASTER flicked on the Center intercom-visaphone in his study. "Dr. Everling, please."

A moment later Everling's face appeared on the screen.

"Yes, Master."

"Doctor, your brilliant success in curing the Lady Ellora seems proof of your claim to have conquered the disease which baffles orthodox science. Therefore, I have arranged for a special world-wide telecast in which I will announce your discovery. You will receive an award of honor."

"But, Master—"

"Please, do not interrupt. The Council will issue you a grant of one hundred and fifty thousand villars annually for life. You will be given funds for research and the training of other physicians in your methods. However, I must request that you make a telerecord of your methods, and of the training you underwent. Also, a translation and photorecord of the ancient document you discovered."

"Master, I—"

"Come to the telecast tower in ten minutes."

The visaphone screen went blank, but Everling remained motionless, staring into it. His hands reached for the switch, then dropped to his side. Slowly he raised his cowl over his head, the green cloth framing his dark, burning eyes.

Adjusting the folds of his robe, he paced slowly across the exquisitely parqueted floor. When the time indicator on the wall showed that five minutes had passed, he paused before

the long mirror to study his image. Straightening his shoulders, his chin high, he left the room.

When he reached the arched entrance to the building, he glanced at the telecast tower, a gleaming needle pointing to the clouds. Between him and the tower was a paved court. He started to run.

The rising wind whipped his robe and leaves scuffled across the stones.

The lives of the inhabitants of the third planet from the sun stopped; the tools, the jests, the scheming, were laid aside. The thoughts of a race were focused on a spire against the sky and the words which came from it:

"This is a special world-wide telecast from the Center. The Master will announce the discovery of a cure for the sickness . . . This is a special . . ."

In markets, in crowded rooms and lonely places, in shops and laboratories, beside immense machines and among the splendor of tropical flowers, men and women silently watched telecast screens. The horror of the sickness had come from somewhere to Earth. But between men and women and horror stood the Master. As was to be expected, he had found a way to protect them.

Lady Ellora, Varden and Korson sat before the screen in the blue bedroom. Instinctively they had met there—by one of those unspoken understandings which sometimes govern life. Ellora had not been surprised when Korson arrived. And if Varden had not come to her then, the ties which hold friends together would have been only cobwebs.

Everling was breathing hard as he crossed the marble bridge, and jerked open the door to the telecast room.

"Master!"

The tall figure in the blue cape turned abruptly. "Yes?"

"I must speak to you alone. At once."

"This telecast is of greatest importance."

"What I have to say is more important."

This was the thing he had feared, thought the Master. Yet he must face it out to the end. He signaled the telecast engineer to hold the broadcast, and went outside with Everling. As they stood on the bridge, the wind took the Master's cape, spreading it like a great wing, and snatched the cowl from Everling's head.

The Master shouted above the vortex of roaring air, "Be quick!"

"Master!" There was desperate urgency in the luminous eyes. "You have solved unbelievable problems. You have saved a world. But you cannot cure the sickness. I can—if I have sufficient time to finish my work here. A bargain, Master! Your secret of rejuvenation for my secret of the cure!"

Clipped, harsh, came the answer.

"You are a fool if you think I would consider such a demand!"

"I am not asking for eternal life. But I must have another thirty years in order to serve the people of the world as you serve them."

As the Master started back across the bridge, Everling caught the edge of his wind-swept cloak.

"Your duty is to humanity. And I am part of that duty. Neither of us can be spared." Everling spoke through dry, cracked lips. "Grant me this!"

"No."

"Then I appeal to you, not as the Master—but as a man. The Lady Ellora is not yet out of danger. I shall be forced to stop the treatments. . . ."

High on the bridge, screaming wind swallowed the last words, yet they were known, blazoned between them like a challenge.

"You may think that I have used an ugly weapon," said Everling. But you have left me no choice. With the method of healing in my hands, I cannot stand idly by and lose my last chance of saving men and women."

Uncertainty and blind rage obliterated the Master's reason. He saw below the waist-high balustrade, a drop of seven hundred feet. His eyes traveled from the chasm to Everling and he started forward, powerful hands spread.

"You will not do it."

The Master knew he could not. He was beaten. Ellora must have a chance. "Part of your duty to humanity. . . ." Was he bound to the figure opposite him, unable to go forward without him? Had they been catapulted together in this particular moment in time for a particular purpose? He was convinced there was nothing to do but think it out, play for time.

"I shall cancel the telecast."

People went back to their daily business. Some wondered a little, shrugged, and added another incident to the mystery of the Master. In hospitals, white faces turned wearily away from now blank telecast screens. Doctors and nurses tried, with hollow, professional inanities, to comfort those with the blue mark.

In the bedroom of the Master's Lady, Varden looked at Korson. "How could he!"

Korson felt suddenly awkward. Forcing a smile, he shrugged. "Some change of plan."

"But this was so important! I can't understand—" Varden broke off, "or can I?"

"Don't worry, either of you," Ellora said quietly. "I know the Master better than you. He has his reasons. Dr. Everling has given the world hope. He is a wonderful person."

"Maybe you're right," Varden said, "but I can't get to whatever's inside that green robe."

"You don't like him? Why not?"

"I don't know. Come on, Korson, let's get out and give her a chance to rest."

A few minutes after they had gone, there was a light knock on the door. When Ellora opened it, she found Tarmo.

"Lady Ellora, I—I wanted to talk to someone. Could I—"

"Come in, my dear." Lady Ellora took the girl by the hand and led her into the room, shutting the door behind them. Sitting on the lounge, she pulled Tarmo down beside her. "I'm afraid it's rather lonely for you here. We must find some young girls for you to meet."

Tarmo was startled, murmuring doubtfully, "I wouldn't know what to say to them."

"Nonsense. You can go to the park. Have a picnic, play some games together. There are a dozen games to learn."

Tarmo's hands, hidden beneath the folds of her robe, twisted nervously. "Is the park far?"

"No."

"Because he doesn't like me to go far from him."

"He?"

"Everling."

"When he understands that you will be quite safe, he will agree." A life such as Everling's would not be easy, she thought. Being father, mother and playmate to a young girl was certainly not simple. No wonder Everling was overly cautious.

The glitter of jewels on the dressing table caught Tarmo's eye and she went to look at the sparkling ornaments, sniffing the faint scents that rose from flasks of perfume and boxes of powder.

"Do you swim in the pool?" asked Ellora.

"May I?" she asked eagerly.

"Whenever you wish. You will need a swimming costume. I'll have one sent to you."

"You are very kind, Lady Ellora." A filmy handkerchief dangled from Tarmo's fingers, on it was embroidered the likeness of a flamingo in brilliant colors. "Do you love birds and animals?"

"Yes."

"The birds here are wonderful. I know them all."

"I'm glad to hear that. But you must make human friends."

"My Lady, I think I have."

"Yes?"

"Korson."

Lady Ellora's arm went round Tarmo's shoulders. "Of course, he's your friend. But you are dear to all of us, and we don't want to lose you."

There was a curious, veiled look about the girl. "Lost . . . Sometimes I have felt I was lost. But when I began to feel it, I sent my thoughts a different way."

Does she merely express herself in a fantastic manner, or is there another reason, wondered Lady Ellora. "Surely you have been lonely? Perhaps unhappy?"

"Never. I have been trained so that I do not admit such sensations. It is sickness of the mind which causes these feelings. And I am very healthy." Moving away from the protecting arm, she studied a mosaic set into the wall with interest. After a moment she said in a low tone, "Did the Master tell you why he stopped the telecast?"

"No. Why don't you ask Dr. Everling?"

"He—he doesn't talk to me as he used to. The Master is a wonderful person, but Everling—"

"I understand. A young woman usually believes her father is the most wonderful man—until she falls in love."

"What is that?"

"I cannot tell you. But you will find out."

"I love the trees and the wind."

"That's one kind. Love is the most abused word in our language. It means a hundred things—everything and nothing. You love an animal or a dear friend. Or one man. But it is still the same word."

"There ought to be more words."

"You are right." Lady Ellora stood up. "You must go now, my dear. I shall see you at dinner."

CHAPTER TWELVE

LONG GOLDEN arms of late afternoon sunlight probed Terra City. They slanted across the shoulders of a tall man standing beside a pool. The man noticed how the sunlight painted the still water with brilliant red and orange reflections from the clouds overhead.

A servant came noiselessly into the patio and switched on a small telenews screen recessed into the wall. Dimly, as from very far off, the voice of the announcer reached the Master's mind.

"Union of North Europe reports more than 1500 deaths resulting from the sickness. Trans-Northland reports . . ."

He went to the set and turned it off. Returning to the pool, he sat on a weather scarred sandstone bench and covered his eyes with his hands. He did not realize Everling had approached until he heard his voice.

"Good afternoon, Master. Have you reached a decision?" The cowl was thrown back and his eyes were as expressionless as two holes bored straight into eternal darkness.

"The secret of everlasting life is not mine to give. It belongs to the world."

"Then why not give it to the world?"

"It is the one discovery that men must not know."

"Why, Master?"

"We are not discussing that point."

"But it *is* a point."

The master nodded.

"You have seen proof," Everling continued, "that my work is the only known solution to the horror of this disease. Certainly it is reasonable to allow me another thirty years to complete what I have begun?"

"Obviously, Dr. Everling, the decision involved is tremendous. The secret has been guarded as nothing else on this earth. If misused, it could turn whole planets into gigantic slaughterhouses."

"I do not understand."

"Of course not."

"The secret will be safe with me."

The Master rose to his feet. "Why do you want it?"

For a moment Everling appeared to be plunged in uneasy thoughts and did not answer.

"Perhaps," The Master continued. "you believe the Council knows the secret. They do not. I alone know it."

Everling moved a little, restlessly, seeming uncertain. "Master, I have given my life for science and medicine. It is true that I am not a World Scientist. But are two silver stars the measure of a man's genius? Is the organization of World Scientists designed to rule—or to rule out what they do not understand?"

"If to be a World Scientist is all you desire, I can arrange for a special order."

"That will neither give me back the years I have sacrificed, nor time to finish my work."

"I have offered you rewards and honors but you refused them."

There was deep, passion in Everling's voice. "It is justice I want!"

"I have searched for it longer than you."

"Your pardon, Master." He was calm, now. "Ultimate justice is something that I—and probably even you—can never understand. Let us rather say that, although I have not received human justice, I desire to serve humanity. Only with another thirty years can I accomplish this."

The Master, his body sagging a little, his hands trembling like those of an old man, forced his answer through stiff lips. "I need time to think. Wait. . . ."

Everling seemed to be observing something of very great importance in the depths of the little pool.

"The Lady Ellora will be waiting, too. . . ."

Without speaking, the Master left him, walking across the patio, past banks of fragrant roses which were beginning to glisten with the evening dew. He entered the low, domed corridor. Here his footsteps took on an eerie likeness to reverberating voices.

Over and over they repeated, "You are the Master. You will have other wives. The secret is not yours to give. Yet, Everling may be right. . . ."

Hollowly, the footsteps seemed to linger behind him, wisps of sound that were trapped and doomed to whisper endlessly.

A little way down the corridor he met Varden, who was carrying a chess board and a box of men.

"Did you go to bed last night?" Varden asked.

"No."

"I thought so. How about some chess?"

The Master shook his head, the pathetic ghost of a smile crossing his face. "You might beat me. If you want to play, Dr. Everling is in the patio. He told me he understood the game."

Varden lingered, his mind a turmoil of questions, his eyes on the face of the man who was both his friend and the Master. That he carried a heavy burden was obvious, and Varden wished to share it. But, as he started to speak, the Master, anticipating his words, turned from him and, with

a wave of his hand that meant dismissal, went on his way.

Tiny eterno-lights, automatically turned on, gleamed here and there among the trees. Everling and Korson were engaged in a conversation which, Varden realized at once, was about to expire.

Placing the box of chessmen on the table, Varden opened it. Korson disclaimed any knowledge of the game, but Everling accepted the challenge with obvious pleasure.

"Most interesting and excellent mental discipline."

Taking a black and white pawn from the box, Varden shook them in cupped hands behind his back, and extended two closed fists. Everling tapped the left. It was the black pawn.

For an instant Varden considered what opening he should use. There was no use trying any of those weird openings the Master was always springing on him. He didn't understand them, and doubted if the Master did. Use something simple—why not queen's gambit?

To his surprise, Everling accepted the gambit. Varden played slowly, blocking every positional advantage gained from the original pawn sacrifice. But somehow Everling developed a remarkably strong position. Everling sat back and smiled.

"You play well."

"I keep in practice, playing with the Master." Varden studied the board, wishing he had castled earlier.

Everling increased the pressure. His handling of the diagonals and his bishops—which he had refused to exchange— was deft. Varden struggled out of one trouble into another. Moving his king-knight's pawn, Everling said, "Check, discovered."

Korson, who had been wandering around the patio, said, "The Master must be a difficult man to beat."

"The Master plays the game to win," said Everling. "That is the only way to play any game."

Suddenly Varden saw it. The last play had been only a nuisance check. There was nothing behind it. One move to escape check, and he would be free to force a bishop exchange. Next the double check with knight and queen—and it was over.

He moved out of check. Everling looked at the board a long time. The stylized wooden pieces reflected the soft glow of the lights. Finally Everling made an ineffectual rook move. He glanced up at Korson. "One who wants to win above all else will win."

Varden forced the bishop exchange and they played in silence for several moves. Then Varden completed his plan by a move which made the passing of a pawn inevitable.

Everling studied his position, smiled, picked up his king, and handed it to Varden. The chief assistant was surprised at the traditional gesture of resignation.

"You have proven my point," Everling said. "My attention wandered—and I lost."

They were replacing the men in the box when Tarmo ran out on the patio, wearing a bathing suit.

"Come for a swim, Korson."

"Good idea." He got up. "Water therapy is the only treatment after being exposed to chess."

Tarmo was already on her way, calling, "Come, Korson!"

Varden watched Tarmo as she ran. Suddenly he felt Everling's eyes upon him. "Your ward is a lovely child," he said.

"She is."

"Or should I say a beautiful young woman?"

Everling did not answer. Now he was staring after Tarmo.

Refreshed by the swim, Korson dressed for dinner and entered the library. He found it empty except for a beau-

tiful and unusual woman. Although he had seen only pictures of them, he was sure she was a Venusian. She had ripe-olive skin coloring, three-fingered hands, and slate-gray eyes. Around her neck was the traditional high, rose velvet collar which concealed her vestigial gill-slits.

Seeing him, she stood up. She was tall for a Venusian. "I greet you, sir."

Her pronounciation was remarkably clear. Only the soft, high-pitched syllables remained of the lisping Venusian speech.

Korson bowed. "You speak our language well."

"Learn, I must. I am secretary to the envoy of Venus. He talks with the Master." Her head turned slightly, toward the closed door of the study.

Sinking again into the deep-cushioned chair, she leaned back languidly, her golden robe accentuating the delicate contours of her body. Korson realized why Venusians were characterized as exquisite.

For a moment, he considered the standard archaeological puzzle as to whether the Venusians had once been Earth dwellers who migrated after one of that planet's periodic cataclysms. It would explain the mythology which inevitably associated Venus with the goddess of love. But the Venusian's gill slits, indicating recent amphibious existence, did not accord with the Earth-life theory. After all, the surface of Venus was eighty-seven and eight tenths percent water.

She smiled with the gracious courtesy of a lady welcoming a guest into her home.

The strange, exotic quality of her entranced him and he came close, his gaze challenging, direct. "You're very bold, Earthman."

"Is boldness unrewarded on your planet?"

"Wisdom rewards."

"I do not understand." His eyes continued to travel over her. "How old are you?"

"Forty-nine Venus years." She smiled at his surprise. "That would be thirty Earth years."

He realized that she was looking over his shoulder. Tarmo's footsteps on the deep floor-covering had been unheard by him, but the Venusian's acute ears had caught them.

She bowed her head in greeting. "I am Venusian. In your words, my name is Zaline."

"I am Tarmo." She was edging back toward the door.

"Stay, Earthgirl." Zaline went to Tarmo, took her arm and, folds of the robe Tarmo wore, she asked, "Why do you not wear finer robe?"

"Everling chose this for me."

"Oh Earth!" Zaline laughed. Slipping her hand into Tarmo's, she pressed it gently. "To make yourself adored, choose for yourself. Jewels, flowers, robes. *My* purpose in life is to attract. That is why I exist."

Tarmo flashed a quick glance at Korson. "I will see you at dinner." She ran out of the room calling, "Goodby, Zaline!"

He watched her go, and looked back at Zaline. "You have taught her something, I think. Perhaps it will make her happy. I'd like to do something for you. Entertain you."

"Tomorrow show me Terra City."

"You've been here before."

"Some of city I see. Gay parts. Not real parts. Meet me outside old rocket junk yard. At the sunset."

The door to the Master's study swung open and the Venusian envoy entered, his face deeply lined, his eyes dark circled. There was an edging of sweat around the conventional high collar.

Zaline made the introduction. "Ambassador Imptoli, this is Korson."

"I greet you. "The Venusian nodded and sat down.

"Good evening, your exellency. I have always wanted to visit your planet. I have often read about it. But I have seen no record of your having anyone similar to the Master."

"Never is need for Master. To make happy our lives we use machines. *They* do not use us. We fight not among ourselves."

"Do you believe the Master is the only one in the universe who does not die?"

"You are a World Scientist. Belief is for children. Facts are for men. I possess no factual evidence that there is one besides the Master who never dies." The Venusian rested his head against the back of the chair. "I have weakness," he murmured. He unfastened the high collar.

Korson gasped as he stared at the brown throat. Between the gill-slits was the mark of the sickness.

Imptoli looked up and followed Korson's eyes. "Yes," he said, "from Earth comes strange gifts. Yet we blame you not. All planets are daughters of the sun. Their fate the same."

Unnoticed, the Master had entered the room. "There is hope, Imptoli," he said. For an instant he thought he should say more. Accept Everling's bargain, now that the scourge had spread to other planets. Why hesitate? Yet, he did.

CHAPTER THIRTEEN

VARDEN maneuvered his way through the crowds in the street. In two hours it would be Carnival night and the pageantry of the world's history would be relived at the Pavilion. With every citizen in costume, the city would assume the appearance of a gigantic stage, and its population, actors.

At the moment, however, Varden's mind was not concerned with the Carnival. He was wondering why the Master continued to withdraw from all his normal associations. Grave and silent, he wandered about his museum or isolated

himself in Laboratory I. Confiding neither in Varden nor the Lady Ellora, he made evasive answers when cautiously questioned. Often Varden found him alone in his big chair, with Flim's great head resting on his knee.

Even on this Carnival day, the Master had spoken only once to Varden, and that had been a brief visaphone message which had sent the chief assistant on his present errand.

Working his way around a man in a sixteenth century French costume who was arguing with a woman dressed as a twenty-seventh century Izonian, Varden opened the door of the Ronding Biological Institute.

Although he well knew that Ronding had never been noted for the orderliness of his laboratory or the length of his temper, Varden was unprepared for the madhouse which he entered. Beakers, pipettes, carboys, spirals of tubing were scattered about the long tables as if flung by the hand of some fretful giant. His feet crunched on fragments of broken test tubes.

Ronding, his back to Varden, faced a little group of technicians. Between bursts of profanity, he was snarling something about an experiment.

"You goddamned idiots should be unloading cargo on Mars. Biologists—hell! You waste my time with the results of this experiment. Why? Because it happened to *be* an experiment. What do I care about it if it doesn't prove anything?"

Ronding paused to suck in a new supply of atmosphere, and one of the technicians said, "That's the way science progresses. You make an experiment and report your data. Then, science—"

"Science. It's a word, nothing else!" Ronding hurled another test tube into the far corner of the laboratory where its fragments joined half a dozen others. "We are not concerned with abstract science. We are fighting the sickness."

Now get back to work and use your heads for a change.

They straggled away and began to clean up the shambles on the tables.

Varden moved closer, grinning broadly. "Trouble?"

Ronding spun around. "Hell's fires—oh, Varden. Well, I've plenty of trouble without you."

"Won't you ever learn that it takes time to make a biologist?"

Ronding stared at the ceiling in despair and disgust. "How did you ever get to be chief assistant? You're worse than those morons over there"—he jerked his head in the directions of the lab technicians—"who claim to be scientists. What the hell are you bothering me for, anyway?"

"The Master asked me to find out whether there is anything you need."

Leaning against a table, he rubbed his eyes with his hands. "There is. But you can't give it to me. Nor can the Master."

"He has instructed the Council to give you what you ask."

Concealing hands dropped from the man's eyes, and Varden noticed they were red-rimmed and very tired.

"Not what I need."

"What is that?"

"I need," said Ronding, "human beings who have just contracted the sickness."

"Haven't you called for volunteers?"

"Of course. They came for a while. But after the Master called off the special telecast, they lost hope and quit."

"You must have already collected sufficient specimens?"

"I need cases of the disease in its early stages. You know how suddenly the mark appears—often on awakening in the morning. Or in the middle of a day's work. Sometimes there is only half an hour between the appearance of the first faint signs and the mark's complete development."

"I would have thought," Varden said, "that the first in-

dication of the disease would cause people to come to you."

"When people get the sickness they try to conceal it—even from themselves. The handful who have come here were nearly dead."

"We can't force anyone to come. The law cannot be broken, even by the Council."

"I know." Ronding extricated two crumpled cigars and shoved one at Varden.

Varden took it and lit his and Ronding's.

"Why did the Master call off that telecast?"

"I haven't the slightest idea." Varden sucked on the cigar and coughed.

"There's something odd about . . ." Ronding's voice died slowly and, as it did so, his eyes became alive—first incredulously, then with expanding realization, and finally with a bright and sparkling certainty.

On the floor before him was a broken beaker. The half sphere of glass had become a mirror which reflected the concentrated image of a man. The man in the reflection was squat and deformed, his body fading away into a vague blob, his head distorted upward into a fantastically elongated face.

The strange trickery of the light and the curvature of the glass had brought the man's throat into exact focus. There, sharp and clear, was the blue mark of the sickness.

Ronding's steady fingers touched his throat and, as he did so, a hand entered the sharply focused area on the broken beaker and the fingers pointed to the blue mark.

He spoke with infinite serenity, "Now I have a chance."

Then he was shouting commands at the technicians.

Varden started to say something, but the words wouldn't go together. An uncontrollable desire to be back in the Carnival throng, to be an unidentified member of the masses, swept over him. The tumult in the laboratory was so furious that no one noticed his leaving.

An ominous clatter met Varden as he entered the Center. He was trying to identify the sound, when a strange figure stalked across the courtyard, arms outstretched. It was dressed in a knight's full armor. Varden stopped the specter from the past with a firm hand against its breast plate.

"Glub?" came a plaintive query from behind the closed visor.

Varden raised the visor. "Which are you?"

"Koom," answered the entombed one.

"Sorry, I lost my atomic torch. You'll need it before the night's over."

Koom gazed at him with icy superiority. "Nothing is sacred to you."

"Why don't you join the percussion section of an orchestra?"

"I prefer to dress with some dignity for the Carnival. It is a traditional celebration. A person should honor it without frivolity. Your clown suit is laundered and pressed. You will find it on your bed."

Varden stepped back and saluted.

Slamming down his visor, Koom stalked away with a fateful clank. As Varden continued on his way, he wondered if the Master knew that his museum was minus a piece of priceless antique war costume.

It was late afternoon when Korson reached the rocket junk yard. The Venusian was standing by the gate. For an instant the guard hesitated. But the stars of a World Scientist were enough, and he swung open the great doors.

Here, assembled as a vast storehouse of scrap metal, was the history of man's effort to escape into space. A hundred types of crumbling ships towered into the sky.

Briefly, Korson explained the saga of Earth's tragic efforts to accomplish what Venus had known so long. Zaline was silent as, walking from ship to ship, he outlined man's

battle for the beyond. At last he said, "Why did you want to see all this?"

"For the sake of one man."

"The ambassador?"

"Yes."

"You love him?"

"Truly, I do."

"What has the rocket junk yard to do with it?"

"Because of these ships there is on his throat the blue mark."

Suddenly he visioned the junk yard filled with jet men, sphere-spinners, magno-balancers, astrographers. Ghostly figures thronging round the battered ships. What would be the ultimate result of all this? Expanding life—or death from the sickness? Oppressed by the mood of the place, he remained deep in his thoughts until Zaline's soft voice broke in.

"Take the Earthgirl She is good."

Korson answered firmly, "I have a reason."

"Reason and love go not together."

He knew he could say it. It would be safe with her, but he would not.

The strange eyes probed his face. "I sense a trouble. But you desire to keep it secret. So I do not ask. It was wrong to come here when he is dying of the sickness. Forgive."

"There is nothing to forgive."

A tiny vibration of sound, on the edge of audibility, murmured in the falling light. It was the day, the hour, the instant when an ancient rocket fin had decided to let go. There was the crescendo of parting metal, and a broken knife-edge crashed to the ground.

It had fallen only ten feet from them. Her three fingers slipped into his hand. "It happens so," she whispered. "Strange is fate."

Staring up at the dark, twisted mass of space ships above

them, she added, "Earthman, in this physical world planets do not mate. Only love and tragedy do. Come, we go now."

Tarmo watched the eterno-lights flicker on the surface of the water as she poised herself on the diving board, ready for the spring The sound of running footsteps caused her to pause and look around. Korson, in his bathing trunks, was chasing Flim, who had made off with his sandals. When she was sure that Korson had seen her, Tarmo dived and swam across the pool.

Korson gave up the pursuit of Flim and ran to the pool, his body arching into the water in a racing dive. Clear to the bottom he went, swimming underwater to the end of the pool where Tarmo lay stretched out on the tiles, and cautiously rose to the surface at the edge. Silently, his arm stretched out toward her ankle. He did not see that she had picked up a leafy branch which the wind had torn from one of the Mozette trees.

The branch thrashed down hard on his hand. Jerking back the hand, he laughed up at her. Tarmo leaned far over the edge, trying to slap his face with the branch. Grabbing the end, he pulled sharply.

Caught off balance, she fell, the water splashing high, a crystal screen around the two of them.

It was no longer a game as their bodies slid together, twisting and struggling. Korson twined his legs around hers, so she could not escape. Tarmo's arms went around his neck, pulling his face closer, her lips lifted for his kiss. Desire and longing swept over him, but before his mouth touched hers, the specter came between them. The fifth day.

Roughly, he gripped her encircling arm, breaking her embrace, and swam away. As he climbed out of the pool, Tarmo called after him.

"Korson!"

He did not look back.

Dressed, Korson sought the library as a sanctuary. Four walls of ancient wisdom and philosophy surrounded him, as did the musty scent which is peculiar to libraries throughout the centuries. He opened a volume and tried to bring his ideas into sharp alignment. This, he thought, is why I came here. It is all I want in the time left to me.

A huge lighted globe of the Earth persistently distracted his attention. Impatiently, he switched it off. His mind at last became absorbed in the book, and he did not hear the door open.

Tarmo was still wearing her bathing suit, over which she had thrown a long cloak. I am sure the sun will rise tomorrow, she thought. As I know that, I know also that he loves me. He must be taught not to fight me any more.

Her hand covered the page he was reading; she pressed close to him, moving her cloak so that it was not a barrier between them.

"I came when you called me," she whispered, and ran her hand lightly through his hair.

He did not move or look up. I could have you now, he thought. But that would leave something only begun. I am concerned only with endings.

"I did not call."

"I heard you thinking about me. In the pool, under water, I heard you."

He stood up, taking her firmly by the shoulders, and moved her back from him. "It's been a pleasant visit. Now, run along."

There was a low, savage tone in her voice. "A little while ago you wanted to be near me!"

"That was a little while ago," he answered coolly.

"You held me close to you."

"Only because you expected it. Because it amused me." He must make her dislike him, even hate him, if he could.

He sat down and opened a book. "Go feed your birds. Play with the dog. I've got work to do."

She could not believe it. She dared not. What has he done that makes white seem black? What have I done? I do not know anything at all if what I felt is false. White is black. Black is white.

Slowly she walked down the long room to the door and stopped to say, timidly, "The Carnival is tonight. Will—will you take me?"

Without looking up he muttered, "I've no time for carnivals!"

It was almost ten o'clock on Carnival night when the Lady Ellora entered Tarmo's room. She found only silence and emptiness. A black domino lay crushed on the floor, and a transparent undergarment clung limply to the edge of the bed.

She sought for some clue as to what had happened. The room spoke eloquently of turmoil and confusion. But why? Yet how ridiculous it was to attempt to fathom the motives or moods of others. It had been tried since time began and still no one ever really knew another.

She left the room in search of Korson, whom she found in the library.

"I'm sorry to disturb you, but I'm worried about Tarmo. She isn't in her room and I haven't seen her all evening. Her costume is missing. Except for this." She held out the domino.

"I can't help you. I haven't seen her since this afternoon." He rose, dignified, yet with a certain awkwardness that did not escape her. "Perhaps the guards . . ."

She was standing near him and he felt her presence as something more real than a physical touch. The essence of her being flowed out to him, surrounding him with its understanding and compassion.

"Why should I call the guards," she said, "when I have

the best of all guards beside me—your love for Tarmo. Go, find her yourself."

Korson shouldered his way through the crowd in the Pavilion. It was between acts of the pageant, and the dance area was jammed with wildly gyrating celebrants. A tall man in a beggar's costume marched by, carrying a girl who clutched a glass of wine, tilting it back in an effort to gulp a few mouthfulls.

Someone doused him with iridescent rainbow fluid. Three men were singing, "Space Ain't so Deep as Other Things." Two attendants stopped a fight. Fireworks laced across the sky. Another fight started while the announcer's voice boomed.

"The second half of the pageant will—"

Then he saw her.

Tarmo was sitting at one of the tables on the balcony which surrounded the open-air dance area. She wore the costume of an Arabian dancing girl and was obviously the cause of a dispute between two men.

Korson climbed the balcony and went to the table. "Tarmo!"

She looked up. "Hello, Korson. Good-by." Moving closer to one of the men she smiled seductively, reaching for his wine glass.

"I've come to take you back."

"I won't go!"

One of the men stood up, scowling, "Take her where?"

"It's none of your damn business!"

"Oh, have a drink and forget it—" He broke off suddenly. "Uh—is she your girl?"

Korson nodded.

The man sat down again and, shrugging, glancing at his companion. "Little family quarrel, I guess."

An Arabian dancing girl was picked up bodily by a man

dressed simply as a World Scientist and carried, kicking and screaming, out of the Pavilion.

In the shadows of the trees, he put her down.

"You wanted me," she said. "You wanted me, Korson!"

He took her radiant face between his hands and lifted it into the moonlight. "Yes, dearest, I wanted you."

Shadows engulfed them.

CHAPTER FOURTEEN

VARDEN was vanquishing a hangover when the Master's voice summoned him from his shower. He stood, dripping, before the visaphone.

"Yes, Master?"

"Come to my study at once."

When he entered the room, Varden found it dim, the drapes still drawn over the windows, the Master a hunched figure in his great chair.

"You know that the Venusian ambassador has the sickness?"

Varden nodded.

"Do you connect the occurance of the sickness on Venus with Dr. Everling's theory?"

Varden was thoughtful for a moment. "In one way, yes. I think you realize that I do not like the man. But I must be honest. His theory that the sickness is partly caused by a lack of struggle would make Venus an almost ideal place for its occurance. Could it have originated there? The life on Venus is certainly the easiest in the solar system."

"I have been reasoning along the same line. Dr. Everling's theory is certainly unorthodox. Yet, who knows?"

Varden shrugged.

"Wouldn't it seem logical," the Master continued. "for me to discuss the matter with the one person who has experience with both Dr. Everling and the sickness?"

"Lady Ellora?"

The Master nodded.

Entering the blue bedroom without knocking, the Master found a tray of breakfast, almost untouched, beside the bed where Ellora lay. Gently he kissed her. "Dearest, you should sleep longer in the morning."

"Always telling people what to do."

Was there a trace of agitation in her manner, he wondered. "And you must eat all of your breakfast."

He saw her fingers nervously touch the silk cord of her bedjacket which was fastened closely about her throat. His hand reached out and her eyes watched, wide and helpless. Jerking the cord, he thrust aside the collar of the jacket. On her throat was the blue mark of the sickness.

A few minutes later, Everling entered the study where the Master sat, apparently engrossed in some papers. Actually he was still trying to control the cold rage that had swept over him in Ellora's room and to think clearly.

The man from Cheenwa stood near a globe of the Earth, idly spinning it, until the Master spoke.

"Dr. Everling, I accept your proposition. I will reveal to you the secret of eternal life."

"When, Master?"

"Tomorrow night at nine o'clock, in Laboratory I. Now—go to my wife and save her!"

In the blue bedroom, Everling took a small amber vial from its plastic case and placed it on the table beside Ellora's bed. Quickly he filled a hypodermic syringe. He glanced at her expectant face.

"Yes," he said quietly, "this nightmare through which you

have been passing will soon be over. Rest. Dream of green hills, clear waters and far places. I shall give you the injection now. When you awaken, it will be to a new and brighter world."

His movements were rapid, but sure. They were the motions of a man in high excitement, yet with the self-control to master it. Holding her white arm, he drove the needle home; his thumb began the slow, steady pressure on the plunger. Ellora's eyes closed, and a half smile tugged at the corners of her mouth.

As Everling withdrew the needle, the buzzer of the vis-phone sounded softly. He laid the syringe on the table and went to the set. The face of the Master appeared on the screen.

"Everling?"

"Yes, I am with her. There is marked improvement. She must rest, now."

"Then there must still be hope."

"More than hope. I will cure her, Master."

Everling turned back to the woman on the bed. "You will slip slowly down, down a gentle spiral, into the depths of sleep. . . . the depths of power . . . the place where you find a renewal of that vitality which is your right . . . sleep . . . peace . . . sunlight in the woods where your footfalls are muffled . . . Remember the days of your childhood . . . long, long ago. . . ."

Picking up the vial, he returned it to its case and left the room.

In the grove of great pines, Tarmo lay on her back, arms supporting her head on a cushion of emerald moss, damp and sweet. She was saying, happily, "We'll have a small house and a big garden. And dogs."

Korson said nothing.

"We *will* have dogs, won't we?"

He kissed her. "Dear heart, we won't have any dogs. We won't have anything. . . . *I am the donor.*"

It must be a joke, she thought. But his expression frightened her and she appealed tremulously, "Korson . . ."

"It is true, Tarmo."

As she realized he meant it, she screamed, pressing a hand hard against her mouth, "No—no!"

He caught her in his arms and she clung to him desperately.

"You must go away. I'll help you! We'll go to Cheenwa—deep in the forest. They can't find us there."

He shook his head. "No donor has ever run away."

She could not mistake the acceptance of his fate, the calm refusal to consider any alternative. She ran from him, then, running to find a refuge—as if a refuge would blot out the horror and it would exist no more.

Everling went into his room and crossed to the mirror over the big, carved chest. Gazing at his reflection, he touched the deep crow's feet beside his eyes and the few touches of gray at his temples.

He heard a low, convulsive sobbing, coming from Tarmo's room, which adjoined his own, and hurried in to her.

She lay face downward on the bad. Sitting beside her, he put his arm around her shoulders. "It surely can't be that bad, my dear."

The calm, rather hoarse tones, familiar all her life, racked her nerves. She looked up for a moment into the curious probing eyes which seemed to bore into her skull. "How do you know!"

Such dominance and vigor were in his smiling face that, if she had not been overcome with grief, it would have dazzled her. "You know nothing!"

"This is a great day," he said. "when I explain, you will forget to cry."

"Korson told me that *he* is the donor!"

"Yes. I knew it."

"I begged him to go to Cheenwa. To hide. But he won't try to save himself!" Springing to her feet, she cried, "He can't go into Laboratory I and never come out again! We love each other!"

"I am sorry."

She dropped to her knees before him and took his hands in hers, pleading. "You can do anything. You always helped me. Help me to save him!" She bowed her head in his lap.

Above her, Everling's face was immobile as he stroked her hair. "You're very young. There will be other young men."

Her head came up; her voice rang with final conviction. "There will be only one love."

He moved restlessly, as one who tries to hold in check a flood of exultation and triumph. Fire glowed in the great ruby as his fingers closed tightly, then loosened to pluck at the folds of his robe.

Her eyes on the red spark, Tarmo cried. "Because of the Master, Korson must die. I hate the Master!"

Everling put his hand under her chin, tilting back her head; she felt the brilliant, hypnotic eyes upon her.

"Soon I shall be powerful. Very powerful. The time has come to tell you my plan. . . . For many years I knew that too much power in the hands of one man was dangerous. A hundred things showed this clearly. Things that went wrong all over the earth. Yet no one was strong enough to rise up and act against him. No one clever enough to think of a way to overthrow him. In the past, nations fell into darkness and decadence under the heels of dictators. It has always happened. It will always happen. But now the entire Earth is at stake!"

He stared past her, envisioning the day, now so near,

when the peoples of the earth would acclaim their hero.

"There must be change—always change. I heard in Cheen-wa that the Lady Ellora had the sickness. I came here, bringing you, young, strong healthy. I said that I had cured you of this disease."

She stared at him incredulously. "You mean I never had the sickness?"

"Only a childhood illness—nothing more. But, so desperate was the Master that he clutched at any hope. And I achieved a bargaining position, exactly as I had planned." He bent over her, closer now, his breathing quicker, heavier.

"But Korson?" She did not fully realize the whole meaning.

"If I save him will you do something for me?"

"Yes—yes!"

"Promise!"

Her gaze was frozen upon the glowing eyes opposite hers. "I promise."

"Before Korson dies, I will know the Master's secret. I will live forever. *I will be the Master!* He has been the abomination of this earth for too long. My task is to end tyranny!"

"How will you save Korson?"

"Before he enters Laboratory I, the secret will be mine, and the Master will either be dead or under my control. Then I can free Korson. The curse of the donor will be over forever. Korson will live—and you will keep the promise you have made."

"What must I do, Everling?" she whispered.

"When I am Master, you will be The Master's Lady!"

He pressed his body against hers, his strong fingers loosening her robe. As their flesh touched, she sank into a black pit of oblivion.

Korson paused before the door to the Lady Ellora's room. Should he disturb her? No matter how it all ended, she

was entitled to whatever peace she could find. Yet he knew that Tarmo would need her badly when he was gone.

The door was slightly ajar. As he opened it, he said softly, "Lady Ellora?"

She was in bed, but her eyes were open. They were vacant, expressionless.

"I want your help, Lady Ellora."

The head resting among the pillows did not move.

"Please, Lady Ellora!"

Still, she did not move nor answer.

"How do you feel?"

"I feel very well, Dr. Everling."

"I am not Dr. Everling. I am Korson." Worried, he studied her breathing and the pallor of her skin. "Do you feel better today?"

"Better today, Dr. Everling." The words came parrot-like from her lips.

Korson glanced at a shaft of sunlight which cut across the bed. "You'd feel better if the sun were shining, wouldn't you? But this is a gloomy day."

"A gloomy day . . ."

He took a cigarette lighter from a pocket of his tunic. Slowly, he passed the intense white light across Ellora's eyes. She did not blink.

He switched off the lighter and glanced at her bare white arm. The puncture mark was clearly visable. And, as he saw it, the sunlight glinting on the syringe caught his eye. He picked up the glass cylinder and tilted it. The few drops of remaining liquid moved sluggishly.

Dropping the syringe into his pocket, he stood looking down at the Master's Lady, speaking as if she could understand him. "This must not be."

Tumult blasted at Korson when he entered Ronding's laboratory. Ronding was inoculating a guinea pig. Korson,

shocked, wondered if it were really Ronding, the great bio-chemist. This haggard, unshaven man seemed to have no relationship with the inspiring teacher he knew.

Korson noticed that Ronding often paused in his work and wiped perspiration from his face. Yet there was some-thing incredible about the man, as if dust on its return journey to dust had already revealed the living core of energy which it had so long hidden.

Korson approached. "Dr. Ronding?"

He turned. "What the hell do you want?"

Korson held out the syringe. "Whatever is in this must be analyzed at once."

"What do you think this is, an elementary chemistry lab? Get out!"

"This is vital to—"

"Get out!"

"The Lady Ellora."

Ronding said something that might have been an apology and lit a cigar. Through the smoke, the bloodshot, weary eyes were as piercing as ever. He took the syringe and carried it across the laboratory.

Only a few minutes were necessary for his analysis. Writing down the formula, he signed his name and handed it to Korson. With his teeth clamped viciously on the cigar, he growled. "If this is connected with the treatment Lady Ellora is getting for the sickness, you'd better move fast, young man!"

Outside the clinic Korson read the formula and notation. The drug Everling had injected was nothing but norcozyne. It produced a state of lethargy, followed by a temporary burst of synthetic energy. It cured nothing.

Once more he saw Lady Ellora, lying helpless in a hyp-notic trance, drugged with norcozyne. Precious time had been wasted, hopes raised—all useless.

An instant later his jet car was speeding through Terra City traffic.

Turning the car over to a guard, he strode through the gates of the Center. In the anteroom he grabbed the visaphone from the clerk and called for the Master. The operator informed him that the Master would receive no calls that day.

He cursed the operator, the gods, everything, and ran to the Master's library.

The room was now as familiar to him as his own laboratory. He looked about, but the Master was not there; only the shelves of books and the glowing eye of the great globe.

A guard stood in front of the door to the Master's study. "Can I help you, sir?"

"I must see the Master. It is very important."

"My orders are to admit no one."

"You must."

"I am sorry, sir."

"Surely, if I write a message, you could step inside and hand it to him?"

"The orders are specific. He must not be disturbed by anything."

"Where's Varden?"

"In the telecast tower, I believe."

Back through the corridors Korson went. As he crossed the court, he glanced up at the tower, and saw Varden crossing the marble bridge.

"Varden!" he called.

Varden waved his hand and came down the curving stairway.

At the foot Korson met him with a grim, set face. "I must see the Master at once! It's vital. But he's left orders that he will see no one—receive no messages. *You* could get to him."

"Not today."

Grabbing the chief assistant's arm, Korson persisted, "You don't understand. This is deadly serious!"

The stocky, ruddy-faced man regarded him with kindly eyes, in which there was a trace of disappointment. It is because of the girl, he thought. He has found he cannot face death; he wants her too much. He wants to live and hope for a reprieve. The best thing is to blast his hopes at once.

Varden's casual, good-natured air gave way to his official manner as he answered, "There is nothing I can do. And if you could see the Master, you would be disappointed."

He walked on past Korson, cool and implacable.

This, Korson thought bitterly, is the absolute end, the final irony. He had done what he could. His hand crumpled the paper with the formula. And after all, nothing mattered to *him* anymore.

CHAPTER FIFTEEN

THE NINTH day of Month 13, year 3097, dawned clear and calm. Sunlight caught the peaks behind Terra City and began working its way down into the valleys. Night mist was sucked away from the cobalt sky.

On the grass behind a one-story, low house that looked like a giant, glistening cube of sugar, two boys were playing a game of their own invention. It involved racing, tumbling and amicable fighting.

Their shouts roused a woman who sat near a window, reading a book of ancient history. She looked out, smiling

at her children playing in the sunlight. How tall and strong and handsome they would be when they were grown!

A group of seven girls in their teens were beginning a picnic. They sang as they put up a net for a game of ball, lusty young voices throbbing in the clear air as they attempted to harmonize. When the net was up, they started the game, calling to each other as the big ball flew through the air.

"Tomorrow's the party!"

"Going with Leveng?"

"I like Jorgex better—"

"What'll you wear?"

Outside the great gate of the Center, the guard was at his usual post, moving a few feet in one direction or the other. His thoughts wandered . . . They come, they go, watching their own feet, all-important feet on the slick pavement. No one really knows where his feet are taking him. . . . The guard jerked to attention as one of the passersby nodded to him.

He decided that it was very possible he might become a poet or a great writer of some kind. He would write a book so fine that it would be placed in the library of the Center. Perhaps in the Master's own collection. Not science, certainly. He was tired of that. Romance, adventure on one of the planets, perhaps. He had always meant to be a wanderer, himself.

The guard would have liked to scratch his neck. However, a large group of people entered the Center, on their way to the museum. He stiffened to formal attention. To a poet they were a flock of sheep, nothing more. To a poet who wished to scratch, they were an even worse nuisance.

After the visitors had passed, the second guard said, "Hi, robot."

"Robots would do better at the gate," growled the first guard as he scratched vigorously. "That's what we'll become, in time."

The first guard did not answer.

After a moment the other man added, soberly, "Have you noticed there's something oppressive about this place today?"

"There is. And I haven't seen the Master for three days."

"Neither has anyone else."

"Something *could* happen. . . ."

In his study, the Master stirred uneasily in sleep, awoke to a half-doze, and discovered that his cloak had twisted uncomfortably about him. His body stiff, he got up with an effort and removed the cloak, letting it fall to the floor. His mind was clearer but, as he slowly crossed to the window, his steps were uncertain, tottering.

His hand, opening the window, was deeply wrinkled, the veins thick and coarsened, the skin spotted with brown. He looked out, and watched Flim who was stalking a bird among the flowers.

It was noon when Tarmo left her room and went down to the garden. The Center seemed oddly hushed; no voices, no bustle of activity. No one moves around me but ghosts, she thought. I feel no pain, no sorrow for ghosts.

A flood of sunlight warming her body made her look up and, raising her arms like a pagan goddess, she cried, "Stop! Stop the sun for one day!"

The sun of the ninth day of the Month Thirteen, was touching the horizon. Korson was reading a book which had been given him by the Master. The book was entitled THE BITTER ONE? A LIFE OF FORONI. The Master had circled a passage on the last page:

Just before Foroni's death in 2907 he said:
"That death does not exist—at least as the term is
understood—that this inevitable happening is merely
a not very radical evolutionary transition is, to me, ob-
vious. I have already presented the evidence and reason-
ing on which my conclusion is based.

"However, as men would suffer any torture rather
than to think, I do not expect them to pay the slightest
attention to anything that I have ever said."

It was evening of the last day. The solar system hurtled
at approximately nine miles a second towards the star, Vega.
Everling stood on the terrace, gazing into the night. He
might have been a cosmic pilot, guiding the solar system
to its proper destination. Already he had come a long way,
and when the new dawn rose, he would have traveled
farther than any other man.

Alone in his study, the Master's thoughts spun out from
a dark core of anguish. Everyone would be in the drawing
room for after dinner coffee, he thought, envisioning their
faces.

Korson and Tarmo loved each other. How many loves are
found too late? How many eager, seeking hearts love, and
are not loved in return? How many ever find the flame for
which they starve? And how many flames joined only when
they went out.

Korson loved Tarmo. In two hours He must extinguish
both flames in LaboratoryI. Varden had told him of Korson's
frantic request for a meeting and he was convinced that the
young man desired an extension of the time allotted to the
donor. Desired it because of the girl. Somehow, though, he
could not understand Korson pleading for a reprieve. . . .

Dressed in a wine-colored robe, her hair caught up in

a net spangled with sapphires, Lady Ellora poured coffee from a golden urn and handed the cup to Varden. It would be a difficult evening for all of them and she was determined to keep the conversation in a light vein for as long as she could manage. "What is this story I heard about your doings at the carnival?"

"Obviously, a lie."

"And last year?"

"Also a lie." He grinned. "I'm surrounded by spies."

Everling walked down the long room to where Tarmo sat. In her big chair she looked like a lifeless rag doll which someone had tossed aside. Her face was as white as the creamy satin robe she wore. He stooped, murmuring to her in a low tone.

Varden turned back to Lady Ellora. "There are times," he said, "when I feel mildly violent toward that man. Like wanting to cut his throat, for instance."

Lady Ellora put her hand on his shoulder. "He is strange, I grant you. Rather barbaric, or pagan."

As Varden lit his cigar, he saw her eyes wander to the door.

"I wonder where Korson is?" she murmured, almost to herself.

Bending his head close to hers, Varden said in a low tone, "I do not want to upset you, but there is something you should know—whether the Master agrees or not."

"Korson." She nodded. "You are not violating a confidence. He is the donor. The Master told me."

"He must tell you everything."

"No. But I like to think he trusts me as he does you."

Varden was silent a moment, then said gruffly "Tonight won't be easy for any of us. I have an appointment in the city. It's business, but I can put it off and stay. . . ."

She shook her head. "What good would it do?"

He shrugged helplessly.

"Talk." She bit her lip to stop the trembling. "Say any-

thing. The space between each of us here is a vacuum."

Over his face came a mask, a bright sardonic smile. He turned toward Everling. "Are we social outcasts, Dr. Everling?"

From Tarmo's side, Everling said, "I'm afraid I was meditating on my past. And nothing is duller conversation than reminiscence."

Varden picked up a plate of sweets and carried it to Tarmo. She took one of the candies. "That doesn't apply to you, Tarmo. You're too young to have a past."

Dully, she answered. "I was wondering why the Master was not with us at dinner."

"He's probably wasting time with that Moon Base affair." Her nails dug into the palm of her hand. Why doesn't the Master come? What has happened? Where is Korson?"

And, like an evoked spirit, he stood in the doorway.

"Sorry I'm late." He went to Lady Ellora and, somewhat hesitantly, bent over her hand and kissed it.

There was only one person in the room he wanted to see, the slender girl in the satiny white robe, with black hair falling upon her shoulders, who nervously twisted a pearl bracelet between her fingers.

"You are beautiful tonight," he said to her. "Like a bride."

Everling gave an angry start of surprise, and broke in quickly. "The reason the Master is not here seems obvious to me. He has undoubtedly shut himself away to work out some difficult scientific problem."

Is the man blind? thought Lady Ellora. This was Korson's and Tarmo's last minutes together. "Dr. Everling, there is something I want to ask you." Taking his arm firmly, she led him away toward the cabinet of music recordings. "One of these came today. It is said to be an old folk song of Cheenwa, and I would like your opinion."

The music was not too loud, but sufficient to create a barrier between them and the young people.

Without looking at Korson, Tarmo rose as if pulled by a magnet. His hand clasped her small fingers and they went across the thick pile of the carpets to a windowed alcove, half concealed by folds of heavy drapery.

If only I could disappear among these folds and take him with me, she thought. But if he knew what I am now, he would not come with me.

In agony, he watched the shadow of the wild, laughing creature she had been. So quickly she has turned from everything in the world, because I am leaving it. He felt the tense, hot hand gripping his own. "Tarmo . . ."

Her whisper was low, but insistent. "I want you to remember something! Anything I do is for you. Anything I have to give is for you. Will you believe that, always?"

If only, she thought with vacant eyes, I could clean my mouth. There is a taste in my mouth as if I had been drinking blood. A taste of iron, warm and hot, as though I had killed and eaten. . . .

She touched his chest, then his face with her hand. "Whole. Quite whole," she said in a tone of wonder. "I don't know what is real, any more. Korson, is the moon blue or silver?"

What caused this melancholy fantasy, he wondered. She is very young. She must not leap from the dreams of childhood to the regrets and uncertainty of old age. "Tarmo, you must not be sorry—not even for yourself. You, too, must remember something. I might have come to this last night without knowing there was a you."

"And if you were free? If this were not the last night?"

His voice was harsh. "There is no escape, and you know it." For the last time, he put his arms around her. "Goodby, beloved."

The music stopped with his kiss.

Slightly apprehensive, Varden eyed Korson as he approached the table where the brandy decanter and glasses

were. But Korson smiled and said, "Do you own that stuff, Varden?"

Lady Ellora's voice sounded feverishly bright. "I'm a miserable hostess."

The clear, dark fluid gurgled pleasantly into Korson's glass.

"Brandy is my favorite drink," Everling said. "An inspiring liquid."

"Does your genius need an aid to inspiration?" asked Korson, with unconcealed sarcasm.

"Relaxation might be a better word. That peace which comes from the gentle glow of the kindly drink."

Korson's laugh was short and curt. "I grant you that certain men are in need of peace. Do you dream, Dr. Everling? Do you have nightmares?"

"I sleep like a child—"

"Of the devil!"

Sharp and quick, with the tone of authority he so seldom used, Varden broke in, "Come, Doctor. You need a refill." Everling followed him to the decanter.

Korson, now alone with the Master's Lady, spoke urgently. "Lady Ellora, I know something of the greatest importance. I must reach the Master. How can I do so?"

"There is no way."

Once more the unfathomable weakness attacked her; she could no longer stand, and sank into a chair. He must hate me, she thought. This tall, imperious, tender young man. She was mistress of the Center, of the place which had doomed him.

He bent closer to her. "You would know how to find him if anyone does. Only two minutes to talk to him—now!"

The luster of her eyes was veiled by sadness. "If there were a way, it would do no good. If you were my own son, I could not save you."

Soundlessly, Everling had come near enough to overhear

the last words. "It is surprising that he would wish to be saved."

An instant after the words left his mouth, the blow struck squarely. Everling staggered back and dropped, sprawling, to the floor.

Darting across the room, Tarmo knelt beside him, terrified that he might not keep his promise to save the life of the man who had struck him down. Her hand touched his hair, his cheek. Korson looked down at them, cold and hard.

"Tarmo, did you ever have the sickness?"

"Yes!"

Everling got to his feet, waving away Varden's gesture of assistance. "Our young friend is zealous in his search for truth. I trust he is satisfied."

Varden scowled, knowing something was behind Korson's action, yet inclined to attribute it to the strain of his last night of life. Both men wanted to spring at each other's throats, but could not find the reason.

"We were all impetuous once," the hoarse tones continued. "Enthusiastic, following the rules, our feet never straying from the wall-defined paths science laid out for us. It is understandable." He bowed to Lady Ellora. "Now, if you will excuse me . . ."

With dignity, Everling walked the length of the drawing room, Tarmo beside him and, in silence, they disappeared from view.

Three pair of eyes avoided each other. Finally, Korson said, "I apologize to both of you."

"Forget it," Varden told him. "Look, Korson, I'd like to stay with you here, for—"

"Hell no!" Korson interrupted. "Do you think I want to play chess?" He held out his hand.

Gripping it, Varden tried to say something, realized he could not, and went out.

The Lady Ellora said, quietly, "I want to play chess."

The sound that came from him was the wordless protest of humanity against a destiny it cannot fathom.

Her frail arms closed tightly around him, cradling his head. Forgetting pride, he sought the woman's kindly strength. It is almost ludicrous, he thought. Both of us doomed. She, tender and sad for my fate, and I for hers.

After a moment he moved out of her embrace, smiling, "We could go out in clouds of glory, with vine leaves in our hair—but we won't.

"Let's do a decent job of it, Lady Ellora. Let's not break the glasses at ten. Lord, I don't know how to say things. I'm only a biochemist—but a damn good one!"

"You are, surely."

"Don't wreck it. And don't wait here with me. Go—now!"

He felt the light pressure of her lips on his. Then she was going away, her slender figure poised, head high.

He was alone, now. Emptying his drink, he poured another. It was the one time in a man's life when he was most free. Free of the niggling, inconsequential happenings of today—any day—free of yesterday, free of tomorrow.

He glanced at a time indicator. The dial markers stood at 9:07.

CHAPTER SIXTEEN

In LABORATORY I, the great machines squatted like shadowy monsters that had been frozen in their death agonies. The wall illumination had been turned down to a faint glow, and the only brightness was the single beam of light focused on the desk.

It seemed to the Master that the tall figure of Everling in

his green robe and pointed cowl was a character from some ancient oil painting; not a man, but a specter that had stalked out of the childhood of humanity.

He looked at the time indicator. It was less than an hour until Korson would arrive. The matter at hand must be finished, and quickly.

From beyond the shaft of light slanting down to the desk, came the deep, compelling voice, "For longer than I can remember I have desired to see the interior of this place."

"Undoubtedly. However, you are here only because I must keep an agreement. So I shall be brief." He placed one hand, palm down, upon the top of the desk and rubbed a long finger over the dry, discolored skin. "What causes men to age?"

"It is a cosmic law of the life force."

"Which I have broken? Men do not break cosmic laws. And I am a man."

"Nevertheless—"

"Nevertheless you are neither a logical philosopher nor a good pathologist. *Men age because of a change in their blood.* That is the reason why all men are not deathless. The only reason.

"The individual organs of the body are potentially immortal. But a man is a unit—not a set of organs. What unified him? It is the ever-flowing river of blood that connects and integrates the organs. A man is as old as his blood."

Everling started to speak, but a motion of the Master's hand cut him off.

"As the various organs of the body take on nourishment and give off waste products, the composition of the blood slowly changes. Each organ poisons the others. The blood becomes that of an old man; eventually, of a dead man.

"That change is absolute and irrevocable. Science, with all its knowledge, cannot alter it. Even the Master cannot."

"But," said Everling, "with massive tranfusions of young blood—"

"It would not work."

"Why not?"

"First, every drop of blood must be removed, and the circulatory system cleaned. Were the smallest amount of old blood allowed to remain, it would act as an antagonist to the new blood. The old man would die as swiftly and as surely as if he had been given a transfusion of the wrong type of blood."

"Also, and this is the strange fact which I do not pretend to understand, the young blood must be from a single individual of the same sex. Remember, you are not simply transferring blood—you are transferring that which holds a living creature together. You are receiving not a set of organs, but a unit.

"Finally—and in this case you were partially right—there is what you called 'life force.' Each organ has its own life force. This can only be renewed by a brief period of apparent death. During that period, the organs will take in energy from the eternal well of youth, and return to the period of their maximum vigour.

"Now, if you nourish those regenerated organs with the blood of a single young person of the same sex, and if that nourishment flows through a cleansed circulatory system, the old person will become young. And that is an actual cosmic law."

Everling was silent a moment. Then he said, reflectively, "It is more complicated than I had anticipated."

"Truth is never simple. Only half truths are simple."

Everling was staring at the Master with growing realization and amazement. "But to do what you have said you would be forced to suspend life!"

"Yes."

"Suspend life!"

The Master nodded. "That is my secret."

"By the use of such a discovery all human beings could have their youth renewed." Everling's tone was biting. "By what perversion of thought does the Council allow you to keep the secret?"

"They do not know it."

"Why not?"

The Master's fingers impatiently tapped the desk. "I did not say that I could make *old* blood *young*."

"But—"

"Think for a moment. If my secret were known, the world would instantly be filled with a race of vampires. Every man and woman would spend half his life struggling, scheming, killing to obtain precious young blood. Every child born would be another potential source. At maturity, he would become a hunted animal. I know which temptations men can stand—and which they cannot resist. Worst of all is the desire for renewed youth."

The cowled head nodded in agreement. "You are right, Master."

"From the very beginning, I realized the possible consequences of my discovery—both for good and evil. Therefore, I did not disclose my secret. I had done my experimental work with animals. Dogs cannot talk.

"In those days, when humanity was disintegrating because of war and the inability to control the machine, the great Conference of Scientists was called. I went before that gathering and proved my discovery—without revealing my methods. Then I proposed that one man, and only one, be made immortal. And that he should be the Master.

"They debated for several days, and finally agreed to my plan. As they had no choice, they selected me as the Master."

"And you have guarded your secret ever since?"

"Until now. If you will follow me, I will show you the key to potential immortality."

Walking across the great laboratory, the Master touched a button and the panels began to drop into the floor. When the first panel was completely down, he pointed to the nude young man in the scintillating mist.

"My first donor."

Everling threw back his cowl, and stared intently at the entombed figure. Then the man from Cheenwa rapped on the plastic cover of the cabinet.

The sound echoed in the laboratory, but the man in the cabinet did not move.

"But," he whispered, "he seems alive!"

"He is neither living, nor dead. His life is suspended, and has been for ten centuries."

"The real basis of physical life," the Master continued, "is not chemical, but electro-magnetic. I discovered a way to make that life force inactive until I wish to reactivate it."

"What is that strange mist around him?"

"That is the fluorescent effect of the force field which I have created in the cabinet. It is that field which suspends the electro-magnet potential, or 'life force'."

"Why does he stand so straight?"

"His muscles were taut when his life was instantaneously suspended. The muscles will remain so."

Everling's thick brows drew together. "Why not kill these men?"

"There are many things which even the Master does not know. One is *exactly* what happens after death." His finger pressed the second button and the panels began to rise into place.

"I believe," he added, "that death is a beginning, not an end. But many of the men in those cabinets did not share my belief. Therefore, I have kept them here, hoping that some day I will find a way to return to them the only life they were sure of. This life."

"Thirty living dead men!" Everling whispered hoarsely.

The panels were down, except for the last two. These two cabinets remained open—and empty.

"You noticed, Dr. Everling, that there was an urn in each cabinet. Those urns contain the old blood from my body which was exchanged for the young blood of the donor. If I can discover a way of making old blood young, my secret can be revealed. Then I can give these men back young blood. And their lives, which I stole."

"What prevents the force fields escaping from the cabinets?"

"The walls of the cabinets are double. Between those walls I have created a second field which balances the primary field and contains it within the cabinet. It took a long while to work out that problem. At first, the fields had to be constantly renewed."

The Master went to the two empty cabinets. Behind him he heard the slow, measured footsteps of the doctor. He became conscious of a queer illusion; from somewhere far off a faint voice seemed to be warning him not to take this final step.

"When the donor arrives," the Master said, "he will strip and enter this cabinet. I will then adjust the force field and the insulating fields. For an instant, the donor's life will be suspended."

"Why do you not adjust the fields before the donor arrives?"

"The fields must be adjusted *immediately before the donation.* An individual's life force is not static, but constantly changing—even from hour to hour."

"When the donor's fields are set, I can release him from suspended animation. He returns to his last moments of life and steps out of the cabinet. I then instruct him how to adjust the fields. Next, I strip and step into the other cabinet. The donor anesthetizes my arm and inserts this needle into a vein."

The Master indicated a large hypodermic needle which was attached to a length of flexible, transparent tubing. The tubing emerged from the inner side of the cabinet.

"After which," Everling said eagerly, "he closes the door of your cabinet and adjusts the fields according to your instructions."

"Exactly. There is only one more step. The donor enters his cabinet, inserts a simliar needle into his arm, and closes his door. When he shuts that door the master switch is automatically closed, and the whole affair is turned over to the time clock, mounted between the cabinets."

"The actual donation," Everling interrupted, "is automatic?"

"Yes. For an hour, the world's only Master is the time clock. After that period, my door is automatically opened, the force fields are shut off—and I return to life and youth."

"How are the fields adjusted?"

"I will show you."

He led the way to a large control panel in the center of the laboratory. The panel was studded with knobs, switches, dials and indicators.

"The adjustments must be unbelievably complicated!" There was something rather like panic in Everling's unnaturally high-pitched tone.

"No, said the Master. "I have simplified them and made everything possible automatic. This was to minimize any chance of error."

A brief sigh escaped Everling. The Master wondered if he had actually heard the sound or not. He was annoyed, for it seemed that he was missing something of significance.

"These are the controls for the donor's cabinet. These are for mine. These four knobs are adjusted until the dials read so."

Swiftly, he instructed Everling. The Master was amazed at the rapidity with which Everling's mind grasped each point.

When he had finished, Everling said, "Is that all?" He was almost mocking, as if a great deal had been made of something quite ordinary.

"Except that every control on the panel is labeled in code. The key to the code is in my desk. I will destroy it after the donation is completed."

Exultation throbbed in Everling's voice. "When will Korson arrive?"

"At ten o'clock—" The Master broke off. "You knew the donor was Korson?"

"He told me accidentally in a moment of anger." A nervous motion of his tongue moistened his thin lips. "Interesting to know that my new blood will be his, Korson's."

"No, it will not!" It was no longer the voice of an old, tired man; it was the voice of the Master.

"That was our bargain!" Everling's voice was suddenly out of control. "Is your word no better than a cheap liar's?"

"I have kept my word. I agreed to reveal my secret in exchange for yours. I should never have made such an agreement, but I was weak enough to place my love for a woman above all else. I have despised myself for it."

"You promised thirty more years of life!"

His method of escape was technical, unworthy, and the Master knew it. "The agreement was to exchange secrets. You falsely presumed that I also agreed to give you renewed youth. Korson offered his life, as a decent scientist should. But *you* wanted to bargain like a merchant."

The trap was sprung. The Master saw a shiver pass over the man opposite him, saw him grow calm again.

"You have disclosed your secret. Now you wish me to tell my method of curing the sickness."

The Master nodded.

"I believe, Master, that I have been treated unjustly. However, I have saved the Lady Ellora, and I ask one favor.

"What is it?"

"May I experience, for one moment, the sensation of suspended life? To you, of course, it is not a sensation, but for me it has a mystical significance. I would like to enter the donor's cabinet while you adjust the force fields."

What possible harm could come of humoring Everling? the Master thought. There was some justice in Everling's bitterness. "Very well. Strip."

It required only a few seconds for the Master to adjust the controls. He suspended Everling's life for perhaps a half minute, then turned off the fields and opened the cabinet.

Smiling, Everling stepped out. "Thank you, Master." Quickly, he dressed.

"Now, Dr. Everling, what is your method of treating the sickness?"

"I will explain at once. However, I would rather talk in more pleasant surroundings. I am haunted by those living dead men. May we go into your office?"

The Master shrugged. The man was becoming a nuisance with his trivial requests. However, he must have his answer. He crossed the laboratory, and took the atomic torch from its niche. As its rays fell on the opalescent disk, the great slab began to swing outward.

Everling's voice came from directly behind him.

"This is *my* secret!" His weapon crashed against the back of the Master's head.

As the aged body crumpled, the torch fell from its hand. Ponderously, the slab swung back into position, leaving Laboratory I once more sealed from the outside world.

When consciousness returned, the Master tried to move, but he could not. He realized that he was bound and gagged, his body propped against one of the machines.

Everling, a heavy wrench in his hand, stood before him. "I will take my thirty years—and more!" I shall not kill you, yet. For the present you are no use to me dead. Alive, you may become one of my most valuable possessions."

Sitting down behind the desk, he lit a cigarette. "In half an hour Korson will be outside the laboratory. I will open the door by the method you so kindly showed me. Korson will suspect nothing—and I shall be armed and prepared. Fortunately my knowledge of science allowed me to follow your explanation and to realize that the donor need not be conscious. *An unconscious donor will serve my purpose excellently.*"

The Master knew that what he said was true.

"You have already set my field, and I know how to set his. Tonight, for the first time in a thousand years, the world will have a new Master!"

Taking the Master's cape from the back of the chair, he drew it around his shoulders.

The man was insane, thought the Master. It was a fitting ending that the Master, who had been created to save the world from its own madness, should be destroyed by a madman.

CHAPTER SEVENTEEN

IT WAS nineteen minutes to ten when Korson heard the tapping of sandals on the parquet floor in the entrance of the drawing room.

As Tarmo came running to him, he called, "Get out. Damn it, get out!"

"I can't go through with it! Not even for you. Korson, the Master must not die. We'd be killing all that's good on earth—"

Roughly he gripped her arm, "What do you mean!"

"I betrayed him—for you. I never had the blue mark or the sickness."

"And you lied!"

"To save you. Everling told me his whole plan two nights ago. He means to kill the Master and become Master himself. He met the Master at nine o'clock in Laboratory I. And he promised to save your life." Abject before him, she covered her face with her hands.

Korson muttered, "I can't get into Laboratory I!"

She raised her head. "The guards?"

"If neither Varden nor I can get in, how can they?" He thought a moment. "There's one chance—Lady Ellora."

Grabbing her hand, he jerked her along with him as he ran out of the room.

The Lady Ellora was lying on her lounge, reading, when they burst into the room. As she looked up at them in astonishment, both saw the livid blue mark on her throat.

"There's little time, Lady Ellora. Everling is in Laboratory I with the Master. He intends to kill him and become Master himself."

Her frightened blue eyes stared incredulously at them. "How do you know?"

"Everling told me," said Tarmo. "It was part of his plan to get into the Center—to pretend he could cure the sickness. I never had it and he never cured me!" A sob choked her. "Oh, my Lady, I am sorry!"

"There must be a way into Laboratory I. *You* know it," said Korson quietly.

Her head turned to and fro in feverish torment. "I cannot tell you."

"Tell us or the Master will die!"

"It is sacred trust."

"I must get into that laboratory before Everling expects me, and take him by surprise. It's my only chance." Korson was uncompromising.

"If I did as my heart pleads, I would let him die . . . so that he could go with me."

"Then," said Tarmo, "you would not be the Master's Lady."

The child has become a woman, thought Lady Ellora. She sat erect, a final spark of vitality flaming in her face. "Korson, have you a weapon?"

"A World Scientist isn't allowed to carry one."

"Get one from the guards—"

"They must not know about this—they might talk. Too dangerous for the world to know of the Master's one weakness."

"Then . . . " Forcing the words through bloodless lips, each one a struggle against her ebbing strength, she continued, "Come closer . . . the combination cubicle is to the right of the door. The combination is 4-92X-9-7-418-K."

He repeated it once, and was gone.

Dropping to her knees beside the lounge, Tarmo's arms went round Lady Ellora as tears poured down her cheeks.

As Korson slammed open the combination cubicle, fear that in the last moments of his life his memory might betray him, made his fingers shaky. But he set the dials which only one other pair of hands had touched before.

Suddenly, the almost imperceptible cracks in the concrete wall began to widen. The massive slab swung inward.

Korson saw the figure of Everling behind the desk, the folds of the Master's cloak hanging from his shoulders. A hand darted out to grab the heavy wrench on the desk.

Everling came around the desk.

Lunging across the space between them, Korson dodged the blow of the wrench. As he came up, half-crouched, he struck Everling's arm a paralyzing blow with the edge of his palm, causing the doctor to loosen his grip on the wrench.

With his free hand, Everling gripped the collar of Korson's tunic, jerking him forward, twisting the collar in an attempt

to choke him. He must not kill the donor, just render him helpless.

Suddenly Korson's powerful leg thrust between Everling's, tripping him, and he went down on one knee. Flinging himself on top of the doctor, Korson smashed his fist into the man's face. Blood spurted from a cut over his eye. Everling, half-blinded for a moment, could only cling desperately to the wrench, feeling his arm slowly, painfully pressed back and outward, further and further.

Hampered by the long cloak, his movements were clumsy and he could not throw Korson off. At the moment he lost his grip on the weapon, Everling sprang to his feet, the wrench landing on the floor several yards away.

Two savage blows, low on his body, knocked the wind out of Korson. His eyes blurred as he saw the other man make a dash for the wrench. One blind lunge brought him forward, to wrap his arms around Everling's legs and drag him down, just out of reach of the wrench.

Everling launched a vicious kick; his boot caught Korson's jaw, snapping his head back. Consciousness dimmed, but he clung grimly to Everling, and slowly inched himself up along the other man's body. Finally, he was in reach of his throat and, pinning down Everling's legs with his own, he thrust his thumbs into the flesh on both sides of Everling's throat. Fury had erased all thoughts from his mind, except one—to kill.

Slowly increasing the pressure of his thumbs, he saw Everling's eyes begin to glaze. Then Korson remembered that it was for the Master to deal with the doctor; he had no right to be the executioner. Within a second of the kill, he relaxed his grip. Everling was unconscious.

Now, with the eyes closed, the face of the man on the floor was cruel, evil.

Hurrying to the Master, he untied him and helped him to his feet. Shocked at his slow, feeble movements, he felt

deep pity for the trembling old man. Pity, and fear that there was too little time to do what must be done.

"Use me, Master. Quickly!"

"It must be quick—" whispered the Master. The grey eyes flicked down at the prone figure in the green robe. "But *you* are not the donor. *He* is."

"What!"

"Korson, make sure that Doctor Everling is alive."

Stooping down, Korson felt Everling's wrist. "He is alive, Master."

"Find his card which shows his blood type."

Korson searched Everling's clothes and brought out the card.

"What is his type?"

"Type A—Rh positive."

"Good," the Master said softly. "That is my type."

"We know nothing about this man's health. And he's a few years too old."

"He is healthy enough and young enough. If necessary, I can ask the Council to send me a new donor ahead of the usual time."

Still, Korson did not move. "*I* am the the donor."

"And I, Korson, am the Master."

The Master sat alone behind his desk in Laboratory I. He had sent Korson to find Tarmo and bring her to him. He wanted them together when he announced the final decision he had made, which would change their lives, and end this strange affair. Dreading the step he was forced to take, he knew there was no other way.

He rubbed a hand across his forehead as if to blot out something. Yet the same few words were repeated endlessly in his mind—the words which, in answer to his first desperate question, had come over the visaphone circuit from the outside world.

"The Lady Ellora is dead."

Placing his hands on the desk before him, he noticed that already years had gone from them. The flesh was becoming firm and smooth. Soon they would be the hands of a young man. Even now, he felt youth's energy pounding through him.

Varden's voice on the visaphone startled him.

"Ronding wishes to speak to you. Says it is urgent!"

"I will talk to him."

Ronding's excited face appeared on the screen, and his voice boomed, "The drinks are on you and Dr. Everling, Master. I have isolated the cause of the sickness! It is damn virus, terrible and unusual, but still a virus. My findings have been checked by the Council. With the cause known, we'll find the cure. You can tell all the other eggheads that it took Ronding to lick it."

"The world owes you a great debt, Dr. Ronding."

"Oh hell!"

The Master was glad that Ronding could not see his face. "Find Varden and stay with him until I come."

He rose and, with light, vigorous steps, wandered about the great laboratory. He paused a moment to look at Everling, eternally sealed inside the swirling mist; then he pressed the button and the panels rose into place. He went into the little room in the corner of the laboratory, and stared idly at the notes concerning his most recent efforts to solve the problem of communication with the dead. Korson's voice on the visaphone interrupted his thoughts:

"We are outside the door to the laboratory, Master."

The beam of the Master's atomic torch found the disk, and the slab swung inward. Tarmo and Korson entered.

She hurried to him, impulsively pouring out her story. "Forgive me, Master! When I first came here with Everling I truly believed I had had the sickness and that he had cured me. Then he told me his scheme and the part I had played.

Tonight I lied to the others, because he said he would save Korson. Forgive—" Her voice stopped as if unseen hands had closed round her throat, and she stood frozen, suddenly realizing the change in the Master.

He smiled, and his rich, calm tones filled the laboratory. "You have never seen me like this, Tarmo, my dear. The old man you knew and the young one you see are the same person. Korson has told me the whole story. Your actions speak for themselves. The matter is ended, except for something I must do. Something which may seem harsh to you. Come."

Returning to the desk, he sat down and looked steadily at the young people.

"No one must ever know Everling's fate. Nor that Korson was not the donor."

"Yes," said Korson. "I understand."

"You will leave Earth tonight, both of you. And you must never return. You may visit any of the other planets and pursue any work you desire. To the day of your deaths, nothing that is in my power to give will be lacking from your lives. But you must change your names and conceal your identities. Every day you live, you must remember that the fate of the Master, and perhaps humanity, is in your hands."

He paused, looking beyond them at the dim shapes of the great machines. Then, opening a drawer in the desk, he took out a thin sheaf of papers. "I prepared this while I waited for you. You will find here a complete background of fictitious identities for both of you. I have selected names, and sketched the major outlines of your lives previous to tonight. Tomorrow I will have this information filed with the proper official quarters. You will leave on the dawn rocket for Moon Base. Your reservations are made." He hesitated. "Korson . . ."

Korson smiled. "I know. It would be impossible for me to conceal my identity if—" As his hands touched his shoulders

to remove the two silver stars, Tarmo tore them off, laughing, and kissed him.

The Master strode across the courtyard, through the tunnel and up the stairway which led to the blue bedroom.

They were all there, Varden, Ronding—even Flim. Automatically, the group parted before him. He glimpsed the awe and wonder in their faces—but he had seen that before.

Bending over the Lady Ellora his lips touched hers and he shivered, feeling their coldness.

Going out onto the balcony he stood, silhouetted against the star-scattered sky above Terra City. There remained only the ultimate problem that was enclosed by the little room in the corner of Laboratory I.

"And what, oh Stars, is your answer?"

For I should know. I am the Master.